"Readers will be utterly enchanted by Dykes's Hepburn-esque heroine who brings the glitz of the Golden Age of Hollywood deep into the heart of the mountains in a last-ditch effort to keep a broken promise. They'll uncover a tale that reminds us all that no matter how impossible things may seem, there's always room for restoration. Unforgettable."

—Amanda Cox, bestselling and award-winning author
of *He Should Have Told the Bees*

"Amanda Dykes is one of the most creative and talented storytellers I've ever had the pleasure of reading. *Born of Gilded Mountains* is a symphony of characters who resonate, pitch-perfect pacing, and a setting that sings. Settle in for a tale worth savoring down to the last note."

—Jocelyn Green, Christy Award–winning author
of *The Metropolitan Affair*

"A mountain-sized treasure of a tale, artfully scripted, skillfully penned. Dykes has outdone herself in this nostalgic and heartfelt portrayal of friendship beyond measure and redemption beyond circumstance. Bravo!"

—Nicole Deese, Christy Award–winning author of *Roads We Follow*

"Amanda Dykes has achieved a new level of storytelling with *Born of Gilded Mountains*. Glimmering in charm and rich in heart, this novel stunned me and compelled me to journey deeper and deeper into the lives of Mercy and Rusty. This is the perfect book to enjoy with friends."

—Susie Finkbeiner, author of *The All-American*
and *Stories That Bind Us*

Born of
Gilded
Mountains

Books by Amanda Dykes

Whose Waves These Are

Set the Stars Alight

Yours Is the Night

All the Lost Places

Born of Gilded Mountains

Born of Gilded Mountains

A Novel

AMANDA DYKES

BETHANYHOUSE
a division of Baker Publishing Group
Minneapolis, Minnesota

© 2024 by Amanda J. Dykes

Published by Bethany House Publishers
Minneapolis, Minnesota
BethanyHouse.com

Bethany House Publishers is a division of
Baker Publishing Group, Grand Rapids, Michigan

Printed in the United States of America

Library of Congress Cataloging-in-Publication Data
Name: Dykes, Amanda, author.
Title: Born of gilded mountains / Amanda Dykes.
Description: Minneapolis, Minnesota: Bethany House, a division of Baker Publishing
    Group, 2024.
Identifiers: LCCN 2023050046 | ISBN 9780764239519 (paper) | ISBN 9780764243196
    (casebound) | ISBN 9781493446605 (ebook)
Subjects: LCGFT: Christian fiction. | Novels.
Classification: LCC PS3604.Y495 B67 2024 | DDC 813/.6—dc23/eng/20231025
LC record available at https://lccn.loc.gov/2023050046

This book is a work of fiction. Names, characters, places, and incidents are the product of the author's imagination or are used fictitiously. Any resemblance to actual events, locales, or persons, living or dead, is coincidental.

Author is represented by Books & Such Literary Agency.

Baker Publishing Group publications use paper produced from sustainable forestry practices and postconsumer waste whenever possible.

24 25 26 27 28 29 30   7 6 5 4 3 2 1

To Joanne, for everything.

A friend is someone
who knows the song in your heart
and can sing it back to you
when you have forgotten the words.
—Unknown

Thank you for singing it back, time and again.
You're treasure, and you're treasured.

The mountains will bring peace
to the people. . . .

PSALM 72:3

HIC
SUNT
DRACONES

MARYBETH'S TREE

RUSTY'S TREE

RUSTY'S CABIN

GOLDEN LEAF
LAKE

GREEN
MEADOW SPIRES

SEA GLASS LAKE

BALANCED ROCK

TELLURIDE

SILVERTON

OURAY

GILCREST MINE

WELCOME TO
MERCY PEAK
YOUR ALPINE HAMLET HOME
POP. 198,199

Prologue

Blood moons were made for pact-swearing. Four boys orbiting ten years old knew it, and so did the mountains standing witness.

They were an unlikely group, but life up here did that. Remote and rugged, so beautiful it'd cut you to the quick just as sure as the peaks sliced the air and brought down the heavens in the form of stars and storms.

Silas Bright led the charge, tonight and always. He was the one rapping on doors, throwing pebbles at windows, rallying troops. Short in stature but he moved worlds, Silas did, with a heart bigger than the sky.

Martin Shaw had come west on an orphan train. Its *chuff-chuff-chuff* had rattled into his spine for so many miles it got caught there for the rest of his life, till everything he did had rhythm and drive. He jumped off that train in the Rockies and ran for the hills: prospecting, digging, working odd jobs until someone lassoed him up into school.

Reuben Murdock was the quiet one. Still waters run deep, they say, and for Reuben it was God's honest truth. Kind and sincere, a gentle giant whose little sister toddled after him like a shadow.

Randolph Gilman was a tall, lean, walking ledger of calculations. He had an affinity for logic in a world that made no sense most times. Head and shoulders above the rest, Randolph could cut a course out of granite, given enough time and numbers.

Those Blood Moon Boys ran with everything they had, Silas whooping when they reached the top of the butte. Dust flew up at their heels as they

11

stopped on the precipice of something so great they could feel it beating in the air. They lit a fire to seal their promise, there on the edge of forever.

"Swear it," Martin Shaw said, hands on his knees as he caught his breath. "Any of us finds treasure out here in these mountains, we all get behind that man. None of this backstabbing, money-grabbing, no-good—"

"Crying crayfish, Marty," said Silas Bright. "That book got you worked up good!" The teacher had been reading *Treasure Island* to them at school, and Martin had piped up nearly every chapter with questions about why people were turning on one another, why maps were the cause of so many problems, why treasure seemed like something good but turned so many to poison—why this, why that, why such things happened around here, too.

"We'll use what we find for good, and we won't get all rotten, and we'll take good care of any claim we find. That's all I'm saying. We should swear it, and quick." He eyed the moon. It'd be a plain old white moon again soon, and then who knew what'd happen to pacts sworn under it. "And we'll sign it in writing, too."

"I think it's a good idea." Reuben Murdock scuffed his foot, words falling quiet to the earth, as his often did. "I don't have the smarts for a plan, but you can count on me." He shrugged a shoulder, the burlap sack slung over it bobbing the neck of an instrument upward. He set the sack down, brought out a guitar. Retreated to where the glow of the fire barely touched him and summoned notes from steel.

"We're the future of these mountains, boys," Martin said. The vision was rising up within him. "You see all those people leavin' in droves. We won't leave. These mountains raised us, and we're going to raise these mountains up from this 'silver slump.' But when we get our hands on something good, it ain't gonna ruin us. Not like what we've seen around, and not like that wretched old book!"

"We can't raise the mountains," Randolph Gilman, literal to his very bones, tried to make the words add up.

"That's not what I meant. In all this mess with the silver crash . . . if we can stick it out, boys . . . five, ten years from now, we'll see this place right."

"In five or ten years, we'll be about . . ." Randolph calculated lightning-quick. "Fifteen or twenty. Do you see any fifteen-year-old sheriffs or superintendents around?" He scratched his head through impeccably combed dark hair.

"Well, *you* won't, that's for sure," said Martin. "Deserting us for that fancy school. You in or out of this?"

"It's not my choice," he said. "I have to go, it's all arranged. And anyway . . . Manchester Meeks isn't so bad as far as schools go."

"Who you gonna play kick the can with around there?" Silas Bright kicked a rock into the fire, causing a swirl of sparks to coil up toward the red moon. It was like him, Silas, to blow off the tension quick as a wink. "Ten cents says you won't find friends there like us." A grin spread across his freckled face. "Don't worry, Rand. We'll keep your place here. Right, Marty?"

Randolph tugged at his jacket, not sure where to look. "I'm not going for friends. I'm going to come back as an engineer. So I can vow as well—as good—as any of you gentlemen—you fellas—that I'm going to come back and help, too. Just watch."

"Good man." Martin nodded. "I swear this place isn't done yet. There's more mining to be had, I know it. You just gotta read this mountain like a story, it'll show us. Our job's just to not give up, even when the others do. So swear it, boys: We will not leave this place. We're gonna be the ones to see it through, someday. Yeah?"

Randolph Gilman was the first one to step forward and stretch his hand out.

Martin let out a whoop. "Yessirree!" He spit into his hand, ready to pump Randolph Gilman's promise into certainty.

"Now you spit, too," he said.

". . . spit?"

"Spit."

"But that isn't how the men at my father's mine seal their contracts. They use ink and wax."

"Listen, if you mean it enough to shake on it, you better mean it enough to give it something from way down deep inside your soul."

"And that's . . . spit?"

"Spit."

Randolph shook his head but took a step closer.

And as the mountains bore witness and the blood moon slipped to white, the boys spit into their hands and shook all around. On their honor, cross their hearts, hope to die, avenge each other's death, brothers to the end, and above all, someday pull enough riches from this dying mountain to bring it back to life.

So when they took their spit-smeared, handshake-sealed promise to the back of a scrap of brown postal paper, wrinkled and peaked like the mountains, and signed their names with the tail feather of a bald eagle because—according to Martin—"it means more that way, like our promise came from the sky or somethin' . . ."

It meant something, alright.

Enough for Martin Shaw, the visionary, to grow up into a prospector who never gave up searching every gully and gulch, every pinnacle and peak.

Enough for Silas Bright, who never knew a stranger and grew up toiling in those very mines, to recount that legendary night to his bride and daughter, all through the girl's growing-up years.

Enough for Reuben Murdock, the gentle giant whose fingers brought magic to strings and who was perhaps the unlikeliest to break the vow—to leave. A man shattered. Gone, they feared, forever.

And enough for Randolph Gilman, bona fide engineer, sole heir to Gilcrest Mine & Holdings, to hang onto that wrinkled charter. Buried beneath decades of ledgers, plans, and a snuffed-out conscience. Sealing the silence of a legend . . . and the whereabouts of a treasure that could change everything.

But a promise meant something in Mercy Peak. And when Martin Shaw came shivering down from the mountain one winter, summoning Randolph Gilman and Silas Bright back to the place of their pact, they showed up. Martin was bound for Denver, to verify he'd found what he thought he found, at a claim he would not yet tell where. But knowing well his own mortality and not willing to let the treasure languish when it could do so much good, he gave the two men each a piece of a puzzle.

For Randolph, a brass capsule, containing a riddle that was useless without a key.

For Silas, that key, in the form of something tucked into a box. Useless, without the riddle.

For Reuben, absent Reuben, a prayer that if the worst happened and these men needed to use the gifts he'd imparted . . . the loss of Martin's own life might prove to be the rescuing of another.

If anything happened to Martin, the men would need each other to find the treasure.

The pact would hold fast . . . come what may.

It had to.

MERCY PEAK

A Screenplay in Three Acts

WRITTEN: 1949
BY: SIDNEY MCGEE

ACT I
THE VANISHING OF MERCY WINDSOR

Scene 1

NEWSPAPER, *HOLLYWOOD HERALD*, SPINS TO A STOP. CAMERA
ZOOMS IN ON HEADLINE.

SILVER SCREEN STAR VANISHES

SECOND NEWSPAPER, *SILVER SCREEN TIMES*, THROWN ON TOP.
HEADLINE READS

WHERE IS MERCY WINDSOR?

THIRD NEWSPAPER, *HOLLYWOOD HERALD*, SPINS TO A STOP.
HEADLINE READS

WHO IS MARYBETH SPATTS?
AFTER DISAPPEARANCE, MERCY WINDSOR'S
HUMBLE BEGINNINGS COME TO LIGHT

ENVELOPE SPINS TO A STANDSTILL AS CAMERA ZOOMS IN.

PAN-AMERICAN YOUTH CORRESPONDENCE PROGRAM
1928

CUT TO CAROLINA SCHOOLHOUSE. INTERIOR—SCHOOLHOUSE WITH
POTBELLIED STOVE IN CORNER, CHILDREN AT DESKS IN ROWS.

MARYBETH SPATTS, 10, OPENS ENVELOPE. AT TEACHER'S
PROMPTING, CHILDREN BEGIN TO READ OPENING PARAGRAPH OF
THEIR LETTERS ALOUD TOGETHER:

CHILDREN (in unison)

> Dear [children all insert their own name],
> It's a pleasure to meet you. Thank you for
> taking part in the new initiative to promote
> friendship, literacy, and cross-geographic
> personal educational encounters through the
> Pan-American Correspondence Program. I send
> you greetings from the mountainous terrain
> of Telluride, Colorado. . . .

MARYBETH, DARK HAIR IN LONG AND WOBBLY BRAIDS
AS IF SHE HAS MADE THEM HERSELF, LOOKS AROUND,
QUICKLY REALIZING HER CORRESPONDENT DID NOT USE THE
SAME OPENING SENTENCES AS OTHERS, AND IS NOT FROM
TELLURIDE. SHE SLIPS A LITTLE LOWER IN HER CHAIR AND
STARTS TO READ SILENTLY.

RUSTY (off screen)

> Rusty Bright, age 10
>
> Mercy Peak, Colorado
>
> 1928
>
> Dear Friend,
>
> What's your name? Mine's Ruby, but they
> all call me Rusty, on account of the time
> I jimmied the lock of the old church door
> to let out a trapped cat. I picked the lock
> with a rusty nail. Carried it (the cat, not
> the nail) to Miss Murdock's over the river
> on Whistler's Bridge. By the time I got
> to Miss Murdock's, that cat was yowlering
> and looking like its stripey orange face
> got stuck in a blast of wind. Miss Murdock

wasn't home, so I picked her lock too, let
the cat loose inside, locked the door good.
You got any pets, Marybeth?

MARYBETH LOOKS UP, THINKING. FADE TO FOOTAGE OF
MARYBETH FEEDING THE SQUIRRELS ON THE HILL BEHIND HER
HOUSE, ITS OPEN WINDOWS DARK AS A WORN CURTAIN RIPPLES
OUTWARD IN THE BACKGROUND. FADE BACK TO SCHOOLROOM
SCENE, WHERE RUSTY'S VOICE CONTINUES READING LETTER.

Miss Murdock asked how I broke into the
church, and she sort of had the same look on
her face as the cat did, with the wind and
fangs and all. I told her I picked the lock
with an old nail I found in the dirt. Then
she saw how tore up my good green dress was
from the cat and her face looked even more
cat-in-the-wind-y, and soon folks all around
were saying how there wasn't much I couldn't
do with a rusty nail.

So that's how I got my name, even though
Miss Murdock says nicknames are vulgar. Says
I need a good woman's influence. Well, I had
that once. Dad says I might not remember my
ma—she died when I was a baby—but that she
loved me big enough to last a lifetime and
make me richer than all the metals he mines
for in these mountains. Then he slides a
slab of corn bread in front of me and says,
"Eat up!" He doesn't know many things to
cook, but what he does is good enough to
make a rock rise up and eat it. Your dad or
ma cook anything good, Marybeth Spatts?

FADE TO FOOTAGE OF MARYBETH COOKING DINNER IN A SMALL
CABIN KITCHEN AND PUTTING IT ON THE TABLE FOR TWO,
THEN WAITING AS THE CLOCK SHOWS AN HOUR GOING BY AND
THE FOOD GROWING COLD BEFORE HER FATHER, A COAL MINER,
TROMPS IN, PICKS UP A ROLL OFF HIS PLATE, AND GOES TO
LIE DOWN. FADE BACK TO SCHOOLROOM.

And now I'm supposed to ask you three good
questions.

Here are the three best questions I could
think of:

One: Why do spiders have eight whole legs?
Eight! Just seems wrong.

Two: Why does Sam Buckley keep bringing
plums in his lunch pail if he doesn't like
them? I take them off his hands, and keep
the pits. His grandfather brought five pits
with him when he came west, prospecting.
Planted them all, and all died but one, and
that's where Sam's plums come from.

Three: What is the meaning of life? I don't
really know what that question means, but
I saw it on the cover of Miss Murdock's
Harper's Bazar. She says she's a bastion of
civility here in the mountain wilderness. I
wonder what that means.

Your new pen pal,

Rusty Bright

p.s. You ever need a place to be, you just
come find Rusty Bright in Mercy Peak. Sure as
your name's Marybeth Spatts, you got a place
here. And don't forget it.

CAMERA ZOOMS OUT. CAPTION READS

20 YEARS LATER

FINAL NEWSPAPER SPINS TO A STOP AS CAMERA ZOOMS IN ON
HEADLINE.

WINDSOR IN EXILE:
WHERE IS THE WORLD'S MOST FAMOUS FACE HIDING?

Folio of Field Notes, Volume I:
Mercy Windsor Disappears

[Property of Sudsy McGee, Hollywood Biographer]

OWN A PIECE OF THE STARS

Los Angeles Times
Advertisements: Real Estate
March 3, 1948

For the very first time . . . Hollywood mansion of legendary actress Mercy Windsor* offered for sale! Celestial Climes, the 23-room mansion, sits on a pristine promontory off Sunset Boulevard. Stylish splashes of color throughout the home's plush, carpeted interior; terracotta tile imported direct from Tuscany; bright white walls and vaulted ceilings make for an unparalleled hosting venue. A modern fireplace creates a sleek statement piece, while two entire acres of citrus orchards, with a plum tree at the orchard's heart, provide privacy from faraway neighbors. Bask in your own tropical conservatory paradise with vibrant parrots, an indoor waterfall, and blooming birds of paradise. Never bother again with those pesky Santa Ana winds! On nice days, enjoy the balmy Southern California weather at your sequence of three linked pools. You'll feel as if you've escaped to a mountain haven, with yet another waterfall descending into a pool through a built-in slide. Gable, Stewart, Garland, and more have walked these halls at Windsor's famous social gatherings. Join their ranks today as the new owner of Celestial Climes.

For further particulars, contact
Burdock & Holmes, Inc.
Real Estate

*No publicity inquiries. Burdock & Holmes strictly represents the property and its owner, Pinnacle Studios, and does not have information regarding Mercy Windsor's whereabouts, motives, or plans.

Wildwood Estate *For Sale* Notice

From Mercy Peak Mercantile Bulletin Board
Mercy Peak, Colorado
March 1948

For Sale: Old Gilman Place

Seven or eight bedrooms, maybe nine, hard to say. Indoor plumbing if you get the water running plus **TWO** outhouses. Elevator (hand cranked). Tunnel to town so you'll never have to be cold(er than you have to). Boathouse on Gold Leaf Lake, if you can repair. Maybe boat or two. Bring hammer and nails. Remote. Lots of acres, maybe 50, going on up the mountain. Owner keen to sell. See Kurt.

HAVE MERCY: THE RISE AND FALL OF MERCY WINDSOR

By Sudsy McGee,
for the *Hollywood Herald*

March 1, 1948—She arrived on a train and was on her first Hollywood set three hours later. In a world where aspiring actresses give up by the dozens each day, and even the contracted ones wait for months or years to be cast in a bit role, Mercy Windsor's rags-to-riches and obscurity-to-fame is the stuff of legends.

After all, who in their right mind would take on a black-and-white ten-minute scene in the last silent film Pinnacle Studios would ever produce? Who, in the age of talkies, mob films, and sensational musicals, with rumors of color films on the horizon, would mark their career *obsolete* before it had even begun?

Here's who: the girl fresh off the train, spotted in a stage play in Denver and brought to Hollywood by Pinnacle Studios president Wilson P. Wilson himself.

No one knew her name.

No one knew her face.

It was the lowest-budget film on their docket for 1938. Slated to open at only a few old theatres across the country. One of which included the vaudeville hall–turned–movie house in a tiny Vermont town where revered reviewer Owen Haskell, of the review duo Haskell and Kline, happened to be visiting his daughter.

The famously severe critic for the *New York Review* was moved until words evaded him. "Go and see it," he said simply. From the man best known for scathing syndicated reviews, those four words were as good as gold, and her fate was sealed.

"The single tear that flooded the world," they called it. This unknown actress, with the face of a waif and hair dark as night, took to the screen with something real. In a medium characterized by caricature, where exaggerated expressions and wild gestures compensated for the lack of sound . . . she made silence her voice.

She embraced it. Dared to be understated—to let the minuscule crease of her brow speak more than the overwrought twisting hands she was urged to employ. To let a single tear splash upon her hand, so empty of her child's grip, and eschew the swoon written into the script.

The director saw something in this quiet rebellion and kept the scene in what he'd called "the throwaway film."

But the scene touched something in audiences, who

spent their rare pennies to see someone on the screen who, like them, would've given anything to offer a table full of food to their children.

Soon, the film was everywhere. Every theatre, for lengthy runs. The people's message back to Hollywood was clear: *Give us more of her!*

Hollywood delivered . . . and a star was born.

They loved her loveliness.

Were won over by her winsomeness.

Touted her timidity.

And the spotlight grew. Roles followed as Cinderella, Guinevere, a Fifth Avenue socialite, a backcountry bumpkin, and a catacombs-traversing heroine in a role invented just to include her in *The Cask of Amontillado*, a role she declined initially due to an aversion to tunnels. Typically agreeable to any filming challenge, her quiet resolve surprised the studio, who in response proposed that a roofless tunnel set be constructed, with lighting and strategic shadows providing the needed illusion of confined space.

She gave that same sincerity in each role until she didn't just live on their screens—she lived in their hearts.

One question, always lingering: Where did the girl come from? Wilson P. Wilson, owner of Pinnacle Studios, has been uncharacteristically reserved with his answers to the press. "Mercy Windsor was a gem in her time on the silver screen," he said. "But after an unpleasant set of circumstances, Pinnacle has found it unavoidable to prematurely end its relationship with Miss Windsor, who is, in fact, in breach of contract."

Rumors include everything from moral scandal to embezzlement. All that's known for certain is that it stems from the filming of *Joan of Arc*, with Windsor in the title role. Pinnacle had already poured untold thousands of dollars into it when it was forced to the brink of cancellation.

The Mighty Mercy has fallen . . . and there does not seem to be anyone to catch her. One question echoes in her absence:

Where is Mercy Windsor?

The zigzag stitch is nearly impossible to undo, Mercy. But that's the beauty of it. It's strong. It mends tears, finishes the frayed edges of fabric cut from its place that would otherwise unravel.

—Mabel Greer, wardrobe mistress of Pinnacle Studios

Mercy Peak, Colorado
March 1948

To get to Mercy Peak, Colorado, a plucky little locomotive known as a "Galloping Goose"—half train, half automobile—carried the rare visitor up the colorful foothills and into the emerald timberline.

The Galloping Geese—motors numbered 1 through 8—had tin-toothed grins in the form of a fender-like feature known as a cow-catcher, a term the locals pretended not to notice, out of fondness for their bovine friends. The rail cars galloped daily past landmarks with assuring names such as Lost Canyon, Sawpit, and Lizard Head Pass.

And tucked into the folds of those mountains, they stopped at Mercy Peak Gulch, as the town once was called, till someone decided *Gulch* sounded like something a rude dinner guest would do and it was off-putting to visitors. Nothing was said about how maybe it was the zig-zag railroad putting people off, how by the time you arrived, your soul was stitched to the mountain for the way you'd white-knuckled your seat and held your breath around hairpin turns and too-high trestle bridges.

And then you'd open your eyes to scenery too good to be true and breathe again, hand to heart. A mercy, indeed.

It was a place as much legend as land. High up there and near unto heaven as a body could get while still alive and kicking . . . yet still more peaks rose impossibly above. And maybe that's why men came in search of streets of gold there, the sort that runs down deep.

It took a heap of courage to live there. A world of men thrummed in the lantern light, deep down below. The mechanical heartbeat of the mountain, veins running in petrified ore, hoisted by man and machine. The people there had each other and not much else. They gathered for Sundays, gathered for rice-throwing and candle-blowing, gathered to celebrate and grieve. Made feasts of dried beans and whatever bounty the mountain offered, not much blinking to notice when the Great Depression hit the outside world, for they'd always lived this way. And if hard times hit, you could bet the folks down the road would mention they happened to have a spare slab of bacon or an extra bag of beans, and would you mind taking it off their hands? It'd do them a big favor.

Winters were brutal and summers a dream, all blue skies and thunder in concert, canyons spilling wildflowers into lakes so turquoise-bright they seemed shot from stars themselves. Stars in canopy over spark-spinning campfires, making the good folks below ache in the chest to see how vast it all was, how small they were, how right that somehow felt.

Summers cast a spell, entrancing you just long enough to forget the hard edge of winter and how you'd sworn, come March, to pack up and hightail it out of there to somewhere you didn't have to slice through ice to open your door or knock icicles off your beard. But then came May, and the snow sighed into waterfalls beneath that high-country sun, tumbling over cliffs, running in rivulets, washing souls with wonder and hypnotizing them to stay a little longer, live a little deeper.

It was into this land of not-quite-spring that Motor No. 7 brought a single passenger. Dark-haired, dark sunglasses, and a dark shadow that seemed to hover over her.

A clattering sounded, followed by the slow screech of wheels upon tracks. The driver hopped out, poking his head into the cargo wagon, where Mercy Windsor perched on the edge of a passenger bench, holding tight to her suitcase.

"Everything alright?" she asked.

"Aw sure, we'll have her back up in no time. Just a little overheating, is all. The Geese hardly ever have any serious trouble." He grinned, proud.

She nodded. They'd had their share of overheating on the jungle roads when they filmed *Embargo*. No need to fear. "If you need a hand with the coolant, I'm happy to help," she said, sliding her suitcase from her lap and standing. He took one look at the way the wind rippled the silk of her dress and scratched his head.

"It's an . . ." What was the term the driver had taught her? "Internal combustion engine, yes?"

The man's eyebrows shot up.

"I could pour, or hold the cap, or . . ." Anything to take her mind off what awaited in Mercy Peak. Or rather, what didn't await. She held her hands out, forgetting about the bandages.

He saw them. She saw him see them. She pulled them back, clasping her hands behind her back.

Soon. Soon, she'd be healed enough to remove them.

"I wouldn't want you to, uh, get your perty dress soiled," he said with a blush.

She looked down. "It's all I have." And it was the truth. It was this or one of the other costumes, and this one was as plainclothes as her costume wardrobe got. "For now." She'd been locked out of her own home, a legal entanglement with Pinnacle Studios resulting in frozen accounts, immediate eviction from Celestial Climes, dayslong deliberations between attorneys over what "breach of contract" did and did not mean . . . and her one possession clear: her entire movie wardrobe, per the infamous costume-keeping clause.

It was fine . . . except for one item she desperately needed, squirreled away on a shelf at Celestial Climes. But she'd find a way to get it back. She had to.

They were soon back up and running, chugging their way up the mountain to Mercy Peak and the end of the line for Mercy Windsor.

The jaunty engine slowed, approaching the depot. Mercy stood in the doorway of the dented tin Goose, taking in the Victorian village with its brick buildings. A hotel so fine it looked like it had been plucked from Paris and planted here in the clutch of these peaks. A clock tower on the town hall, a mercantile. In the distance, snow blew off the peak like a phantom flag, frozen in a ripple. Her courage rippled, too.

It was different, coming to Mercy Peak this time around. A little over ten years ago, she'd been here and gone before twenty-four hours had passed. Before anyone had even known she'd made the trek across the country, left everything she'd ever known, to get to a place she'd dreamed of coming all her life—only to turn right back around and leave.

A woman thin as a rail and with the posture of one, too, laid a measuring tape between lampposts and scribbled down notes. Across the cobbled street, two white-haired men sat on a bench, engrossed in conversation as if they'd worked all their lives to do just this. The measuring tape snaked loose in a twist, and one of the men hopped up, holding it down with his foot, doffing his cap at the woman. All without missing a beat in his soliloquy about how the trout weren't biting in the river, and had the other man tried Jake's Cove yet?

A sign at the end of the depot in fresh white paint with crisp black letters caught her eye.

Welcome to
MERCY PEAK
Your Alpine Hamlet Home
Pop. 198

The engineer with bushy white brows offered his hand, pulled it back when he realized it was streaked in engine grease, wiped it on a handkerchief that he stuffed back into his overalls pocket, and helped her down. She pulled her wool sweater tight against a shiver, planted her scarlet silk heels on the weathered platform, and breathed deep.

"Is that a new sign?"

"Priscilla Murdock's doing." He tipped his head toward the woman, who had neatly coiled her tape and was now examining an empty flowerpot outside a shop, *tsk*ing at a crack and jotting something down. "The town's trying to get people to come out here. Not much in the way of mining anymore, and things have been . . . slow. So, they put up a new sign, and Miss Murdock said *alpine hamlet* sounded nicer than *gulch*. But to me, hamlet just sounds like breakfast food that's a heap too small, and I can't see how that's much better. Whatever you call it, Miss Murdock was born and raised here, just like most of us. The gulch is in her veins, whether she likes it or not." The woman, dressed in a long wool coat and a fine hat with a feather, walked at a clipping pace with a hint of a limp. "Maybe even more than most, good Lord bless her." He tilted his head to study the sign with Mercy. "Nice sign, though."

When she asked whether she could reach Wildwood Estate by foot or if she needed a taxi, he guffawed. "Ralph'll take you," he said. He saw her into the mercantile—*"heart of the town, where anything that's got to get done, gets done,"* according to her guide. Here she saw a man named Kurt about the keys and was introduced to Ralph, a kind-faced older gentleman who looked wary when she named Wildwood as her destination but was happy enough to lend his Model T to the task.

She arrived at the gate of a stone-and-timber estate with pinnacles and points aplenty . . . with broken windows and boarded-up doors, too. The earth squished and punctured beneath her stiletto heels. *That's right, mud,* she thought. *Cover up the old life. Here, we start anew.*

Gripping the rusted bars of the ornate iron gate, she sent up a silent prayer that this place—though she knew nary a living soul here—would do for her what the mud did to her shoes.

"Ma'am?" Ralph spoke over the throaty idling engine of the Model T that wore its mud splatters like badges of honor. "You sure you'll be alright in there?" He scratched his head as the hem of blue chiffon trailed in the mud, forming its own question mark.

"I—" She cleared her throat, put on a smile, told herself the old lie. *I'm ready.* "I'll be fine."

He didn't look convinced. "Ain't a soul stepped inside that place in years. Mr. Gilman was a strange one toward the end. And the house shows it."

Mercy gulped. "How so?"

"Ever hear of the Winchester House?"

"The place with stairs and doors that lead nowhere?" California lore whose fame could rival the silver screen.

He nodded. "This here's a bit like that. Mostly it's just a big house, but Gilman got a little paranoid. He brought in a blacksmith from nobody-knows-where, in a private car, even though we got the best blacksmith right here in Mercy Peak. Made this place into something of a puzzle. The man had ghosts in his past, no doubt about it, and people think they finally caught up to him. He had his share of secrets, sure, but most just think he went a little crazy, in the end. Guilt, probably."

"Guilt?"

Ralph waved. "You don't want to know all that your first night here. You'll get an earful from the town soon enough. And this place'll clean up right nice." His smile was unconvincing. "But if you need a place to stay till it's fit for living, might be Miss Ellen in town has a room open. She poaches a mighty fine egg."

Mercy faced the man and reached for his name in the place she filed them, carefully, in invisible rows. How many words had she memorized over the years? How many lines, in how many scripts? Too many to count. She'd decided early on that the least she could do was make names the first thing she remembered. People mattered, even if she was verifiably the most alone soul in the universe this evening.

"Thank you for your kindness, Mr. Mosely." She pinched open her red clutch, pulling out a crisp bill and offering it.

The bearded man scuffed a foot awkwardly in the mud and waved off the gesture. "Aw," he said, swatting his hand through the air, "no need, ma'am."

"But you drove me all the way from the depot."

"Folks around here take care of each other. Have to, or none of us would make it. Life in the Rockies can be . . . well, rocky."

This, she knew. And hadn't quite figured out yet how to make a home and stay hidden in a place where people knew things about one another.

"You call me Ralph, and you let me and my Nancy know whenever you need a thing," he said. "We're only two or three miles down the mountain."

"Two or three miles," she said, a laugh tumbling into her voice. When was the last time she'd been more than twenty feet from another human?

"Close, right?" Ralph grinned. "Once you leave town, folks are usually five or ten miles apart at least, on the old ranches and mining shanties. Tucked all up in these hollows and crannies. Just where you think a man's never set foot, you'll find a barn and a cabin and likely a warm fire most nights. There's more people than you'd think out here. The folds of these mountains, they keep souls well. Done so for us, anyway."

He stroked a beard as if wondering what to tell. "Listen, you holler if you need us, we'll hear ya. Or just honk one of the horns in the old truck. Guess it's yours now, too, eh?" The man seemed to be doing his best to tamp the slightest twinge of envy in his voice. He eyed the rusted green vehicle covered in brown pine needles and tucked against a pine tree outside of the estate's rock wall, its front end poking forward like a curious onlooker. It was green like the woods, with a faded logo in goldenrod that said *Legacy Timber*. The logo struck Mercy with an odd familiarity, and she tipped her head, studying it.

"Beauty, isn't she?" Ralph said. "Mr. Gilman leased some of the timberlands to that company. They stripped the forest, hauled the trees to who-knows-where, and left him with that broken-down truck. Couple of the guys got it running at one point, but it's been some time. Suppose . . . it's yours now?" He seemed hopeful.

"I . . . suppose it is," she said. *Whole kit and caboodle*, Kurt had said. Everything at Wildwood was hers. Her voice sounded so uncertain and suddenly Wilson P. Wilson's voice was in her head. *"You decide your tone, Mercy. You want to be the Queen of Sheba? Get that quaver out of her voice. You're not a mouse, Mercy Windsor."* She certainly felt like one now, but she pulled back her shoulders and took a deep breath, her old trick to "get that quaver out."

"Thank you, Ralph. I really do appreciate it."

Ralph opened his own cab door, and it creaked so loud it set her teeth to clenching. "I'll bring some dry firewood in the morning. Gets cold up here nights, 'specially March. Winter hangs onto spring for dear life."

"That's very kind. Thank you again for the warm welcome. You do Mercy Peak proud."

His smile widened, and he doffed an old newsboy cap before ducking in and rumbling down the winding road, forgetting, thankfully, to inquire after her name.

If he'd asked, what would she have said? She had taken a great many roles over the years. Leading lady to Gable, Bogart, Stewart, Crosby.

But underneath all that . . . who was she?

Once, in another life, her name had been Marybeth Spatts.

She needed a place to call home.

But Rusty Bright, who'd promised her one . . . was dead.

CHAPTER 2

1928
From Marybeth, age 10

Dear Rusty,

I've never had a pen pal before, but I'm so happy I do now. Did you know we both live in cabins, and both in mining towns? Only it sounds like your lot mine metal and gems and such. We only have coal around here—thick and black, and it seems like it chokes the life right out of people from the inside out. Least that's how it is with my pa. He's mined all his life. There's a picture of him with my mother, who died a long time ago. He has this smile in it, and sometimes I trace it with my finger because I've never seen that smile in real life. Like he was a different person. But that smiling man, he's in there somewhere. It's not his fault he got swallowed up by the man who's my pa. And Pa's alright, just a little rough around the edges. It's the drink that makes him the way he is.

I liked hearing about your dad. I'm sorry about your ma not being there, either—maybe our mothers know each other, up in heaven. Wouldn't that be something?

From,
Marybeth Spatts

p.s. Remember that cat from your first letter? Whatever happened to it, and whyever did you pick the Bastion of Civility to give it to?

p.p.s. I started writing down interesting words and looking them up in the big old (and I do mean old—it drops a little more away into dust every time I open it) dictionary at school. Bastion *means someone holding up certain values and such, but it also means a part of old towers, like from castle times, that was extra strong for when it got fired on. Does Miss Murdock have something to be afraid of, maybe? Maybe that's why she's a bastion.*

February 1932

Dear Marybeth,

Do you know we've been writing for near on four years now? Feels like we should have a celebration about that. Got any ideas? That's your department. All I can think is we both jump up and down real fast at a certain hour so we're both excited, at the same time, across the miles. You'd come up with something a lot better, like "Let's both watch the moon rise and here's the reason why, it's a real pretty reason." Write back and tell me because I'm no good at pretty reasons. Especially right now, things in Mercy Peak are in a pickle.

I'm really sorry about your pa. I hope you get to see that smile of his come back one day. Maybe you have it? You know how people say, "That beauty's got her mother's complexion," or "That rascal's got his uncle's penchant for trouble!" . . . well, maybe you got your pa's lost smile. Check in the mirror or maybe a puddle or some such. I like puddle reflections more than glass 'cause they ripple up my face so I can't see my freckles. Dad says there's nothing more beautiful, that the sun sprinkled my face with love. I'm not so sure.

But the thing about Dad is, if he says something, I believe it. Here's why.

Once, there were four men:

1) My dad, Silas Bright, a man who's lived most of his life underground, but for all that darkness, still sees light wherever he goes.

2) Martin Shaw, like a brother to my dad. They mined together years and years before Martin took off prospecting in the hills. That man had prospecting camps all over this mountain! But he was happy out there under the stars. Said if nothing else, he got to sleep under silver, and that was rich enough for him.

3) Randolph Gilman, who downright scoffed at the thought of stars being as good as silver. People say he has the Midas touch.

His grandfather was the one who found the vein of gold that up and turned the Gilmans from paupers into princes, and Randolph made them kings.

4) Reuben Murdock, brother to Priscilla Murdock, the Bastion of Civility. I don't know much about him. He vanished up into the peaks before I was even born.

Well as luck would have it, Martin Shaw eventually found what he was looking for: a last holdout of treasure. Gold, silver, no one really knows. Why? Because a couple of months ago, he took his pack mule and left for Denver to go "secure financing" to create a mine.

But wait, there's a fifth character in this tale: winter. Most people hunker down for the dark months—these mountains don't get so green in the summer without all that fierce snow piling on in the winter first. Avalanches, ice storms, blizzards, sometimes even thunder snow. Fiercer than any fairy-tale beast, these peaks shiver with all the rumbling things in winter.

Martin Shaw knew this. If anyone could weather all that, it was him—he prospected all the year round, up the heights and in the depths and all the places in between. So the journey to Denver didn't scare him. But he'd also been in his share of scrapes, including an avalanche, and knew his own mortality. Knew he needed a safeguard, some way to pass on the whereabouts of his pay dirt, should he up and ~~croak~~ perish. But also a safeguard that wouldn't rob him while he was gone on his trek to the city.

So, he split up the information. To Randolph Gilman, the man who was shrewd and rich and would know how to make things happen for the vein and the town, he gave some kind of capsule with a clue inside about how to find the location. No one knows just what the clue was. But the clue was useless to Gilman without the bit Dad got.

See, to Silas Bright, my dad, his truest, oldest friend, he gave the other half of the information. Dad has what Martin was worried Randolph doesn't: Integrity. Loyalty. Martin gave Dad a secret code— a key to the clue. A length of leather that somehow holds a clue. But in order to make sense of it, he'd need whatever clue Gilman had.

I know what you're thinking. You're probably jumping up and down and asking, "Why didn't he just tell it all to your dad if he was the good one?"

Well, Martin was sharp. He didn't want a target on his best friend's back. Because his best friend, as it happens, is raising a daughter (me!) who needs him sorely.

So, he split up the information to protect his find, protect himself, protect his friend, and let his discovery live on if he should up and ~~kick the bucket~~ *perish.*

Martin Shaw waited until the skies were clear and blue, loaded up his pack mule, strapped on his snowshoes, and took off for Montrose, where he planned to hop a train to Denver. Montrose is far, but Denver's a whole world away. Dad and I saw him off, along with Randolph Gilman. Then me and Dad came home, and he cooked corn bread in the skillet (tell you how on the back of this letter. And when you come, we'll make it. When you come, Marybeth Spatts, confetti will fly!)

That night, a storm blew in. We sat by the fire and listened to the wind howl and chinked up cracks in the cabin with rags until we could patch them better.

"This is a bad one," he said, and I knew it, too. He paced back and forth, looking at me, looking at the door, looking at me, looking at the door. I could tell he wanted real bad to go after Martin. Those two had been pulling each other out of scrapes ever since they were little tykes. Martin saved Dad back in that avalanche I mentioned. Dad had it in his head that he owed it to Martin to do the same, if he ever needed it—said sometimes Martin risked too much. But he didn't want to risk his own life, on account of me. Finally, I stood up and said, "You go get him, Dad. I'm fourteen years old! Not a child anymore."

He laughed at that. Laughed, Marybeth! Then I jutted my chin out and drew myself up and marched him over to the door. "You'd been risking your life in the mines every day for three years by the time you were my age. I'm fine here. And you'll never rest till you know he's safe."

Well, he went, finally. Said he would only follow as long as he could see tracks and wouldn't go longer than a few hours. He wrapped up good and went out into that night with such a vengeance. I think it was him making the cold shiver and not the other way around.

As that storm howled and blew through our valley in swirls and drifts, I worried more for that man than I ever had before. Chewed my nails down to stubs and would've bit off my own fingertips without even noticing if he hadn't burst through the door when he did. The storm tried its best to burst in, too, coming all around him and him shielding me from its gusts, just like he always has.

He shut the door. Pressed his back against it. Lifted his head slow, and when he met my eyes with those blue ones of his that were always so calm, I saw only heartache. He shook his head so small, and I knew.

"Dad," I said, and rushed over to get him out of his layer of snow, and the layer of ice under that, and the layers of jackets. He was in a trance.

"It—doesn't make any sense," he said. "He's crossed that ridge a thousand times . . ." And wouldn't tell me more, not for days. When the storm finally let up, there came a knock at our door, and I thought for sure it was Martin, there to say it was all a joke, he was fine.

But it was the constable. Hat in hand, saying could Dad come in to tell them again what happened?

What happened? I wanted to scream it. I followed them down the mountain. Paced outside the sheriff's door while Dad went into that brick building and upstairs where I could see him through the window, solemn, shoulders sagging, sitting across from the constable, who nodded every now and then and leaned forward at last, saying something grave. I saw a third man, bowler hat on, step toward them and plant his fists on the table, shaking his head and saying something else that made everyone in the room tense up.

Dad came out looking worse than before. People looked sideways at him on the street. Some of them crossed the street to walk on the other side. Oh, did it make me mad, Marybeth. Nailspittin' mad. I wanted to go after them and demand they explain themselves. But I slipped my arm through Dad's and pulled him close.

When we reached the trail home, I finally asked him what happened.

You've never seen a man look so broken. He shook his head.

34

"When I found Martin . . . he was already gone. In a bad way, looked like he'd fallen and hit his head on a rock. I wrapped him up and led him back on the mule, took him to the sheriff. . . . But now they're saying maybe—maybe I—" He swallowed, looking white as a ghost. "Folks aren't taking too kindly to me right now, Ruby girl. But whatever they say, I never would harm Martin. Never in a million years, never for a million treasures."

"'Course you wouldn't!" I said, stomping my foot and turning him to face me, willing my words to stop those tremors coursing through him. "Those people know you. Once the shock wears off, they'll know. You wait and see."

We're still waiting, Marybeth. I sure hope I'm right.

Dad still goes to the mines. Still goes down in the shafts, still risks his life every day for these others who look at him like he's dirt. I know one day they'll see. They have to. But I hope it's before it's too late. I hope it's while he's still walking this earth and can be free of this shadow cast over him by Randolph Gilman's accusations. He's the one who went to the constable, questioning Dad's story. Insinuating—look that word up—that Dad wanted Martin's treasure all for himself.

I say, it's more like Gilman wants it all for himself. I told Dad as much. He didn't like the idea . . . but I can tell he's thinking it, too.

Truth be told, I think plenty of people around suspect Gilman . . . but tensions are so tight you could snap 'em with a twig. Some don't want to get on Gilman's bad side for fear of what he'll hold over them. Some are angry at those who won't take a stand against Gilman, till the town's becoming one big tangle, and Dad's at the center of it. Dad, who's always been the glue to hold everyone together, is in the middle of the biggest rift of all. It's tearing him apart.

But he's also not a saint. He mounted a telescope on top of the cabin, some old pipe thing he built with Reuben Murdock a long time ago. He pointed right at Wildwood, Randolph Gilman's fancy good-for-nothin' house. More like a castle than a house. I said, "Gilman's going to think you're watching him." To which he said, "Yep." He never goes up there. He spends his mornings watching the sunrise, his nights watching it set, and never once even blinks into that telescope. Says he doesn't want to let that

man take from him anything more than he already has. Says the
best he can do to get back at him is let it go. Says Gilman might
be building an empire, but that he himself is building something,
too. His bricks are just invisible. I don't entirely know what he
means, but he'll tell me in his own time. It's his way.

For now, he just wants to let the truth come out when it will.

So that's the story, Marybeth. What do you think of Mercy
Peak now? Not such a fairy-tale town after all, huh?

Maybe when you come, we'll sleuth it out. We'll find proof
that Dad was innocent. He has to be.

Promise?

Write soon,

Rusty

p.s. I hear you wondering if this means that treasure is still
out there. I bet it sure is. We'll find it when you come. Us or no
one, right?

✳ ✳ ✳

Dad's Skillet Corn Bread

Just make regular old corn bread, but add a smidge
of nutmeg but not so much you know it's there.
Doesn't make sense, but it makes a difference.

Cook in skillet until it holds together like a bread
should. No pudding-like nonsense.

Spread butter on it or it's nothing.

Drizzle honey, if you want.

Done.

(Eat it while it's hot!)

✳ ✳ ✳

Dear Rusty,

Well, we're a pair. Things do seem awful dark right now. And
when it's dark, the moon comes out.

Do you know why the moon is light?

36

It's not. It borrows its light from the sun. Seems like when I've been down, you've been the sunshine and I borrow your light. When you've been down, I can bounce some of the light from my world into yours, even if it's just in letters.

But what do we do when both our worlds are dark?

We do what you said. We both go out and see it. We defy the dark. When we might want to bury our heads under a pile of blankets and shut the world out—we venture into that very world. Climb a hill, a rise, a peak. Find the moon when it's big and full. And we look it full in the face. Midnight my time, ten o'clock yours, next full moon. And we'll sit there and we'll point to the moon and we'll say to the dark, "Look at that! That moon doesn't even have any of its own light and still it sears you straight through to your heart. You will not claim us!" And we will know we're going to make it through.

Deal?

Marybeth

p.s. Yes. I promise. When I come . . . we'll find out the truth. It's us or no one.

* * *

Dear Marybeth,

Deal. See you at the moon.

Rusty

When you come, Marybeth Spatts, confetti will fly!

—Rusty, age 14

March 1948

A pale sliver of twilight moon watched on as Mercy gripped the rusty gates of Wildwood.

"I'm home, Rusty," she said. "Home at last." With a shove, she pushed the creaking gates, shoved hard when a berm of old leaves and pine needles attempted to barricade her entry.

You ought to see the old Gilman place, Rusty had written once. *Like one of those storybook castles, all rock and timber. Most everything's rock and timber (or brick) around here, but the Gilman place is something else. First off, there's a big old gate, like giant teeth at the front of a mouth. I bet you feel like you're being eaten alive if you ever pass through them. I wouldn't know, I sneak in the back way. Wildwood land goes on and on up the mountain behind, farther than any old Gilman has ever gone. They're too busy running the town and visiting exotic places like Washington, D.C., and Paris, and Denver. And over the whole gate there's a name written. They named that place Wildwood. They bring up hunting parties, and they got all kinds of lanterns hanging in trees for fancy balls, and their faraway people from Washington and Paris and Denver come all this way and dance in fabric that swishes like they brought their own wind with them. Don't they know we got plenty of wind already? I climbed a tree and watched 'em, don't tell. It's a good tree, I've been up there before. Ned Roberts said he once saw Randolph Gilman poring over an unrolled bunch of big papers, like a map, and now everyone here wonders if Mr. Gilman's got some new secret mine up his sleeve that he's not breathing a word about. I went up the tree last spring to see if I could snatch a glimpse of the paper or the mine. Didn't see either, but I nearly got busted when I dropped some of my Cracker Jacks and they landed in a lady's champagne. She got one of the nut clusters. Maybe she needed them more than me. All they had to eat at the party was something called* foie gras, *which kind of sounds like you're choking when you say it. . . .*

If only Rusty could leave her a trail of Cracker Jacks now, lead her into this place. She passed beneath the sign that now said WILD OOD. The middle *W* had spun downward and was clinging on by a shred of dignity and mountain force.

"Wild Ood," she said quietly. "What's an Ood, I wonder?" She knew very well that there was no such thing, but the word made her laugh, and the laugh gave her courage.

A breeze twirled through the gate after her, scooping a pile of crispy leaves from their hiding place beneath the eaves of two round stone turrets, towering two stories each with a stone wall attaching them each to the house at some length. They created something of a court-yard, where a few sad torches stood akilter, like tired doormen who once stood guard to the gilded world within. From her dress pocket, Marybeth took a key, entrusted to her by Kurt Pike at the mercantile earlier that day, acting as agent for the heirs of the old place, long absent from here. She'd gotten curious stares all around, and she knew what it seemed like—she in her silk dress, new owner of an estate. If they knew she was down to her last fifty dollars, the rest of everything frozen in banks in Los Angeles County . . .

But she'd make her way. She had to.

The key caught on her bandage, and she pulled in a breath.

Nothing for a battle wound like fresh mountain air, Rusty had once said.

Unwinding the bandages with care, she slowly flexed her fingers in, then out, giving the angry red palms a chance to breathe. It hurt . . . but at least she could feel now. Hurting sometimes meant healing was at work.

She slipped the bandages into her pocket and tried again.

Inserting the key into the ornate brass doorknob, which was mono-grammed with a scrolling *G*, she pulled in a breath. Closed her eyes. Saw a quick succession of three doors slamming behind her.

First, her childhood home. A shanty in a mining town a world away from here. She'd left in the dead of night at eighteen, belongings gathered in a kitchen towel and knotted at the top like the runaway she was. Just a train to hop, and a nightmare to leave behind. *Slam.*

Second, the door to the home of Rusty Bright. Best friend of her heart, whom she'd never even seen face-to-face. *Slam.*

And third, the golden doors of Hollywood. Barred irrevocably to their once and former Golden Girl. *Slam.*

She turned the key. Rested her forehead on the solid wood of the old door and willed every last wish she had into the next action. She turned the knob—and nothing happened. She jiggled the key, but it was jammed. She leaned into it both ways, but to no avail. With the sun behind the mountain and light beginning to fade, panic started to rise in her. What would she do if she couldn't get in?

"Be reasonable," she tried to coach herself, but heard the uncertainty in her own voice. *Do better.* She cleared her throat and put on some polish like she would under stage lights. "There are other entrances, surely. And if worse comes to worst, you can sleep outside. It isn't the first time you've done that in Mercy Peak—"

The odd howl-laugh of a coyote pack cut her off, too close for comfort. She yanked her red satin heel off her foot and whacked the key from the side until a satisfying *click* sounded. She threw herself into the door, pushed it open, tumbled inside, and shut it hard. Her shoulders heaved as she caught her breath, opening her eyes. In her hand, her shoe was heel-less now, its stiletto likely lying in a bed of pine needles outside in the dark.

A shiver traversed her spine. She'd traded the cold March air of Colorado for the frigid air of what felt like a glorified tomb, cavernous and cobwebbed.

The rock walls were thick. The door was thick, like the tree it had been cut from was as old as Eden. The windowpanes, diamond-cut and seamed in lines of lead, were thick. It had the air of a vault and it all felt wrong.

What did vaults hold? Treasure.

And what did Wildwood hold?

A shadowy creature skittered across her feet. She leapt backward and made a mortifying screechy sound. Something shuffled in a pile of old papers in the corner. *Use what you got, Marybeth,* Rusty used to write to her. *Don't matter how poor you are. You got rocks? Build a castle.*

You got shoes? she might have said now. *Defend yourself.*

Removing her remaining shoe and holding it up, she approached the corner and narrowed her eyes through the darkening grey light.

And then it launched, sending an explosion of paper scrap confetti in its wake and screeching more fearsomely than Mercy had. It skittered across her feet again, and she threw her shoe, missing as it disappeared.

"Just a mouse," Mercy spoke. Her voice echoed high and solitary, a cold reminder of her utter aloneness.

When you come, confetti will fly.

Mercy tried to release a dry laugh, but it morphed into choked tears. "Is that the confetti you had in mind, Rusty?"

The decade-old ache, deepened by time, bloomed inside. What she'd give to see Rusty's forward-slant handwriting. She'd loved how it leaned, like it was pushing into the wind and would not be stopped. Just like Rusty.

Catching a glimmer above her of a chandelier, she fumbled around for a light switch. It clicked to no avail. There were gas lamps on the walls, in addition to the odd electric fixture throughout, but only three of them in the foyer worked, causing shadows in triplicate, eerie and orange.

A stone hearth directly opposite the door reached from floor to ceiling, two stories up. Above the hearth, where great families for centuries might have hung oil paintings of patriarchs, Randolph Gilman had instead displayed an illuminated manuscript. Its borders illustrated small scenes, presumably to demonstrate the meaning of the text in times when many could not read. In ornate letters of yesteryear it read,

Philosophiae Naturalis Principia Mathematica
I. Newton

Mercy skimmed the text, making what sense she could of the three laws that followed. Things about forces, uniformity, action, reaction . . . it intrigued her, but not as much as the sole fact that a millionaire had chosen this, of all things, as his home's defining piece.

She thought of him, living all alone in this remote place. And somehow, the thought made her feel lonelier still. The walls of the cavernous, maze-like place seemed to close in on her.

She'd felt that way before. This time . . . she wouldn't be driven out. She couldn't. She had a promise to keep.

Is Randolph Gilman man or machine, Rusty? He sounds awful
cold and calculating.

—Marybeth to Rusty, age 14

Mercy was bone tired. She'd found a small bedroom—likely a servant's
quarters, judging by its simplicity—and shaken out each and every
blanket stored in its cedar chest, piling them atop the bed and burrowing
beneath their weight and warmth. But her mind raced, and she knew
it'd be hours before sleep would come.

She rose and wrapped tight in one of the blankets, coaxing an old
oil lantern into flame. From her belongings, she brought out a paper
worn soft: Rusty's map, one of many she'd sent over the years. This one,
her best depiction of Wildwood Manor. Rusty had made the maps in
duplicate—one for herself, one for Mercy, so they could hypothesize
across the miles together. Rusty was sure Gilman had something hidden
at Wildwood, a proverbial "smoking gun" that would prove once and
for all what had happened to Martin Shaw.

She'd sketched the gate, the house, with one long wing to the west
and one long wing to the east. Two stone turrets stood sentinel in the
back, creating a courtyard of sorts around an ornate well. On the bottom
half of the page, Rusty had labeled the inside of the house: the spiraling
stair, the butler's pantry—Mercy had had to look up *butler* and *pantry*
in the disintegrating school dictionary. She'd written in the location of
the library, a pool, a conservatory, the kitchen, the *summer* kitchen . . .
the list went on and on.

Mercy traced the familiar lines, smiling that her friend had held this
paper, had thought of her when nobody else in the world had thought
of her. As she traced the roofline, she paused.

There were no stone turrets at the front of the house on this map. Only in the back.

Mercy narrowed her eyes. "Did you miss them, Rusty?" But Rusty never missed anything.

This map was fifteen years old.

What had Randolph Gilman needed new turrets for in the past fifteen years?

Carrying the lantern, she made her way back to the foyer and around a bend, trying to map the place mentally. This should be it—and it was marked by a door remarkably plain, in contrast to the other carved behemoth doors throughout the house. Opening it with a creak, she entered a long corridor—the inside of the stone wall that had created the front courtyard outside. Her lamp illuminated steep steps, which she took slowly as her own shadow bounced in odd lines in the flame. Finally, she reached a single arched door. This knob mercifully opened without protest, but the contents of the room beyond offered little answer. The turret had two windows, and upon one ledge sat a pair of binoculars. Mercy picked them up and peered through the window, making out only the dark edge of the mountain to her right, which rose up in sudden height around the border of Wildwood.

Moving toward a telescope positioned by the other window, she bent to the eyepiece. At first, she saw nothing. But then slowly, vaguely, a soft glow came into view—that of a window in a cabin across the box canyon that Wildwood occupied. She watched for a while and spotted movement within. A person, though she couldn't make out who. It took her so by surprise that she backed up in haste. What was this . . . Gilman's own personal lookout? Ralph's words about the man growing paranoid rang true.

She left that turret, circled back to the foyer, and found the entrance to the left corridor quickly. Identical to the first turret—stone corridor devoid of doors, except for the arched one at the end. Only something here felt . . . different. Moonlight spilled from a circular window near the end of the corridor, tossing a silver carpet before her, past cobwebs and spinning mites.

"See you at the moon," she whispered, her promise with Rusty offering enough courage to take just one step. *Just one step.* The same phrase she'd been saying since the day she set foot on the train as a girl. *Just one step, and then one more.* Like always, the trick got her to the single door, oaken and carved in swirls and vines. Hand to the knob, slow and steady, she could almost hear Alfred's voice from offstage: *"Glance over your shoulder,"* he'd bark. *"Big eyes. That's right, now let your hand hesitate upon it, as if something unseen is pushing it back from the doorknob. As if you've got no clue in the world what's behind that door. It might just eat you alive, but you've got to open it or die trying."*

And that was how it felt. Except now as she reached for the knob, there was no staged pause for an unseen audience she'd never know. There was only her, and the cold brass weight of the knob that would not budge in her grip.

The moonlight glinted off it as she pulled her hand back. Bringing her lamp near, the amber glow landed on a mechanism just above the doorknob. Tarnished brass, a row of letters engraved darkly on side-by-side turning wheels.

"It needs a password?" Mercy murmured. She knelt, hanging the lantern on the knob. The carefully engraved letters currently spelled *GISNEL.*

Randolph Gilman had erected a stone tower and locked its door with a six-letter password. Possibilities flitted through her mind—all of them too long—*WILDWOOD*—or too obvious. *GILMAN?* She turned the wheels to try the word, but the knob did not budge.

She stood, pacing the length of the corridor. A trick she'd used when learning lines, letting the rhythm of her feet carry her thoughts.

"Randolph Gilman," she said aloud, and tried to summon everything Rusty had told her about him over the years. "Oldest of the pact-makers. Went away to school. Heir to Gilcrest mine. Engineer. Enjoyed math. Paranoid. Accuser." She scrunched her nose, shaking her head . . . she was missing something. These were all things he did, things that happened to him. But what had made the man tick? Who *was* he?

She tried a few last-ditch combinations—WLDWOD, GLCRST, and the like. But when the guesses started to be completely contrived, she decided the best way to keep on was to let it rest. At least for the night. Perhaps in the morning, her mind would be fresh enough to enter that of Randolph Gilman and discover what was inside.

I'll save your seat.

—Rusty to Marybeth, age 11

Mercy awoke to strangeness all around her but kept her eyes closed.

Closed to the world, to the knots in her stomach, to the fact that she was a traitor, pure and simple. Living in the house of Randolph Gilman, who'd been the source of Silas Bright's undoing. Never mind that it had been the only place for sale in Mercy Peak. Never mind that she had every intention of doing something *good* with this place, if it was the last thing she did. Maybe it would ease this burning ache inside of her, even just a little, after all these years of missing her friend.

The ache was nothing new; it had been her companion as long as she could remember. In her younger years, it sprang from a solitariness she wasn't even old enough to know was an oddity. She didn't know it was strange for a little girl to be up before dark, packing her father's lunches and seeing him off for the day.

"Take care, Pa," she would say, and watch him lumber down the path, pail in hand, wishing always that he would turn and wave—or even just look at her. So she would wait, and when the wave never came, she'd go back inside to tuck her own small lunch into a dented bucket she'd rescued from a stream down the hill.

Most days, the longings followed her young form like a shapeless fog; she didn't want to give them words, because when she did, they felt bigger than her, and that scared her. But some nights, lying alone, only the crickets outside for company, the longings tiptoed out of her heart through the growing lexicon of her mind, clothing themselves in words.

What would it have been to have someone rock her cradle? Tuck the blanket up around her?

How would it sound to have a lullaby of your own and not have to snatch one out of the night like a bandit, hearing a mother in the next shanty sing to her baby and pretending for a moment you'd had a mother, too?

How would it be to have someone, just once, say to her, "Take care, Marybeth," and mean it?

The questions broke her heart because she knew her chance was gone. She'd been born outside that chance, somehow.

Rocking to sleep . . . blankets tucked about her . . . lullabies . . . "Take care, Marybeth" . . . That sort of love just wasn't meant for her.

So mornings came, and she packed Pa's lunch, and she did it all over again each day. She told herself the questions—childish things—would fade in time.

But they never did. They were drowned out for a time by the clamor of Los Angeles . . . but here, with only echoes for company, the old ghosts came flying back.

When you want to shut out the world, go out into it instead. Rusty's words to her, back when her world had gone dark at Pa's mine. And here she was once more. Then again, she'd also sworn that she'd never have anything to do with mines, not ever . . . and here she was. Living in the home of a mine baron.

"Go out into it instead," she said aloud.

Her bare feet obeyed, emerging from the blankets. The floor creaked an off-key welcome and unfurled for her a pathway of light spilling from diamond-paned windows, the kind that dripped with age and time.

And then she pulled those feet back fast. Sun-splashed paths on time-worn wood weren't supposed to feel like—like ice.

She shivered against the chill of the air and looked around.

Sunlight did spill in, illuminating the room that was pitch-black when she'd finally retired the night before. But in place of gleaming, storied floorboards, the lighted path she had imagined was crossed in shadows. That of a lamp, tipped and leaning upon a bookshelf. The books from that shelf, scattered like fallen birds upon the floor. In the corner, a washbasin perched on the edge of a dresser, while its pitcher lay in a heap of broken pieces, slicing the air as dust mites swirled in and out of them like tiny mountain peaks.

What . . . had happened? By the layers of dust gathered, the havoc had been caused long ago.

From her suitcase, she layered on two sweaters and the warmest garment she could find: a hooded red cape lined in fluff of white, from a mountain Christmas musical with Bing. She pulled it on, feeling ridiculous. She'd thought this home was going to be a fairy tale—the closest thing to a happy ending she might yet find—but she, in her riding hood, was the closest thing to something from a fairy tale here.

In each room, she found not vestiges of a storybook, but pieces of a nightmare.

The butler's pantry, ransacked. The silverware flung this way and that, splayed in sharp angles. Who would raid the silver and leave it there?

The kitchen, a window broken, a skillet nestled in the greening grass just outside it. Who would break a window . . . from the inside?

The upside-down and inside-out questions continued. An indoor pool, empty of water but littered with sheet music, papers, receipts.

A conservatory, plants long dead, tiles removed and not replaced, jingling a terra-cotta tune beneath her feet.

It was all so odd . . . but it could be righted.

Until she stepped into the room she had longed for. Rusty had once spoken of glimpsing the library. *Books as high up as the sun, Marybeth, and a ladder all around to roll on. I rolled it. I know you wouldn't do that, you'd go straight for the GIGANTIC dictionary that has its very own stand like it's a preacher at a pulpit. But I did, Marybeth. And I screeched with delight before I could stop myself. The housekeeper came running and shooed me off with a feather duster out those double doors. Someday, I'll sneak you in there and stand guard while you read that big old dictionary to your heart's content, even if it takes a whole hour.*

Mercy stopped before two doors of great oak, carved in a scene depicting forest nymphs dancing among trees. She placed her palm against the wood and felt a tug of hope.

Here, in this room, was her heart. She knew it. Rusty had planned to bring her here, to sneak her in, and hadn't she done that? Perhaps by means of nearly all of Mercy's savings not frozen by Pinnacle, but she'd gotten her here. If Mercy hadn't come here all those years ago . . . If losing Rusty hadn't sent her riding a train to Denver, where she'd seen that advertisement for auditions on a bulletin board . . . she wouldn't be standing here now.

"I'm here, Rusty. I made it at last," she whispered. Pushing the doors open in opposite directions, she took a deep breath and stepped in.

A tornado had swept through here. Or something just as bent on destruction. Shelves were tipped, books splayed every which way, a mahogany filing cabinet—or what remained of one—sat gaping and blackened where a fire had consumed everything inside and, by all appearances, had then been doused.

Who would do this?

Looking at the hall of stories that was empty now, she was slammed with understanding too deep. She, too, knew what it was to have every story of your life, every role you'd played, go up in flames.

Stepping back out, she closed the doors, leaned against them, and pressed her eyes shut. "Lord, help me," she murmured. Partly a confession near unto surrender, and partly a prayer of desperation.

The clanging of a bell sounded so loud and sudden, she jolted. Eyes wide, she looked all around.

"H-hello?" she called. Was someone in here with her? Was there a bell tower she hadn't seen, or . . . ?

It clanged again, and she thought it sounded like it was coming from outside. Making her way across the floor, she paused at the front door. *Put on your polish, Mercy Windsor.* It wouldn't do to be seen at her wit's end. Quickly she removed the red cloak, brushed her dress smooth, squared her shoulders, and spread on her stage smile.

She opened the door to a smile so warm it seemed to blow the chill right off the morning. A tarnished brass bell, the likes of which she'd seen crown the faces of old steam trains on set, stood beside her on a post. An interesting choice for a doorbell, but Wildwood was full of surprises.

"So it's true!" the woman said. Strands of silver hair scattered among gold framed her face, escaped from her braid like a snatch of mountain wind had set it free. "Tongues were wagging in town that someone was staying at Wildwood, but nobody believed anyone would do such a fool—" She stopped, shaking her head. "There I go, getting ahead of myself again. I always do get things out of order." She set a large picnic basket down and offered her hand, which Mercy shook. "I'm Willa Jones, and I thought if there was any truth to the rumor, someone up here might be a touch hungry by now."

Savory smells wafted from the basket—ham, fresh bread, and other things that mingled into such a symphony that Mercy's stomach joined in with a growl.

Mercy's cheeks burned hot, but Willa only looked delighted. "Come in, if you like," she said. And then recalled what she was inviting the woman into. "It's in a bit of . . . disarray . . . but—"

Willa waved the thought off, stepping in like it was old territory. "We all know about this place, dear girl. Don't you worry. Now if you don't mind my taking over the kitchen for a minute or two . . ."

And she was off, Mercy trailing behind, opening doors for her, clearing a spot on the kitchen counter. Willa nestled the basket there, planted her hands on her hips, smile undaunted. "Well," she said brightly. "We'll have this put right in no time. The window might take some doing, but—" She paused as if catching herself running ahead again. "You sit." She gestured to the small table, the one place Mercy had dared to clean so far. "Plates . . ." She skimmed the cupboards, where shelves were cobwebbed and scattered with dishes both broken and whole. "Plates are overrated," she said with a wink.

How that woman managed to pull an entire feast from such a small basket, Mercy would never know. A coffee can that produced a loaf of steaming Boston brown bread. A simple enamel dish—the likes of which she hadn't seen since she'd left North Carolina—revealed a thick slice of ham, browned to perfection, alongside two fried eggs. She'd even brought a crock of butter and a small jar of jam. "Blackberry," she said. "Harvested last summer, up by the falls—" She clamped her hand over her mouth. "Well, the cat's out of the bag. That's your property now, but it seemed a shame for the berries to go to waste. I do apologize. . . ."

"I'm glad you rescued them," Mercy said. "I hope you still will."

Willa paused her busywork, looking with fondness at Mercy. "If that isn't the nicest thing . . . They're wrong about you, in town. I told them there had to be more to you when they said you were a city slicker who'd—" She caught herself. "You like coffee?" She poured from a thermos into a blue tin camp cup speckled in white.

"Won't you join me?" Mercy said. "There's enough to go around, and I'd love to learn more about you."

Willa's smile was kind. "I ate hours ago," she said. "But friendship, that's fare there's always room for." She pulled up a chair and carried the conversation with gentle ease, allowing Mercy to eat.

Daughter of a sea captain, she said she was, born on the high seas and whisked away to these mountains when their ship had nearly capsized "in a tempest to tell of, time without end," she said. "Father swore he'd get his family as far from the sea that tried to end us as he possibly could, and put mountains on all sides, too. It was a good life, growing up here."

Mercy nodded. There were times as a child when she'd imagined she could feel Mercy Peak's meadow grass beneath her own feet, even as they were pinched inside too-small saddle shoes.

"The big secret is"—Willa leaned in conspiratorially—"when I was a girl, I wanted nothing more than to see that ocean I was born on. Seems it was trapped in my bones, and never went away. I'm like a conch shell, you might say. I didn't let on; it would've undone my father terribly. That storm did something to him. . . ." She shook her head. "He was a dear man. An ocean is a small price to pay to guard the heart of a man like that." She drummed her fingers in a nearly musical trill on the simple table. "But enough about me," Willa said, looking as pleased at Mercy's nearly empty dish. "How was your first night at Wildwood?"

"A little strange, to be honest," Mercy said. She wasn't sure what to disclose about the locked room, or how much Willa already knew. Still, it felt nice to have something of an ally. "I'm curious about the turrets in the front of the house. They seem . . . newer than the rest? The rock is a slightly different shade of grey."

Willa shook her head slowly. "That," she said, "is a byproduct of Randolph Gilman's steady demise into eccentricity. You know about the wall he built around the headwaters of the falls, I presume? And the tunnel?"

"The tunnel . . ." When she'd read the ad, the dark place out of view of the world at large had drawn her. But in all the flurry since arriving, she hadn't had a chance to find it yet.

"The Gilmans ensured they could always get to town. The town is here because of them, after all, and the senior generations of Gilmans were cut from a different cloth. The original Mercy Peak Gilman, Randolph's grandfather, never forgot where he came from. He built this place alongside the lake so that even when he couldn't traverse the winter road of mud and ice, he could cross by boat and snowshoe the rest of the short trip down into town to see how the people were faring. And when he couldn't get in by boat, do you know what that man did? Strapped on ice skates. Randolph . . ."

She shook her head. "As I said, he was cut from a different cloth. Fed from a silver spoon, and though he was smart as a whip, he lacked the fortitude most men of this mountain had. He wanted a way into town that wouldn't subject him to snow, or ice, or even the heat of summer . . . so he had a tunnel dug. What condition it's in now is another matter, but to your question—that's where the rock came from. Those were added only a few years before Randolph died, God rest his soul. I was always a smidge awestruck by him when we were young—but even so, my heart went out to him. By the time I was old enough to start school, he was getting ready to leave it for his fancy school back east. Some of the boys tried to include him in their adventures and shenanigans, but he always seemed a bit on the outside. Too solemn to fit in with them, too young to fit in with the businessmen he emulated. Seeing the way he walled himself away here at the end, I wonder if he wasn't doing the same thing back then, on a smaller scale. Everything had to make sense for him, follow the laws of nature to a T."

"Hence the display of Newton's Laws?" Mercy said.

"Precisely. Nothing escaped the man's notice, everything meant something literal. His friend—or foe, nobody's quite sure—Martin Shaw, those two couldn't have been more opposite. To Martin, everything was telling a story, everything was majestic, everything was a metaphor. 'The universe pours forth!' he used to say whenever he saw something remarkable. And it could've been anything. Once, he was watching an ant carry a load and shaking his head in wonder. 'It's moving mountains,' he said. And Randolph, watching the same scene, said simply, 'It's an ant and a speck of dirt' and walked away, leaving his friend lost in his own reverie. Anyhow."

She flung a dish towel over her shoulder. "No one knows much beyond that; he'd sent the servants away long before he built the front towers. Whether for want of solitude or want of funds, it's anyone's guess. But there was evidence even back then that the Gilman coffers weren't so full any longer. People speculate about the towers, what's in them. Kids like to say there's a mummy up there. One of the towers is locked, you know." Mercy concealed her surprise at Willa knowing this. "People tried . . . well, you've seen the state of this place."

"A little worse for the wear."

Willa's laugh filled the room. "Ransacked, more like. There are those who were none too pleased with Randolph Gilman. He liked to keep whatever 'leverage' he could about anyone he could hold it over. They all wanted it back after he died. Receipts, accounts payable that were paid long ago but never recorded as such . . . But the new owner of Wildwood promises to be a welcome change."

Willa changed the topic, chattering on and insisting on staying to clean up the kitchen. "No need to entertain me, dear, just go about your day as you normally would. Not right for a girl to have to put this place to rights all on her own . . . When things fall apart, people should rush in, not run away. Consider this my 'rushing in.'"

Thanking her so profusely that Willa asked if she was going to have to shoo her out of the room with a broom, Mercy made her way back to the flagstone foyer. At every turn, something cried out to be cleaned or fixed, made right.

Most of all, the story of Rusty's father.

"Rusty . . . what do I do?" Her heart twisted in the silence that followed. Sometimes she thought that's what hurt most—the sudden severing of everything Rusty. Her indomitable voice, her vibrant spirit—no warning, no good-bye. Just gone. The silence, cruel.

She recalled Rusty's description from the time she'd been discovered roaming the estate and had been called in by the housekeeper to help chase out a squirrel.

Light floods in from a billion windows, like someone built that welcome-room-tower-thing for the sole purpose of holding sunlight captive and wrapping visitors all up in it.

Mercy opened her eyes.

She blinked. Blinked twice. And again, trying to get her eyes to work with the darkness before her.

A holding place for light? She shook her head and laughed dryly. Every window was boarded, except for the circular one so high up it only illuminated the top of the stairs. It felt like a prison cell. She'd been in enough on set to recognize the dank air of hopelessness.

Paint peeled, mites settled, bits of the floor were cracked like the flagstones were burrowing up, trying to make their way back outside to the mountain from which they'd come.

But the big picture window, front and center, was boarded up from the inside. Different wood—older than the rest, by appearances. As if whatever captive this prison had held . . . had hammered himself in.

That, at least, she could take care of. She might not be able to put this whole place to rights overnight but she could always do something, no matter how small.

And that was enough. It would have to be.

Back in her room, she opened her suitcase and pulled out her most treasured possession: the folio. It was where she kept the letters and maps. How Rusty had loved her maps.

Mercy rummaged through them, landing at last on the one depicting

Wildwood Estate in all its glory, with an arrow prominently pointing at the tree where Rusty liked to watch Gilman's soirees.

MY SPOT, she'd written in all capitals.

YOUR SPOT, she'd written in the tree next to it. And then, in parentheses, *(I'll save your seat)*.

She searched until she found the crooked drawing of a barn and a garden shed, then went to track it down and find a hammer.

Outside, the morning air washed over her like water from a mountain brook. Crisp, clean, clear. It was sweet, tinged with the scent of pine, sage, and fresh-fallen rain. A smell so lofty it seemed to billow up inside of her, unearth something from beneath the dregs of disillusionment.

It carried her swiftly through overgrown trails as a woodpecker's beat beckoned her to a weathered barn. She tried the padlock with all the keys on the ring given to her at the mercantile, but to no avail. This man and his locked doors . . .

She walked on, puzzling again over what he might have used as a password in the turret room. Willa said he was literal. What did one need to open a door? A key . . . but that word was too short. Which seemed to be the case with every other literal possibility she thought of as she walked on. *Word. Code.*

Perhaps . . . *answer?* Or maybe he was less literal, and it would be his hero's name—*Newton.* Or *tunnel,* a nod to where the tower stones had come from? Or perhaps simply *letter,* to signify that letters were needed to unlock the door. Feeling hopeful, she picked up her pace. At least she had a few possibilities to try when she returned.

The garden shed proved a sight easier to access, as it had no door at all. Or rather, its door had fallen on its face in the mud, laid out like a warped wooden welcome mat. She stepped over it, climbing into the vine-covered building. She rummaged through crates of tools and nails, stopping and nearly swallowing her own stomach when she stumbled into a corner of stacked crates marked *TNT.* Quick relief came when she realized they did not, in fact, contain dynamite, but sat empty.

Still, she moved a bit slower and more carefully until she found a hammer, trying not to wonder what Randolph Gilman had been doing with crates of TNT.

Shaking off the scare, she emerged dirt-smeared and ready to accomplish something. But the sound of trickling water stopped her in her tracks. She turned, searching. Moving to the far side of the shed, where she had a clear view of the steep-rising mountain above, her breath caught. For there, through the trees in glinting white splendor, was a waterfall. Frozen into daggers of ice that were both majestic and terrifying.

Mercy dropped the hammer at her side, narrowly missing her toe. She snatched it up and closed the distance, tilting her head to take in the nearly musical performance of droplets. The ice gleamed with the melting sheen, and by the look of things, this petrified place would be roaring to deafening life in days, or even sooner. She reached out, taking hold of it, wondering if she'd ever be able to place her hand here once it was flowing in full force.

A smile tugged at her face. What was happening? She was holding a waterfall. Literally gripping it, frozen in time, in the palm of her hand. Of all the things she'd done . . . all the places she'd been . . . all the roles she'd played . . . never had she even thought to dream of such a thing.

It felt as if this place were whispering some truth to her, something she didn't quite know how to hear yet. And it felt so foreign. Perhaps . . . a bit like joy.

Back inside Wildwood, she stood before the boarded-up picture window, and as her first act of restoring this downfallen place, she let the light in. Pried the board loose and lowered it to the ground, she could see that the window wasn't broken at all. She set to cleaning it, with a towel and water from an actual hand pump in the kitchen. As layers of grime gave way, newly released light set the chandelier above twinkling, casting color here and there, despite the cobwebs. And she couldn't help marveling at the view it afforded. Who in their right mind would cover up such a vista?

She could see rooftops of the village poking up like timid onlookers from below the rise that created the basin of the lake. Tallest among them was the pinnacle of the clock tower.

Mercy smiled, recalling Rusty's account of how Randolph Gilman had "generously commissioned" the clock tower addition to the town hall, only to nearly come to fisticuffs with Martin Shaw over it, claiming Martin was a lousy stonemason, clockmaker, and metalsmith, and that he'd gotten carried away with its ornateness and was taking too long. Martin claimed anything worth doing was worth doing well and challenged him to find another stonemason/clockmaker/metalsmith all rolled into one man. They'd each huffed off, leaving the town gawking.

How many other stories were held down there in the streets and within the canyon walls of the mountains, rising around the village like a fortress? The layers of strata tilted upward in diagonals, as if the whole mountain were trying to say, *Look up!*

She did. To the right, at the head of the little Victorian village with its grid of streets, brick buildings, and gingerbread cottages, there rose its namesake. *Her* namesake. Mercy Peak, its point a little jaunty and oh so strong. But it was the sight on the left side of the box canyon that arrested her most of all.

The little cabin she'd glimpsed from the turret last night. Humble, solitary.

There was something odd about it—a dark line emerging from its boxy form at an angle. She squinted but couldn't make it out. Remembering the binoculars, she scrambled down the corridor to the turret to gather them up. Returning to the window, she held them up to her eye, shifting around the red-tinted landscape and searching the evergreens until—there.

The little cabin sat stout and secure . . . with a telescope perched upon its roof, pointed right at this window. She could just picture Rusty's father securing it tight to withstand any mountain storm. And even though he never used it, she had a hunch Rusty clambered up on that roof to keep her own eyes on Randolph Gilman many a time.

"Hi, Rusty," she said. Oh, what she'd have given to speak those words to her friend and not just a hollow shell of her friend's life. Still, seeing the cabin that had raised that girl, the one who'd pulled Mercy out of her own forsaken life, given her courage to take the next step and forge a new path . . . it was a comfort.

And here she was again, sorely in need of that courage.

Armed with her handful of six-letter words, she went to face the locked turret door once more. Running her hands along the stone of the wall, she couldn't help thinking of the irony—stones being removed from the earth to make way for a tunnel, only to be used up top to create, in essence, another tunnel.

Kneeling to face the spinning letter discs, she tried the words one by one, heart sinking when the latch refused to budge. She laid her forehead on the door.

"Think," she said. Whatever was inside, it had to be something that could help unearth the truth of what had happened. Perhaps Gilman had found a new vein of gold, after all, and had hoarded his spoils up here. Visions of overflowing treasure chests, stacked bars of gold, a floor covered in glimmering coins danced in her head. She laughed. This was not a movie set.

At this rate, she'd have to force her way in. What had that first tenet of Newton's Laws been? Something about how nothing changed, unless forces were acted upon it . . .

She picked her head up, hope shooting through her. *Forces.*

Moving her thumb over the first wheel, she dialed in the *F*. Then, with care, the *O*, the *R* . . . until all the letters lined up in a row. She stood, gripped the scrolling handle, and pushed down.

A deep *click* sounded, and her pulse responded with equal magnitude.

The door creaked open slowly. Shafts of sunlight speared reams of slow-swirling dust. She was looking at the workshop of a genius . . . or a madman. On a drafting table to the left, a large paper sprawled—the schematic of what appeared to be a train.

Hanging from the ceiling from strings at varying levels were note cards all in neat rows, spinning in the dusty light shafts. A black trunk rimmed in brass brads was shoved up against one wall, locked with a heavy padlock.

And as the light shafts landed on the cold stone walls, Mercy stopped short. Was that . . . writing? On the wall? As if Gilman had run out of paper and in a fevered moment of revelation had written on the walls themselves.

She recognized math when she saw it but was quickly swallowed up in symbols and equations she had no idea how to interpret. Triangles, coordinates, dashed lines, words like *trajectory* and *equal and opposite reaction*. There were tools laid out on a desk with care. Two compasses—one pointy, mathematical sort, next to one round, navigational sort. A magnifying glass. A stack of papers, their top corners fluttering as she moved by, as if timidly waving. She bent over them, thumbing through and skimming their contents. *Timetable of Trains*, *Lode Claim Certificate of Location*, plentiful graph paper, all with varying graphs and arcs upon them . . . and a map. Anchoring them to the desk was a brass cylinder of some sort, seamed in the middle like a capsule.

Mercy picked it up. She felt like an intruder and yet . . . was this hers now? "You bought this place," she said into the quiet and couldn't resist the tug to open the capsule. It squeaked as she twisted, then opened to reveal a small scroll of aged paper.

She carefully unrolled it, setting the capsule pieces on the desk behind her with a *clink*.

In ink-blotted script that looked as if it belonged in a tale of pirates and swashbucklers, riddling lines unfolded.

> *Flightless in flight,*
> *she seeks revolution.*
> *Tunneling blight,*
> *she keeps the solution.*
> *Coil the lash tight,*
> *begin restitution.*

Mercy's stomach fluttered.

"Here you are," a cheery voice said, and Mercy startled. Willa's bright smiling face peeked around the door. "I looked everywhere for you. But how did you manage to get this open?" She gasped at her next thought. "Wait till they all hear."

"If it's all the same to you, I think we'd better wait awhile before we tell them," Mercy said.

"Right you are," Willa said. "They'd all be knocking on your door uninvited—" She raised her hand in a sudden laugh. "Well, like me, I suppose. Anyhow, I'm popping back into town and wondered if you'd like to come. I could show you around a little, make introductions—oh my," she said, noticing the contents of the room. Mercy spun to face her. "So, there isn't a mummy hidden up here after all."

"No," Mercy replied. But there were reams of paper scraps, all wrapped around the mind of a man she did not understand. "But it might not be too far off."

CHAPTER
6

March 1932
From Rusty, age 14

Dear Marybeth,

Composition day is the best because Miss Templeton gives us all three sheets of paper instead of just one. I write real small (see?) so I can take an extra one home. Sometimes things pop into my head and I fair itch for a place to write them down. Dad's given me all the old paper he can find. We don't want for much; the mountain gives us near everything we need to live: fish, pine nuts, fresh spring water. We keep a goat for milk, we bring in supplies from town plenty. I wouldn't say as we're poor exactly. We're pretty rich to get what we need from right beneath our feet. But there's not always extra for paper. So, pardon my small writing.

Spring's coming in slow—like a tug-o-war with winter. We'll get a March full of blizzards, an April that teases daffodils, and then some more snow just when we thought we could shed our winter coats. Crocuses pop up, snow melts, and streams show up that only come during melting and mud season. Birds snatch threads from the clothesline to go build their nests, little bandits. You'll see it someday. When are you gonna come, Marybeth? Maybe when we're old, like twenty?

Speaking of threads in trees . . . there's talk lately about Randolph Gilman. He's getting strange as the years go on. Acting different. Walking his woods at night. Measuring things that have no reason to be measured, marking things on papers. People call it "eccentric," and Kurt down at the store wondered out loud the other day what the man's will said. Said it seemed like his days might be numbered.

It's got me thinking. About life and death and all. If I ~~die young~~ expire from this life prematurely, know this:

1) It was foul play, had to be. Suspect Ned Roberts. He glares at me when I eat peanut butter and honey sandwiches and all he has is dried beef.

2) Aunt Bess, God rest her soul, once said I'm full of vim (what is that?) and vinegar, and it's going to be the death of me. So vinegar could be the culprit. Is it poison in large amounts?

Write soon,

Rusty

p.s. Don't tell a soul: I'm sending this package to you for safe-keeping. Dad and me don't trust Randolph Gilman farther than we can see, and you know why. I saw him hiking the timberline up above our cabin last week. That man's never set foot so high on the mountain his whole life. Doesn't go down into his own mines, doesn't care how the conditions down there are so bad. He just keeps to his ledgers like Ebenezer Scrooge. He's gotta be scouting around our place for the box from Martin Shaw. Dad's away working over in Idarodo mine, and I'm getting that box out of here, to the safest place I know, where Randolph will never look, and I'll be able to find it if I need it.

Please keep it till we untangle this whole mess together one day, or till I write you to get it back. Promise?

Dear Rusty,

I promise. I'm not letting it out of my sight. What's in it, anyway, a belt? Sure looks like it—just kind of simple, with no buckle. I like it.

And, Rusty, you know you can write all the letters you want. I'm sorry I'm slow to answer sometimes. It's tricky with Pa and all.

You just had a birthday . . . and I have a gift for you! It isn't much—most of it was got from the teacher a few months back and I've been saving it. I asked her if I could have Peter Schneider's old composition book. He colored blue in some of the speckled white spots on the front, and he got a D on his essay inside, and then he never came back—I think he might have moved away. So it was just sitting there on her desk for months and months, and it just hurt my heart to see it collecting dust when there are your words, swimming about in the mountain air without a paper to land on except when the teacher gives you a few sheets to write to me.

I covered it up so you don't have to look at Peter's blue speckles, and now it's yours. Happy birthday!

Promise not to let it collect dust, Rusty. Or I'll start calling you Dusty, and that's a promise. Use it to collect your thoughts instead. They're good ones.

Marybeth Spatts

Dear Marybeth,

Is it a belt? Your guess is as good as mine. I thought it was a single horse rein when I saw it. Dad kept it coiled up in that box. I caught him puzzling over it a few times, and neither of us can figure how a length of leather could be the key to a clue. Is it a measuring tape? The length of a man's stride? A code, awaiting its decoder? We'll find out someday.

Now, about your gift. How do I love it? Let me count the ways!

1) A whole composition book? Please thank Peter Schneider for up and flunking! I have kept his essay entitled "Why Grits Should Win the Nobel Peace Prize" for posterity. Sure, he might've got a D, and the teacher might have called it "preposterous" in mean old red ink, but you know, he has a fair point. They got grits down at the diner, and I'm going to see if they can rename them after Peter Schneider.

2) What's that burlap from that you covered it in? I like how you cut out the picture of a sun rising over cornfields. Was it corn? Did you do that on purpose because corn makes grits? You're a clever one, Marybeth.

3) I love it so much that once it's filled, I intend on hiding it in the dungeon beneath the church so no one will ever find it but you (so you have to come). I guess it's the storm cellar, but dungeon sounds more exciting. Not much call for using it, and the only other thing down there is a surplus of Mr. Vick's pickled beets, which he brought to a church picnic seven years back and "somehow" ended up down there instead of at the supper. (Miss Ellen is the "somehow." She says it was an act of mercy.) My journal shall be there beside them, and you are my sole heir, and it is your inheritance. Inside the journal, I'm also going to hide the last clue I have about the belt-rein thing. But you won't need it. We'll sort it all out together someday. I feel it.

I hereby beqweeth these things to you irrevocably. I just learned that word, and it means "for keeps."

If anyone in this life was ever for keeps, Marybeth Spatts, it's you.

Anyhow, I love my journal to pieces. No, really. I love it so much I cut it to pieces. You think I'm joking? Open up the parcel within for proof, if you please. I will wait right here.

See? I couldn't keep all that glory for myself, Marybeth. You're probably thinking things like "How could she? I spent all that time making that just for her, doesn't she know how hard that was? Doesn't she know how much courage it took to ask the teacher for that notebook? And how on God's green earth does she know all these questions I'm thinking?"

I just do, Marybeth, because I know you and I love you for all those questions. Love you so much that I had to make this because I'm not the only one with words bursting to find a place to land. You've got your dictionary words. You go through life picking up meaning wherever you go, whether it's in these words or every stinking sunset.

So, that tiny volume, made from the lower left corner of my de-luxe burlap cornfield D-graded journal, stitched together at the spine by a shoestring I pilfered from a shoe that I found in a shed at Wildwood that nobody was using or ever will use, is the one and only . . .

BRILLIANT LEXICON OF (the) ORIGINAL MARYBETH SPATTS

See? See how I stitched the letters right on for you? BLOOMS, and a flower to match. Don't you get after me saying there shoulda been a "t" in the middle. It sort of ruins the effect, you know?

I put your first few words in for you.

You can put in whatever words you like from here on out. It's small enough it should fit in your apron pocket. You just promise that no matter what, you'll never stop hunting for all that meaning. Okay?

I need to know you're out there doing that. I skip right over the meaning most times. I see a flower and think, "Hey, flower, you're dumb, growing in the middle of the road there." You'd see that same flower and think, "You brave thing, growing in a crack where nothing else would dare."

That's something, Marybeth. And something's something. Remember that.

Rusty

p.s. Speaking of blooms, when you come, remind me to take you to Willa Jones's cottage. It's all built of stone and sits on a ledge of mountain overlooking the river, with green grass rolling down and red roses climbing up and music spilling out the windows. Willa likes music. And she'll like you, and you'll like her. Some things you just know.

BLOOMS

(Brilliant Lexicon of the Original Marybeth Spatts)

ENTRY NO. 001

Keeps

As defined by Ruby Adaline Bright:

(1) Something you hang on to, no matter what.

(2) Marybeth Spatts

Just rip the bandage off. Do the hard thing and get it done, and that's courage. You'll think then you can start living, but the truth is you've been living all along. That's what Dad says. So every morning I eat my stupid porridge that makes me gag. Courage!

—Rusty, age 10

April 1948

Keeps.

That's what Rusty had thought about Marybeth . . . but it wasn't true. Not according to Hollywood. Not according to her pa. The old ache burned, and she tucked the letter under the brass bookend she'd polished that morning.

Since last week, she'd puzzled over the rhyme she'd found in the turret.

> *Flightless in flight,*
> *she seeks revolution.*
> *Tunneling blight,*
> *she keeps the solution.*
> *Coil the lash tight,*
> *begin restitution.*

Most of it she could make neither heads nor tails of. But that last part—coiling a lash? She knew exactly what the "lash" was. It was what she'd thought so long to be a belt. It was the one thing she had left of Rusty. It was her most cherished possession, the truest part of her. So much so that in every role she'd ever played, she'd "coiled that lash" around her own waist, over some costume or another. Staking a proclamation to the world—or perhaps just to herself—that there was a piece of Marybeth Spatts under all those lights, all that makeup.

It was that writer, Sudsy McGee, who'd noticed it first, after four or five films. And he'd made quick work of announcing it to the world. The headline was printed on her heart.

WHAT SECRET DOES THE SILVER SCREEN QUEEN WEAR?

He'd gone on to chronicle the scenes in which he'd spotted the belt, movie by movie.

She'd been consumed with anger. What right did the man have to discuss her possession with the world? She'd locked it away in a safe, determined never to bring it back out.

Only her anger had quickly turned to shame. It *wasn't* her possession, not really. And he was just doing his job.

Her only comfort had been that Randolph Gilman, if he was still alive, had no clue that Rusty Bright had sent her the length of leather. And even if he did . . . he certainly had no clue that Marybeth Spatts had crossed the country and assumed another name. She'd felt secure for the belt in that, at least.

That was, until the day her dressing room had been broken into while on location in Chicago. She'd worn the belt as usual, tucked carefully beneath a drape of a dress for a soiree scene. But the director would have none of it, despite her best attempts to convince him. She'd retreated to her dressing room, coiled it up with care, and hidden it in an empty shoe, only to backtrack and place it in her handbag for the scene instead. After the scene, she'd found the lock to her door was broken. "Happens sometimes, miss," the janitor said as he fixed it, but the wary look on his face said otherwise. And so did a single upside-down tapestry pillow on the gilded settee.

From that day on, she'd gone to great lengths to keep it with her, or locked in a safe inside Celestial Climes, behind locked door and triple-locked gate. There was only one person on earth who would go to such lengths for an otherwise ordinary length of leather. She couldn't rest, knowing her one connection to Rusty, the one area where she hadn't yet failed her, was at risk.

She'd hired a private investigator, who reported that Randolph Gilman, last in the line of Mercy Peak Gilmans, had passed away—*perished*, Rusty would've written in—just that week. But that he had hired someone who'd been making inquiries from Swickley's Crossing to Elitch Gardens, had tracked Rusty's connection to her—and the belt—all this way.

And now Gilman was gone.

She'd never met the millionaire . . . but did he have a single person in all the world to mourn him? The thought wended around her heart until her short-lived relief was overshadowed by sorrow.

There had been no further incidents regarding the belt, other than Sudsy McGee's investigative journalism that made it into a piece of Hollywood lore.

It felt like the last thing on earth that was hers had been snatched from the depths of her heart and fed to a ravenous public, and all for a headline.

But in her next role, the voices of anger and fear had quieted enough for her to remember why she'd worn it in the first place: as a silent proclamation to the unknowing world that Rusty Bright would never be forgotten. And now, too, as a way of holding sorrow on behalf of the man who had no one to mourn him. And as a proclamation to herself that somehow . . . she would keep her promise.

She didn't have the belt now. An employee of Pinnacle Studios had bundled up the few possessions that were entirely hers when she'd been disallowed from Celestial Climes. That night, in a tiny motel room far off Sunset Boulevard, she'd dug frantically through the small bag. Her heart shattered afresh when she realized what was missing.

It was then, in her blackest moment—no home, no family, no friends, no single cherished possession—that she faced her choice.

Read the signs loud and clear, and admit defeat.

Or sell every possession that wasn't locked down and tied to Pinnacle Studios, and do the only thing she could think: buy Randolph Gilman's estate and track down that clue.

Now she had the clue—the riddle—but no key.

But somewhere in a church basement, there might be a clue.

Today was the day. She finished dusting off a massive dictionary on its carved pedestal. Wiping a rag one last time over the edges, she flipped the pages. Its crinkly whisper fluttered to a stop, letting her run her finger down as she searched until she found:

Vim [vim]: n.

energy and enthusiasm. Synonym: dynamism.

A dry laugh tumbled from Mercy. "Dynamism?" A word she'd never heard in her life before this moment, and yet it latched onto her memory of Rusty like an indelible stamp. *Dynamism.*

Pulling the BLOOMS from her apron pocket, she wrote as much.

ENTRY NO. 187

Dynamism
As defined by Marybeth Spatts
(1) Vim, energy, enthusiasm
(2) Ruby Adaline Bright

How she missed her friend. What she would've given to tuck this entry into a letter and send it on its way to be delivered by Galloping Goose Motor 8 into her friend's dusted-up hands. She smiled even as the coals of grief glowed to life. Over time, that's what grief had shifted into. No longer a zombielike walk through terrain that felt foreign and impossible to breathe . . . but now, a place where somehow, grief-embers and smiles knew how to impossibly entwine, wrapping up memories together.

She could just picture Rusty clambering down into a church cellar, looking over her shoulder every three seconds like she was engaged in espionage. In fact, when Mercy had played international spy Evelyn Eve in *Embargo* and Alfred had ordered take after take of her rounding a shadowed alley corner looking furtively over her shoulder, it was Rusty who'd helped her deliver at last, when the director kept swatting down her attempts like tennis balls at the country club.

"*Too quick!*" he said. "*Too slow.*" "*I said furtive, not fake!*" "*I said* spy, *not* cry!" Mercy had pressed herself up against that brick wall of a false building, closed her eyes, breathed in, and pictured Rusty squirreling away that journal next to Mr. Vick's pickled beets. She'd opened her eyes, tried again . . . and delivered. It was a scene that some said won her the Academy Award, and all she'd wanted to do when accepting that gleaming trophy was to thank those pickled beets.

Mercy closed the dictionary with a thud, turning to walk through the sunlit swirl of dust that resulted.

She checked her list. Every item crossed off was like breath for parched lungs.

-Fix broken locks

-Find broom—sweep floors

-MOUSETRAPS, lots. Find out how to set them. Do I need cheese?

-Stock pantry—keep under $5. Saltines? Maybe peanut butter.

-Sensible shoes

-Normal clothing

-Something to fix truck mirror

-Better backing-down-the-driveway skills. (Which aisle would those be in?)

-Magical replenishing of funds

-Someone to tell jokes to so I don't have to write them on to-do lists to myself. Wish Rusty was here.

-Gas for truck

-Get a job (move this to top of list)

-Keep promise

She thought of the things she'd done this morning, her third day here, and wrote them down just so she'd have something to cross off, no matter how small. *Rehang washed curtains on first floor. Check waterfall melt. Feed rabbits.* She crossed them off with a satisfying swash of her pen. The last one was a stretch; she'd discovered a warren of rabbits living beneath the stone barn and had taken to bringing them her meager scraps. They didn't need it. . . but it felt good to have someone to care for.

Coming down from Wildwood's long driveway, the view of Mercy Peak was so beautiful it almost hurt. The town was laid out in a small grid, with the one winding road slipping through it like a river, and the actual river hugging it from the other side, at the base of the peak. All the cross streets stretched in between like neat stitches, as if to bring some order to this wild place with its mounding, pinnacled layers of red-tinged mountains draped in greenest pine.

The church, located on the outskirts of the town with a meadow opening up behind it, was like something from a painting. Part stone and part white clapboard, its simple steeple at a slight tilt, like a hat doffed in greeting.

Mercy nodded back as she approached. Her breath puffed in the cold air, and the only sound as she drew near was the hymn of the river in babbling harmonies.

Peeling paint around letters on a sign proclaimed the *Chapel on the Rock*, and Mercy slowed her approach. It was, as its name implied, built upon a gargantuan rock—and built of stone itself, with the appearance of having grown, stone by stone, out of its very foundation.

She knew the church would be empty. There was a traveling preacher who came once a month, sometimes twice, sometimes stayed a month when snowed in. But he was over in Durango just now, Angus at the mercantile had said. Just to be safe, Mercy checked the door, which was locked.

Unless things had changed, the dungeon—or storm cellar, rather—wouldn't be.

When she'd first come to Mercy Peak, seen the funeral and fled these mountains, she'd been so pulled asunder that she hadn't recalled the journal until she had reached Denver and spent her last penny. *I'll come back*, she'd thought. As soon as she could—as soon as she'd saved enough money.

But when she finally had more than two pennies to rub together, suddenly it was the other commodity that she was short on: time. *I'll get back*, she'd promised. *As soon as there's a break in filming.*

But months turned into years of plane trips, film sets, rehearsals, fittings, premieres, an endless cycle of leapfrog-type duties. Film one, debut the previous one. Film the next, promote the last. And so on, in a dizzying vortex that had made her tired to her very soul. Every time she ascended the metal stairs to board a plane, she wished she was descending stairs down into an obscure storm cellar in the San Juan Mountains, where treasure awaited her. Sometimes, when the vortex threatened to swallow her, she would close her eyes and picture the journal. The quiet. The cool of the cellar. Just knowing it was there, tucked into the folds of the mountain in peace even as the world raged on in chaos, was a comfort to her.

But she was here now. At last.

At the back of the church, the building traipsed off its boulder foundation, onward over the earth and down into an outside stairwell. The stone clambered around an alcove where a half wall protected the stairs from the elements.

She placed her foot on that first step and closed her eyes.

At last.

No clunk of high heels on metal airplane stairs.

No glide of sparkling navy slippers atop a red carpet.

Instead, a step down as her worn boots, pilfered from a wardrobe at Wildwood—too big for her, but welcome in their roominess—gave a mellow *thud* upon the steps until she rounded the corner and stood in a sea of winter-spiced leaves before a weathered door.

Gently lifting the evergreen tendrils of the vines that covered the back of the church, she took the rustic door handle in hand and pushed.

It didn't budge.

She pushed again, this time putting her shoulder into it.

After a furtive glance over her shoulder that would've put *Embargo*'s Evelyn Eve to shame, she threw her whole self into it, bursting through the door with a tumble.

Pitch-black cold swallowed her up. Sickness climbed up inside her, the old nightmare suddenly there—*whoosh*—across the miles and years. The mine that swallowed up her daddy in unseen ways, swallowed up her childhood, swallowed up her life.

"Put on courage," she muttered. Paint it on like layers of stage makeup, wear it even when it didn't go down deep. That's what she knew how to do. That mine was half a country away and a lifetime ago.

A deep, slow breath, and she opened her eyes, her own shadows scattering to the far corners.

Her eyes adjusted until she could see the simple room. Three chairs lined up neatly in various states of disrepair—a splintered leg, an unfastened back where hung a man's worn hat, a wobble that sounded a lonely greeting as Mercy brushed past it. A crate perched on one, containing folded-up blankets and a book placed squarely on top. Her pulse quickened. Was it the journal?

Running her hand over its worn dark cover, she knelt, nearing to read it in the shaft of door light. *Swift Rider: Adventure at Chimney Peak.* A well-loved book of comics, by all appearances, featuring a boy on a horse, holding a wooden slingshot painted with a blue streak. *Swift Rider and Blue Lightning Conquer Peril in the Sky*, the subtitle read.

Not the journal, then. With her eyes adjusted now, she could see the room was only a glorified cavern, spanning half the length of the church above until it met up with the foundation boulder. Small in the grand scheme, but large enough that she'd have to go deeper in.

She crossed to the only other furniture in the room: a tilting set of shelves secured to the wall behind it by ropes, like anchor lines. And there, like a beacon of hope, the unmistakable glint of a glass pickling jar containing Mr. Vick's pickled beets.

"Hello, old friend," she said, smiling. "We meet at last." She was being ridiculous, but she *did* owe them a proper Academy thank-you.

And then—as she shifted the jar ever so slightly . . . there it was. The journal, waiting for her like a promise, and suddenly her throat was closing, eyes swimming.

She lifted her hand. Hesitated, letting her fingers hover over it as she blinked back those tears. The hand that had written her all those letters, the hand that had told her to come home here, the soul that had given her courage when she'd had none of her own . . .

That hand had been the last one to touch this journal.

This was the closest she would ever come to taking hold of her friend's hand. To seeing the one who'd loved her best, loved her most, knew her deepest.

A silent sob slipping out, she let her hand rest upon the cover. Burlap. Strong and rough around the edges, built to hold life. Like Rusty Bright.

Mercy picked it up, held it to her heart, wrapping both arms around it like she was embracing her dearest friend at last. And all at once, she was pulled in by a surge of gratitude and a swell of suffocating grief.

Rusty was gone. Still.

But her words . . . were here.

She should do a thousand things with this book. Hike it to the very tip-top of Mercy Peak, to read it in the place that was grandest, clearest, most untainted by the world below. Find Rusty's old spot in the tree overlooking Wildwood, read it there, where Mercy knew she'd written in it, keeping a tin box of pencils in the hole of that tree.

But instead she just knelt. Right there in an old church basement, hugged by the cold walls that held back earth, and opened it.

BE YE WARNED!
This here's the property of Ruby Adaline Bright and no one else.
(Unless your name's Marybeth Spatts, in which case, hi at last.)

And there was her friend. As real as if she had stepped into the room herself.

"Hi at last," Mercy sighed, whispering a disbelieving laugh at the words before her.

IF YOU READ THIS, and you're not me (or Marybeth), then a fate worse than vinegar is sure to befall you!

First things first. Miss Murdock had a kangaroo rat come around her garden Wednesday night, and folks say she jumped a mile high. Did you ever think Priscilla Murdock, the Bastion of Civility, would depart earth and take flight? She's no angel, and the words she spoke weren't so angelic,

*either (says Ned Roberts), but that might be the closest any of us come to
seeing her fly like one. . . .*

The stories went on. Talk about town festivals, talk about the new
candy at the general store—Boston baked beans, which happily turned
out not to be beans at all—and yes, there was her friend. The same
precocious mix of heart, warmth, pith, a little bit of bite and laughter,
too . . . and the subtlest undercurrent of surprising wisdom.

Time left the room as Rusty's words filled it, ushering minutes or
an hour or more into an abyss as Mercy sat on that leaf-scattered floor
and soaked in the essence of her friend. Laughing, crying, running her
fingertips over words that made her miss Rusty so much the ache beat
against her ribs for a way out.

At last, she closed the book. She would save these entries, ration
them like the treasures they were.

Oh, but the clue! She'd been so carried away in her friend's words,
the warmth of getting to spend time with her in some small way, she'd
nearly forgotten why she'd come.

She flipped to the back of the journal, expecting an envelope or a
note—perhaps another riddle or rhyme. Certainly not expecting what
she found—a seam ripper. Taped to the back cover, no explanation.

With care, she peeled it from behind the yellowed tape, whose grip
gave way into a crisp *snap*. Mercy held up the tiny tool, examining the
sharp point at the end. This was her clue?

Her stomach dropped. The length of leather . . . had a seam in it.
Mercy had presumed it was just the design of the belt or whatever it
was—edges sewn together to give both sides a finished look.

All this time . . . all these years . . . all the millions of people she'd
worn it in front of . . . had there been something inside?

She'd sent a telegram yesterday from the post office inside the mercantile and prayed it would prove fruitful. It was her only hope for
reclaiming the belt, save breaking into property she was legally expelled
from and causing a surefire hullabaloo in doing so.

She tucked the seam ripper safely in the journal, stood, and brushed
the bracken from her dress. She went to brush the dust from her dress
where she'd hugged the notebook, but there wasn't a smudge.

Odd.

Pulling it to herself again, she spotted the illustrious pickled beets,
alone and forlorn upon the shelf, and remembered her other task.

She straightened the jar so that its *Ball* inscription faced forward, like she was straightening a gentleman's bow tie for a grand event. She cleared her throat, retrieved a tea towel–wrapped object from her basket, and closed her eyes to remember that night, up in front of all those people, all those flashing cameras, that red carpet, the Academy.

She'd thanked the Academy duly, and the director, and Wilson P. Wilson. But inside, she'd secretly known that two unspoken sets of thanks were the truest for that Oscar.

She spoke them at last. The first, in a whisper.

"I'd like to thank my dearest, oldest friend, Rusty Bright. My inspiration."

She dashed a wayward tear from beneath her eye, pulled in a breath as she looked at that gold-painted statue, so austere that Mercy stood taller just looking at his posture. And beholding all of its gravitas, she bequeathed it to its new owner. "And I'd like to thank Mr. Vick's pickled beets."

She stood the statue in his proud stance beside the ancient beets, and something bubbled up inside Mercy. Somehow the ceiling felt a little higher, the room a little wider. But as she placed the statue there, she narrowed her eyes. This shelf harbored more than just a light coating of dust. The shelf, the jar—but not the journal.

Unease crept up her spine, and she turned, scanning the room to ensure she was, in fact, alone.

Had she read the room so wrongly? A quick look around confirmed that it really did appear to be just the odd scattering of stored items. But what if the hat and blankets and books belonged to somebody?

"Stop that," Mercy said, halting her imagination. "You're not in a movie. You're in a sleepy mountain town, in a church cellar, and people store things here. That's all."

She gave a curt nod to the beets, a wary parting glance at the Oscar, and made her way out, securing the door behind her.

Back up the stairs upon the carpet of leaves and out in the open, she blinked in the sun and breathed deep, some sense of normal settling back over her. Things always seemed in better order in daylight: time stepped forth in its onward march, hats and crates resumed their place being merely forgotten items, and her heart beat glad and grateful. But as she rounded the corner of the church to make her way out onto the hard-packed road, she stopped in her tracks.

There, pulling a ladder from a winter-weary shed, was a man. Clad in red plaid like a lumberjack and whistling something happy. He leaned the ladder against the church and climbed. Who was this? The preacher? Should she apologize, offer to put the journal back? Maybe make a break for it?

Just walk on, some voice of reason urged.

She hugged the journal tight and took a small step.

"Good morning!" he said.

She turned, but the man wasn't facing her. He just worked away, pulling up shingles, throwing them to the ground. He looked a few years older than she was, with hair the color of chestnuts and a kind face.

"Good morning," she said, stepping into the role of a townsperson. *Townsperson Number Two.* That could be her. How refreshing to just be one of the people, not anyone who anybody paid any mind to or knew anything about—

"Marybeth, right? You find what you were looking for?"

He looked over his shoulder, and she searched for any bit of accusation or offense on his face.

Neither was there. Only a quick smile as he descended the ladder and crossed over to her, taking off a worn, thick glove and sticking out a hand.

"Casey Campbell," he said. "Pleased to meet you."

Mercy took his hand tentatively. "Like the soup," she said, stalling.

"Like the soup," he repeated.

"You . . . knew my name," she said. "I don't recall being introduced—"

He waved his other still-gloved hand and seemed a little like a bear with a big paw. A friendly bear, but looming all the same. "You've been here what . . . two days? Three?"

"And a half," she said.

He looked amused. "But who's counting, right?"

She thought of her tallies scribbled on a notepad—tiny victories—and blushed.

"Newcomers around here usually make the gossip headlines in the first three hours. Three days, and you're nearly guaranteed to be known in every house from here to Silverton. Maybe farther."

His gaze locked on her mud-caked boots, oversized and clunky beneath the sheen of her green dress. "Yep, they've all heard of you."

She didn't know what to say.

The friendly bear of a man shrugged, putting his glove back on. "Don't worry. It was me they were spreading word about six months back. Funny, a person picks this place to come because it's quiet, maybe a place to disappear for a while—"

Her cheeks burned harder.

"—and finds themself center stage."

She gulped.

"But," he clapped his gloved hands, a cloud of dust billowing and catching morning sun, "they're a good crew, for all that. Starts to feel like home at some point, if you can stick it out." His gaze dropped to her boots again. "You'll stick it out," he said, as if pronouncing a verdict.

"What makes you think that, Mr. Campbell?"

"Please, just Casey. I don't know," he said, shrugging as he hoisted a crate of what she assumed were shingles. "You've got grit."

"Grit?"

"Yeah, well, at least your shoes do. And I've got a hunch there's some of that in you, too. Enough to take you down into a spooky cellar and find yourself some great reading material." If there hadn't been friendly mischief in the kind crinkles around his eyes, his words could've pinned her with accusation.

And it hit her. The hat. The crate. The tidy room and this man's rugged but tidy appearance, plaid shirt buttoned up, dark beard closely trimmed.

She stepped back with the realization, pressing a hand to her heart. "I'm sorry," she said. "*Swift Rider*—that was your book?"

Something softened in his demeanor. "My kid brother's. He was a big fan. Used to have me read that to him every day."

In the echoes, Mercy knew his use of *was* didn't mean he was away at camp or some other temporary place. It was the same *was* as Rusty. Her heart ached.

"I'm so sorry," she said again. "I didn't mean to intrude—"

Another wave of his gloved hand as he approached the ladder. "You've got as much a right as me to be in there," he said. "I'm up in the hills and peaks more often than not, work to do up there."

"You're a . . . prospector?"

He weighed the proposal, tipping his head side to side. "In some sense, yes. Not prospecting for gold or jewels. More like . . . the future."

She narrowed her eyes, wary of the way he dodged her question. But who was she to take issue with cryptic answers?

"Skiing," he continued. "The wave of the future for these parts. At least a few of us think so. I'm surveying the mountains for some possible slopes. Preacher lets me camp out in the cellar when I'm down here in the valley, in exchange for a few odd tasks." He nodded to the crate to make his point. He paused then, looking down as if unsure. "Do you know her?" His voice steady, but with an upturn of hope at the end of his question, the uncertainty digging a hole between them that quickly filled with a fondness for his meaning.

"I . . . did. In a sense." He inclined his head, inviting further explanation. "She's . . . gone."

And her heart split, speaking aloud of Rusty for the very first time. And yet for all the ache, it felt . . . right. She had held her friend so close to her heart all these years, never speaking of her to anyone. It felt too sacred, Rusty too dear, too close. No one would understand, not by any fault of their own, but because—*how*? How could they know, in a spoken paragraph or two, all that built between them, with all those letters flying across those years? A pair of sisters, who'd never met. No one could understand that.

But this man did. At least a little. She could see it in the regretful quirk of his mouth. "I heard that from people in town," he said. "People around here sure miss her. Guess I just . . . hoped to meet the one who wrote all that. Seems like she was a good kid. Reminds me of my brother in some ways."

"You read it? Past all those warnings?" Mercy smiled. "How ever did you dare?"

"I could be wrong, but she seems like the sort to be thrilled at someone defying that warning."

"I believe you're right, Mr. Campbell," Mercy said.

He blew out his cheeks. "Guess I owe you an apology, Miss . . . Spatts?" He narrowed his eyes. "Or is it Windsor? I've heard it both ways."

The simplest question, the most impossible answer.

"Guess it's none of my affair," said Casey Campbell, climbing up the ladder. He stopped on the third rung, looking sheepish. "But you're sure—I mean, is there any chance she—" He stopped himself. "Never mind. Enjoy that reading. Glad to see it's made its way home."

Not sure what had flustered him so, she offered a good-bye as he went back to his work, and Mercy turned to face the looming task at the top of her list: Find a job . . . with no practical skills to speak of.

Folio of Field Notes, Volume II: *Mercy Lands in the Mountains*

[Property of Sudsy McGee, Hollywood Biographer]

Interview with Mercy Windsor

Interview Transcript of Biographer Sid "Sudsy" McGee
with Mercy Windsor, screen name of Marybeth Spatts

DATE: February 27th, 1948

LOCATION: The Brown Derby Restaurant, Vine Street, Hollywood

ORDERED: S. McGee: Corned beef hash and pot roast (purportedly
C. Gable's preferred dish here), crème brulee (extra crispy)
M. Windsor: Cobb salad (at place of its invention—work
into article?), grapefruit cake

Sudsy McGee: Miss Windsor—or is it Miss Spatts? Which do you
   prefer?

Mercy Windsor: Simply "Mercy" is fine.

SM: I think your adoring public would agree there's nothing "simple"
   about Mercy. You're a sensation!

MW: If I may, sir—

SM: Certainly.

MW: On the topic of pseudonyms, isn't "Sudsy" a rather—singular—
   choice?

SM: [in a pleased tone] Well now . . . Can't claim the credit for
   that one, I'm afraid. Given name is Sid, short for Sidney. But

someone along the way once said I leave no stone unturned in my work as Hollywood's unofficial biographer, that I scrub until I get up all the dirt. Sid turned into Suds . . .

MW: And Suds turned into "Sudsy."

SM: Sudsy McGee, humble biographer, at your service.

MW: That's an interesting profession. Most writers around here work on screenplays.

SM: Can't say as I haven't thought of that, Miss Windsor. But it's got to be just the right story, you see. Perhaps someday. But for now, with all the other writers so . . . illustriously occupied, as you alluded to, that leaves a very comfortable niche for my work.

MW: I confess I was surprised by your contacting me, Mr. McGee. There's not much in my story to tell, so if you're planning a biography, I'm afraid it'll be a short one.

SM: [laughs uneasily] Much as I'd like to write your biography, Mercy Windsor, it's a risky career move just now. Frankly one I can't afford. People aren't taking too kindly to those associated with you.

MW: I've noticed.

SM: But I'd be remiss if I didn't document this . . . *time* . . . in your life, for posterity, if nothing else. My own notes on the auspicious history of Hollywood would be incomplete, and one never knows when one might need a particular little fact down the line. Are you going to eat that? [points fork at grapefruit cake]

[A pause]

MW: There is nothing like the Derby's grapefruit cake. One of life's best pleasures. Please. [Mercy signals waiter, who divides cake and gives Mr. McGee his own portion.]

SM: One of life's best pleasures, alongside Golden Flaxe cereal. Right? [grins, pleased with what appears to be a joke.] Although word has it you pronounced it *flack-see* on the first take of the commercial. Can't say as I blame you. Whose bright idea was that . . . *creative* . . . with spelling *flakes*?

MW: [silence] That was clever, Mr. McGee. And the spelling is a mystery whose answer I likely shall never fathom. But as I'm sure you know, Golden Flaxe and their parent company have severed their partnership with me.

SM: *Severed* seems a severe word.

MW: [clears throat, shifts in seat] *"Discontinued their partnership with me"* is the official phrase.

SM: [taking pen out, clicking top, poised to write] What'll they do with all those cereal boxes with your lovely face on them?

MW: I imagine they'll discontinue those. As they've done with me. Well, then, Mr. McGee, we'd best get to it. You had some questions?

SM: Miss Windsor, your recently filmed epic with Pinnacle Studios is impressive. By the numbers alone . . . [Shakes his head in wonder. Opens notepad, taps paper with pen as he lists items.] Fifty thousand tons of white sand imported from Mexico. Over a million props, over a million pounds of plaster, and the battle scene alone cost over a million dollars. It included untold thousands of extras—

MW: People.

SM: Pardon?

MW: People. You said "extras." If it's all the same to you, Mr. McGee.

SM: It is. I mean, it's a fairly standard industry term—

MW: It isn't to me. They are not a countless, nameless, faceless mob. They're— [voice catches] They're people. [murmured]

SM: [narrows eyes, scribbles something down] And yet you walked out. You decided that untold thousands of *people* didn't matter, and neither did your executives or the cast and crew. That it was all yours to [circles hand in air] throw away. Leaving those dedicated directors to piece together the last sequence out of cut footage you had already filmed. Now, now, I can see this is upsetting you. But all I really wish to know is—all your adoring *public* really wishes to know is—why?

[A lengthy pause. Sudsy eyes Mercy's cake, which is untouched. He tips his head at it, a formality, and she pushes the plate toward him.]

MW: Every person's work can matter, Mr. McGee. But I wasn't thinking about dollars, plaster, or props. I was thinking about one single person. And yes, I do believe she was worth far more than a million of any of those things.

SM: For someone who is "simply Mercy," it would seem there is nothing simple about you, Miss Windsor-Spatts. [points fork at last bite of cake]

[A pause. Mercy pulls plate of cake toward herself and fixes her eyes to Sudsy's.]

MW: Let me save you the trouble of scrubbing out every last corner of my life. As to "throwing it all away"—I know what it is to be thrown out. And what happened on the set of *Joan of Arc* was exactly the opposite. I challenge you, in your scrubbing, to unearth that. If you dare. [pulls in a deep breath and leans back] Mr. McGee—

SM: Sid.

MW: Mr. McGee, it isn't that the people didn't matter. They do matter. That's the point. And that is all I am at liberty to discuss. You can see Pinnacle Studios's attorneys and inquire about their nondisclosure clause if you would like to take it up with them. It is out of my hands.

SM: And what is in your hands, Miss Spatts? [He nods to her bandages.] Not a contract anymore, certainly. Which leads me to another question everyone wants answered: What now?

MW: You were right. There is certainly nothing simple about mercy. I come to believe more and more that mercy is the most scandalous scandal of all . . . and I am a grateful recipient of that gift. If you discover in your "scrubbing" that my story is one of scandalous mercy, then I suppose I shall count that an honor. Good day.

[Mercy picks up empty plate. Gives polite nod as chin almost imperceptibly trembles. Swerves at door and exits through kitchen.]

Interview with Neighbors about Mercy's Arrival

Interview with Ralph and Nancy Mosely, closest neighbors to Mercy Windsor in Mercy Peak, Colorado

Ralph: How did she seem that first day? I don't know, tired, I guess? Most folks are after making the trip up here. What was she wearing . . . can't say as I recall exactly. Something sorta windy. Kinda billowy, you know, like a parachute or somethin'. That girl's gonna need a parka real fast, or a campfire. She'd best be careful, though, the timbers of that old Gilman place are liable to go up in flames— and maybe that'd be better, starting fresh. Build something new. Easier than fixing what's broken and old, you know?

Nancy: She can do it. We'll help. Everyone will help.

Ralph: I thought she'd have a tough time breaking in. Seemed sorta standoffish, and around here when you're standoffish, folks are standoffish right back. Makes it seem like you're hiding something, you know?

Nancy: [hoots] She's not standoffish. I knew it right away. She might seem it, but she has a way of burrowing down and springing up on you before you realize how close she's got. Why, her second day here, I saw her using old Gilman's binoculars to nose right into the town's business. Leastways the Bright cabin across the canyon. Probably looking right at their telescope with her binoculars. [rolls eyes and laughs]

Ralph: And how'd you see that from way over here?

Nancy: [looks reluctantly at spyglass perched on windowsill]

Ralph: In any case, she got that truck running and that's a mountain miracle if I ever saw one.

Nancy: She might've got it running, but she ran it straight into a tree—twice!—trying to back it down the Wildwood driveway. Knocked the side mirror right off until it dangled like a broken arm. What kind of person can fix a broken-down car but can't back it up?

Ralph: She's a mystery, that one. [appears wistful, whistles low] That poor truck.

WESTERN UNION

MARCH 3, 1948
TO: HOLDEN HUXLEY
PINNACLE STUDIOS BACKLOT—HOLLYWOOD, CA
FROM: MERCY WINDSOR
WILDWOOD MANOR—MERCY PEAK

SOS FROM YOUR PAL WHO SAVED YOU FROM BEING STRUCK BY LIGHTNING ON SET DURING MUSICAL NUMBER. CALLING IN FAVOR. KINDLY FORWARD SMALL BOX FROM FORMER CLOSET TO POST OFFICE AT MERCY PEAK COLORADO. MUMS THE WORD HOLDEN. I MEAN IT THIS TIME . . . ASSUME SPY ROLE YOU DO SO WELL. HOPE YOU ARE WELL.

WESTERN UNION

MARCH 5, 1948
TO: MERCY WINDSOR
WILDWOOD MANOR—MERCY PEAK
FROM: HOLDEN HUXLEY
PINNACLE STUDIOS BACKLOT—HOLLYWOOD, CA

SOS RECEIVED. 10-4, WILL ACT ASAP. WILSON IMPOSED
CURFEW ON ME AFTER AN INCIDENT INVOLVING A
MONKEY COMING OFF SET WITH ME. ONCE I CAN GET
OUT FROM THE WATCHFUL EYE YOU SHALL RECEIVE
YOUR PACKAGE. HOW DO YOU FEEL ABOUT MONKEYS?

Kurt Pike's Interview Notes

Interview Notes of Kurt Pike, owner of Mercy Peak Mercantile
Date: March 4, 1948
Interview #2 for clerk position

Lady, newcomer, Mary Jane or Marybeth, check on that.

Skills: Says she's a Jill-of-all-trades and master of none, learned
enough to ride a horse but not jump one, mix a pie but not bake
one, but can swing a hammer and paint signs, some kind of stage
set background. Likely down from Elitch's in Denver, maybe couldn't
catch a break in show biz.

Priscilla Murdock wandered by. She took one look at the girl and
her eyes got as wide as saucers and she lit out of here like her
feet were on fire. Not ten minutes later, she was back with some
sort of woman-magazine, holding it up at me from behind the girl
and pointing at the cover of it. Pointing at Mary Jane, pointing at
the cover, mouthing words I couldn't make hide nor hair of. Odd
duck, that Murdock woman.

Anyway, I put the girl to the test, had her stacking cereal boxes
into a display, got a deal on 'em, don't know why. Golden Flaxe,
fancy new stuff we don't get much of, but the company had a deal,
something to do with the boxes not being fit.

She looked like she'd seen a ghost at first but got over it right quick and stacked 'em neat as bricks and looked mighty proud when she showed me. Didn't have the heart to tell her she'd faced 'em all backward.

Update: Hired her on. Started her at a quarter an hour, same as what I paid the Jenks kid. She's not as strong, but it seemed fair. Been here a week now. Strange, she handed her pay right back, wondered if she could just work for trade, needed supplies. Started by grabbing a box of saltines . . . and then went back and got Boston baked beans from the candy aisle.

I'll catch you if you ever fall, Rusty.

—Marybeth, age 13

April 1948

Kurt wandered in from the storeroom, clipboard in hand. He peered up over his reading glasses, spotting Marybeth where she stacked cans of cranberry sauce. "Payday, mountain girl," he said.

"She has a name," Kurt's brother, Angus, spouted from the postal counter across the room. "Marybeth Spatts, Swickley's Crossing." Angus gave her a wink. As the postman, he'd handled her words as much as Rusty had. *"Marybeth Spatts?"* he'd said her first week. *"Rusty's Mary-beth? Swickley's Crossing?"* Her eyes had pricked with tears. Someone on the earth knew her after all . . . and not for the spotlight, but for the scraggly writing of a ten-year-old girl on an envelope.

Mercy returned his wink with a smile as she set an armload of cans on the top shelf. He occupied the northern one-third of the store, while Kurt occupied the southern two-thirds. An incident some years before had caused them to paint a line down the floor that neither of them crossed during business hours, and of which they never spoke.

They shared the same salt-and-pepper hair, but other than that they were as different as night from day. Kurt was tall, efficient, always on the move, and—apropos to his name—curt. Angus was shorter, passed his days greeting people, sitting in a creaky old wooden rolling chair that he launched into action with his feet, sliding this way and that as he stuffed mail into boxes. He always stopped his work to ask after people's husbands, wives, children, and pets, how their sugar snap peas were faring, or whether the baseball team stood a chance against Ouray or

Durango this year. Every now and then, he would stop his rolling short, scramble over to a paper pad, and scribble something down.

"Payday, *Miss Spatts*," said Kurt. "What'll it be this week—money or goods?"

"I brought a list," she said, pulling it from her apron pocket. "I can gather it up on my break and see if it reconciles?"

Kurt stared. She never could tell what he was thinking. It unsettled her but she held his gaze, refusing to be the first to break. He held out his hand for her list. "I got time," he said. "You keep facing the cans."

She nodded, handing him the list, which he promptly started to read aloud in a monotone voice. "Saltines . . . mousetraps . . . cheese . . ." He wrinkled his nose. "You sure you want cheese? Tracy Bascomb brought in a batch, but it's smelling ripe. Probably fine if you eat it within a day, but if you don't—well, just don't."

"It's for the mousetraps."

"Don't bother with cheese. Something that smelly will scare them off. Use peanut butter. What else you got? Cornmeal, milk, eggs—you gotta get yourself a chicken. Baking powder, salt . . . nutmeg?"

The rattling current of Angus's chair rolled front and center to his desk. "Nutmeg? Cornmeal? Sounds like you're fixin' to make Silas Bright's corn bread!"

A surge of joy rose at the mention of the man's name, as if he had been Mercy's own relative and not a miner she'd never met. "You know it?"

Angus whistled. "*Know* it? Why, that corn bread warmed us all up come winter, every one of us in this valley. Don't know who I miss more, Silas or his corn bread."

"Angus," Kurt said.

"I'm kidding. You know I'd give anything to see him again. We all would."

"He sounds like a remarkable man," Mercy said, eager to keep the Bright family as the topic of conversation. She bit her lip, then asked, "And his daughter . . . Rusty? I gather the apple didn't fall far from the tree?"

"Ha!" Kurt said. "*Remarkable* is one word." He shook his head, but was that a smile pulling on the stoic man's face? "Miss that girl. The day Angus had to deliver that death notification, so much changed around here. Wish she—"

The bell over the door rang, and in came two young girls with matching blond braids. Something about Kurt's words tripped around inside

Mercy . . . *death notification*. They punched the wind right out of her. But as she tried to breathe past it, she shook her head. Why—and to whom—would the postman deliver a death notification?

Silas, she knew, had died of a winter sickness several years ago . . . and Rusty's mother had died when Rusty was just a baby. The very fact of sharing that loss was part of what had bound Mercy and Rusty fast. Rusty's beau, Sam, had been states away, working for the Civilian Conservation Corps. So who would have been left . . . ?

The questions lined up—how, why, when. Her mind pushed away the scene of anyone having to deliver news of the loss of a soul so vibrant. *Death* and *Rusty* just didn't go together. Even after ten years, Mercy couldn't reconcile it.

"Jenks girls," Kurt said. "Here for peppermints or malts?" Kurt, gruff as he was, didn't seem the type to run a malt counter, but once in a while, and especially when he'd had good fishing that morning and was therefore in a good mood, he'd pull out the malt machine, hand-cranking it with a straight face and a twinkle in his eye.

Today the girls requested the peppermints, and Kurt helped them at the register, saluting them as they dashed back out the door with red-and-white-striped sticks in their hands.

"I was also wondering," Mercy said, as Kurt returned to packing her order, "do you have any sort of strong tape?" She'd seen something in use recently on the sets, like an adhesive sort of duck cloth. "Something very strong to fix something broken." Like a side mirror on an old truck she'd lovingly dubbed Big Green.

"You're wanting that stuff by Revolite," Kurt said.

Mercy nodded. "Revolite." She followed him to the end of an aisle that had a few tools, spools of string, bolts. And tape.

"Here you have your cloth tape—mind, it's a sight cheaper, and you can make a good tape yourself. Just a matter of melting some rosin and rubber together and soaking it."

Mercy furrowed her brow. "Rubber," she said. "Do you sell that too?"

Kurt laughed. "I wish. Rubber's hard to come by out here in the best of times. Add a war shortage on top of that . . ." He shook his head. "Nope. Just find an old bicycle, grab the inner tube, melt it down, you'll be all set."

Mercy pictured herself standing over a cauldron like the witches in *Macbeth*, stirring up a concoction of rubber and rosin and cackling in the air as she lowered the cloth strips into it.

She gulped. "And . . . the tape by Resolute, was it?"

"Revolite. Sure, that's your other option. They started sending this after the war. Used it on ammo boxes for the soldiers so they could open them quicker. Now they're using it on everything from patching up soldier gear to sealing up air ducts, of all things." He chuckled, shaking his head in awe. "Thing of beauty right there. Wish it came in silver so it'd blend in with pipes and such. Maybe someday." He stared at the object in his hand dreamily, looking downright smitten. It was the most emotion she'd seen play across Kurt's face yet. "You can do anything with it, mark my words. But it's a pretty penny, compared to that." He nodded at the plain roll of cloth.

"I'll take it," Mercy said, snatching it up a little too quickly. Kurt's eyebrows shot up, more in respect than surprise. Her face heated. "Goodness knows there's plenty to be fixed around Wildwood." *And on certain lumber trucks.*

"Smart," he said. "Get it while you can. Phinneas Trent likes to hoard it, buys it up whenever he's in here. But you let me know if you need more." He looked side to side to see if the coast was clear and whispered, "I keep a secret stash in the back." He winked. And inexplicably Mercy's heart soared. Had she just cracked the cold, indifferent armor of Kurt Pike?

This tape really was a miracle.

Kurt went to go get a "fresh roll," as if that was somehow better than the ones on display, and Mercy picked up a broom and started sweeping. Outside on the sidewalk, a woman paused at the door, leaned in close enough to see through it. Upon spotting Angus, she kept walking.

Odd. What could that mean? She couldn't imagine Angus having an enemy. Or perhaps she'd just had the wrong store. She'd been wearing denim pants, big boots that looked like they knew the mountain well, caked in mud and pine needles. Green blouse, sleeves rolled up in haste. She had the look of a woman who could do things, make things, make things happen. Perhaps she'd meant to find the hardware store instead?

Or maybe she was after the coveted Revolite tape.

"Lunch," Kurt said, reentering the room and tossing the roll of treasure to Mercy. She clutched it tight. "Be back in an hour."

"Hey." Angus stood. "You went first yesterday."

"So?"

"What do you mean, 'so'? That means it's my turn today. We always take turns."

"Bye." Kurt grabbed his hat, plopped it on his head, and took a long stride toward the door. Angus launched up from his chair and ran across the room to block the way.

"Line!" Kurt pointed at the line, which Angus was standing on.

"What is it, roast beef day at the diner? You worried Jimmy's gonna run out before you get yours?"

Kurt's jaw twitched.

Angus leaned in, jabbing his brother in the chest and narrowing his eyes. "I knew it." They locked eyes for a split second, then both made a mad dash, tangling up in a scramble at the door. "I'm not getting stuck with Preposterous Pete's grits for lunch!"

"Well, neither am I!" Kurt elbowed his way past Angus.

"Um—" Mercy stepped closer. The men didn't see or hear. "Excuse me," she tried again, louder. To no avail. "Boys!" They both froze, staring at her. "I mean—gentlemen." She paused, their last words registering. "Wait . . . did you just say 'Pete's grits'?"

"Sure, why?"

Mercy laughed. Rusty had actually had the grits renamed? Leave it to her.

She became aware of two very hungry men, doing their best to wait patiently for her to talk. "I just wanted to say that if you're comfortable with it, I could mind the store and post office while you both go."

They blinked. First at her, then at each other.

"Roast beef waits for no man," she said.

"She does know the ropes now," Angus said.

"Mostly," Kurt said.

"And she's right about the beef."

"Fine. But I'm not sitting with you."

"Yeah, y'are." Angus gave a small *whoop* and out they went, into the sun and the promised land of roast beef.

Not two minutes later, the door jingled again, and in came the green-bloused woman.

"Hello," Mercy said. "Anything I can help you with?"

The woman stopped, turned reluctantly. The look she gave Mercy said she wasn't impressed, or perhaps didn't have time to be bothered. "Who are you?"

"Oh, I'm Mercy—" Drat. She was trying to revert to her true name, but old habits died hard.

"Mercy? In Mercy Peak."

Mercy bit her tongue, not sure what to say now. She nodded.

"How original." She pulled in a breath and released it. "Is that why you came here? Your name matched the place?"

Mercy opened her mouth, about to explain it was the reverse—the place had loaned her its name when Wilson P. Wilson insisted she needed something more *punchy* for the screen.

The girl looked around furtively, forgetting her question. "Kurt and Angus gone for lunch?"

"Yes, but they won't be gone terribly long. If you need them . . ."

"I'll be quick."

She turned swiftly, looking over her shoulder out the window, instead of at the shelf, as she reached for a can and tossed it into her burlap bag. Repeated the process throughout the low aisles and crates, as if this was a well-rehearsed dance. Would Mercy ever know the store this well? Her own legs were dotted with bruises from run-ins with crates and corners of shelves.

Watching enviously the way she breezed through the store like she could do it with her eyes closed, Mercy did a double take. The woman was rounding a corner, looking backward out the window again, unaware that there was a new display in her path.

A display of backward-facing boxes of Golden Flaxe.

"Look out—!" Mercy said.

But it was too late.

The boxes exploded from their circular structure, where they'd been stacked like a very straight Tower of Pisa. When Mercy had been there to film *The Italian Escape*, she'd spent a long time staring at the leaning tower and trying to picture it straight and sure. Something in its tilting form had reached inside Mercy and pulled out all her compassion until she wished to prop it up.

Stacking its facsimile out of forsaken cereal boxes was no rescue, but it had been a private tribute to it, a note from afar when she had no one else to write to.

And now . . . the tower crumbled. The woman, too, losing her balance as she tried to avoid crushing them—all while fifty versions of Mercy's heavily made-up face grinned like a breakfast-touting maniac with bright red lipstick. The green-blouse girl lost her balance, arms circling in a last-ditch attempt to stay upright. Mercy grabbed for her, catching her hand but not holding on hard enough as it slipped back out. She went tumbling down on top of three or four boxes, whose corners jabbed awfully, judging by the grimace on her face.

"What in blazing tar—?"

"Are you alright?" Mercy stretched her arm out to help her up, but she turned away.

"I'll be fine," she said fiercely—and somehow unconvincingly.

"I'm so sorry. Is there anything I can do?" Mercy retracted her hand and watched as the girl finally looked at her longer than a second, taking in the green kerchief over Mercy's dark hair, the flowy dress she wore under the store apron.

"What are you, Cinderella?"

"Pardon?" Mercy's hand flew to her kerchief, patting it self-consciously.

"You look like you're dressed half for work, half for a ball."

One of the boxes spun a slow circle on the hard floor and Mercy stepped in front of the dizzying cardboard slow dance. She was pictured in a blue dress, one heel kicked behind her as she stood near a table, lifting a spoonful of cereal from a bowl to her cherry-red lips. *Delectable Golden Flaxe make the most nutritious breakfast!* she said in a cheerful speech bubble. *One of life's best pleasures!*

Before Mercy could stop her, the girl grabbed the box to get a good look at the thing that had taken her down.

"Today I forded a stream, outsmarted a rattlesnake, guided my pack mule through snowbanks that looked like they'd give way at any second. And this is what takes me down? *Golden flack-see.*" She read it with the preposterous tone it apparently deserved. "Who ever thought of eating breakfast out of a paper rectangle? Not our most appetizing invention yet as a human race."

"Well, it does say *crunchy* on it." Mercy offered a sheepish smile and tapped a finger on the back of the carton, where it said CRUNCHY AS ALL GET-OUT! "Please, let me help you up," she said again, extending her arm.

The girl pushed off the ground. "I don't need help." Then, as if regretting her bluntness, she offered a slightly more subdued "Thanks anyway." She snatched two of the crumpled boxes, stuffing them in her bag. "I'll pay for the destruction," she said, heaving a sigh. "I can always feed it to my goat if it tastes like cardboard."

"It's . . . surprisingly tasty," Mercy said. "If you enjoy very sweet things."

The girl mumbled something in return.

"I'll pay for it," Mercy said. "And you take as many boxes as you'd like. I'll—I'll even unbox them, so you only have to carry the bags home and aren't bothered with the, um, crunchy corners."

The girl narrowed her eyes, as if trying to decide if Mercy was trustworthy or just crazy. "You're funny," she said dryly.

Mercy quirked a smile. "All of your laughter says as much."

"Where are you from, anyway? You speak a little . . ." She paused. "Funny."

"Oh, that—it's just a habit. A learned accent."

"From where?" She began stacking boxes, and Mercy helped.

How did one explain the transatlantic accent? Mercy slipped into it by accident sometimes when tensions were high, her acting instincts kicking in. "A little bit of everywhere, I suppose." That much was true. The girl slid the last three boxes over, and they both stood, silence swimming between them and looking for a place to land.

"Can I help you find anything else?" Mercy asked.

"Maybe I should be asking you that. You seem a little lost yourself." She swallowed. She thought she'd been hiding it so well.

The girl shook her head, looking remorseful for the first time. "I'm sorry," she said. "Words are always popping out of my mouth before I get a chance to smooth them out. It just—it seemed like you were looking for something." She paused. "Are you . . . new at the store?" As if that answer weren't obvious.

"Yes," she said. "But I do know how to run the cash register; Mr. Pike showed me that much. Are you ready?"

"As I'll ever be."

Mercy rang her up, scribbling notes on the receipt pad and doing calculations, keenly aware that her hands were being studied. The bandages were gone, her skin healed but a curiosity. They were mottled here and there by the dark vestiges of the burns, yet untouched by the calluses that marked those of Mercy Peak women, who worked hard all the year round to survive this rugged place.

"You alright?"

The question took her off guard, and she nodded, words evading her. No one was going to give her a script. She was going to have to learn how to speak for herself here.

"Listen." The woman set her burlap sack on the floor a moment. "Don't you fly away. People come here, and sometimes they can't make it—life's different in these mountains. It can feel like you've disappeared."

"That's what I'm hoping," Mercy mumbled.

The girl narrowed her eyes. "People are so tight-knit, they've grown up holding each other's secrets until the fabric of it all—well, it's so tight, it's tough to break through. But you stay around if this is where you want to be. Because when it's all said and done, the people 'round here hold more than each other's secrets. They hold their pain and joy, too. And those stitches can only be made by time."

"Are you . . . stitched in?"

"It's complicated." She strode to the door, turning one last time. "Don't you fly away," she said, pointing at her and then making her exit, the bell clanging behind her.

MERCY PEAK

A Screenplay in Three Acts

ACT II
SCENE 1: THE VANISHING OF RUSTY BRIGHT

CAMERA PANS DOWN OVER ALPINE MOUNTAIN PEAK, CONTINUING
TO THE RUST-COLORED MOUNTAINSIDE FORESTED IN TREES AND
ON TO THE VALLEY AND TOWN BELOW. FADES TO A SHOT TAKEN
EVEN FARTHER DOWN TO MINING TUNNELS BENEATH.

NARRATOR

> Mercy Peak thrummed with life, above and
> below the earth. In mountains shaped by
> winds and waters, where men steadily tapped
> their hammers in dark tunnels below.

CAMERA FADES TO MONTAGE OF YOUNG RUSTY BRIGHT ROMPING
THROUGH THE MOUNTAIN MEADOWS, FORESTS, AND CREEKS.
CATCHING CRAWDADS BENEATH LAKE DOCK, WRITING LETTERS
UP IN A TREE.

> Aboveground, a pair of perpetually bare
> feet gave the mountain melody a lilting
> lift. Swishing their way through tall summer
> grasses to pull crawdads from a lake.

CAMERA PANS OVER THE TERRAIN WITH A PROGRESSION OF
MORNING TO EVENING, WINTER TO SUMMER.

Rusty Bright grew up like the pines and red
stone walls around her, the canyon a refuge
from the fierce winds that swept the outer
faces of the mountains. She trounced in and
out of people's days, bearing crawdads or
kittens, wildflowers or berries, painting
everyone's world with color.

The year of correspondence between schools
came and went. Rusty Bright and Marybeth
Spatts kept on writing. Rusty Bright met
Motor No. 8 like clockwork.

Rusty sits on boardwalk in front of depot,
tapping her fingertips on two overlapping
knots of wood and eagerly watching for Motor
8 to appear. The Galloping Goose sways in,
and Rusty greets driver Phinneas.

RUSTY

Got a letter for me today, Phinneas?

PHINNEAS

Gotta give it to Angus, and he'll give it to
you. Protocol, Miss Rusty.

RUSTY

Lunch, Mister Phin. [Holds apple out in
exchange for letter. Snatches it away with a
backward-glancing thank-you and wave as she
runs down the platform.]

PICTURE ZOOMS IN ON ILLUSTRATED VIEW OF WILDWOOD
ESTATE'S WOODLANDS. ILLUSTRATION FADES TO RECORDED
FILM FOOTAGE.

RUSTY, 12, OPENS ENVELOPE WHILE PERCHED ON A CLIFF
OVERLOOKING A ROARING WATERFALL. EATING HER OWN APPLE,
CYCLING THROUGH LAUGHTER, ANGER, INDIGNATION AT WHAT
SHE'S READING. SHE PULLS OUT A PEN AND PAPER FROM HER

WORN RUCKSACK, DUSTS OFF THE SURFACE OF A ROCK, AND
BEGINS TO WRITE.

RUSTY'S VOICE FADES IN.

>When you come, Marybeth Spatts, you'll see
>all the places I've read and written to you
>about in the letters. My tree. My cabin.
>The big meadow. Gold Leaf Lake—the Wildwood
>shore, it's better, and I can sneak you in.
>And right here, at the flat rock by the
>falls. You'll think, "What a place! And to
>think I've already been here ten or fifteen
>times without ever setting foot here!" When
>you do set foot here, you'll be home. That
>old Carolina cabin's just a wooden prison.
>Doesn't matter what a place looks like—
>jail cell or palace, it's what's trapping
>you that makes it a prison or not. You're
>gonna get out of there, away from that
>mean old man of yours. You didn't tell me
>before about the switch. Can you get out of
>there when he comes home like that? Hide
>somewhere safe? You have the biggest heart
>of anyone and I know you want to take care
>of him . . . but who's taking care of you,
>Marybeth? Come here to Mercy Peak, and I'll
>take care of you. You've been taking care of
>that man all your life. High time someone
>looked after you.

NARRATOR

>The letters of Marybeth Spatts, in fact,
>visited those favored haunts twenty-three
>more times before she would set foot there
>herself.

>Meanwhile, Rusty continued to grow as the
>pines around her reached higher and their
>roots went deeper. Those bare feet continued
>to dot the mountainside with escapades,
>joined with growing frequency by another set
>of feet, belonging to one Sam Buckley.

CUT TO MONTAGE OF SILHOUETTED FIGURES AT DIFFERENT
STAGES OF GROWTH. CLAMBERING UP TO TOP OF WATERFALL.
TALLER AND OLDER, TRAVERSING AN OVERGROWN ROAD.

> In a windswept waltz over the years, Rusty
> Bright and Sam Buckley, purveyor of lunch
> pail plums, grew together until they were
> inseparable.

CUT TO SCENE OF HIM DIGGING WITH A SHOVEL, STOPPING TO
WIPE HIS BROW AND LISTEN AS SHE PACES, READING ALOUD
FROM A PAPER. HE LAUGHS AT SOMETHING SHE SAYS AND SHE
PICKS UP HER PACE, PLEASED.

> She read him letters to her faraway friend
> and spoke of seeing her someday, this sister
> she'd never had.

> He'd lie back on the grass and look up at
> the clouds and grin at her. "It'll happen."
> Two words, but they filled her with hope
> . . . just as he did when the day came to
> say his own good-bye. . . .

CUT TO SCENE AT DEPOT; THEY STAND WITH THE TWO KNOTS
IN THE DEPOT PLANKS BETWEEN THEM. BEHIND THEM, A
POSTER READS: *CIVILIAN CONSERVATION CORPS: A YOUNG
MAN'S CHANCE TO CHANGE THE WORLD.* SAM'S GREEN UNIFORM
MATCHES THAT OF THE ILLUSTRATED FIGURE ON THE POSTER.

SAM

> I'll be back. [strokes thumb over Rusty's
> cheek]

RUSTY

> [jaw working] Not soon enough . . .

SAM

> [warmly, catching her hand] Rusty Bucket,
> you're the most independent person I've ever
> had the pleasure of butting heads with.
> You're going to be fine without me. You
> never needed another soul in your life—

RUSTY

>   [struggling to mask her amusement at his
>   words with a glare] Lies, all lies.

SAM

>   [laughing, growing serious, shaking his
>   head] I'll be back before you know it.
>   Twenty-five dollars a *month* . . . just think
>   what that could mean for us. I'll be back.

RUSTY

>   [resolute] You'll be back. [single tear
>   betrays her. Sam strokes it away with thumb
>   and lifts her chin.]

SAM

>   Wouldn't miss it for the world, Rusty girl.
>   You'll see.

NARRATOR

>   What "it" was, only Rusty knew, but she
>   held that promise tight to her heart in the
>   months to come.

CUT TO CONTRASTING MONTAGE: SAM PLANTING TREES, RUSTY
WATERING A GARDEN. SAM BUILDING STONE BRIDGES, RUSTY
WHACKING A LOOSE NAIL DOWN ON WHISTLER'S BRIDGE. SAM
TOASTING BEANS OVER A CAMPFIRE, RUSTY STIRRING CAST-
IRON POT OVER HEARTH FIRE.

>   It was his letters Rusty awaited, too, then.
>   Gathering crawdads and berries, biding time
>   until the two souls who loved her would
>   set foot on those planks. When the letter
>   came at last from Sam that she'd been
>   yearning for, she tore down the road, made
>   arrangements with the preacher. Put on her
>   Sunday best on the appointed day, gathered
>   up a clutch of wildflowers for her bouquet,
>   and went to the depot to meet her groom.

CUT TO RUSTY AWAITING GALLOPING GOOSE, DRESSED IN HER
THREADBARE FINEST, BOUQUET IN HAND. A PASSENGER EXITS,
THEN ANOTHER. SHE CRANES HER NECK TO SEE, BUT NOBODY
ELSE COMES. ZOOM IN ON HER LOWER LEGS/FEET, STANDING
AT THE TWO KNOTS IN THE WOOD, ONE FOOT AKILTER. SHE
LINGERS A MOMENT, THEN THE HAND HOLDING THE BOUQUET
DROPS TO HER SIDE, UPSIDE-DOWN BLOSSOMS STILL IN HER
GRIP, PETALS FALLING TO COVER ONE OF THE KNOTS.

> Into mountains shaped by winds and waters,
> Rusty's feet carried her. Bearing invisible
> shackles in place of their one-time lilt.
> She wore the peaks' shadows like a veil of
> mourning . . . leaving only echoes of herself
> in the valley town below.

You scared the life out of me, Marybeth Spatts!

—Rusty, age 12

April 1948

Mercy opened the door to Big Green, and it gave an outright anguished cry, testament to the way the temperature had dropped this afternoon. Kurt had sent her home early, likely taking pity on her state of mind when she expressed her desire to buy all remaining boxes of Golden Flaxe, and asked if he would take payments.

Sitting in the cab, she reviewed her small notebook—people she'd met, details she wanted to learn and remember. *Stitches*, that outspoken girl had said. If Rusty was here, she would've called her a blabbermouth. Mercy snickered. Perhaps the girl had known Rusty. Mercy had been so flustered, she'd failed to ask the questions that were becoming familiar friends now: *What's your name? And your favorite thing about living in this beautiful place?* People lit up at that question, and she had filled a page of notes about it already.

-Angus Pike—likes pike fish.
-Vivian Rubio—keep deviled ham stocked for her. Ask after her nephew working the Camp Bird mine.
-Sally Riley—recommends popovers from the bakery.

The list went on, and something fluttered inside Mercy. She'd traveled the world, lived a thousand lives—or seventeen and three-quarters, rather, if you were counting exactly by the number of roles she'd played. She'd shaken the hands of soldiers, met the president, and laid her hands in a cement star that would never again see the light of day.

But she'd never yet fished for pike, or had a popover by a stream, or eaten a deviled ham sandwich.

Perhaps life was not over after all.

She turned the ignition, and nothing happened. Popped the hood, exited with the door's groan, jiggled the cables to the battery and tried again, firing the engine up, and thanking heaven above for the jeep trouble they'd had repeatedly on the set of *Embargo*.

Up the street, two gentlemen sitting on a bench in front of the bakery gave her a hearty applause—and it tumbled over her with joy a thousandfold what auditoriums full of applause had once meant to her. Riding the spritely joy of the moment, she turned and gave a curtsey, then drove Big Green away.

But the wave of confidence disappeared when she rounded Second Street and pressed the brake to slow before the hill.

The truck sped up.

She pressed harder, the brake pedal hitting the floor of the truck with a cold, hard *clack* and not a bit of resistance—and the truck went faster.

Mercy's eyes wildly scanned the scene before her. A few cars parked in front of houses built long before cars existed, a child playing in the yard to the left, and at the bottom of the hill, someone crossing the street, attention fixed to a picnic basket.

Mercy's heart pounded. Her foot pounded, too, again to no avail. She leaned on the horn, and it uttered not a sound. Thoughts came so fast they were wordless—there was no time for them to take enough shape. But they felt like wild gnats flying at her.

Roll down the window and yell.

No time.

Open the loud door; it'll give warning!

No time.

The truck grew faster.

The hill grew smaller.

The basket lady grew closer and closer until she looked up, frozen. Their eyes met for a split second. It was the cereal-box toppler. Mercy swerved, bound for a hedge that she hoped might somehow stop her.

A tangle of jostling, bouncing, creaking ensued—and was that a cat yowling? The truck blazed into the hedge and the ditch beyond until *thwack*—the far bank stopped Big Green, and Big Green's steering wheel stopped Mercy.

"She okay?" a voice said. Mercy lifted her head. The world spun.

Something hot and wet dripped down her forehead. She touched a hand to it—blood.

"I told you not to fly away," said the cereal girl through the rolled-down window. "You okay?"

Mercy nodded, brow pinched. "I'm so sorry . . . the brakes . . . are you okay?"

The girl waved off the question. "Takes more than a runaway truck to get to me. I'm fine."

"Get the cat!" said another voice, this one shrill.

"Miss Murdock, there's a bleeding human being here. The cat will be fine, and she's yours anyhow—"

"You had the picnic basket. It's your cat. Take it!"

"Who puts a cat in a picnic basket?"

"Who breaks into a house to leave a cat behind?" An exasperated sound.

The scene swayed a little before Mercy as she pulled a handkerchief from her pocket and pressed it to her forehead.

"For the last time, that's not my cat! And if you don't retrieve it, some coyote will thank you come nightfall. You're all bluster and blow, but you're the same girl who drove a racoon out of town on your bike when everyone else wanted it good and dead. Don't think I don't remember those beady little eyes, smirking at us from your knapsack."

The older woman seemed to be growing taller, crossing her arms and staring down the younger one, who stood unmoved. These two were forces well matched. But their words began to warp into each other strangely as the scene before her blurred. The next thing Mercy knew, she was standing on a patch of tall-growing grass, held up by the two men who'd applauded her earlier. "Best get her over to Miss Ellen's. She'll know what to do. She has that *tele*phone," one of them enunciated proudly. "In case we need to call Doc."

"I'm alright." Mercy winced as she took her first step. "Just a scratch." She'd fainted on-screen at least ten times. It didn't feel anything like this.

She took another step. "Really, I—" The ground tipped on its axis, and she nearly crumpled. The men caught her.

"Go get that cat, Rusty Bright," the shrill-voiced woman said.

"R-rusty?" Mercy said, closing her eyes and swallowing back the wave of nausea brought on by the dizziness. "Did she say Rusty?"

She must have heard wrong. Thoughts swam at her sluggish and odd, trying to piece themselves together in her cloudy state.

She twisted, squinting to see a blurred figure retreating with a picnic basket, hollering after a cat.

"Wait!" Mercy cried. But as she lurched forward to chase the apparition, her head pounded with the force of a gong, and the dizziness pulled her down into a sea of black.

Muffled voices swam around her. Mercy lifted her eyelids, entering an unfamiliar world. Where was she? Things were a little blurry, but above her, light twinkled through a crystal chandelier. Was she playing Queen Victoria again—back on the Windsor Castle set? She must be. Or maybe—Daisy Buchanan in *The Great Gatsby*. Hadn't she had a ceiling like an upside-down wedding cake?

She blinked, clearing her vision, and saw instead a ceiling tiled in an embossed white floral motif. Deep woodwork crowned the bright room, framing windows, scaling stairs. On one wall, bookshelves climbed from floor to ceiling. On another a player piano, its scroll sitting still. Hooks upon the wall were draped in various dusty jackets and men's hats. As the details played out, her mind began to clear, too.

This was no movie set.

"W-where am I?" she muttered, feeling a bit like Dorothy in *The Wizard of Oz*. Memories started to come back—Big Green, plummeting down a hill. People shouting, truck bumping, and then—

Rusty. Had she dreamed it?

Mercy sat slowly. A grandfather clock ticked, a teapot sat on a wooden stool, steam rising, and the whole room wrapped her in the welcome warmth of a bygone era. Everything orderly, nothing cobwebbed or burned. A world away from Wildwood.

As if the keeping of this house was somebody's living work of art. Which begged the question . . . who lived here?

"Hello?" she said, and got up, approaching a doorway that spilled light and the musical jingle of silverware. She entered a kitchen where a woman knelt, head inside a cabinet, speaking aloud.

". . . meat on her bones, poor thing. Now, where's that pan . . ."

Mercy cleared her throat lightly, not wanting to startle the woman, who promptly shrieked, bonking her head on the cabinet.

"Leaping lizards," she said. "That certainly was fast! Ralph went to see if he could fetch Doc but said he's up at Silverton today. Could be some time. Look at you." She bustled toward Mercy. She was pink-cheeked, red-haired, and exuded sunshine. She raised a hand to Mercy's forehead.

"Something cold," she said, and bustled herself over to an icebox, chipping off a chunk of ice with what looked like a tiny pickaxe and hammer, kept right inside the door. She rolled her eyes up in light-hearted explanation. "Behind the times," she laughed. "It's what we are around here. The rest of the world has refrigerators that plug in, and heaven knows what else. But this icebox has been serving up cold drinks to miners for almost a hundred years now, and nobody told it that its time was done, so it just keeps going. Besides, I don't trust a contraption that tries to replace ice with electricity. It just seems wrong! Here." She wrapped a towel around the ice and handed it to Mercy. "Painful, is it?" She grimaced, and Mercy winced as she pressed the ice to her forehead.

"Just a bruise, I'm sure," she said. The woman looked dubious and eyed the marks on Mercy's hands while she was at it. She'd become accustomed to hiding them in the folds of her skirt, but that was useless now. Best just to let the question hover, unanswered.

Mercy took in the room, where a table stretched the length of a whole wall, plates set for at least a dozen people. This was no ordinary house. Something Ralph said when he'd deposited her at Wildwood tugged at her memory . . . a woman in town who might have a room open, could poach an egg extraordinarily. "Miss Ellen?" Mercy ventured.

She paused her bustling, setting a sack of flour on the counter. "Now, how did you know that? I know we haven't met; I'd remember a face like yours," she said. "But now you mention it, there *is* something awfully familiar about you, Miss . . ."

Mercy swallowed. There was no movie house here, she reminded herself. Likely Miss Ellen never had seen her. "Marybeth," she said, extending a hand and unschooling it from its posed habits. Miss Ellen wrapped her hand in both of hers.

"Well, Marybeth, I'm Ellen Rogers."

Papers rustled in Mercy's mind as she shuffled through Rusty's letters long held there. *Miss Ellen's got hair even redder than mine—mine's just sort of brown-red. She's got the best plum pudding around, even though plums and pudding don't seem like they should go together in any universe, and puts on a record of violin music every night at dinner. Don't those miners all look so refined, sitting up tall when Bach's tunes start to play? You can see 'em through the window from down by the creek.*

"It's a pleasure, Miss Ellen," Mercy said.

Miss Ellen tilted her head. "You're not from around here," she said. "Here. Have a popover." She said it as if that would fix that fact. "Come on outside. The evening's warm for April, and you're about to see the burst."

"The burst?"

She nodded, curls bouncing. "You'll see." She seemed to relish this little piece of private information. Was it something from one of the mines? Some explosion to signal the workday being done?

Ellen led to a table for two on the grass overlooking the river, and they sat. "Tell me, Marybeth, do you have relatives in town? The hotel closed fifteen years ago; not much call for it once the trains stopped. Visitors trickle in once in a great while. . . . I'm the only lodging, poor souls." She chuckled.

"Lucky souls," Mercy smiled, lifting the china teacup to her lips and relishing Ellen's laugh in return. "You've created quite a haven here."

"Oh, it's not much. There's hardly a place on earth you can't make a soul feel a little better with a place to sit and a warm drink in their hands."

It was much more than that, and Mercy knew it. She suspected Miss Ellen did, too, but just smiled, encouraging her to continue. "But you . . . already have a place to stay?" Mercy suspected Ellen already knew the answer.

Mercy swallowed her tea and gave a tentative nod. "A place called Wildwood . . . Do you know it?"

She lurched forward, pressing her lips closed around the sip of tea. "Know it? We all know Wildwood." She said it with familiarity, and then something else. A somber flicker over her features. "Are you . . . a relation of the Gilmans?"

Her tone was friendly but tentative, and Mercy felt an immediate distancing between them. Miss Ellen shifted in her seat, casting a glance around, as if they were being watched.

"No," Mercy said, and the woman's shoulders eased a little. "I confess I've never met them. There's a good bit of work to be done to . . . spruce up the house." She pursed her lips, pondering whether to confess the next bit. "When people find out I live there, they seem . . ."

"Wary? Suspicious? Treat you like you've got the plague?"

"Well, yes, frankly. I was wondering if there was something I might do to let them know I'm . . . safe."

Ellen considered. "I'm tempted to say time is the only cure for their suspicion," she said. "Randolph Gilman sowed distrust for decades, and in the most subversive ways. A foe dressed as a friend, and it didn't just betray trust. It broke hearts. People won't be quick to embrace anyone who they think might have ties, but they also won't judge you entirely based on where you live, or who you're connected with. Time will tell . . . and perhaps you'll find a way to show them you're friend, not foe."

"How does a person do that? You seem to excel in the art of making people feel safe."

Miss Ellen beamed. "That means more than you could possibly know." She thought. "All I can think is it boils down to simply opening the door. That looks different for each person . . . and I have no doubt that the people—and Wildwood, and your own heart, and the good Lord who made them all—will show you just how to do that."

Mercy would've preferred a tidy script and a quick result, but the truth of Miss Ellen's words resonated. "Well," she began slowly. "Wildwood is in no state to welcome people quite yet."

Miss Ellen's laughter burst forth like a sunrise.

Mercy felt bewilderment spread across her face. *Placid. Look placid.* She'd been doing it since she was a girl, covering over the storm inside. But Ellen caught her look too soon, and laughed all the more for it.

"Oh mercy," she said. Now Mercy's cheeks heated—she knew, then? Who Mercy was? "Mercy me," Ellen continued, dropping her palm to her lap. "You do have a way of polishing things up nicely. Anyone in their right mind would take one look at that place and run the other direction. And no one would call that monstrosity a house. The Gilmans always called it the manor. One of their many manors—and that was the *only* manners they had, if you catch my drift."

The statement seemed a door cracked open, and Mercy stepped through it with care. "They . . . weren't kind?"

Ellen looked to the sky, where early evening clouds were mounding. She sighed, and her spritely spirit sobered. "They were complex. To the outside eye, they were all decorum and grace, even generosity. When I was a girl and the influenza swept through, do you know what they did? They planted a whole field of potatoes in the lot where the Browns' house had burned down three years before. Wanted to help provide for the town during a time of hardship, they said. Parents were so ill, children would dash down to the lot, pull up potatoes enough for their families, roast them over the fire the Gilmans' man kept going on the lot, and take them home to feed the ailing."

"What a beautiful gesture," Mercy said. There were times she'd have given anything for a corner potato lot.

"Yes . . . but as I said, they were complex. The Browns owed a great debt to the Gilmans and were unable to pay it. No one could ever prove that they had the house burned down, but we all knew. Then the son—Randolph Gilman, the most recent of the Gilmans—put up a town hall for us all right there. Tied the crime scene in a pretty bow, you might say."

"Weren't they ever prosecuted?"

Miss Ellen blew her cheeks out. "It's hard to prosecute someone when the entire town—lawmen included—are under their thumb, and when the town exists in the first place because of their mine. It was a company town back then, and the Gilmans were kings. They owned everything. When the last of them were gone . . . you could almost feel these granite peaks heave a sigh of relief." Her forehead pinched, then she seemed to remember herself. "If people seem a bit standoffish when they find out where you're living, you just stick it out. They're only remembering what it was to live under a cloud like that. Gilmans . . . they knew how to keep the upper hand. Some say Randolph Gilman kept meticulous records."

"Finances?"

"You might say that. Money owed, secrets kept, any and all things he could hold over anyone's head."

"So they were afraid of him."

"More afraid of his book than of him, I think."

Afraid enough to ransack the house? Mercy rubbed her head, trying to add it all up beneath the pounding inside.

"Is there anything I might do to help allay their concerns?" Her words were measured, surface-level exactions that were a result of having to walk on eggshells in her former life, where anything she said could and would be used against her in the court of the newspapers and public opinion. She sometimes felt like a walking legal document.

Ellen's eyes sparkled as she studied Mercy. "Well," she said, "relax, if you can. You're home now. That is—if you mean Mercy Peak to be your home?"

Home felt a dream too far to speak. Had she ever had that? "I hope so."

Ellen nodded. "Treat it as such. Live here like you mean it. You have to around here. It won't happen overnight, but you're not the first newcomer. It just takes time . . . and you can't make the time go faster with a plan of attack. You just watch, and if you're willing to live the long story here, you'll see this place soften to you. I promise."

Mercy's eyes stung, and she lifted her chin, breathing slow. The way to keep the tears from falling was to look up—this she knew from crying scenes timed to the second.

But Ellen didn't have a timer. No regard for when tears should or shouldn't come. And the tears were following her lead, welling up to heights impossible to contain. Ellen's hand was on hers before she knew it, and—instead of running at her to touch up her makeup or saying "Cut!" and demanding a fresh take—she only squeezed her hand gently.

Mercy let out a shuddering sigh, laughing at herself. "I'm so sorry," she said. "Crying in front of a perfect stranger . . ."

"I'm not perfect, and we're not strangers. Now, ready for the burst?" She pointed toward a dip in the ridge. "There's a place just there where when the sun sinks just into that crevice, the ridge cuts the light loose and it pours out like you wouldn't believe. A crack opened in the mountain wall some years ago after an avalanche," she said, somber. "None of us were ever the same after that avalanche. When the mountain cracked open, it seemed like our hearts did, too, even wider—but then we saw what it made way for. Watch . . ."

The pale sun seemed to move more swiftly at the ridgeline. And just as Ellen said, when it reached the crevice, light seared in a last, luminous outpouring so bright it burned.

Ellen clasped her hands together and shook her head in wonder. "It never gets old. It's too easy to miss, when you get used to it, but it's always there. Sure as the sun. It's beautiful on its own, but knowing it came after a tragedy too great for any person to bear . . . it's a daily reminder that light will break into our darkness." Her eyes held a sheen.

"It's beautiful," Mercy said. She'd blinked past plenty of blinding set lights, but never anything that transported her this way.

From trees all around the property, an evening chorus of birds rose around their silence. The light, the song, the peace of twilight, it all seemed to lay itself down in invitation for Mercy to step out and ask the costliest thing.

"May I ask you a question, Miss Ellen?"

"Please do!"

"When the truck wouldn't brake, it was charging toward somebody. A woman, about my age, I think. She had a basket with a cat in it. . . ." She heard how ridiculous she sounded. She shook her head, rubbing her temples. "Never mind. I must've hit my head harder than I thought."

"Rusty Bright," Ellen said, without missing a beat.

The breath went out of Mercy. She blinked, and blinked again, searching for something to say, some way for that thought to settle down and make sense.

"R-Rusty?"

"Yes, ma'am."

"Rusty Bright?"

"You look like you've seen a ghost, dear. Rusty's alright, if that's what you're worried about. She's got her share of troubles, but today she walked away without a scratch—a miracle, considering. But that's Rusty for you."

Mercy slumped in her seat. "Rusty's . . . alive," she whispered.

"You really did have a scare today, didn't you? I don't believe there was any mortal danger. You swerved in plenty of time, to hear it told. But it certainly is kind of you to be concerned. Mind you, she's done her best to erase herself from this town, but it's not that easy. You belong to Mercy Peak once, you belong forever. She disappeared up the mountain after Sam Buckley was killed."

Mercy sucked in a breath, the words slicing. "When—when was he killed?"

Ellen thought. "1936? 1937." She mused for a moment. "It must've been '37," she said. "He'd been gone for some time with the Conservation Corps by then." She shook her head, eyes glistening. "Some sort of accident. It wasn't always safe work those boys were doing. But Sam had made his peace with that. Work that comes with a risk . . . it's just a way of life around here."

"And . . . was he buried here? In the cemetery?"

"Yes, ma'am. It snowed that day . . . early snow, as I recall."

Mercy's mind raced. She had watched that snow that night from where she'd huddled beneath the covering of Whistler's Bridge.

"October," she murmured.

Miss Ellen tilted her head. "That's right," she said. "The whole town came. How we loved that boy. There's never been another kinder. Only Rusty didn't come . . . but we didn't blame her. She'd taken to the mountain and wouldn't budge from her cabin. The snow came down, and the girl went up, like some sort of trade. We lost two young souls that day. Rusty, poor thing. Up there alone in that cabin, which she'd been sprucing up—" Ellen laid her hand on Mercy's arm. "Like you! Sprucing up a place. I bet the two of you would get along swimmingly. Anyway, she'd been fixing up the old Bright cabin for the day he returned, the day they would wed. Do you know she took some cast-off old, red-checked tablecloths from the Daughters of Esther and sewed them by hand into curtains? She pricked her fingers a dozen times at least and brought them to my parlor more than once for my help untangling knots. Rusty was never the domestic sort—too busy running wild in the hills, catching toads and climbing trees. But for her Sam, she'd do anything."

Ellen trailed off, talking about the time Sam and Rusty had sheltered with the whole class of Sunday schoolers in a cave during a cloudburst, keeping the young ones safe. But all Mercy could hear was her own heartbeat, carrying with it two words:

Rusty's alive.

I enjoy the current iteration of you, Rusty. You're sharp as nails, but something's making you gentler, too. Like that word? *Iteration.* It's going in the lexicon.

—Marybeth Spatts, age 15

Rusty

Cabin's Log
April 3, 1948

Strange things are happening around here. Spring's off to a terrible start for the plums—they burst forth in blossom like crazy, only to have a cold snap shrivel up half of the blossoms. I'm ashamed to admit it, but when I went to check on my little ring of plum trees and saw the crisped petals, I dropped to my knees like I was Scarlett O'Hara and wept. I never cry. Not when I should, anyway. But there I was, knees in the dirt, soil digging in, wilty flowers in my palms. My hands felt emptier than ever, and it just hit me. It's not the plums. It's not the blossoms. It's what they signify.

Thank the good Lord no one was there to see. Only . . . that same night, I saw a burst of black smoke go up, right where I'd been kneeling. My stomach twisted at the thought of fire getting those trees. I ran like a jackrabbit, bucket in hand, ready to go douse it . . . and found not destruction, but salvation.

Someone had stuck a pot of some kind right in the center, full of fire, with a chimney-like stack on top. I could feel the warmth myself as I drew near, and I knew it was to keep the frost away. There was no one there, just a note scribbled, speared to a branch. It said, "For the plum blossoms. This should ward off the frost."

Who did it?

Don't know if I want to know.

Then the strange things continued.

I went down into town yesterday. I'd put off the trip as long as possible, but my supplies were getting pretty low. Long story short, I near got hit by the old Gilman truck, with no Gilmans around for a decade now, and by some highfalutin nincompoop who fainted at the first sign of trouble. And even before that, was thrust a cat in a basket (same cat, gotta be old as dirt by now) by Miss Murdock.

The cat is currently yowling from the bedroom. I'm sleeping in the kitchen, lest he abscond into the night and become coyote food. He gets the bed . . . but I get the fire. Fair enough.

I escaped the truck, but Miss Murdock's basket could use some tending to. One of the lids is flapping loose. And if that basket is all the payment I'm to get for taking in that wildebeest, then I'll be mending it with some fishing line.

Wonder what The Traitor would say to that story. Sometimes I wish I could write to her. But then I remember she disappeared without so much as a word—right when I needed her. She always said I was the strong one. She thought she needed me.

Guess she'll never know it was the other way around.

Guess she'll never hear about the cat and the basket.

I hate it. I hate that she's gone, hate that I don't know where, hate that she just clammed up and didn't even think to tell me why, not unless a letter got lost in the mail. But even if it did . . . wouldn't she have written again?

Marybeth Spatts wanted to vanish—and vanish she did. So as a last act of friendship, which she'll never know about, I'll respect her wish and erase her from my story.

Trouble is, she just sticks around. Something happens like the cat incident, and who do I want to tell? Sam, who's gone, and Marybeth, who left.

At least I can hope for a smidge of peace for a few more months, now that the trip to town is said and done. . . .

Rusty set down her pen, propped her chin on her hand, and thought. What a strange day yesterday had been. It had started pretty normal. In spring, when the snow melted so fast the earth couldn't keep up with soaking it all in, the gully flowed past the cabin with a veil so furious it looked pure white. "The Chute," they called it, for the rest of the year it was near-empty, or only a trickle. When water slowed, kids took to chuting themselves down it like a great big waterslide, near the foothill.

In another life, Rusty had led the charge, whooping all the way down. Now . . . she took the mountain by foot come spring. Tromping right through rivulets and mud-cloaked memories, averting her heart from the ache that sprang up. Every spring, Rusty arrived at the bottom of the mountain with her skirt muddied, and two words came over the town:

Rusty's back.

Miss Ellen would swipe the day's pie from her own kitchen, much to the boarders' chagrin, and bustle out to the boardinghouse yard with it.

John Bowman over at the stable would hide most of the extra horseshoes and keep a watchful eye, as if Rusty was still twelve years old and liable to steal them in the middle of the night for her impromptu game of "knock down the icicles by throwing horseshoes," which ended up in a bruised elbow, a black eye, and a symphony of clanging that woke the whole town. Over the years, though, when it became clear Rusty was not her former self, John Bowman began to leave out a horseshoe or two . . . just in case. But there they stayed, rusting over, which seemed about right.

When Rusty came down, Will Travers would step from the smithy with his ash-stained apron and say, "Well, if it isn't Rusty Bucket." His cheeks always colored when he remembered that was what her classmates called her when it became clear she'd someday marry Sam and be Rusty Buckley . . . and when he remembered why that would never happen now. "Sorry, Rusty, I didn't mean—well, I mean—what I mean is, you're a sight for sore eyes! Come in by the stove for a coffee like old times, eh?"

And Priscilla Murdock would come out of Danube Cottage, with all its flowers and picket fence, holding up the black cat with its eyes wide and its legs pinned rigid into the air like weapons, and say, "Take him, will you?"

Each year, Rusty took the pie with murmured thanks and a pasted-on smile. Each year, she gave John Bowman's horseshoe pile a wide berth. And always, she scratched the head of the stray and said, "Be good for Miss Murdock now, will ya?"

But in all of it, that lilt in her flying feet was gone.

In that way, yesterday had been no different. She'd hovered at the edge of town, looking over Main Street while looping her arm around the rough trunk of a pine tree. "Here goes nothing," she said, tromping down the last incline and into the street. Taking that held-out pie and mustering a smile in return. Declining that coffee.

Angus and Kurt Pike emerged from the mercantile, which occupied the corner space in the long brick row of shops that looked like they'd plunked down in the mountains from some European village. They jostled down the boardwalk toward the diner like they were in some kind of shuffling race, Kurt elbowing Angus at one point.

And then there had been the kerchief girl, and the cereal boxes, and the cat, and the truck—

She blew out her cheeks. It was good to be home. Alone.

Tap-tap-tap.

Who would be here? Nobody, that's who. Must've been the wind flinging some pebbles at the door. Right where someone would knock. All in a row, just so.

"Quiet," she said, not that the wind would listen. It never did, but she talked to it plenty and found in it a force as strong as the gusts that blew in her heart all night sometimes. It was a good companion.

She retrieved a handful of dried leaves and twigs from her tinderbox, laying it beneath the stubborn pyramid of logs. Trouble was, this wood wasn't seasoned—but she hadn't planned on going through her winter's supply so fast, or spring being so blasted cold. She struck a match and watched the pile ignite, smoke beginning to curl.

Tap-tap . . . tap-tap.

The cat yowled, as if to tell her to answer the door already.

Fine. Whoever it was, she'd send them packing.

Rusty stood, dusting her soot-covered hands on her plaid shirt, and straightening the red handkerchief she wore on her head. The girl behind the wheel might have lost her mind, but Rusty had liked the green kerchief she wore. She wasn't much for fashion herself, and even if she was, she'd buck trends like her pack mule kicked the stable walls. But that girl would never know she'd inspired Rusty to tie her old bandana around her hair.

She opened the door. There stood the kerchief girl. No kerchief, but it was her alright, wide-eyed like a deer in the headlights.

That was ironic.

"What, no truck?"

Kerchief Girl swallowed and appeared speechless. A bruise blossomed purple on her forehead, beneath a scratch.

Rusty raised her hand on the edge of the door and leaned into it, waiting.

Kerchief Girl looked to the left, then the right, as if to check for spies. She wore a dress as green as the pines but with a sheen that had no business being out here in the woods.

Rusty raised her eyebrows. She wasn't going to break this silence. If that girl was going to drive at Rusty in a truck with lousy brakes, then she could find her own way into a conversation. Likely with an apology.

"R-Rusty?" she said at last.

Rusty just stared.

"Rusty Bright."

"That's right."

And then . . . nothing. She looked lost again, like she'd not only lost her way in the woods up here but maybe in the world, too.

Something stirred in Rusty. Pity, or even . . . compassion? Blast.

"Mercy!" She hit on the name at last, victorious. "Like the peak. That's you, right?"

The girl stammered as if that was the hardest question in the universe. Sheesh, maybe she'd really hit her head hard.

Rusty took her hand down from the door and stuffed both hands in her pockets. The truck was nowhere in sight.

"How'd you get up here?"

She looked relieved for a question she could answer. "I walked," she said simply.

"Probably a good thing you didn't get behind a wheel," Rusty said, and winced. That sharp tongue of hers . . . it was so fast she couldn't stop it sometimes, and the girl's cheeks were pinker than Red Mountain at sunrise.

"Look, it's okay. I know you didn't mean to. That old truck would be a death trap for anyone. What were you doing in it, anyway?"

"I . . . it's my only way of getting around, just now. Or—*was*, rather."

"How'd you get ahold of the old Gilman truck? Not that they'd touch that thing with a ten-foot pole. Too fancy for that."

Mercy didn't seem to know what to say. Was that dress silk? It looked fancy. As fancy as a Gilman, come to think of it. Rusty hung her head. She'd done it again, stuck her big fat foot in her big fat mouth.

"You're one of them, aren't you?"

"I'm . . . ?"

"Sorry. I shouldn't have said that about the ten-foot pole. Are you a cousin, or what? Long-lost sister? Distant relation come to claim your inheritance? Hate to break it to you, but the Gilman place isn't exactly a prize, in its current, um . . . iteration." That had been a Marybeth word.

Something on Kerchief Girl's face changed at that last phrase, and she swallowed. "No," she said. "No relation, I'm afraid."

"No call to be afraid of that. So? How'd you get the truck?"

"I just . . . bought the place, that's all."

A stifled snicker escaped through Rusty's nose. "I'm sorry," she said. "It's just you say that like it was easy. To buy the home of a millionaire— and one that isn't exactly primed for habitation."

"It was anything but easy." Mercy's features relaxed, and a laugh bubbled out. Kind of melodic. "And yes, it's a wreck."

Rusty straightened a bit. Maybe she was being too hard on her. Maybe she'd hardened up more than she realized out here on her own. There was once a time when she'd have brought a pot of crawdads and a sack of pine nuts to anyone new in town and made sure they knew they had a friend. This girl had come all this way on foot; the least Rusty could do was give some semblance of a welcome.

"Well, come on in," Rusty said. "Care for some water?" She opened the door wider and fetched a tin cup from its hook as Mercy entered, looking tentative and out of place. She clasped her hands in front of her and took in the surroundings. The fireplace, the tiny table with its wobbly leg. Two chairs—one that had been empty for years now.

"Make yourself at home," Rusty said, pumping water into the cup. "Not much to speak of, but it's a roof over my head, and that's all I need." The cat yowled from the bedroom.

Rusty placed the cup in her hands, expecting to see disapproval on the woman's delicate features at the sound of a wild animal contained. Instead . . . was that a stifled smile?

"If you came to apologize," Rusty stepped back, leaning on the counter and crossing her arms in front of her, "there's no need. I appreciate the gesture, but—"

"I really am sorry," she said. "I'd never forgive myself if I'd hurt you in any way." A flicker of a furrowed brow, as if she wasn't sure how much to say. Good gracious, speaking was hard for this woman. It was a wonder she'd made it this far in life. If she was this tongue-tied in front of one person, imagine if she ever had to give any kind of public address.

Compassion stirred. Maybe she'd come to Mercy Peak for solitude. That, Rusty could understand.

"What made you buy the Gilman place?" Rusty asked.

She gripped the cup like it was a lifeline. Stared into it and then placed it on the table. "I . . . always wanted to see it," she said at last, not meeting Rusty's eyes. "I used to picture how it looked when they had their balls, the lanterns hanging from trees. The finery of the people's swishy skirts sounding like wind."

Rusty narrowed her eyes. That was a strange description. Something she'd have said, a long time ago.

The woman hesitated, then continued. "I once drew a picture of a little girl up in a tree, watching it all. I used to wonder what she thought of, sitting there for hours, eating her box of Cracker Jacks."

Silence billowed. Mercy lifted her head slowly, until her eyes met Rusty's. They were wide, searching. Hope and fear swam in them.

The words socked the wind out of Rusty. She breathed shallowly. "I only ever told one person that story."

Mercy's hands clasped. Hands that—if what was dawning over her turned out to be true—had written her probably twelve novels' worth of words, a decade and more ago. She nodded and opened her mouth to speak. "Rusty, I—"

Rusty held out her hand to halt her. Now she was the one tongue-tied. She pressed her eyes closed and shook her head.

A long silence passed. Mercy tried again, taking a tiny step forward in old leather boots that were way too big, way too worn, and didn't fit her fine dress one bit.

"I've wanted to meet you my whole life. Ever since that first letter, Rusty, and I thought—I thought it wasn't possible, but—"

Rusty shook her head more adamantly. "You're not her."

The Imposter dropped her hands to her sides, her green dress swishing like the wind, like all those fine ladies and gentlemen who were always absconding with Cracker Jacks.

Her mouth wobbled a little. Rusty felt bad—but then promptly felt anything but bad. This woman held more pieces of Rusty than anyone else in the world . . . and she'd left her to fight on her own, without so much as a word, like she was nothing but a bucket of ashes to be tossed out.

"You are not Marybeth Spatts."

The Imposter pursed her lips, her silence saying otherwise.

"Marybeth Spatts would never"—she raked in a breath—"vanish for ten years without a word to someone she claimed was as good as a sister." Her words were measured. Because the moment she let them break through the thin thread of restraint, there would be no stopping the lava flow.

The Imposter nodded slow, dropping her head. "I can explain," she said, and her voice sounded hollow. The lilt of hope that had been there before was gone. Rusty's doing.

"Was it pirates?" Rusty put her hands on her hips and challenged her with a good long stare. "Because unless it was pirates, and unless you've been tied up somewhere all this time, or lost at sea, there's no possible thing you can say that will undo the way you disappeared. Or possibly prison. Were you in prison?"

She stammered a little, looking torn before saying, "Well . . . there were pirates for a short time, but I don't suppose you'd count them, they were just part of a—"

"Do you know I wrote to the undertaker?" Her breaths were getting shallow, not enough room to go deep with the churning inside. She'd best be careful, or she was liable to erupt. "I thought, 'There's no way Marybeth Spatts would do that.'" She laughed with no trace of mirth. "She died. It's the only explanation. Do you know how it feels to be convinced that your best friend in all the world has died?"

The Imposter's eyes opened wide, and she looked ready to speak. But the coming eruption inside was rising, and the words wouldn't stop. "Of course not." Rusty stepped closer and the Imposter flinched. "Because you just disappeared without a thought about me. So maybe I cared more about you than you did about me. But I did, Marybeth. I cared. And you didn't die. That's what the undertaker said. That you'd just left. Got on a train, he said. So I thought, 'Maybe she's coming here.'" A mirthless laugh. "I needed you."

Rusty's voice cracked at the confession, and it was too real. She pulled back. Tamped down the lava. Folded her arms over her chest. "I thought maybe the train didn't make it. Maybe you were lost—I telephoned rail stops from here to North Carolina, worrying about you. And now . . . what? You're just standing here, like none of that ever happened?"

"I can explain—"

"You'd best be on your way back down the mountain. Sun goes behind the peak early here, and there's all sorts of shadows and creatures to tangle with. Good luck."

Marybeth ran a thumb over her hand. "I'll stay, if it's all the same to you, Rusty. I'd like to explain."

"You can *leave*, if it's all the same to you."

"You once told me that growing a backbone looked like staying when you want to leave sometimes," the Stubborn Imposter said.

"Well, I certainly wasn't imagining *this*. And I also said courage looked like leaving sometimes. I was trying to get you out of that poisonous house. This"—Rusty flung her hands out, gesturing at this room, this moment—"is different." She marched to the door and flung it open.

The Obstinate Stubborn Imposter stayed put. "If you're bound and determined not to hear me out, Rusty, then I can't leave without you at least knowing—"

"I don't need to know a thing."

"But if this is my one chance to tell you—"

Rusty pulled the door open as wide as it would go, relishing the glorious screech of the hinges. The Obstinate Pigheaded Stubborn Imposter winced . . . and still stood firm. Crossed her arms over her chest to match Rusty.

Pride swelled inside Rusty. She wanted to clap Marybeth Spatts on the back for standing her ground.

But her stomach soured, too, bitterness oozing. Her closest companion, these past years. She clenched her teeth and seethed. Bitterness, she well knew, held its slithering power in the way it silently summoned other things. Doubt. Fear. Anger.

Even when something tugged at her inside, begging her to see its irrationality. *Hear her out.*

But the anger came bubbling up inside her anyway, unheeding. Anger boxed up that voice real quick and hammered the lid shut.

"Fine. Stay as long as you want. But don't expect me to stay, too." She crossed the room in three strides and placed her hand on the bedroom door. If this was the last time she ever saw this person, she wanted her to know. "You near killed me, Marybeth, going silent like that."

Marybeth's eyes welled with tears. They locked gazes, and blast it, Rusty's vision got blurry, too.

This was where Marybeth should be spouting explanations. Asking important questions, like where was Sam Buckley? Why was she all alone out here when he'd promised to marry her?

The answer sank hard and fast and nearly knocked her over. Marybeth knew.

And still she'd stayed away.

The hot tears welled up fierce, and she turned to face the door, dashing her eyes and turning the knob. With a twist, and an open, and a slam, this would be done once and for all.

She twisted the knob.

Pulled the door open.

Stepped inside.

But before she could seal the moment with a slam, a shrill yowl unfurled as a black blur darted past her.

Oh no.

"Get the door!" Rusty hollered in a panic.

Marybeth sprang into action. Time slowed as the black dart raced against the green dart of Marybeth, who clearly saw she would never make it to the door in time.

Rusty lunged after the cat. Marybeth tipped a chair over, sliding it across the cat's path.

The cat screeched to a halt and veered around it, its tail whipping tightly as it made to escape.

By this time, Marybeth and Rusty were both springing for the door. The cat beelined like there was no tomorrow. All three reached the portal to the outer world at the same time, and in a lickety-split second that could have been choreographed, Marybeth scooped up that cat and Rusty slammed that door shut.

They looked at each other, both breathing hard.

Not to be foiled, the wild thing writhed and wriggled and flipped and finally sprang up.

Marybeth cried out, retracting an arm in pain. The cat flew from her arms, latched onto the red-checked curtains, Rusty's one foray into domesticity. That darn cat clawed his way up, snagging here, shredding there, yowling all the way.

Now the cauldron that was Rusty's stomach was boiling over with anger. At Marybeth for being here. At Marybeth for being gone. At Sam for being gone. At the curtains, for reminding her. And at the cat, for shredding that reminder to bits.

It clung to the top and swung like a pendulum. Marybeth crept up from behind and waited, like a mountain lion for its prey.

Pretty impressive, actually. Too bad Rusty hated her.

The curtain swayed.

The cat clung.

The seam gave a defeated *pop*. Followed by a *pop-pop-pop* as the whole thing came down, right into Marybeth's arms, the rod clattering to the ground as she held that cat bundled like a baby. She fell backward with the momentum, and Rusty rushed over, helping her up by the elbow.

Marybeth struggled to her feet and offered the curtain-cat to Rusty, like a midwife putting a swaddled babe in a new mother's arms.

"Well," she said, a little breathy.

"Well," Rusty said in return. The cat was oddly still, as if it liked this cocoon. It breathed in and out, and Rusty held it close for fear of what it'd do to the universe if released.

"I'll go," Marybeth said, her voice holding a wobble that she covered over quickly. "But in case I don't get the chance again, Rusty . . . I want to thank you."

Rusty swallowed, throat burning. She drilled her gaze into the floorboards.

Marybeth pulled in a ragged breath. And for the first time, Rusty wondered what the last ten years had been like for her. Maybe Rusty wasn't the only one with a story to tell.

"You were a friend to me when I had none other in the world, and it . . . *you* . . . changed everything for me."

Was that a good thing? A bad thing? Curiosity bubbled and she held her tongue. People said strange things about curiosity and cats.

She made herself look anywhere but at Marybeth, the girl who borrowed light from the moon when the sun was nowhere to be found.

"You know you once told me that if I came to Mercy Peak, confetti would fly."

Rusty's eyes snapped up, and behind her swimming eyes, a spark of mirth shone through as Marybeth dipped her head toward the cat.

"Maybe your flying cat just got himself a name." She stepped to the door, opened it, and paused. "I hope we can talk sometime, Rusty. If you find you can bear listening, I can explain. Or at least—please, read this."

Rusty let out a dry laugh. "You wrote me a letter?"

"We know how to speak in letters."

"It's about ten years too late."

"I thought this might happen—"

"Oh, you think you know me so well—"

Mercy put her hand up, halting Rusty's words and finishing calmly. "So I brought something from long ago. Just in case."

She put a letter on the table and eyed the cat, as if to warn it away from the thing. "I know it won't undo the past. I should've been here for you. But I can see my presence in your cabin is causing you pain, and that's the last thing I want. So . . . I'll go. Just—I'm . . . I'm so sorry." Her voice grew thick. "About Sam. And . . . for not being here. You deserved better."

She took three steps. Paused and turned. Appeared to deliberate.

"Oh, and Rusty?" Her voice was different. A hint of mischief. "I could use some help picking a lock, if you know any experts."

Rusty smirked.

"A mysterious black trunk. I'm sure you wouldn't be interested."

And with that, she was gone.

Marybeth, age 15

Dear Rusty,

Here's the latest entry into the lexicon:

Dodo Bird: Flightless island bird recorded by Dutch sailors in 1598. Has since gone extinct.

I guess flightless birds are the ones that go extinct. That makes sense to me.

Things are hard here, Rusty. Most days Pa doesn't speak a word to me—and when he does look at me, it's as if to say, "What a waste you are." He despises me.

And the times he does speak . . . I can't repeat the words. They cut deep. Maybe I deserve them. I try to do what's right, but the beast still comes out.

One night it got so bad, the yelling—he had fire in his eyes, and the bottle in his hands. His eyes landed on me, and it was like his hands searched the universe for a place to lay all the blame for every demon he harbors—and found me. I backed up to the wall. The logs felt so cold, but so secure, bracing me. I closed my eyes as the bottle flew toward me and shattered right beside my shoulder.

I don't know if he was aiming for my heart—but it felt like that's where it sliced. No drop of blood was shed, no tear was dropped. Tears make it worse, so I stopped those up a long time ago. I don't guess I'll ever let anyone see me drop a single tear again, in this life.

I don't know what to do. If I was a bird, I wouldn't just be flightless—I'd be the kind whose wings never even grew in.

Maybe I was never meant to have any. I look around sometimes and feel like all I can see is chains. So heavy I can feel them cinching deep where my breath comes in. When I breathe deep, that hurts, too.

At the mine they say the explosives get more explosive as they get older. Nitrocellulose, they call it. I hear that, and I think, I wonder if Pa is made of that. Because in some ways, the more time that goes by, the worse it gets.

But I don't see a way out. And even if I could . . . I can't leave. For all his faults, I think if I left, it would be the end of that man. And I can't do that to him. He's still my father.

It feels a lot like an island. And I feel a little like I'm going extinct. I'm invisible . . . unseen. I don't really care much about being seen, Rusty, I never really have. I prefer it in the shadows and wouldn't know what to do with a spotlight. But something inside aches at the thought that these four walls might be my life, and nothing more. It would be nice, I think, to know that somebody knew me.

Pa doesn't.

You do. And I'm so thankful. I wish I could know you face to face somehow. It's so alone here. If I just knew that someone close . . . knew me.

But I don't think that will ever happen.

How pitiful that sounds. But it's the truth, so I'm leaving it.

I stopped by the school—I so miss being there!—and saw the textbook open to the page about the Dodo bird. She said the rest of the class laughed at its name. I tried to smile, but I just felt sad.

Don't worry about me, though. I'll be okay. Even flightless birds are—or were—there for a reason.

Right?

Marybeth Spatts

✻ ✻ ✻

Dear Marybeth,

1) Never *is a terrible word. Don't say it.*

2) FLIGHTLESS BIRDS ARE THE MOST SUPREME BIRDS.

You know why?

Two words: Flightless. Bird. *They seem impossible together.
What do they call that, an opposite phrase. Oxenmoron? Something like that. I remember it sounded like dumb oxes but actually meant something that seemed like it shouldn't be possible,
like a perfect imperfection. That's what makes it beautiful . . . like
anything could happen.*

Like a flightless bird.

Like a PENGUIN.

*Penguins have purpose! I've never met one, but I mean to one
day, and when I do, I intend to shake its flipper good and hard
and tell it that it makes people smile just by the way it waddles.
A smile is pretty hard to come by sometimes, so I'd say that's
downright miraculous.*

*Penguins have purpose, and anyone who says otherwise is
going to make me mad. Scratch that—spitting mad. Scratch that
again—nail-spitting mad!*

*Flightless birds are the best, Marybeth. Don't you doubt it one
second. But you know what? I think you do have wings. And one
day you'll take flight.*

*I do know you. I wish the whole world knew Marybeth Spatts!
You'd probably crawl into a hole and hide if that ever happened. So,
I guess it's just me, and I guess that just means I'm the lucky one.*

*Nothing to report here. Sam brought me three plums last
Tuesday. One was too soft, so we splatted it at the back of a
fallen-over shed on Wildwood's back forty. It splattered us both,
and we fell over laughing. Here's my tip: Go splat some fruit
somewhere. Doesn't matter what kind and doesn't matter what
you splat it at. You'll just feel better. It's the eighth law of thermo-
dynamics. Think Randolph Gilman knows that?*

Rusty

*p.s. Mr. Travers the blacksmith clips his chickens' wings so
they won't fly the coop. One of them was so fast he could never
catch her, and he named her Jezebel, telling her she'd get eaten
by dogs if she got out and that she'd better let him clip her wings.
Guess which chicken flew away into the wild blue free, not a wild
dog in sight?*

You'll fly, Marybeth.

Folio of Field Notes, Volume III:
Fire

[Property of Sudsy McGee, Hollywood Biographer]

Interview with Tabitha Greer

Sudsy McGee: Hello, Tabitha. Thank you for answering a few questions today. How is it that you're not in school?

Tabitha Greer: It's Saturday.

SM: So it is. I don't know where my mind is, my apologies.

TG: You should draw it a map.

SM: Pardon?

TG: If you don't know where your mind is, you should draw it a map so it can find its way back. Miss Mercy taught me about drawing maps. And her best friend when she was my age taught her.

SM: And what is your age, Tabitha?

TG: It's Tabbie. And I'm ten.

Mabel Greer (Tabitha's mother): Going on twenty-five. [laughs]

SM: And . . . Miss Mercy's best friend's name, back then?

TG: [shrugs] She never said. But she looked happy when she talked about her. And a little sad, too. She said she was like a sister.

SM: What's that you have there?

TG: Oh, this? [She tilts a book out that she's been clutching close to her.] It's only the very best story ever written. A fairy tale. *The Light Princess.* Mr. George MacDonald wrote it. I kept asking Miss Mercy to make it into a movie, but she said she's not in charge of that. [sighs wistfully] I just *love* the scene when the prince dives into the lake to save the princess. Only she didn't want saving. It's funny!

SM: It does sound entertaining. Tabbie, I understand that Miss Windsor saved you? Could you draw me a map of what happened at the soundstage?

TG: [shrugs, takes paper offered, thinks, starts to draw] Well, the fire started here, by the castle set.

SM: You were an extra on the set?

TG: [nods] That's right. Me and my friend used to sneak over the fence and play on the backlot. We got caught and were about to get a big scolding when Miss Mercy saw what was happening and worked out a deal that we could be extras whenever they needed kids in the background. Got us pay and everything.

SM: And did you like the work?

TG: I liked being with Miss Mercy. And the studio cat. The work was fine, I guess. I just look around curiously at whatever's happening, and then they give us some money.

MG: Miss Windsor has been very protective of my Tabbie. . . . There've been times when they thought she might do for a big role, and Mercy just seemed so torn. She told me, woman to woman, it wasn't much of a life for these kids who grow up in the spotlight. She has close friends who grew up that way and are grown now and hurting from the inside out. She says Tabbie has talent, though. And the pay for the extra roles has helped. It's just the two of us, and I have work in the wardrobe department, sewing. We get by, don't we, Tabbie?

TG: You bet!

SM: And what did Mr. Wilson say about the fire?

TG: He said, [lowers voice and plants hands on hips] "Roll film. We'll use the fire footage someday. Nothing's wasted." He got the crew rolling in the street outside and got the whole thing on film.

SM: I see. Thank you, Tabbie. Do you hear from Miss Windsor?

TG: Who?

MG: Miss Mercy, sweetheart.

TG: Oh! No. I miss her something awful. She used to let me sit with her up in the rafters where she watched the orchestra practice. Mama sometimes, too. [clamps hands over mouth] Oops! It was her secret place she could go when she wanted to disappear for a while. I wasn't supposed to tell. . . .

MG: [stroking Tabitha's hair] It's alright, Tabbie. She's safe, wherever she is, I'm sure.

124

FIRE AT SOUNDSTAGE 8
SILVER SCREEN QUEEN TO BLAME?

**America's Sweetheart under Fire
for Valentine's Day Conflagration**

BY S. McGEE

February 15, 1948—Building 9 at Pinnacle Studios in Hollywood, California, has been destroyed by flame. On February 14, a night security guard reported smoke rising from the roof of the famed soundstage, which is fifteen feet higher than the studio's other stages. Owing to its height, it is reserved for the movie industry's most demanding film sets, such as the one that had nearly finished filming there: *Joan of Arc*, starring Mercy Windsor. Windsor, 30, is the "doe-eyed ingénue" who broke upon an astonished world in her debut role and came to be famed for her delivery of "the single tear that flooded the world." She was reported to be in the building late that night when the fire broke out. She narrowly escaped, together with a child who sustained mild injuries.

"It's a very unpleasant situation," Wilson P. Wilson, owner of Pinnacle Studios, says. "One doesn't like to speak badly of anyone, least of all someone so well-loved as Miss Windsor. Stage lights are notoriously hot and set construction materials often highly flammable. It's understandable that there must have been much weighing on her mind. Regarding the rumors circulating about her state of mind—and sobriety—we can only say so much. You understand. Every effort will be made to keep Miss Windsor in the Pinnacle family, but her contract is the bottom line, and it is currently under review by our legal department. In the meantime, Pinnacle Studios offers its heartfelt apologies for the black smoke that clouded your blue skies this week. As recompense, we are offering complimentary admission to all Pinnacle films showing at Highland Theatre this Saturday, until capacity is full. Pinnacle loves you, Los Angeles. Never forget."

═══ PURCHASE ORDER ═══

Pinnacle Studios Purchase Order No. 20556
For film set: *Joan of Arc*
10/10/1947
(Check mark indicates approval by Mr. Wilson)

√ Plaster: 10,000 pounds
√ Legacy Lumber: Misc. lumber in the amount of $3,000
~~New sprinkler lines estimated to cost $2,000~~
√ Import white sand for set: $2,000

Pertinent Correspondence between Wilson P. Wilson and Mercy Windsor

12/12/1947

Dear Mr. Wilson,

Thank you for the wonderful opportunity to play Joan of Arc. It is the role of a lifetime and a great honor to get to bring a voice to someone in history who I so deeply respect. You have orchestrated a truly enchanting world with the ornate sets, costumes, and props. I deeply commend you for that.

However, it has come to my attention that there may be some oversight with safety. I understand that set construction is a finely tuned balance of budget, safety, and effects. If I may venture to say so, Mr. Wilson, the excellent script and the details you've already poured into the set design are exquisite. They are enough.

As you know, owing to the extra height of Building 9, its west end is home to one of Pinnacle's film vaults. You're aware, I'm sure, of the high flammability of nitrocellulose, of which film is made.

Building 9 has sprinklers, but they are weak. I have seen them tested. They will do nothing to prevent a disaster if the volatile film should be compromised. More importantly, countless lives are on the line if this situation is not rectified.

You often express your deep adoration for Los Angeles. Without a doubt, that certainly includes the employees on your beautiful backlot. If I can be of assistance in helping to ensure their safety, please count on me.

I am sure it's merely an oversight, easily corrected.

Sincerely,
Mercy Windsor

12/15/1947

Dear Miss Windsor,

You forget your place.

I made you.

I pulled you out of obscurity at a Denver theatre housed at a <u>zoo</u>, of all places, and gave you the stars.

Be sure that the stars are a price you're willing to forfeit if you speak of this again, whether to myself or to others. There are negligible numbers of people who would be in jeopardy if anything were to cause the set to be compromised—which it won't be.

Film as we know it would not exist without the innovations of Pinnacle Studios. We are pioneers. I have been in this business longer than you've been alive. The film reels housed in Building 9 are older than you, my dear. If there was anything dangerous about them, it's most certainly dissipated in half-lives upon half-lives. Speaking of life spans, if you care anything for the life span of your career, you will cease and desist your ill-directed efforts. If you're smart, you'll leave the righteous fighting to Joan of Arc.

Just play your part.

Wilson P. Wilson
President and Founder
Pinnacle Studios

Mr. Wilson,

Nitrocellulose grows less stable and more volatile with time.

The smoke alone can be lethal, especially in confined places. If it does not kill, it destroys in other ways. Trust me—please. I, more than most, know it. I have seen it.

I cannot keep my silence.
If nothing is done . . . I will not complete filming this role.
It is the one thing I can do on their behalf.

Marybeth Spatts

Miss Spatts,
Read your contract.
Play your part.

WPW

CHAPTER
11

Marybeth, age 14

Dear Rusty,

I don't know how to start this letter. There's no good way to say this.

It's burning inside me like a cattle brand, and it gets hotter and deeper every day, and I'm near to bursting if I don't tell somebody.

Pa last week at supper said the rats were running at the coal mine. He laughed, said some of the men quit on the spot. "The rats know when something's comin'," they said. Pa swigged his drink and said he'd been around a lot longer than any dirty old rat and no rodent would make him live life any different, much less miss out on a day's pay when the mining's good. He refused to listen to the rats. Just like when he told me to "shut my trap" about the snowstorm last winter, that it'd be fine. And that if I had something to say, I shouldn't whisper it. "No room for scared mice here, Marybeth Spatts. Spatts is strong. Speak up if you got somethin' to say."

It's just that Pa always spoke up enough for both of us, his voice so loud sometimes it shook the walls and shook me, too. I didn't like to speak up. Maybe my quiet would pull back some of his loud.

But the rats running . . . that wasn't right. I knew it. And I knew he knew it, too. But they offered more pay, and Pa wanted that.

I couldn't sleep that night.

In the morning I got up before the sun so I could see him. I cleared my throat. I had the words. I'd worked all night on them.

"Don't be a fool, Pa," I was going to say. "Don't go. Go to the fishing hole instead. It'll still be a good day of work." That's what I was going to say.

I stood up. I opened my mouth. "P-pa."

He turned slow and squinted, finally seeing me in the lantern light over by the table.

I cleared my throat. The words stuck.

"Well?"

Spatts is strong, I told myself.

He pinched his brows together. Heaved a big sigh that made his shoulders drop. I was letting him down again.

"H-have a good day at the mines," I said. That was courageous, too—that's what I told myself. Swallow back my fear. I always find the fear, and telling Pa to have a good day even though the fear was roiling like storm waves inside me—that was a different kind of courage. That's what I kept telling myself. But . . .

"Rats runnin'." The words skittered across my mind all day, like the words were rodents themselves. Scritching and scratching until Miss Walker told me to sit still in my seat. But I felt like something was trapped inside, something deep and burning. It stayed as I walked the road home, and the whole world felt restless. Tree leaves trembling, winds blowing soft and then hard, like it couldn't figure out what to do with itself, just like my hands couldn't figure out what to do with themselves.

I don't know how, but I knew. Something was happening down there under our feet. Rumbling like it held a great fire in its belly—because it did.

And then it happened. I do not have words to describe it, Rusty. I should probably tell it like it was a dragon breathing fire up from below, but a dragon seems too nice for what it was.

The sound near blew my ears out.

The shake nearly toppled me.

And I ran for the mine. The sounds got worse. Men yelling like I've never heard, and you know that's saying something. Metal on rock, men and machine trying to move earth and get her to open back up, like she was Hades releasing captives.

I always felt odd, thinking of men beneath the earth, their hearts beating away somewhere down there. That's nothing com-

pared to thinking of men trapped next to other men dead, next to other men half-alive.

"Give them up," I said. "Give up the men." I spoke it strong, like a Spatts. I took my voice up when I got to the clearing and watched on, one of the men pointing, telling me not to get closer. "Give up the men," I said, and said it again louder. A prayer, a plea—over and over till I was shouting, but no one would know it, for the sea of women and kids and other men who'd gathered, wailing and praying.

I fell to my knees. Pa was down there.

So I yelled like a Spatts, but I was ten hours too late. I should have yelled that way at him in that lantern light. Because now he might never see the light again. And it's my fault.

I clawed at the ground. It got blurry, I couldn't see, and the taste of salt and dirt ran into my mouth, tears running down and dust rising up until someone—I don't know who—pulled me back. One of the men who quit yesterday, one of the ones who listened to the rats. He pulled me into himself and wrapped his arms around me to hold my flailing arms close to my stomach so I wouldn't hurt myself, and I shook like the earth. I looked up at the sky, desperate for something real and true and good that wasn't shaking. Desperate for the sun or the sky or the trees—

And saw only coal-black snow, raining down. Covering the world.

They said something about a cave-in being one thing, but a cave-in that falls into a storeroom of old explosives . . . that's something else.

It's all I know, Rusty. They're still digging. It's been four days.

Rusty, age 14

Dear Marybeth,

Spatts <u>is</u> strong.

Don't you give up. Whatever's happened, you take a breath, right now. Feel that? That's life, real and true. Now take another one, even slower, even deeper. Feel it? That's life, real and true.

Keep on doing that. Pick up the pencil—you might not feel like it, you might feel like crawling in a hole yourself. It's okay if you do for a minute, but you gotta climb back out because a hole

is no place for Marybeth Spatts. Pull in that air, one more time.
Pick up that pencil.

Talk to me.

What happened?

Whatever it is . . . I'm here.

Love, all the way down to the deepest darkest holes and back,

Rusty

Dear Rusty,

I'm sorry for the bad paper this is on. I got your letter because
the teacher brought it over, even though I haven't been to school.
I'll probably never go back. Pa always said girls had no place in
school anyhow, and now . . . well, he needs me here.

They got him out. He's in a bad way . . . all bandaged up on
the outside, but I think it's even worse inside.

He wants it dark in here all the time. Hardly eats a thing, and
when he hollers for food and I bring him something, he takes a
bite and hollers some more that it's not right, not done, not good.
Throws it across the room, plate and all. Doesn't matter what it
is. Except I made him your dad's skillet corn bread yesterday. He
ate that.

Do you want to hear something ridiculous, Rusty? I've never
told a soul, and never meant to. But everything in me is all
splayed out anyway . . .

I used to have a dream. It was a small one, I thought. Some
kids dream of seeing the world, or being somebody, or climbing
tall mountains. For me, my wish was so small, but so impossible.
I just wrapped my heart around it and held it tight, for nary a
soul to ever know.

I wanted a lullaby.

It looks so silly, written upon paper. But I'm sure, if I'd known
my mother, she'd have been the sort to sing her babies to sleep.
Only . . . she only ever had one baby and only lived to hold her
once. There wasn't even enough breath for a lullaby, to hear it told.

Pa used to sing, people say. I've never heard him, not once.

I used to sleep with my window open a crack to feel the
breeze, and there was a time when the neighbors had a baby. The

132

mama would sit out on their porch in a rocking chair and sing a song, just for that baby. It drifted in my window and right into that crack in my heart that was holding a place for a lullaby. I borrowed it, Rusty, and maybe it was stupid. I wouldn't begrudge that baby her lullaby, but I floated on it awhile, I admit it.

Sometimes now, sometimes when it's pitch-black, so far into the night you can almost touch the morning . . . Pa cries. Like a baby, Rusty. He just shakes under his covers and cries. I wish I had a lullaby to give him . . . but my voice is gone. I didn't use it that day to keep him out of the mine, and now I can hardly wrap it around simple words to speak, let alone a lullaby for a man engulfed in a dark abyss. But somewhere deep inside me, I still wish for one. For him.

I put my blanket over him the other morning ever so quiet, thinking to help with his shivering. I tried to do it without him knowing. He'd hate me seeing him cry like that.

But he saw me. His dark eyes found mine in that cold silver moonlight, and he reached up a hand and took mine. As his shoulders shook, he said, "I'm sorry."

Half of me wanted to crumple into a pile myself and hold on tight to those words—the nicest thing he's ever said to me my whole life long.

But half of me got so angry, Rusty, I'm ashamed. I wanted to stand up and yell back at him, "For what? For not listening? For going in like a stubborn mule? For getting yourself crushed, and making sure my life was crushed, too? For all the drink, all the yelling? What are you sorry for?"

But the truth is, even deeper down, under all those questions shooting around my imagination like bullets . . . I'm the one who's sorry.

Doc says Dad will never mine again. He's lucky to be alive at all, but he'll never be the same. He'll never work, maybe never walk again. So I'll work. And I'll care for him. And this will be my life.

All those dreams we had, Rusty . . . me coming to Mercy Peak. Us being together at last. Taking on the world together . . .

They're gone.

I'm sorry, Rusty.

I should've spoken up that morning about the rats.

Maybe someday we'll be together.
Maybe someday we'll climb Mercy Peak together.
Maybe.

Marybeth

Dear Marybeth,
This'll be quick—I'll write a longer letter soon, but I want this to get to you in time.
Do you get the radio there? Put on the Edie Valentine Radio Hour. That lady's got a voice like an angel, and whatever song she sings when you put it on . . . I hereby dub it your lullaby. For you to keep, or for you to sing to your pa, or just to sing away the ache for a minute or two.
Don't let go.

Rusty

Dear Rusty,
I wish I had words to thank you.
I did what you said, and a song came on . . . "Stars shining bright above you . . . Night breezes seem to whisper I love you" . . . It went on, all about birds singing in trees and dreaming a little dream.
It was simple in so many ways.
But to someone who cannot dream, who has never had a single voice say to her, "I love you" that song was the sound of hope.
I tucked it away, and I hum it under the stars, and I wonder big questions that won't fit inside my heart. Does the Maker of those stars think of me? Does He whisper in the night breezes, "I love you," even when no one else does?
I do not know. But it is a thought, and it is a hope, and I will hold to it.
Thank you, my friend.
And while I cannot dream, I hope you will. Dream not of me, but for me. Dream for both of us. Dream a beautiful life for yourself, and live it, Rusty. Live it so big.

The thing about prospecting is, you gotta look for what isn't there. Crack between rocks? Go deep. Because something was there, once, and you'd best find what it was. That's where the treasure is, if it's there to be found. Look for what's not there.

—Martin Shaw, local prospecting legend

Rusty

Read your letter.

The voice in Rusty's head was incessant.

Four days. Four days, that blasted envelope sat on that table.

On day one, Rusty turned her back on it and rolled her eyes at Marybeth's attempt to lure her with the mystery of a lock that needed picking.

On day two, she shoved it in the cupboard—the table was too good for it. She did not think of the lock at all, except to tell herself not to think of it.

On day three, she pulled it back out and stuck it on the table again— the cupboard was too safe a place for the Traitor to hide. She chronicled what type of padlock it might be, based on the Gilmans' resources and history. She envisioned something old and crusty and glorious. Her fingers thrummed the table, thinking how they'd coax such a device open.

On day four, after Confetti the Cat batted it her way and it spun like a pinwheel, catching red-tinted sunlight through the now-shredded curtains, her fingers betrayed her, and she opened the envelope. The tear of the paper felt good, rending the silence. And then her eyes betrayed her, too, dashing over the lines before she could stop them.

ELITCH'S ZOOLOGICAL GARDENS, the stationery spelled out in letters that looked like they'd been built of twigs. A lion and a monkey bookended the words in muted colors.

DENVER, COLORADO
October 1937

She stopped. Gulped down her toast. October 1937? The paradox month. It was imprinted forever on her heart, and it was blurred forever in her memory. It was when she'd lost Sam.

Dear Rusty,
    It's been four days.

"Well, that's downright spooky," Rusty said, looking around as if the Traitor were hiding in the cupboard herself. "How'd she know how long I'd let this letter sit here, Cat?"
Confetti licked his paws and looked drolly up at Rusty.

Four days since I got to you and left you, all in the same moment. Words—these things that made you and me . . . they have nothing to offer me now. I reach for them to try and put some kind of structure around this oozing ulcer of grief inside of me, Rusty, and—they can't do it. This will be short. I can't send it, anyway, knowing you're not there to receive it.
    Still, I'm going to come back to Mercy Peak someday. I promised before, and I promise it now.
    When I asked in town where to find you, they got all teary-eyed, and the lady with blond curls who was there to buy flour to "make a cake for the family" shrugged her shoulders and couldn't speak. The man there—I'm supposing it was your Mr. Angus, who has handled all our letters over the years—he shook his head sadly and said that the households of the Brights and the Buckleys were in mourning. That there'd been an accident, and it was best to give space, though if I needed to, I could find them at the graveyard that afternoon for the funeral.
    I couldn't believe it, Rusty.
    I wouldn't.
    You wouldn't dare to—I can't even write the word. Three short letters makes it feel so cruel.
    You wouldn't dare to . . . perish.

Rusty shook her head. Leave it to Marybeth Spatts to be flipping through the dictionary in her head at a time like that, to make the word *die* sound both gentler and ridiculously dramatic.

A dry laugh escaped her clenched teeth.

(You'd laugh at that word if you read it).

Rusty clamped her mouth shut.

You wouldn't dare. And I defied it to be true. I had to see for myself.

I spent one night there. I climbed up the foothill a bit. There was a path and a clearing with a big boulder balanced right up against a tree. From there, I could see down into the graveyard, Rusty, but it hurt so much to look down there that I didn't. I looked up at the sky instead, saw how rain clouds were mounding, and that felt right. For the very sky to grieve you, who held the wind inside of you all your life. It came, the rain, right on my lifted face. At some point, it turned into snow, twirling down out of the dark. I followed your map to Whistler's Bridge. You said we'd sleep there someday . . . so I did. I traced the beams above, one by one beneath the covered bridge. Shivering through and through.

You said Mercy Peak would be home, Rusty, but with you gone, I'd never felt so alone. My heart broke so wide open, whatever was left inside spilled out, and I think I left it right there in the shadow of that mountain.

It wasn't until after I'd climbed on that Galloping Goose back out of the mountains—a different one from the one I'd come on—that I remembered what you left me in the dungeon of the church.

Churches don't have dungeons, Rusty. I wish we could sit together and laugh at that, and I'd say it's a storm cellar and you'd say I could call it what I liked, but if it had spiderwebs and was underground, a dungeon by any other name was still a dungeon.

I'll go back someday for my inheritance, Rusty. But for now . . . I will honor you by not going back to Swickley's Crossing. Pa's gone, slipped away into eternity. I sat in that room I've lived in all my life and felt carved out and empty . . . and could nearly hear the shackles fall to the ground.

If I could've seen them, I might've just picked them up and clamped them back on, if only for the familiarity. I've known nothing else.

But you were in my head, telling me to fly.

So I did. Or tried to.

I don't know where I'll go, Rusty. I don't have much I can do or offer to the world. I came to Denver because it was the farthest I could get on the train with what I had left. I've found work feeding the elephants at Elitch's Zoological Gardens, and I know you'd have a hoot about that. They have a summer theatre, too; they mentioned putting me to work there sweeping or selling concessions.

I wish I could tell you.

I wish so much. I wish I could see you. I wish I could tell you what I never said. That you're not just my friend. You're my sister. Not "were," but <u>are</u>. You always will be. That doesn't just stop, just because one of us moves on to heaven.

I want to ask you why. I want to ask you how. I want to beat the ground and tell it to give you up, give you up, just like it gave up Pa all those years ago when I did that.

But it gave me back Pa a whole lot worse than he was.

And I don't begrudge you where you are. But I miss you, Rusty. No way around it.

It's been four days, Rusty. And I'm still digging.

> *Your sister,*
> *Marybeth*

Rusty blinked, eyes hot and wet. Ignoring the twisting going on inside her. "Of all the . . ."

She flipped the page over, sure there must be more. Only a watermark of an elephant, trunk raised, greeting her. It may as well have sprayed her with cold water for the way the letter rattled up her insides.

"That's the most ridiculous thing I've ever heard," Rusty said aloud. "She thought I was dead? Well, that's just . . ."

What? What was it? Nonsense, that's what. Did that mean that all these years of silence could've been avoided if she'd just asked a question or two more when she'd come?

But she'd come.

And that was Marybeth—she gathered things up and held them in close, when they jarred her. Some people exploded, some imploded. Marybeth was the latter. Would she hold her own nature against her?

And would Rusty have had the presence of mind to ask questions in a situation like that? Likely she'd have exploded, not imploded, but she had to admit . . . she would've been too busy exploding to ask questions.

Something pricked inside.

Did that mean that right when Rusty had needed her most—she'd *been* here?

Something pricked even deeper.

Did that mean she'd been on Motor No. 8, just hours before it had disappeared? Rusty had scoured this canyon, its rises and ridges and canyons and cliffs, looking for that thing. For the one letter she hoped it still contained. But like everyone else who'd searched for the long-lost engine . . . she just kept coming up empty.

Rusty pressed her eyes closed, remembering the night too well. The somber service, honoring her Sam. She couldn't face everyone but couldn't miss it. She'd watched on from a hillside, hidden by trees. Across the valley from where Marybeth, apparently, had watched on, too.

She'd boarded up this shanty tight, and the wind had been cold, pressing through cabin cracks she hadn't known were there. She barely noticed the cold, though. . . . It matched the way her insides shook as she tried to hold back the sobs, knowing that the moment she gave in, they'd pull her under, well and good. And she might never resurface.

That was the night she locked the tears up so tight they'd never budged.

And Marybeth Spatts—the friend she'd longed for—had been a stone's throw away. Out in the cold.

Something in that felt soft around her heart.

Drat.

Soft things could slither under cracks, make their way into fortified chambers. She pushed the soft thing away and straightened up, reaching for the familiar cloak that would lock it all out: anger.

She found it easy and fast as it writhed around, feeding on falsities. Her logic tried to tame it.

She came. She didn't know. She'd been grieving, too.

But the anger drove her on. Rusty cinched her black wool coat around her tight with an old belt and stepped out the door where the April air slapped her cheeks with life. Up the mountain her clunky boots splatted against spring-thaw mud, sliding here, catching there as she skirted the far end of the canyon on the high path. It was the long way, but it was her way and afforded her the best view of the village and valley below.

She picked her way over rocks that crossed the river above the waterfall, shaking her head for the thousandth time at the stone wall Randolph Gilman had erected around its headwaters. The man was an enigma. Certainly the falls were on his land . . . but did he really have to proclaim it visibly to the world?

She traversed her own zigzag path down to Wildwood, across its woodlands, and around to arrive at the front gate of WILD OOD. Sounded like some sort of fearsome varmint. Mercy Peak needed a creature of lore. Loch Ness had her monster, but all they had around here was the Slide-Rock Bolter, and that belonged to all of the Rockies.

It was a debate she and Sam had loved to banter. He was a devotee of the whale-like monster said to haunt the peaks of these mountains, curling its double-grappling-hook tail over ridges to secure itself, then letting go to slide on a river of slime from its mouth, down toward unsuspecting miners and passersby.

"*That's a whale of a tale,*" Rusty used to say, and Sam would laugh every time.

"*Top it. I dare you.*"

"*Why should we have to share a tall tale with all of Colorado? Mercy Peak deserves her own.*"

"*Then make one.*" He'd pushed his glasses up, the unmistakable sign of a challenge.

"*You can't just make up a tall tale.*"

He'd shrugged. "*Someone had to make them up.*"

"*Or did they . . . ?*" Rusty had narrowed her eyes and scanned the timberline, stopping suddenly and making her eyes huge. She'd grasped Sam's wrist and made every single muscle in her body tight, gulping.

"*Quit it, Rusty Bright. You've never been afraid in your life. Make up a proper monster, and then we'll talk.*"

Turned out some monsters were far worse than the saber-toothed, crazy-eyed creatures. Some monsters were vacuums. The place left behind.

Sam was one.

And she was about to face the other.

Rusty paused only a moment, hauling in a breath.

At the door, she knocked once. Nothing. Twice. Nothing. The words were piling up now, ready to launch like a spring the second the door opened. *You couldn't write? Double-check? Triple-check? If it'd been you, I'd have quintuple-checked and beat a path to Swickley's Crossing to see your headstone for myself before I dropped a tear. But you just gave up?*

The windows were open. A curtain blew out breezily, looking airy and fine. Not like the shredded mess at her place. Was there no justice in the world?

Before she could talk sense into herself, her hand was on the door handle, the embossed brass *G* cold in her hand like a reverse cattle brand. A quick turn, and in she went.

"Marybeth Spatts!" she hollered, and her breath puffed in clouds around the words. Criminy, how cold was it in here? Felt twenty degrees colder than outside.

A muffled sound from deeper inside.

"Marybeth Spatts," she said again, this time with only half an exclamation mark.

"Rusty?"

That was a very strained voice.

"Spatts?"

Rusty hoofed it down the hall, setting a bowler hat spinning on the floor as she bumped it with her ankle, and slipping on a stray bit of sheet music. What had Marybeth been thinking, buying this disaster?

She gulped a little. She wasn't exactly faultless for the state of things here.

She followed Marybeth's voice up the left turret stairs and down the hall, nearly stopping in her tracks when she saw the door open. She'd tried to crack that lock more times than she cared to admit. How had Marybeth gotten in?

Inside, light poured in over a scene that dropped Rusty's jaw. There was her petite pen pal, holding up a bookcase with her back and trying—unsuccessfully—to right it as it attempted to crush her.

Indignation against that bookcase rose, sending Rusty flying in, sliding under the bookcase beside her.

"On three?" she said, and Marybeth grimaced as she nodded her agreement. "One—two—" and they both heaved, walking the behemoth back up to its place against the wall.

Rusty brushed up against Marybeth's elbow and jerked away just as quick. Marybeth crossed her arms, biting her lip and straightening her kerchief. She was dirt-streaked and disheveled and dressed like one of the Gilmans' party guests, in some chiffon getup that looked more like a cloud than a piece of real clothing.

Marybeth caught her look and blushed. "I know," she said. "I realize my clothes aren't quite up to the task. But it's all I've got."

Rusty tried to wipe the bewilderment from her own face, but she was never much good at camouflaging things. "Maybe try the attic," she said. "Whole heap of clothes up there, if they haven't been eaten by moths. Gilmans left it all behind."

Marybeth looked surprised. "Thank you," she said hesitantly, and wiped her face, smearing more dirt across her upper lip, this time in a perfect moustache.

Rusty snickered, then clamped a hand over her own mouth.

"What is it?" Marybeth raised her hands to her cheeks. "I must look a fright."

Rusty composed herself. "You look just fine," she said, "if you're campaigning to be a stunt double for Charlie Chaplin."

Marybeth's eyes grew round as donuts. She whirled to find her reflection in the glass pane of a framed picture and rubbed her face good.

"Was there a reason for your visit?" She turned back, looking so hopeful that something twisted inside Rusty, choking out her perfectly planned speech.

Rusty cleared her throat. Marybeth waited, hands clasped behind her back.

"To be frank, I came here to squash you, metaphorically, but it seems the bookcase beat me to it."

She expected Marybeth to bristle in defense, but instead a flicker of amusement stole across her picture-perfect features. "That was funny," she said, and waited again.

She had to hand it to her. She'd always thought Marybeth had a certain meekness to her. And true, there was gentleness and refinement, but somewhere along the way, her pen pal had picked up a good dose of grit, too.

It disoriented her. She grasped at straws, trying to take hold of her planned speech. "You . . . um . . ." Drat. *Don't sound so wishy-washy.* "You shouldn't have—"

Marybeth tilted her head, and for a second Rusty glimpsed the look of a little girl in her—a little girl who clawed at the ground, begging it to give up the miners . . . only to receive one so broken that he broke her, too.

Here she was, all grown up and poised in front of her with some kind of polish she'd never had during their letter-writing years. As if she'd been hibernating in a frozen palace of an ice kingdom somewhere all this time.

"You shouldn't have tried to move that bookshelf by yourself. What were you thinking?" Rusty said.

"I was thinking of a mountain woman who lives three hundred and sixty-five days of the year in a cabin all by herself and likely fends off bears and chops down trees and I don't know what else," she said. "Where I come from, we call those tall tales. Around here, that's called Rusty Bright." Marybeth lifted a slender shoulder. "I just thought if you could do all those things, I could unload these books and move a bookcase a little."

"What was so important? Why'd you have to move it? Seems there's a thing or two more pressing here than arranging furniture."

"I know." Marybeth looked ready to spill a whole bushel of beans, share some big secret, but then something stopped her. "I was just . . . looking for something."

"For what?"

She looked torn. Glanced over her shoulder back out into the hall-way. "I'm not sure how to explain. . . ."

"Try me."

"Very well." There was that polish again. "Oh, but first—Charlie Chaplin's stunt double auditions are at that frame over there." She lifted her chin and breezed past Rusty, a twinkle in her eye.

A quick look at her reflection revealed a hand outlined perfectly in bookshelf grime, right where Rusty had clamped down her own laugh-ter at Marybeth's moustache. She scrubbed it away and turned to face Marybeth, who clacked her way across the wood-planked floor. Even her shoes were otherworldly, with heels so high they could qualify as Rocky Mountain peaks.

From a precarious stack of books teetering to unwieldy heights from the floor, Rusty picked up a spine-cracked volume. "*The Light Princess*," she read. There was a bright white paper marking a page—evidence of recent reading.

"Oh, here." Marybeth held a hand out. "A . . . friend of mine loved this book. I haven't finished it, but I promised her I would someday."

"A friend who keeps her promises," Rusty said drolly. "Imagine that."

Marybeth's shoulders fell, and she hugged the book tight like it was a shield. Something crawled up Rusty's throat, tasting an awful lot like remorse.

She cleared it away and picked up the next volume. "*Fearsome Creatures of the Lumberwoods, with a Few Desert and Mountain Beasts.*" She couldn't help the smile that came. "Sam borrowed this book from the Gilmans once." She'd caught him sounding out the half-Latin, half-fantasy name for the Slide-Rock Bolter when he was ten. *Macro-stoma saxi-perrump-tus.* He'd beamed with pride when he squished the syllables together and sounded like a scientist. The memory was good and hard and true.

Rusty ran her thumb over the edges, cracked it open, and it fell right to his favorite entry. She laid her palm upon the page. Had he been the last one to touch this book? Likely so. Mr. Gilman wasn't the type to pore over glorified fairy tales.

"Was it a favorite of his?"

"He kept it three years, till I'm sure Mr. Gilman had no earthly recollection it even existed. But Sam had a heart of gold and returned it all the same." She closed the book firm and fast, the *slap* of the pages jostling her back into the moment.

"Keep it," Marybeth said, her eyes gentle. "Please."

Rusty put it down. "I didn't come to talk about Sam."

"Oh, but I don't mind—" Marybeth's voice was kind. "I—I feel like I know him, from your letters. Just a little, but still . . . I was so sorry to learn—"

"Anyway, what happened with the shelf?" Rusty cut her off. She hadn't come here to talk about Sam, least of all to Marybeth Spatts. "And what *is* this place?"

Marybeth clamped her mouth shut, dropped her gaze as if she could see her attempt at connection writhing to a slow death on the floor between them. But taking Rusty's cue, she pivoted and returned the conversation back to the task at hand. Thank goodness.

"I don't know where to begin, except . . . remember the capsule with a clue that Martin Shaw gave to Randolph Gilman?"

Rusty furrowed her brow. This was not where she'd thought this conversation would go. "Yes."

Marybeth bit her lip, reached for something on the desk behind her, and handed it to Rusty.

Rusty narrowed her eyes, looking from Marybeth to the brass cylinder no longer than her palm . . . and twisted it open. She pulled out aged paper, and began to read:

"'Flightless in flight, she seeks revolution. Tunneling blight, she keeps the solution. Coil the lash tight . . .'" Rusty's voice trailed off.

". . . begin restitution," Mercy finished.

"Is this—?"

"The clue your father had the key to. It has to be. Don't you think? I can't make sense of any of it, except for the lash part. I've looked all over this room."

"Which is what . . . a mad scientist's laboratory?" Rusty took in the odd collection of tools, equations, charts, plans, graphs. Lengths of a heavy chain, hanging on a hook. A magnifying glass laid neatly upon oversized papers on a drafting table.

Rusty leaned in, studying the papers. "What was a mine baron doing with the schematics for the Galloping Goose?" she asked. "All this locked up so tight . . . he had to be trying to find that treasure all on his own."

"No doubt about it," Marybeth said. "I've been puzzling on it and can't make much progress, but I thought opening that trunk might help shed some light on things. Only I don't have the key, so I was searching the bookshelves . . ."

"And climbing them, I suppose?"

Marybeth gave a sheepish smile. "To no avail. Still no key. Did you come to help me pick the lock?"

"I came to pick a bone with you," Rusty said. Then, more subdued, "And yes, to pick a lock, too. But this—this means—"

She paused. This could mean everything. They had the riddle. They had the key.

Wait a minute.

"Where's the belt?"

Marybeth went white.

"Tell me you have the belt, Spatts."

"I have the belt!" she answered a little too fast. "I do, it's just—a bit of a distance from here. I already have someone working on it—"

"A bit of a distance?"

"A few miles away . . ."

"A few miles?"

"In Hollywood."

Rusty blinked.

"California?" Marybeth clarified, looking sheepish.

"I know where Hollywood is. What's it doing there?"

"It's safe," Marybeth hurried to say, avoiding Rusty's question. "I know exactly where it is. And I guarded it with my life, all these years, just like I promised."

Rusty nodded, slow. *Give her a chance. Be fair.* That blasted voice of reason inside, and it sounded an awful lot like Marybeth Spatts.

"Alright," Rusty said, with measured calm. "Maybe it's like you said. Maybe there'll be something we can use in the trunk."

Rusty pulled out some tools from her pocket, and Marybeth knelt beside her, silent.

She clicked along, bending a nail under the force of the trunk, inserting it, trying it this way and that.

"What do you think the rest of the riddle means?" Marybeth asked. "'Flightless in flight, she keeps the solution . . .'"

Rusty thought, the mechanical workings of the lock calming her. She blew out her cheeks and shook her head. "Martin Shaw was a Renaissance man. Nearly everything on this mountain has his fingerprints on it. He worked in the smithy, the roundhouse, worked on the tracks, sometimes the mines, worked masonry around town, built pieces of this mountain into everything. But mostly, he was just up in the heights, prospecting until he had to come back down long enough to stock up on what few supplies he needed. He lived mostly off the land. He came west on an orphan train, hopped off in the Rockies, and had been chasing gold since he was a kid."

"He sounds like a tall tale," Marybeth said.

"That he was. That's what happens when the mountains raise you. To hear my dad tell it, everything held a touch of the fantastic to him. A musical note wasn't just a musical note, it was a miracle of sound waves and resonance, and he'd been seen to shed a tear or two in the streets outside the opera house, listening to the orchestra while watching the stars. But just as quick, he'd stand up for justice if it cost him his life. He was courage and kindness, strength and selflessness."

"Hmmm."

Rusty stilled her hands. "'Hmmm' what?"

"He sounds an awful lot like someone I know," Marybeth said, looking at Rusty with eyebrows raised.

Rusty's cheeks colored. She wasn't any of those things. If she was, she'd have been able to save the people she loved, who were now all gone. Flustered, she doubled down on her lock-picking until a hefty *click* sounded and the aged lock dropped its weight into Rusty's palm.

She smiled, threaded it out of its latch, and leaned in with Marybeth when she opened the lid.

"Well, that's no treasure," Rusty said, disappointment flooding her voice.

"No," said Marybeth, picking up a round tin, one of at least ten. "It's a film reel."

"It's a lot of film reels," Rusty said, and began to read the labels. "*Ascent to Peril Peak. The Italian Escape. The Seventh Hour. The Country Bachelor. Embargo . . .*" And what looked to be a projector, a hefty metal apparatus standing like a bookend, holding up the reels in a neat row.

This didn't make any sense. The old opera house screened old silent films every now and again, with Willa Jones on piano to accompany, but Randolph Gilman had never once attended. "Maybe he was planning a donation to the town for their film screenings?" Rusty shook her head. "That doesn't fit Gilman at all, though. When he made donations, they were hefty, and visible, like a town hall or a new bell for the firehouse, always engraved with plaques about Gilmans. And his giving stopped years before he died."

Rusty looked at Marybeth, who was uncharacteristically silent . . . and white as a ghost.

"These weren't for donating," she said with quiet conviction. "He was looking for the belt."

Rusty scrunched up her nose. "In film reels? Who would coil it up in one of those? I thought you said it was safe—"

"It is. But . . . the man knew exactly what he was doing. And exactly who had the belt, apparently. These . . . are my movies."

"You collect movies?"

"No, I—well, in a sense, I suppose. I mean, that is—"

"Spit it out, Spatts," Rusty said gently. Her tongue-tied struggle was kind of endearing.

"I'm in those movies. And I used to wear that belt in every movie I was in. I know it's silly, I just—I never wanted to forget."

Now it was Rusty's turn to be tongue-tied.

"You're . . . a movie star."

"It doesn't matter." Marybeth blushed.

"And you wore the belt . . . for the whole world to see?"

"For you. And to keep my promise. I was so lost, Rusty, I just—I needed to know I was still doing something for our promise, no matter how small."

Silence crept around them.

"Oh."

"Someone once broke into my dressing room. I was sure they had to be looking for this . . . sure it was Gilman. I don't know how he found me—I had a different name there."

Rusty thought back to their collision at the mercantile. "Mercy."

Marybeth nodded. "Mercy Windsor."

"After Mercy Peak?"

She nodded again. Then, seeming eager to change the subject, asked, "How could the belt be the key to that riddle? It sounds like it's to be wrapped around something. Coiled. What would it be? We can figure out the rest of the riddle while we wait on the belt."

"Flightless in flight, she seeks revolution . . ." Rusty said. She stood, moving back over to the drafting table. Marybeth followed, and they both stared at the schematics.

There, sketched in black-ink precision, was the jaunty vehicle that had carried their letters over the miles for so many years.

"The Galloping Goose?" Marybeth said.

"Flightless in flight," Rusty said.

Mercy laughed. "Of course! Can we go to it? Is it on the rounds today?"

Rusty's smile vanished.

"Not exactly," she said. "This is Motor Number Eight."

"I remember," Mercy said. "It's the one I came on, the first time. I traced that number around and around with my eyes, all the way across the highest trestles, so I wouldn't have to look out the window. I remember thinking—" she laughed lightly—"that eight seemed such a friendly number. No sharp edges."

"It was a friendly engine," Rusty said. "My favorite, actually."

"Your favorite? Why?"

"Well, they're all different. One through seven are all different from one another, and eight was only ever meant to be a rescue train, to be sent out if one of the others was in trouble. Thing is, there's trouble on the tracks more than you think out here, and it ended up being out so much they just put it into regular circulation. I always liked that. That something that set out for one life ended up in one entirely different and making all the difference for people like us."

"Let's go to it," Marybeth said. "If it's not out, I'll drive us."

"I don't know if I'd survive another encounter with you behind the wheel of that truck."

"Very funny," Marybeth said, face flushing. "Ralph Mosely fixed the brakes, and I'll have you know I once won an award for my driving in a chase scene."

"In a stationary car on a stage somewhere, I imagine."

"Doesn't matter. About that Goose . . . do you know where it is?"

"That's the thing," Rusty said. "Nobody knows. It disappeared. The same night you came."

CHAPTER

13

Mercy

May 1948

Three o'clock rolled around, and so did the regulars who convened every afternoon at the Mercy Peak Mercantile. They'd talk about weather, wars, and wives, and almost all of those roads led inevitably to the topic of fishing. Mercy hadn't figured out how the fish phenomenon quite worked logistically, but in the last few weeks had learned all the best places around for cutthroat, pike, and rainbow trout, and had been duly sworn to secrecy.

Kurt and Angus pulled up chairs to their respective sides of the line around the woodstove in the center of the building. An iron gate surrounded it in hexagon, keeping people from tumbling into it, and—perhaps its real purpose—its ledge providing a rail that served just fine for holding mugs of piping hot black coffee.

"Here you go." Mercy slid the camp kettle onto the woodstove. They'd been singing her coffee's praises since last Thursday, when she'd spent thirty precious cents on an envelope of ground cloves and put a pinch in the coffee while it brewed. Kurt had sniffed the air and said, *"What in tarnation is that smell?"* And then he'd tasted it and in whispered wonder said, *"What in tarnation is that smell?"* as he guzzled it down and slammed his camp mug down with a *clink*.

"Thank you kindly, Miss Marybeth," Angus said, pulling up two more chairs as Kurt pulled in an extra, too. Only five men ever sat here, but they always had an extra, and it always sat empty. She'd thought about asking about it, but whatever the story was, she felt instinctively that it wasn't an outsider's to pry about.

Someday, maybe they'd volunteer the tale.

The door over the bell jingled and in came Hudson Jenks, a miner

150

over at the Camp Bird mine, and Ralph Mosely. Casey Campbell, like the soup, dashed in after them.

"All I'm saying," said Ralph, "is that it could've driven off a cliff. It's the simplest explanation."

"Yeah, but it's *boring*," said Hudson, picking up the conversation as if he'd been there the whole time.

Miss Ellen rounded the bread table, basket on her arm, and shook her head. "Here we go again. Brace yourself, dear," she said sagely to Mercy as she continued shopping.

"How can a fourteen-thousand-pound vehicle of steel, forged in the fires of our own mountain's ingenuity, plummeting to its death and disappearance, be boring?"

"Well, it would be *bore*-ing a hole in the earth," Kurt said dryly.

"Wouldn't it be 'disappearance and death'?" Hudson's dark brows scrunched.

"That's what I said," said Ralph.

"You said 'death and disappearance,'" Kurt said, standing to greet his visitors. "How could the thing fall, and then crash, and then disappear? Did it get up and fix itself and drive away? And besides, who was driving it? Phinneas sure wasn't. He was at Sam Buckley's service."

She followed the back-and-forth of the men's conversation, her gaze like a ping-pong ball bouncing from one to the next. They had to be talking about the Goose. She asked as much, trying to sound casual as she slowed her work of lining cans of green beans on the shelf.

All five looked at her, surprised. "I don't mean to intrude," she said, "I just heard something about it disappearing the other day. Do you know what happened?" She didn't mention that she and Rusty had spent the past two weeks scouring every map they could find and trekking into woods and gullies alike, conducting their own continuing search.

"It was robbed, back in '37."

"I . . . heard something about that," Mercy said, unsure whether to reveal she'd apparently been its last passenger ever.

"Yes, ma'am," Angus said. "An October no one will soon forget."

"Train heist," Hudson said, thumbs under his suspenders and looking a bit proud that Mercy Peak had been the site of something so sensational.

"The Great Train Robbery, you might call it," said Angus.

"You fools got it all wrong. You make it sound like someone robbed the train!" Kurt rolled his eyes.

"Well, in a sense, they did," said Ralph, taking his seat, and his coffee, too. "Up and stole the whole thing!"

"You're all giving her the wrong idea."

"Who did it?" Mercy asked. Maybe they knew something Rusty didn't.

"Not a clue," Kurt said. "That's the mystery of it all. We're just spouting theories." Raising a finger, he leaned forward and said, "The game's afoot. We consider ourselves sleuths, along with the rest of the M.P.C."

"M.P.C.?"

"Mercy Peak Citizenry. Folks. All of us. You're a part of the M.P.C. too, now," Angus said, and Kurt gave him a look like he wasn't so sure.

"Anyway, no one knows, that's the mystery," Hudson said. "And the M.P.C. loves a good mystery. They all pretend they want to know, but what they really want is to keep on not knowing and make a big to-do about it."

Mercy nodded. "Did they destroy the cargo? Or perhaps . . . hide it somewhere?" Rusty had said there was a mailbag on board . . . and confided her secret hope that there might be one last word from Sam. If she could find that mailbag.

Kurt shook his head. "That's the problem. They didn't steal the cargo—they took the whole ding-dang train!"

"Language, Kurt," Miss Ellen said from the crate of apples.

"What?" he said. "It's the noise the train made. *Ding-dang*, you know, the bell."

Miss Ellen rolled her eyes and tossed an apple a few times in her palm, as if considering pelting him with it.

"That's *ding-dong*, you ding-dong." Ralph elbowed Kurt in the stomach.

"You mean the new postmaster over in Silverton? That's Dean *Long*," said Hudson, and Mercy couldn't tell if the younger man was serious, or just as mischievous as his three older counterparts. He was tuning up his fiddle, looking amused.

"Now, stop that, boys." Ellen stepped forward. "Goodness knows that postmaster deserves our respect, coming to territory like this, with people like you to contend with. Next time I see Mr. Ding—"

Kurt snorted. Angus dipped his chin, trying to hide a smile. Ralph pointed at Miss Ellen, eyebrows to the sky, and Hudson studied the ceiling, lips pursed, trying to remain neutral.

"You said it!" Ralph said.

"*Dean Long*," Miss Ellen enunciated. "Next time I see him, I'm bringing *him* a piping hot rhubarb pie just for this conversation."

"How do we get on that list?" Kurt was dead serious.

Mercy finished straightening the green beans and went on to the corn. Appropriate, for this conversation. She stifled a smile at that thought and cleared her throat. How horrified Miss Ellen would be if she could see the mirth Mercy felt bubbling up at the men's banter.

"They—pardon me, Miss Ellen." Mercy redirected her gaze to Kurt. "They took the train?" She knew it from Rusty but wanted to glean any new information she could.

Kurt nodded.

"They absconded with the Goose," Angus confirmed solemnly.

"And no one really knows who did it?"

"Nobody knows, dear," Miss Ellen said. Her basket was full, but she kept browsing the canned goods, keeping a nonchalant ear on the conversation. "Train robbers around here historically have just been men after a fortune. But the Geese aren't known for hauling gold or ore. Just usually mail and the occasional visitor. Uranium during the war, but it was very hush-hush."

"But how does a whole engine disappear?"

"That's the question of the century," Angus said. "Or at least the last ten years. There's a lot of theories."

"The fire theory," Kurt said, ticking off a finger.

"We call that one 'Our Goose Was Cooked,'" Ralph said with a wink.

Casey piped up. "Don't forget your canyon theory. Someone pushing it over the edge of a cliff somewhere."

"That's the 'Goose Flew the Coop' theory," chimed in Ralph. He whistled low. "Wouldn't that have been a sight. First and last flight."

"The buried in the forest theory." Kurt tipped his head in thought.

"We call that, 'Goose Bumps,'" Ralph said seriously.

"The mine shaft theory."

"The—"

"Give her a break, fellas," said Angus. "Trust us, Miss Spatts. There are as many theories as there are pine needles on these mountains. Have people searched? Sure. Problem is, every one of those theories has a thousand and more possible locations to match. Need a canyon? Take your pick! A bump in the woods? We've got a bunch of woods and a bunch of bumps, too. Fact is, Motor Eight could be anywhere."

"Or nowhere, if our goose was cooked." Ralph folded his arms over his chest. "Only real clue we have is that—" He gestured to three chain links, strung together in a single line and hanging from a nail by the door. "The smoking gun."

"H-how could a chain be a smoking gun?"

"Well, a few years back, Motor Number Three tried to run away, too. Some think the brakes just gave out. Took off faster than a speeding bullet down the incline. They kept throwing big chains like that on the track, trying to get her to jump the track and come to a stop. Only problem was, the track was so straight, she'd jump and just land right back down on them, over and over, till they finally got that runaway Goose to derail and stop. After Motor Eight disappeared, Hud found that length on the side of the track between here and the top of the canyon."

"You think someone derailed her?"

"Can't be sure. People find all sorts of old chains and machinery out here all the time, from the mines, or building the Million Dollar Highway. The mountains hold a lot of innovation. But it seemed too strange to be a coincidence, finding that severed as it was. No other lengths around, like someone took pains to clean up after themselves, but missed that bit right there. Still, never a trace of her has been seen since that night."

"And what if someone finds . . . her?" Mercy asked, curiosity piqued, and trying to match their way of referring to the Goose as a "her."

"We got an award waiting for them," said Hudson, plucking a fiddle string as he twisted its tuner. The notes got higher and higher, like the instrument was bracing for what was to come. "A golden goose, as it were. Not real gold; Will Travers worked up a brass trophy, but it shines as good as gold. We call it the Nobel Geese Prize."

Angus beamed at this, and Mercy had a good guess who'd been responsible for the name.

"They give the trophy to someone new each year, someone who's done a heap to help people around here. But if anyone ever finds that engine . . . you can bet the trophy'll go to them. Come on down this evening to the requiem tonight, and you'll learn all you want to know."

"And a whole lot more," Kurt said dryly.

"The requiem?" She was almost afraid to ask.

"Sure. It's Motor Eight's birthday, the day she emerged from the doors of the shop and took to the rails. The requiem's a ceremony where we pay our respects and remember. We might not have a lot out here, but we know how to honor what treasure we do have. And sometimes . . . that's a train." Angus picked up the kettle and poured coffee for the others.

"Diesel engine, you mean," said Kurt.

Angus raised his cup to his brother in agreement. More instruments emerged, ending the conversation in a plucky chorus of tunings and trills.

Mercy saw to Miss Ellen at the cash register, and as the woman left and bustled up the street, Mercy let her gaze wander the horizon. It wasn't exactly the right word—*horizon*—the walls around the box canyon that wrapped up the village like a Christmas gift and drew the gaze on up into the blue sky. But she knew that tucked into and beyond these walls were hidden forests, trails, hills, and terrain that she'd come to know intimately in the form of Mr. Gilman's map.

Mr. Gilman, who had a fascination with the Goose himself. Had he been on his own wild goose chase? Perhaps tonight she'd find out more.

CHAPTER
14

Sam says he wants to buy me a diamond ring someday. But for
now he says he's got another plan. It's not a lot, but it's something,
he says. To which I say, something is something!

—Rusty Bright, 16

Mercy

"Requiem." Rusty said the word like she'd just eaten a live beetle. "I
don't think I can go to that." She closed the door of her cabin swiftly.

Mercy felt the sting in her cheeks from the air current created by the
door. Hollywood should hire Rusty; they'd never have need of another
brush of rouge again.

Mercy knocked again. There was something freeing about the stub-
bornness of Rusty's door. It wasn't going anywhere, and neither was
Rusty, and neither was Mercy. It gave Mercy a boldness she hadn't
known before, and an odd sense of comfort. Mercy hadn't found a
home in Rusty like she'd always hoped, but her knuckles had found one
in the ancient wood of her door, and that was something.

"Something is something," Mercy muttered and knocked again,
harder. "Why aren't you going?"

"I can't hear you!" Rusty said in a singsong voice.

"I didn't know you were a soprano," Mercy said. "And a lovely one
at that. You know, Hudson Jenks said they're looking for a soprano for
the Independence Day choir. I could mention your qualifications to
him, if you like."

"You wouldn't." Rusty's voice was muffled through the door, closer
this time.

"You'd have Hudson and probably all the choir filing up this mountain, knocking on your door. They sure do want that soprano. . . ."

Mercy waited. If her suspicion was correct, then in five . . . four . . . three . . . two . . .

The door flew open. "Don't you dare. I want nothing to do with the I.D.C. of the M.P.C."

"What's to stop me? He'll be at the requiem tonight, and it really would be no trouble at all to—"

"You wouldn't."

"No need to thank me; it'll be a pleasure, really. I'll just head on down. You'll know where to find me if you need to stop me for any reason."

"Why, you—that's blackmail!"

Mercy shrugged. "We've done every other type of mail there is. I'm on a mission to try new things." She turned to go, letting her confident footfalls in the soft dirt send up puffs of dust that danced with the sun.

A moment, and then a second set of footfalls came, pounding down the path and cutting Mercy off. Rusty planted her hands on her hips and squared up. She looked frustrated, but there was a hint of something else there, too. Respect? Mercy crossed her arms and set her shoulders, waiting.

"Don't you remember when whoever it was took that thing?"

"The choir?"

"The Galloping Goose."

Mercy's gaze dropped. "The night of Sam's burial."

"So you know why I won't go. I will never dignify that person—the lowly, good-for-nothing—" The rage cracked, and through it came her brokenhearted whisper. Enough to break Mercy's heart open, too. And then Rusty picked up the cloak of her anger once more, clearing her throat. "Who would use a funeral as a decoy? Of all the low-down—" Rusty bit her tongue, face so red she looked liable to combust.

Mercy's hand landed on Rusty's shoulder, who looked at it like it was a foreign object, fallen from the wilds of the planets above. And Mercy wondered—how long had it been since her friend had known the warmth of a human touch?

She let her hand stay there, despite the urge to pull away beneath Rusty's baffled scrutiny.

"It's alright," Mercy said, eyes wide to show sincerity. "You don't have to go."

Rusty's shoulders dropped in relief, and she appeared all spent of words.

"And I won't sic the choir on you."

Rusty stared at the ground, shuffling a laced-up dusty boot. "They're not a bad bunch, you know. They like their Jell-O salads a little too much, but they're good people. And fine singers."

"Why, Rusty Bright. Was that a compliment you just paid?" Mercy feigned shock, spinning in a circle, studying the ground this way and that.

"What's that you're doing?" Rusty twirled a finger at the ground. "Stop it."

"I'm just—the ground. It's going to open and swallow us, I'm certain." Mercy let her best transatlantic accent come out in full force. "Do be careful, now, it could happen right beneath you!"

"Oh no you don't. Stop with all that fake talk."

"It's just that you've unbalanced the cosmos with your sudden magnanimity, and if the ground doesn't gobble us whole, why I—"

Rusty whacked Mercy on the arm, and Mercy laughed. "That *was* a compliment."

"It was no such thing," Rusty said with all the conviction of a Jell-O salad.

"You forget," Mercy said, "I know your words perhaps more than anyone on God's green earth." She winked. And soared when she saw the flicker of recognition in Rusty's eyes at a phrase from the very first line from the very first letter Rusty had ever sent.

"You don't have to come, and I won't sic the choir on you, but hear me out. Did you see the chains in the turret room?"

"Yes, and they've been giving me nightmares ever since. Chains in a turret room? What was Gilman doing, reading *Frankenstein*?"

"Are there chains in a turret room in *Frankenstein*?"

"Who knows?"

"Boris would know; I could've asked him when we danced—"

"Who's Boris?"

"Oh, just—well, he played Frankenstein's monster."

"You danced with Frankenstein's monster?"

Mercy tipped her head side to side, weighing an answer.

"Your life is strange, Marybeth."

Behind Rusty, Confetti the Cat leapt up to the cabin window and assumed a watchful stare, placing one paw upon the windowpane.

"I'm not the only one," Mercy said, stifling a smile and gesturing so Rusty would see. "Seems you've got yourself a supervisor there."

Rusty rolled her eyes. "All I'm saying is, the chains in the turret were creepy. Like a torture chamber or something."

"The men were saying how they believe chains were thrown across the track to derail the Galloping Goose. Hudson found a small length of severed chain after the disappearance."

"The nerve of Randolph Gilman. I'd be willing to wager he stole it just to ensure my dad—or me, I suppose—never had a chance at solving his riddle. He made the Goose disappear."

"Sort of like you, sending me the belt?"

"Yes, only he disappeared a massive piece of machinery. I wondered . . . he wasn't at Sam's funeral. He was never at anyone's funeral, but still. He had the opportunity to take the Goose. Just . . .to where? I've been all over Wildwood and never seen a trace."

"We'll find it. We have to. I'll start by going to the requiem. If you're certain you don't want to come—"

Rusty took a small step back. "All those people . . ."

"They sure love you, Rusty."

Rusty nodded. "I just don't know how—I mean, it's been so long . . . and they'll want to talk about Sam, and I just—"

"I understand."

Rusty hesitated, her bold exterior wavering. "I know you do," she said, sincere. Almost an olive branch offering, and Mercy smiled gently.

"I wouldn't mind scouring Wildwood a bit, though, if it's all the same to you," she said, some of her former pluck returning.

"Scour away."

Later that evening, Mercy stood at the top of First Street and watched as people trickled into the clearing below Balanced Rock Overlook. A breeze rustled through the aspen leaves above her in a silver shiver. A path meandered down the slope, with kerosene lanterns swaying from tree branches and hands alike, easing away the edge of dark. Down below, Hudson Jenks plied his fiddle till it released bits of "Oh, Shenandoah" onto the lifting breeze.

Mercy was getting bolder with her wardrobe alterations. Looking down at her blue gingham skirt, she laughed. Mabel, the wardrobe mistress, had worked up the dress with its ample fairy tale–like layers as a prototype for a German folktale about a village that only appeared every century, and only for a day. Wilson P. Wilson had envisioned her as the leading lady who would fall in love with a visitor who'd stumbled upon the enchanted village.

"You've outdone yourself, Mabel." Mercy had been delighted at the creative combination of folk fabrics and Victorian fashion. Mabel had laughed. *"They'll need all the help they can get with a story name like* Germelshausen. *What a name for a village!"*

Mercy had been enchanted by the premise, but the film hadn't come to be; there were concerns in the war years over its reception in England and America, with the folktale's German roots. *"Unless they rewrite the thing and place it somewhere else, that story will never see the light of day,"* Mabel had said, bundling the prototype into Mercy's arms. *"Who knows, maybe I'll be working up plaid dresses or lace ruffles instead of gingham someday, if they move the story to the Highlands. You take it. You never know when you'll have need of a picnic dress straight out of the Brothers Grimm."*

With a pair of scissors, Mercy had stripped away the layers of petticoats and shortened the hem to just below her knees. Although the end result had her looking a little more like a tablecloth than a fairy-tale character, she was certain it was less conspicuous than blue chiffon and more elevated than her "lumberjill" outfit of worn plaid and too-short slacks that she'd scraped together from Miss Ellen's ragbag and the attic offerings of Wildwood.

"If you could see me now, Mabel," Mercy said.

Coral streaked the sky, and she moved to read the plaque near the place where the oblong, oversized grey boulder balanced upon a larger one beneath it. From some angles, it looked ready to tumble down and crush anyone in its path, but to hear it told, it had stood stalwart for centuries.

From this valley
upon the 7th day of October, Anno Domini 1937,
the Rio Grande Southern Railway Galloping Goose Motor No. 8
did take her last ride,
and sigh her last sigh.
Into these mountains has she gone,
to whereabouts unknown
and thence unto glory.

"To whereabouts unknown . . . and thence unto glory" came Angus's baritone voice beside her. Mercy started.

"Awful lot of highfalutin words to say *lost*, if you ask me," said Kurt, drawing up beside them.

"It's a plaque!" Angus retorted. Then, more gently to Mercy, "We like our plaques around here."

"*He* likes our plaques. He writes most of 'em."

"Well." Angus drew the word out as if to say, *It's nothing, really.* "Just a hobby."

"Who has 'plaques' as a hobby?" Kurt shook his head. "We've got 'em now for near every landmark. Whistler's Bridge. Balanced Rock. Ruby Rock. Larkspur Ridge. He's got one for the Three Trees, but he can't get up that steep of a mountain to mount it anywhere—not that anyone would see it way up there."

"The Three Trees?"

Angus jumped in. "It's three trees so evenly spaced, they don't look real. Halfway up the foothill of Mercy Peak, right at the steep part. Some people name star formations—we name our tree formations. We've got others, too. There's the deer, the bow, the—"

"She gets the point," Kurt said. "And he'd write plaques for 'em all if given the chance. Next thing you know he'll be writing poetry about rocks." He shook his head.

"I think it's wonderful," Mercy said, and Angus beamed. "And very helpful for a newcomer like me. If Mercy Peak had more visitors, they'd all be thanking you, too. It's such a beautiful place." She watched the sunset streak in pinks and blues. "It's a wonder you don't have more people visit."

"We sure could use 'em," Kurt said. "We've tried a few things to attract more visitors. Commerce is slow, with the mines drying up over time. But it's hard to get the word out and give people something they think is worth the trek to get way up here. Their loss."

Mercy looked down at her gingham dress, recalling the fairy tale. "And yet a far-removed place, up in the heights and untouched by time, has an irresistible charm to it in times like these," she said. "If people knew . . ." The bud of an idea tugged at her.

"Well, missy," Angus said, "you ready for your first Mercy Peak festival?"

"*Requiem*," said Mayor Bernard, coming up behind them and carrying a very official-looking leather folio. "Though we do like our festivals."

"I'm ready," Mercy said.

Angus and Kurt offered her their arms. She looked to the left, and to the right, and couldn't bring herself to choose one. She looped her arms through each of theirs, accepting Angus's help with the plate she carried, dangling a canvas bag from the crook of her arm, and they descended the hill.

The last time she'd been arm in arm with two men at once, it had been Cary Grant and Jimmy Stewart on the set of *The Philadelphia Story* as a stand-in for Katharine Hepburn one day when Katharine was delayed in wardrobe. She'd been contractually on loan to MGM for a month from Pinnacle—her first time—and the strangeness of being checked out like a library book had made her feel even more out of place in that world than ever. But both the men had been gracious in the face of her newcomer stumblings, God bless them. They'd bantered in such good humor as she'd faltered in matching their long strides and all the tension had fallen away.

This time she had to shorten her strides, though she was coming to learn she was in the company of princes among men.

Soon the path morphed from the dull grey-brown of dirt to the warm distinct red of Colorado earth that ribboned through the terrain. A blink and her vision turned to memory, her clunky boots flashing into a vision of navy silk stilettos, so pointed at the toes that Mercy had joked to Mabel that they should be considered weapons, and young Tabitha had promptly picked the pair up and started fencing the heels against each other.

The dusky red of the path morphed into the mirage of a deep red carpet. Discs of camera flashes everywhere flashing, flashing, and Wilson P. Wilson's voice in her ear, hissing to *"give 'em a smile to write about, sweetheart."* All eyes on her. Her breath coming short, wishing she could see even one of the people behind all those flashes. Meet someone's eyes, and see a person—not a lens, a screen, a barrier between her and the rest of the world. She'd grown to love being a part of bringing people respite and re-enchantment through a story on-screen—but this part made her feel cold and isolated. *I made you,* Wilson had said in his letter. And although she dismissed the letter on the surface easily enough, his words were banded deep inside. Wasn't there some truth to it? He'd built her into a shell of a person. Herself, only pretend, and she could never live up to that mirage. Marybeth Spatts had nothing on Mercy Windsor.

"You alright?"

It was Kurt, looking uncharacteristically concerned. She'd stopped right in the middle of the path, shoulders rising and falling in quick, shallow breaths.

Blinking, she found his face. Eyes green-grey, searching with kindness. Angus, on her other side, waited in concerned silence, not a rush in the world.

A swift look around revealed no camera flashes. The only lights, those of the swinging lanterns and, far above, the twinkle of the first rising stars.

Slowly, she nodded. "I think I am, yes." The corners of her mouth played upward, reaching for this newfound truth.

"Okay to keep on?" he said.

"Yes," she said, something bubbling up inside her. What was happening? This place . . . it had a hold of her. It seemed to grip her past, hold it against her present, and say, *now look.* But what was she supposed to see? She wasn't sure. It felt somehow hard . . . but good. Like cold, fresh air, blowing something new her way.

The evening was a simple affair, and yet all of its simple parts cogged together into something that stirred Mercy's heart with a whimsical ache. Children played chase at the outskirts of the clearing. Stringed music came by turns from Hudson on the violin, Kurt on the banjo, Angus on the mandolin. And Casey Campbell showed up with a guitar, to boot. His fingers didn't fly with the skill of the others, but he jumped in with a hearty strum of any chords he knew, and they were all the merrier for it.

Casey Campbell. She recalled his talk of surveying the mountains for future ski slopes. Would he be able to help decipher the graphs and charts in the turret room?

People filed in, all of them with some dish to share, filling the communal table with a mosaic of stoneware and crisp, sun-dried dishcloths covering piping hot offerings. Mercy nestled her plate into the mix and grimaced. It was gilded china, the only thing in the Gilmans' butler's pantry, and out of place among the cast iron and Pyrex casseroles.

"Whatcha got there?" A kid sidled up to her, with two slightly older replicas of himself hot on his heels. He licked his lips eagerly.

"Oh! Um, well, it's . . ." She withdrew her own clean dish towel, revealing the plate with toasted bread slices topped with a concoction of savory whipped cream, chopped fresh-caught, lemon-broiled trout, and garlic-braised dandelion greens. It'd been a long time since she'd plied the fishing pole or foraged for greens, not since her Swickley's Crossing days, but it had come back to her quickly. She had only one chance at a first impression, after all, and with not much to spare in the way of coin, the stream behind Wildwood, a dandelion patch, and some dill from the winter-mangled vestige of a potager garden she'd uncovered near the courtyard had obliged nicely.

"Trout blossoms," she said, and immediately heard how truly terrible that sounded. "Or . . . fish toast." That was worse. She'd been trying to copy salmon mousse hors d'oeuvres served at one of the Sunset Boulevard soirees she'd attended. But *trout mousse* didn't have the same ring to it. The boy's head tipped farther to the side with each of her monikers. "Um . . . stream flora?"

He nodded. "Neat!" He plunged his hand toward the plate, and Mercy's heart skittered with joy. And then his hand soared cleanly over the fishy offering and into a basket of cornmeal pancakes, of which he grabbed a fistful.

His brothers followed suit, one making for the deviled eggs, and the other, unable to choose, stuffing a pancake into his mouth and taking deviled eggs into both hands, leaving Mercy with a rakish wink. The full plate of trout blossoms looked up at her, bewildered.

She abandoned them as quickly as she could, hoping they'd just vanish amid the increasing collection of pies, bowls of fresh applesauce, two pots of chili, baskets of popovers, and two more versions of cornmeal pancakes.

Back in the clearing, Ralph Mosely doffed his newsboy cap to Nancy, and the couple took a waltz among the greening grasses. Millie Pike hung her apron on a tree branch, leaving a pot of beans over a campfire in the care of Miss Ellen, and tapped on her husband's shoulder. Angus's red cheeks appled in a smile at whatever she whispered to him, and he laid down his mandolin, letting his bandmates play on as he took his bride for a spin.

It was all so simple, so very ordinary, and yet that was what struck Mercy most. That their ordinariness belonged to one another, here. That the belonging *was* so very ordinary, filling their days to the brim, until it seemed to climb up like a tide, climb the slopes of these mountains, and spill over into the sunset. Which, at present, ridged the horizon with searing brightness. It was a gold unlike Mercy had ever seen, as if its climb over the mountains refined it into its purest, most urgently benevolent form.

AMANDA DYKES

Mayor Bernard gave a small speech, and Mercy listened at the edge of the crowd to the peculiar history. He said something very close to the plaque at Balanced Rock, and then handed the "stage"—a bare bit of earth beside a creek running through the meadow—to Phinneas Trent.

A suspendered man stepped up to the stage, wearing overalls and a freshly pressed grey flannel shirt, his beard grey and thinning white hair combed.

And Mercy knew him.

He'd been the first one to greet her, here in these mountains. Flopping that hand in a wave, then back down on his steering wheel. The driver of the Galloping Goose. One of the few people who'd seen her a lifetime ago. His hair had been wild, raked by the wind through his open windows, and it had suited him. His boots had been dusted with adventure, shirt collar unbuttoned to welcome the wilderness, too. He seemed a man born to tumble over these ridges day in and day out, one who'd found and settled into his calling.

He'd taken care this night to comb every hair, button his collar high, and shine his shoes. Out of respect for his beloved Motor No. 8.

His hands were stuffed in his pockets, shoulders up high. His gaze dropped as he took a deep breath, raising his head and giving a nervous laugh before he said a word. Pulling out a hand, he flopped it in the air in a wave, then stuffed it right back and gave a sheepish shrug. "Guess most of you know I'm better talkin' in small places. Not much for public speaking."

"We all know you got plenty of words, Phin! Lay 'em on us," someone hollered.

Laughter rippled over the gathering, and Phinneas Trent seemed to ease into it.

"Well, you asked for it," he said. He talked about the origin of Motor No. 8, and in his matter-of-fact way, he made the discs and sheets of metal seem like something fantastical. "Fact is, that was a magic Goose in some ways. The stuff of storybooks, you might say. Brought me and my Viola together, long after the time most folks give up on finding true love."

Here, he tipped his hat to a woman in the audience who stood in a brass-buttoned skirt suit of navy, looking official, every bit the no-nonsense stickler and not at all who one might conjure as the soul mate of this sentimental engineer. But at his words, her solemn expression flickered into a girlish smile that melted Mercy's heart on the spot. She didn't know how an engine could have played a part in such an unlikely love story, but clearly it made Phinneas love Motor 8 all the more.

Phinneas Trent blushed. "Aw, well, you all remember. Anyway, Goose Number Eight brought you your goods, your news, your people. All those turns of the wheel . . . they meant something. And I know when they stopped, that meant something, too. We didn't just lose the old girl," he said, voice thick. "We lost what she carried."

Phin surveyed the crowd, then, as if seeking out particular faces. He paused on the face of Hudson Jenks. Then up at the eastern slope, where Rusty's cabin sat. A few sniffles sounded, a handkerchief or two dabbed at eyes, and Mercy read it like a script. There was more they understood here than she did.

Phin continued, "Call me crazy—"

"We do," someone shouted, and the sniffles turned to warm laughter.

"But I know she's out there. I might've hung up my driving cap when she disappeared, but I haven't stopped searching. And I hold on tight to hope that you who were waiting . . . you'll get what you were waiting for in that lost mailbag. Don't give up."

Silence billowed with currents strong.

His eyes landed on Mercy and narrowed. Out of all the people he'd ferried into these mountains and out again over the years . . . surely he wouldn't remember the bedraggled, life-weary girl whose only possessions were a bag just as worn and a last shred of hope.

He did.

After conceding the stage to a lone bugler, he approached her. "Always thought you'd find your way back here."

She gave a weak smile, and he nodded encouragingly.

The solemn, brassy notes of "Taps" began. Hands went to hearts, and Mercy followed suit, her own palm feeling the *thud-thud-thud*.

But then, something curious. When the bugler reached the last three notes of the song, he played the first two in solemn succession . . . but let them fade away. No third note played, except in their imaginations, where it resonated with a poignant ache. It was so melancholy, the absence of that final note of conclusion, Mercy yearned for it.

As hands dropped to people's sides in a moment of silence, they began to cluster into small groups of quiet chatter, a few of them trickling toward the food table.

She turned to face Phinneas Trent. "What happened to the last note of the song?" She didn't mention how its absence left her with the urge to chase it into the woods, to find it and haul it back, bring a sense of resolution.

"That one note is our way of holding out hope," he said. "This requiem, we do it each year, and we finish it off with that one missing note. Our way of telling her we're holding her story for her till we find its ending. Someday, when we do . . . then we'll play the final note. Give her a proper send-off. 'Spose if she understood any language, I think it'd be the call of a horn."

The evening had grown dark, and the M.P.C. were proving they liked lingering just as much as they liked gathering.

"You know, I thought about you sometimes over the years. You worried me, showing up all white-faced and lost, like the wind brought you here. And then you just . . . vanished."

Mercy nodded. "A little like your Motor Eight."

"*Our* Motor Eight," he said. "She's all of ours."

"I can see that," Mercy said, smiling at the scene before them. "It's singular, really. All of you gathering for a machine." The words out, she realized they could easily sound incredulous. "I mean that in the best way," she said quickly. "I think it's wonderful how you make things . . . matter."

He thought on that for a bit.

Somewhere Hudson Jenks struck up with "Eightsome Reel," and a passel of hoots and hollers sounded as kids started jigging with all of the joy of the Scottish traditional and none of its traditional order.

"That one, especially, felt the loss something fierce," he said, lifting his chin at Hudson.

"How so?" Mercy asked. Questions always felt to her an intrusion, but she was learning that they didn't have to be. They could be a stick laid in an ever-growing bridge, crossing the canyon between people.

"You ever hear a fiddler like that?" he asked.

She watched his fingers fly, the way they lit the air on fire. She'd seen and heard the best of music from her perch in the rafters of the recording auditorium at Pinnacle, where she'd been privy to unparalleled compositions long before the world was ever allowed to hear them. And she'd been moved deeply by those performances.

But Phin was right. There was a raw force in the movements of Hudson Jenks that was unlike anything she'd ever seen.

"He was a shoo-in for some fancy music school back east," he said. "He picked up a bow at seven years old, and we all knew that kid had something special. This town could get to making a ruckus so loud at the town hall, and when the mayor couldn't get 'em calmed down, someone would plunk Hud Jenks up there. He'd start playing, and something about the music coming from the hands of a little tyke, well, they'd calm right down like it was some sort of siren song. We all knew a talent like that would take him far away from us.

"The Jenkses—mining family—didn't have much, but they were bound and determined to find a way to send him to that school. The three big brothers pitched in soon as they were old enough to go into the mines. Hud tried, too, but they wouldn't let 'im, said it was too dangerous. So, he took a job up top, sorting rocks in the rock pile. The sisters grew spuds and sold 'em to Angus and Kurt at the store, and Kurt always slipped 'em an extra nickel or two, sometimes more. Scrimped and worked and saved, all of them. Hudson got to feelin' guilty about it all once he got older, saw their little house and all of 'em packed in, saw that pile of savings 'going to waste,' he said. Tried to get 'em to divvy it up or use it to grow their house, but they'd have none of it. Then came the day he was old enough to apply to that school. All six of those Jenks siblings showed up with Hud to hand his application over to Angus and send it off into the world, along with all their hopes. They saw it to the depot and waved the Goose off, like they were partin' ways with some dear relative."

Mercy had so often thought of hers and Rusty's letters landing and taking flight on the wings of the Galloping Goose, but she'd given little thought to other missives that had come and gone from this valley. Words bringing the world to this little haven tucked within these box canyon walls, bringing or breaking hope.

"He . . . didn't get in?" Mercy couldn't believe that. His own three daughters joined hands with his bright-cheeked wife, Daisy, all four of them dancing in circles to his golden thread of music, matching gold-blond hair flying behind them.

Phinneas shrugged. "He got a letter one day. I took it to the Spires myself, seeing as they'd all been bustin' at the seams to hear."

"The Spires?"

"Green Meadow Spires—the Jenks place. You know it?"

"I haven't had the pleasure."

"Ah, well, you should. You will. No place like it. Anyhow, I thought for sure it was the news they'd been hoping for—had a shiny seal on it and everything—and I didn't think they'd waste something like that on a 'we didn't pick you' letter. All those Jenks sisters and brothers, they gathered around young Hud as he opened the envelope with those fiddle-playing hands. Kid went white as a ghost, eyes like saucers, gulped, and didn't speak a word. Coulda heard a pin drop. Mr. Jenks, Hud's dad, was the one to finally say something, and it was just one word. *'Well?'* I remember it because I thought a word never held so much hope and pride in one little sound. But that was Mr. Jenks. Didn't say much, but he always meant something good when he did."

Mercy leaned in. Phinneas noted this and looked rather pleased, hooking his thumbs into his suspenders and beaming at her.

"An acceptance?" Mercy coaxed him.

"An audition. Kid and his dad took themselves all the way up to Denver. Outta here on Number Eight, then all the way up on the train. He'd never so much as set foot off this mountain in all his born days, and there he went, white-knuckling that fiddle in a backpack his mama stitched by hand out of her husband's old wedding suit, best thing they had. He was a sight, the bow sticking out of that backpack like an antenna. Up he went to Denver, and to hear Mr. Jenks tell it later, he played that city spellbound. They even ate at a castle."

"A castle in Denver?" Mercy searched her mind, trying to think of what that might be.

"Palace, I think." Phinneas waved his hand. "All I know is it sounded awful high and mighty for being named after the color of dirt and being shaped like a piece of pie, to hear him tell it."

Phinneas's words stacked up into a picture that made Mercy smile. "The Brown Palace." She could just picture the two Jenks men, sporting their mountain best and standing in front of the fine hotel, one of Denver's landmarks.

"So the audition went well," Mercy said. "But he didn't get in?"

Phinneas shrugged. "Jenks clan showed up together every week on long change Sundays—that was the day the brothers and the dad had long enough out of the mines to come all the way down to town together, when the men working nights switched to days for a couple of weeks. Every long change Sunday, they came on down, Sunday best, went to church, came up to Angus after with hope painting their faces like sunshine. After a time, they dropped away bit by bit, starting with Hud. Made excuses not to stay and talk with Angus, other than a quick greeting. Went to ready the horses for the trip back out to their homestead up the canyon. Mrs. Jenks, his mother, started staying with him so he wouldn't be alone. One by one, his sisters started to drift off on Sundays to other activities.

"It was his father, hat pressed to his chest every time, who kept on coming. *'Any word yet?'* shifted to *'Don't suppose there's a letter in this week?'* and finally to just a look. That man could ask a whole lot with just his eyes, and they held that flicker of hope long. It was Hudson who finally asked him to stop. Both of 'em hung their heads in the street, just a few words exchanged. *'Think it's time, Dad'* was all Hud said. Tried to say he was sorry. Angus said he heard the boy's voice near break wide open. But that father just put his arm around young Hudson and said, *'Don't you stop playing, son. A gift's a gift, plain and simple. Not just when someone sees it. Audience or not, God gave it to you, you give it to Him. Simple as that. You keep on, and He'll take those notes wherever they were meant to go. Must be He meant them for the wild and free, not stuck in stuffy old concert houses.'*

"So, that's what he does, to this day, though his pa's not around to see it anymore. He plays for his cows—has a fine herd up at their place. Plays for weddings. Plays for the requiem. Plays if someone's sick. Figures if he can play, he's meant to share it, so he does."

Mercy watched one of the older couples dancing, the way a woman who was winded with laughter pulled her husband to the side to clap to the rhythm and twirl a raven-haired grandchild who came to take her hand.

"The letter never came," Mercy murmured.

"Never did. Not unless it was in that bag when the rail car went missing, and I guess we might never know. I had that bag locked up in the Goose during young Sam's service—intended to deliver it to Angus right away after . . . but I was too late. Even if we ever find Number Eight, it's been a decade. These mountains . . . not much could survive out in the elements all those years. 'Specially paper." He sighed. "There were others' hopes tied up in it, too, though no one really knows what might be in the bag. Joe over there, he was waitin' for word on his brother in Boston, who died of consumption. He won't say as much, but he sure was hopin' for one last word from him. Thick as thieves, they were." His eyes scanned the crowd, then he pointed when he found Miss Murdock sorting salad forks from dessert forks and laying them in neat rows. "She clams up every time that bag is mentioned. Not to mention . . ." Now his gaze rested on Mercy. "Folks say you're living up at Wildwood?"

Mercy nodded. "That's right."

"Old Gilman place, you know."

"So I've heard."

"Gilman was sure a strange bird there toward the end. Mind if we mosey?" He patted his stomach and pointed at the food table.

Mercy dashed to catch up. "You say Randolph Gilman was acting strangely?"

"Yes sirree, pacing the town at odd hours, measuring strides when he thought no one was looking. Somethin' fishy about all of it if you ask me. Speakin' of fish, what's that?"

He lifted up the near-full plate of trout blossoms.

"Oh, it's um—well, I guess you could call it trout mousse."

"Trout *mousse*?" Phinneas let out a low whistle.

"I know, it doesn't have the same ring to it as salmon mousse, but—"

"Trout's not your problem. It's the other word you got a problem with."

"Mousse?"

He nodded gravely. "Unless you mean a creature with antlers about yay high." His arm stretched far above his own head. "Around these mountains? You'd best choose another word. Hey!"

He hollered, pointing his voice at the people. "Fresh-caught trout going to waste over here. Caught by none other than our newcomer, Miss—" He squinted an eye and peaked a brow, looking at her.

"Oh—M-Marybeth. Marybeth Spatts," she said.

He put the plate down, and it wobbled to a stop. "Well, I'll be . . . not the one who wrote to our Rusty all those years?"

"Guilty," she said, clasping her hands behind her back and watching in awe as people clambered over to the trout.

"Caught by Mercy Peak's own Marybeth Spatts," he announced to the crowd, who were mostly already gone. Even so, Phin's words caught her up fast. *"Mercy Peak's own . . ."*

"Rusty always said you'd come," he said. "I miss her old man something fierce. Might be the best man this town's ever known."

"You knew him well?" Mercy smiled, setting to work folding towels and placing them in their empty dishes, lining them up. She always did better at gatherings when her hands were busy. "What was he like?"

"Knew him long before he was ever a father. We were schoolmates, way back when."

"Is that so?"

"Sure is. He was younger than me, but we got into a scrape or ten together, let me tell you." He cocked his head, studying her. "You know, I always thought there was some link between you two."

"Me and Rusty?"

"You and Silas Bright."

Mercy blinked. That was unexpected. "I'm sorry to say I never met the man."

"Yes, but—do you remember when you rode in the Goose, back when, and I think I told you I had a spare seat up there since Mr. Gilman wasn't riding that day?"

She searched her mind. It was all a blur, after the shock that had met her once she'd arrived. But she did recall recognizing Mr. Gilman's name and thinking it odd that a man of his means would choose the Galloping Goose as his means of transportation. She and Rusty had always joked about him traveling in a chariot of silver. "I remember I was surprised to learn he rode with you regularly," she said. "You called it something like his 'usual seat.'"

"That's the thing—it was more than unusual. He never rode in old Eight—or any of the Geese—all his life, till the last year or so, before she disappeared. And the day before you came, Mr. Gilman was full of questions about Silas."

"He was asking about Rusty's father?"

"Sure was. Strange, too, since the men never spoke."

Mercy nodded. "From different worlds, I suppose?"

"Different universes, more like. If Silas Bright hung the moon, Randolph Gilman sat enthroned on it, or so he thought. But it was more than that. In fact, they were friends, way back. You know about the uh . . ." He looked around over his shoulders, then leaned in, lowering his voice. "The Incident?"

Rusty had written all sorts of Mercy Peak news to her over the years—the mouse in Miss Murdock's orange cream pie; the fire at the *old* old smithy, not to be confused with the old smithy; the time Sam accidentally knocked out Jacob Skinner's tooth with a wayward baseball and felt bad enough about it he mucked stalls for a month—Jacob's job—and let Jacob keep the pay. But she knew he could only be referring to one incident.

"I think so, yes," she said.

"Well, you'll understand, then. It was just strange. He'd asked me all about others before, especially Martin Shaw . . . but never Silas. Silas Bright and Randolph Gilman hadn't spoken for years, and then one day long after Silas had passed, Randolph Gilman hops into Motor Eight, asking all about the man and if he ever rode with me, what his riding habits were, that kind of thing."

"Riding habits?"

"Wanted to know if he ever got off the engine any place strange, or did anything to the motor, or tinkered with it at all."

"And did he?"

"No, ma'am. Hardly rode at all, except just to say hello every now and then. Silas was always big on stopping to say hello to people. Even me. He'd hop in once in a while just to listen to me drone on. Good man, he was. Raised that little girl up with the strength of these mountains in her. Anyway, Gilman showed up, asking all about Silas Bright, then didn't show up the next day. That's how you got that seat. Seemed his questions still swirled all around that cab, and there you were, this wisp of a thing, sitting right in the center of those questions. Always struck me, somehow."

Hudson's fiddling drew to a close in the distance.

The mayor rang a bell, and everyone gathered for the awarding of the Nobel Geese Prize. Miss Ellen, the winner last year, was summoned forth to present it to this year's winner, Kurt Pike, who refused to come forward until he was shoved by Ralph Mosely.

On a stage of earth, beneath a canopy of stars, with a score of scattered laughter, Mercy watched a story unfold more enchanting than any the Dream Factory of Hollywood could have produced. Even the applause of the people, drifting up to meet and mingle with that of the aspen leaves, felt ethereal.

It was a living stage, this place.

And others should see it.

The thought came fully formed, unbidden, flying at her like a starling peeled away from its flock. In a flash she could see it: an audience seated in this hamlet, torches lighting the way like they had for Randolph Gilman's parties. Forest finery, like Rusty used to describe—people come from afar, weary of the bustle and press of life. Parched for respite, ready to be swept away into a story. Given the gift of hope.

Keep on playing.

Mercy shook away the words. Those words had been given to Hudson, offered by his father.

Not her.

So why did her chest ache like she'd just stumbled upon something that felt remarkably like . . . purpose?

Folio of Field Notes, Volume IV:
The Blood Moon Boys

[Property of Sudsy McGee, Hollywood Biographer]

PACT
1894

*We, the undersigned, ~~right here at the~~ in the witness of the blood
moon and all the mountains, do solemnly swear to be good ~~keep-
ers~~ stewards of any riches this mountain ~~gives us for keeps~~ does
bequeath into our keep.*

> *Spat and signed,*
> *Martin Shaw*
> *Reuben Murdock*
> *Silas Bright*
> *Randolph Gilman*

1896
Manchester Meeks Academy

Dear Father,
   *In Truman Hall today, the professor spoke of the laws of phys-
ics. Suddenly, the universe seemed to fall into place, under the
rules of a man named Newton. Martin Shaw is always on about
his riddles, but when I stack his mind up against a mind like Sir
Isaac Newton, I almost feel badly for him. He seems to be stuck
in a world of questions when a world of answers is at his fingertips. It won't serve him well in life, poor fellow.*

Using some of the concepts we've been learning, I have some plans in mind for the mine that I hope to propose to you when next I'm home. It's with economy and efficiency in mind, just as you are working for.

Your son,
Randolph

AVALANCHE ABOVE EMERALD GULCH

San Juan Special

March 8, 1904—An avalanche tore through the Mercy Peak wilderness, southeast of Sea Glass Lake, starting at about four in the afternoon on Sunday. It tore over the train tracks, taking out the depot at Ridge Pass and narrowly missing the boardinghouse at Gilcrest mine, where hundreds of miners slept. "That roar woke me from a dead sleep," said Jim Greystone. "Thought the whole mountain was splitting open."

Four young men were traversing the back country. Though caught in the slide, they narrowly survived. After rescue efforts by citizens of Mercy Peak and boarders at Gilcrest mine on the slope, a girl of twelve was pulled from the snow. She had been trapped for four hours and is under the care of Doc Swenson, who says he hopes very much that she will pull through.

Letter from Martin Shaw to Randolph Gilman,
recovered from turret room

March 15, 1904

Randolph,

I should never have drug you fellas up there, chasing into an adit that we could've waited to see. I thought the snow was fine; I can usually spot a slide-ready mountain from miles away. I got too confident, too eager. It's my fault. Thank God that girl survived . . . but Reuben's blaming himself. Thinks he almost killed his own sister, not looking out for her. He's saying things like she'd be better off without him. The avalanche might've broke his sister's leg, but it broke something in him, too.

I'm going to make this right. I swear it.

Martin

Rusty, age 16

Dear Marybeth,

You'll never guess.

Alright, knowing you, you just made five guesses already. Right? Quit that! Let me just tell the story, will ya?

It was Independence Day. The town was festivaling, as only Mercy Peak can. They brought in a circus. The animals couldn't get up the narrow gauge railway in the Galloping Geese— although I think a Goose carrying a bear would've been a sight to behold. Anyway, they were too heavy, and the circus people thought they'd get stuck. So they led them up the hill on foot— giraffes and all! Sam took me and held my hand all the day long. Held my hand, Marybeth! I'm telling you, I always thought that nonsense was just for other people, but there's this beating in my chest when Sam's around, pulling up his crooked smile with his dimple, like he already knows whatever mischief I'm thinking before I ever speak it. His eyes twinkle—green like the pine trees, behind his glasses. When he took my hand, I yanked it away, thinking that'd be it, the end of us, all our adventures and joking and whatnot. It'd get all mixed up and ruined. But he just smiled and waited and held that hand out like he was some kind of Prince Charming asking a princess for a dance. My hand found my way back to his, and oh.

That boy has calluses.

When people say swoon, *are they talking about the stomach-tumbling, tongue-tied, acrobatics-going-on-in-your-chest that happens when Sam's calluses are wrapped around your hand, all strong and rugged and warm?*

Don't hate me, but I think I mighta swooned.

Anyhow, there was bunting slung from every tree like the ladies committee thought the trees were some of those southern debutantes you were talking about, with frills and lace coming out their ears.

We don't have debutantes, but we got trees that look like they might fall over, busting with bunting.

Were there fireworks, you ask?

Is Mercy Peak riddled with miners who love to explode things?

If you can answer that, you'll know.

Sam said he had a surprise. He borrowed a pack mule from the Peak View mine—Mr. Gilman's being real kind to me for some reason I can't figure—and led me on it like I was Mary and he was Joseph.

We were up on land that's nobody-knows-whose. No, really, no one knows. It's nobody's, officially. Gilman land stops at the river, and so does Bright land. The river belongs to no one. Winter of '29 dumped so much snow that it changed its course. First it just got bigger, then it shifted like a snake, away from Gilman (can't blame it) and onto Bright land. Cut some of our land away from us and left what used to be river to dry out in the sun and belong to nobody.

Well, that's where Sam took me. No-man's-land.

It had rained hard that afternoon. And then, like a good July monsoon, it let up in the early evening and left the sky on fire with colors the likes of which us mere mortals should only wish to dream of. The forest was alive with smell, those pines just dripping the scents of soil and spice and life into every molecule of air.

The ground was still damp, so Sam unrolled a blanket on it, deep blue with yellow lines of plaid. "Like you, Rusty," he said. "Sunshine in the night."

How does that boy say so much with so little?

He flung it out like it was a sail, and it rippled in the wind and settled on the ground. We watched the stars and ate plums, of course, and he told jokes and I laughed, and I tried jokes and he groaned.

Then, when the fireworks started in the valley below, he stood and pulled me up, too, like we were standing at attention for all that color and majesty.

He turned to me, my hand in his.

Calluses. Swoons. Who am I???

I engraved his words on my memory so I wouldn't forget. They're too good to be forgotten. Just like him.

He said someday, when I was older, and he had more to give (doesn't he know he already is everything I could ever hope for?), he wanted to be mine forever. And for me to be his, forever. He wrapped his hands around mine with so much goodness and warmth, Marybeth. Not like he was going to hold me tight till I was crushed, but like he was going to be there, always, to be mine and no one else's.

He said he didn't know if he'd ever have enough to give me a ring. And that he didn't want to wait to give me a ring, that he wanted to give me a promise now.

"So, here's your ring," he said. Oh, how wide did his smile get, dimpling his cheek deep and lighting up those green eyes. He gestured all around, like he had some great big secret.

I turned in a circle and didn't see anything.

"Come on," he said, and led me to the edge of no man's land. "Here." He knelt and put my hand on the soil. Then we moved a little and did the same. Again and again, until we'd made a circle around the whole bit of land, where river currents used to rush and fish used to swim, and now only sun beats down. Every place he put my hand, he said, "Here. It's part of the promise."

And at the end, when we'd formed a big circle with the places he laid my hand on the earth, he leaned in close and hugged me tight and whispered in my ear. "It's your ring." He said he'd planted the pits of my plums, the same ones his family grew, the same ones he won my heart with all those years ago. He planted them in a ring. He said he's not scared of a promise that's slow to grow. That promises don't hurry.

Pick me up now, Marybeth, 'cause I near fell over dead when I understood.

That I was his someday-forever. That someday, forever, we'd be together. When these trees begin to grow, when they're maybe knee high or waist high or I don't know what . . . that boy's going to marry me, Marybeth.

Right there in the middle of our ring.

Now, how's THAT for a wedding ring?

Say you'll come, Marybeth. When someday comes, say you'll be here. We'll do something special before I get married—camp out or something. Is that what brides do? And then at the wedding, you can stand by me, wear a ruffly dress and all that. I don't even care if there's lace on it; you can wear all the lace you want, scratchy old stuff, and I won't even give you a hard time about it. It'll be you and me and Sam, and everything'll be right.

Signed,
Rusty Bright
(Sam's Rusty)

BLOOMS
(Brilliant Lexicon of the Original Marybeth Spatts)

ENTRY NO. 89

biv·ou·ac (noun)—a just-for-now camp, no tents around, just you and the stars. Made usually by soldiers, sometimes mountain men. And sometimes Marybeth Spatts.

Mercy

June 1948

"This is a terrible idea," Mercy said.

"What?" Willa stood back, stopping just short of the lakeshore, where waves lapped at her heels. "It's splendid! What could be terrible about this?"

She shook her head, smiling at the scene before them. They'd worked together all afternoon yesterday, down here by the boathouse that stretched out over the lake's surface so that a person could row right in. Several miles of the shoreline of Gold Leaf Lake fell on Gilman land, and Mercy had discovered that of all the rooms in that great manor house, it was at the boathouse she felt most at home.

Perhaps it was because within a single week, she had it tidied and put to rights. It did not overwhelm her with impossible tasks every time she entered . . . unlike Wildwood proper.

Or perhaps it was from her role as the Lady of Shalott, who had

181

found her unlikely freedom from a spellbound tower in lying in a boat. Mercy had done so many takes . . . it had been one of her favorite roles. Granted, she was sailing unto the character's death, but for those solitary moments in that boat scene, the cameras were positioned at a distance in what everyone at Pinnacle called "the swamp," a watery corner of the backlot that could be used for a jungle—or an Arthurian river—in a pinch. She'd been alone, on the water, beneath the trees, right in the middle of the concrete jungle of Los Angeles . . . and she'd felt peace there. As if the role belonged to her, and not the other way around.

Or perhaps the reason reached further back, to the place beside the creek at Swickley's Crossing. When, for a few moments each night, she could slip away from the cabin, her own prison, and listen to the water, watch it tumble wild and free, and she would feel content. Even if she could not leave, the water would journey forth and see the world. The chorus of midnight frogs and crickets singing beneath starlight had sung peace to her heart in ways all the orchestras in all the opera houses in all the world never could, beautiful as they were.

Whatever it was, the boathouse had become home this week. She'd brought blankets and pillows down. And after nights unable to sleep inside Widlwood for the way her mind wouldn't stop, she'd slept at last, in a boat anchored to the sides of the boathouse, in the company of the gentle lap of waves against its sides. It was silly, but it felt like a cradle, with the gentlest of hands to rock it. A notion perhaps best fit for fairy stories, but it reached inside her heart to a place she tried not to go: the place that missed the mother she had never known, whose hand had never rocked her. It had seemed a dream long lost, and yet here she was, thirty years old, being rocked to sleep by the Almighty himself.

The thought cradled a scar long hidden in her heart . . . it ached, and it healed, as it rocked and rocked.

The boathouse had become a place of unseen healing . . . and it seemed the perfect place to fulfill at least one promise to Rusty.

When she'd confided in Willa her idea to make Rusty's campout dream come true, right here in the boathouse, Willa had leapt into action. Mercy had thought to keep it simple: a campfire on the shore and two canoes in the boathouse, tied up and inlaid with bedrolls and pillows aplenty.

But Willa had cleaned and brought down the Gilman silver, prepared the silver teapot with hot chocolate to be warmed over the campfire, stuffed a picnic hamper with the fresh bread she'd coached Mercy through making, as well as preserves from last year's berries. In the icy shoreline, she'd placed a large, galvanized bucket, and inside it held a carafe of lemonade and a tin of egg salad from the chickens that Ralph and Nancy Mosely had brought for Mercy to keep in the hutch near the barn. Suddenly, it was an affair fit for queens.

"Will it be too much?" she asked. She'd confided in Willa what it all meant, the accidental fallout between the friends as close as sisters. "Will it just . . . hurt her even more? I'd scrap it in a heartbeat."

"The risk of 'too much' is better than the regret of 'too little,' I think," Willa said. "Trust it. Trust your friend. See what happens."

The crunch of approaching feet upon pebbles, and Rusty was there. "What's all this?"

"Well, you girls have a lovely time unearthing ghostly mysteries and whatnot," Willa said, leaving with a cheery wave.

Rusty studied the scene, puzzled. "I thought we were working on Gilman's calculations. When you weren't up at the house, I came looking."

"We are!" Mercy said, a little too happily. "It's just—well, I've been sleeping here," she blurted out, not ready to reveal what she'd planned.

Rusty's eyebrows pinched. "In the boathouse?"

Lapping evening waves filled the silence. "It's a long story. But yes."

"There are two bedrolls here."

"I thought—I just—" She hated when she did this. Every time her heart got too close to the surface, her words choked into half sentences. This was where acting came in; she could slip into someone else's shoes, put on their heart. Speak in sensical terms.

She took a deep breath. It was risky . . . but Rusty deserved the risk.

"I promised you once we'd camp out," she said. And waited.

Rusty's perplexed look lingered as she searched her memory, and then she froze. Her mouth dropped into a frown. She knew exactly what occasion Mercy referred to.

"We don't have to," Mercy said. "I know it isn't the circumstances you thought they'd be. . . . I wish I could make them right. But this . . . is one small thing I could give."

Silence.

"If you'd like it."

Rusty looked conflicted, nodding slowly. "Well, we gotta eat, I guess," she said, looking at the bucket on the shore.

She didn't say anything about camping out . . . but Mercy would take it.

"Wonderful!" She pulled the dishes out of the picnic hamper and started to lay them on some of the bigger rocks.

"Why are there three plates?" Rusty asked.

"Oh! Well, you know all of those triangles and trajectories up in the turret . . . I've been trying to work out what they all mean. I've got a few theories, but I'm no math genius, and I thought it couldn't hurt to bring in some help."

Rusty bristled. "Bring someone in on the treasure hunt?"

"Not exactly. Just . . . the hunt for the Goose. What do you think?"

"Depends who it is."

As if on cue, the tree branches behind them rustled and down tromped a tall, plaid-clad form.

"Casey Campbell," he said, "and you're Rusty Bright." He stuck his hand out.

She just looked at it.

He just waited.

Rusty might've met her match. At length, Rusty placed her hand in his and stared, apparently not knowing what to do with the way hers was swallowed up in his. She gave him a once-over, taking in his plaid and denim, the scuffs of dirt that bespoke hard work.

"You crawl out of one of the old prospector shacks or something?"

"Sometimes, yes," he said, nonplussed. "Sometimes I sleep under the stars, sometimes in the church basement. Just wherever, really. I've been wanting to meet you."

"Me? Why would you want to do a thing like that?"

"Anyone who can warn people off with a 'fate worse than vinegar' is worth meeting, in my opinion."

She pulled her hand away. Narrowed her eyes. Looked at Mercy, who shrugged and looked back at Casey Campbell.

"You didn't read that old journal," she said.

"Didn't think you'd mind."

"It *said* I would mind."

"Well, you weren't around. And besides, I like vinegar. Pickles, especially. They're a miracle. You take a cucumber—the blandest vegetable alive—and soak it in vinegar, and—" He snapped, loud and crisp. "Just like that. A punch of flavor in your sandwich to wake you up." He shook his head in wonder.

Rusty shook her head, aghast. "*Who* are you?"

"Casey Campbell."

"Like the soup," Mercy volunteered, finger in the air.

Rusty looked wary. "Why are you here?"

"In Mercy Peak? I'm surveying some of the old mining trails to see what might be turned into ski runs and lifts. Actually, I was hoping you could help me. I've been looking for a particular trail. . . . They said in town it used to go to a tram they used at an old mine. I thought it might be converted into a ski lift, if some of the infrastructure is still good. We'd lease the land, of course, if you"—he dashed a glance at Mercy, then back at Rusty—"were agreeable to it. Whoever's land it's on, that is."

Rusty just stared at this man, who was talking to her as if she was a business partner, an old friend, and a hero, all rolled into one. "It's not much more than a deer trail now," she said. "Up to the old Sunnyside mine and Sea Glass Lake."

"Maybe you could show me sometime this week?"

"Why me?"

He shrugged one shoulder. "I've heard you know the mountain like the back of your hand. And besides, I told you," he said. "Vinegar. I like it."

Rusty Bright was speechless. Mercy tried not to be so full of mirth, but it was quite the show. Casey went on grinning, and Rusty went on staring, flabbergasted and slightly horrified. The meal unfolded in a smattering of suspicious looks from Rusty and affable grins from Casey, with Mercy making commentary on birds, trees, fishing boats— anything to fill the silence.

"Shall we take a look at the schematics?" Mercy said when the plates were clean, desperate for a little help filling the silence.

"Yes!" Rusty jumped into action a little too quickly and led the march back up to the manor.

In the turret room, light spilled over what had, to Mercy, looked to be the etchings of a madman. Letters and numbers strung together in equations that, having left school at fourteen, she had no frame of reference to decipher. Dotted lines rising and falling with no explanation, no labels. Dimensions labeling sides of mysterious sloping rectangles. All of it in neat rows on oversized paper hung from walls, until the figures spilled off of the paper and onto the stones themselves.

The three of them stood side by side, hands on hips, elbow to elbow, in a great and stretching ponder.

"Hmmm . . ." Mercy released an almost-sigh, trying to find her way over the terrain of these scrambled etchings for the thousandth time.

"Hmmm," said Rusty, with a smirk that said, *"Yep. I see what you were up to, Randolph Gilman."*

"Hmmm," said Casey, with a lilt of surprise and respect.

Both girls turned in surprise to face him.

"'Hmmm?'" Rusty repeated. "As in . . . this makes sense to you?"

Casey narrowed his eyes. "This"—he pointed at an equation—"makes it seem he was working on some sort of trajectory."

"Those hieroglyphics there?" Rusty pointed to the etchings.

$$y = h + x * (V_0 * sin(\alpha)) / (V_0 * cos(\alpha)) - g * (x / V_0 * cos(\alpha))^2 / 2$$

"It's math used to figure out the trajectory of an object in motion."

"Math is a foreign language," Rusty said hopelessly.

"Math is a miracle," Casey said. "It's the fabric of the universe, lassoed into numbers and boundaries, with which all of existence can be written, given the right forms and functions." He looked a bit giddy, and Rusty clearly struggled to hide the smile that tugged at her mouth.

Mercy spoke. "About this miraculous foreign language . . . what does it mean?"

Casey took his time moving through the room, taking in the Galloping Goose schematics, the map of Wildwood and the box canyon, the formulas.

He paced. Muttered a little, stopped. Stroked his dark beard, paced some more. "I'm guessing we're working under the presumption that this guy stole the Galloping Goose, yes?"

The girls nodded.

"Because . . . ?"

Rusty and Mercy entered into a silent conversation, an exchange of heated expressions that, if translated, would've said something like, *Should we trust him?*

What other choice do we have?

And that's a reason to trust him?

Do you have a better suggestion?

They turned to face the man, who was in danger of a case of whiplash from following their silent conversation with a furrowed brow.

"In its simplest form . . ." Mercy began, and then stopped, stuck.

"We believe there's hidden treasure in this mountain, and that Randolph Gilman stole the Galloping Goose because it holds the key to where that treasure is." Rusty folded her arms, finished.

Mercy's eyebrows shot up. She hadn't planned on saying it all, but there it was.

Casey drew his mouth down and nodded, thinking. "Very good reason for math. And that does help explain it. If I were a greedy villain intent on making something massive disappear . . ."

And for the first time, at the man's succinct summation of Randolph Gilman, Rusty looked a little starry-eyed in the presence of Casey Campbell.

He took a breath. "Tell me what his goals would have been."

"Steal the Galloping Goose," Rusty said.

"But preserve it as much as possible," Mercy said. "He knew it had something to do with a riddle he'd been given, but as far as we know, he didn't necessarily know what parts or functions would be needed in order to decode his riddle. He likely had some guesses . . . but we think he wanted to preserve its structure as much as possible."

"And hide it. He wanted to hide it," Rusty said. "Entirely and quickly, where no one would look."

"Hide it from whom?" a jovial voice said behind them, causing all three to turn.

Mercy jumped, hand flying to her chest, at the smiling face that beamed at them.

"Holden! What are you doing here?"

"You bade me come," he said. "So here I am."

"H-how?"

"Frank said I could use the helicopter," he said, as if the answer should have been obvious.

"Holden," Mercy said, becoming acutely aware of Rusty's and Casey's stares. She pulled him to the far edge of the room. "I'm grateful for your help—truly. But . . . didn't you see the part about being subtle? Like a spy?"

His brows bounced twice, a telltale sign that he was particularly proud of himself. He leaned in and lowered his voice. "Spies use helicopters." He winked. "Don't sweat it, sweetheart. Nobody blinked twice, nobody knows where I am, and nobody cares! I'm on suspension again." He rolled his eyes. "Can't work for another three weeks, or till WPW says—you know how *that* is, don't you, Murse? Say, suspension doesn't look half bad if it comes with a castle like this." He looked around. "How'd you manage it?"

"You're . . . sure nobody saw you, that you weren't followed?" Mercy knew certain journalists were intent on tracking her down, not letting her out of the limelight.

He waved a hand. "Not a soul. We had to put down a few times for gasoline, but nobody's the wiser, sis."

She breathed a little easier, though she didn't believe his reassurances. It wasn't that Holden would lie, but having grown up essentially raised by the studio, he was a bit oblivious when it came to things like the press. They were just a part of normal life, almost invisible.

It did her heart good to hear the actor call her *sis* again. They'd starred opposite each other in numerous films. He could leave the audience weeping and heartsick, pulling out gravitas and depth for every role . . . and then slip just as quickly into his easygoing, oblivious, fun-loving self offscreen, an accidental comic relief on every soundstage.

"Anyway," he said again, "you needed this?" He whistled an alert, pulled a hand from his pocket, removing a box and tossing it in the air so it twirled.

Mercy caught it, clasping it with both hands. "You found it?"

"Or my name's not Holden Huxley!" he said, and she could almost see the diamond-twinkle when he smiled.

"Your name's *not* Holden Huxley," she said.

His smile vanished. "Shhh," he said, looking furtively at Casey and Rusty, who were both staring at the box.

Mercy could nearly feel her friend's quickly calculating mind piecing things together. She crossed the room and held the box out to Rusty, who took it slowly.

She swallowed. "The belt?"

Mercy nodded. The moment swam in significance, airy and weighty all at once.

Completely oblivious to that, Holden Huxley strode over and pumped Rusty's and Casey's hands in succession. "Pleasure to meet you, folks," he said. "You were saying when I arrived that this Gilford wanted to hide an engine from somebody?"

"Gilman. And yes, he wanted to hide it from me," Rusty said. "Well, my father, primarily. He knew we Brights had the other piece of the puzzle, and that we needed his piece as much as he needed ours. Martin Shaw hoped the men would work together, but . . ."

"Randolph Gilman ensured that would never happen," Mercy finished.

"Oh?" Holden braced his arm on the wall and leaned in.

Casey, looking between Rusty and Holden, cleared his throat. "How'd he do that?"

"He accused my dad of murder and sowed suspicion among the very town that loved and raised us both."

Casey nodded slowly, clearly trying not to show the shock this registered. "I see," he said. "Well . . . from what I can tell, and this is all conjecture . . ."

"Please, conject away," Rusty said.

"It looks to me like he pinpointed this place in the narrow gauge railway. Here"—he tapped a map on the wall—"at the top of the rise, where it turns a bend just above the canyon wall up there." He pointed outside.

"That's exactly where the window in the other turret faces," Mercy said. "The Goose comes by there twice a day, once in each direction."

"So why that spot?"

Casey moved to look at a map of Wildwood, all of its outbuildings and timberland, the terrain of the canyon. "The canyon narrows here."

"Right where the bend in that track is," Mercy said.

"So he wanted to—what, make it jump the track?"

Casey scratched his head. "Something weighing that much would drop to the ground and bury itself faster than you could blink, and in the process make itself flatter than a pancake." He shook his head. "If he was going to do something at the head of the box canyon like this . . ." He moved down the line of Gilman's scribblings and stopped at a carefully arcing line. "He would've wanted it to have some lift."

"As in . . . he wanted the Galloping Goose to . . ."

"Fly." Rusty finished Mercy's sentence.

"That's preposterous," said Holden emphatically, as if he'd rehearsed his part.

"Ludicrous," said Rusty.

"Ridiculous," said Casey, but he was growing more excited as his eyes darted over the schematics. "Either ridiculous or very, very ingenious."

"He was a genius," Rusty said. "A dirty rotten scoundrel, but a genius. Schooled back east, and even then he was so smart he was leaps and bounds above the rest, to hear it told."

"It would've taken a lot of planning and a lot of work, but . . . if he'd built some sort of apparatus to guide the Goose off the tracks here, onto some kind of rail ramp—which would have had to be in place, and hidden, potentially for some time prior . . ." He thought. "If he did all that, it would use her momentum and speed and give her just enough incline to harness that power and lift her into flight. He—or whoever he hired to help him—could have bailed out just in time and then the Goose . . . she could've feasibly arced right here—"

All three looked at the map, then at the ceiling. It would've been almost directly above Wildwood.

Mercy closed her eyes and could see it. Thousands of pounds of metal, hovering midair, wind whispering as dark cloaked it, hanging for a split second before floating, in all her seven-ton splendor, before arcing into her descent . . . or demise.

"—and landed here," he said. "On this ledge." He traced the arc and stopped at the opposite canyon wall, where a ledge reached out like a landing strip . . . but not far enough.

"Wouldn't it have crashed into the canyon wall, then?" Rusty asked. "Become flatter than a pancake—in a different direction?"

"Yes," Casey said thoughtfully. "Unless . . ." He moved to face the etching of a rectangle, drawn at a slight downward angle, with the words *tailings to slow* written beneath it. "He was in the mining business, yes?"

"That's right."

"So he'd have had the tools and knowledge—or manpower and funds to silence that manpower—to dig for himself a tunnel . . . right about here." He tapped at the canyon wall at the outcropping in question.

"A mine," Mercy said.

"In essence, yes. But instead of taking something out of it . . ." Casey trailed off.

"He meant to put something inside," Rusty said.

"Tailings to slow . . ." Casey mused. "He might've lined the place with some sort of gravel—"

"Mine tailings?" Rusty said. "Or the crushed rock from the Goose's tunnel."

Casey nodded. "To slow the Goose, soften its landing."

"If you're right," Mercy said, "that means the Goose is on this property . . . right as we speak. But wouldn't people have noticed something like that? An opening in a mountain where there hadn't been one before?"

Something played at the edge of her thoughts, begging for her to see something, to understand . . . but what?

"He could've covered over it easily enough. Camouflaged it with brush," Rusty said. "Or maybe stacked rocks to blend in with the mountain, or . . ."

And then it hit her.

"Covered over it completely." Her heart skittered, the memory of her hands wrapping around a crystal wall of water, frozen in time. "Like a curtain."

Rusty and Casey were looking at her, not following.

"Willa Jones said that Randolph Gilman built a wall around the headwaters of the waterfall at the top of the mountain. Why would he do that? The water still flowed through, the cascade is still there . . ."

Rusty's eyes grew round as dinner plates. "He changed its course," she said. "He put some contraption up there, or dug a dam, or some such."

Mercy tapped the waterfall on the map, where it fell just to the right of the ledge. "He moved a waterfall . . .just a few yards." She shook her head in wonder. "If we're right about all this . . . that means it's been within our grasp all this time," said Mercy.

And for the first time . . . Rusty smiled. Slow and wide, a glimmer of mischief mixed with adventure in her eyes. This was the Rusty Mercy knew.

"Well, what are we waiting for?" she asked.

CHAPTER 17

Rusty

The waterfall blasted the walls around Rusty's heart with a roar that rattled her bones. She was leading the climb down from the top; they'd found overgrown stair-like outcroppings descending to the ledge, but the going was slow. The rocks were slippery, the height stomach-dropping. A fall would be . . . unforgiving.

Stay away, the relentless water seemed to say. But that was *her* line. For the past ten years, it had been easier to roar people away, seal them off, stay aloof up in these heights, than to face the waters below. The sea of community, compassion, currents she knew were kind . . . but that terrified her even more than the frigid grip of isolation.

It meant being seen. It meant being known. It meant letting people in. For that, she'd have to open the door—and there was no telling what would come out. Easier to stay frozen . . . something this waterfall knew all about. When it began to melt, the sheer force knocked the remaining icicles loose with unleashed power, and everyone below had better look out.

It was exactly what Rusty was afraid of. *Stay cold*, she told her stubborn heart.

The waterfall was fully awake now, having thrown aside every last ice dagger, with only the shimmer of frosty diamonds clinging to the peripheral rocks. The beauty struck her so hard she felt it inside—and that scared her, too.

She lifted her face, the mist from the falls settling over her with a rush of unbidden memories. Writing to Marybeth about this very mist, how someday she'd feel it, too. Or Sam, picking up her hand and twirling her into the spray. She, laughing at her own clumsiness, and the slipperiness of the rocks.

Oh, the memory hurt. But oh, was it beautiful.

"Stay away," she said under her breath, echoing the refrain of the waterfall's force.

"What's that?" Casey Campbell's voice at her side startled her, causing her to lose her balance on the slippery rock. He braced her elbow until she'd found steady footing.

She bit her tongue to keep from directing the same words at him. He was too . . . *nice*. She didn't like the way he was always smiling, the way his eyes creased just slightly at the corners, looking friendly and kind . . . nor the way they seemed to find her, often.

"Nothing," she said.

"Should we go back?" Marybeth came behind Casey, with Holden Huxley lagging behind, distracted by every bird that flew by and pointing out every fox and deer below.

"What?" Rusty asked.

"Should we go back?" Marybeth raised her voice. "I don't see a way through."

She was right. There were diamond-sprinkled tendrils and trickles of water at the edges but in the middle—right where they needed to be—the waterfall was impenetrable. If they tried to leap through, there was no telling where, how, or whether they'd land.

Rusty nodded and pointed back up the way they came. They climbed the precarious terrain, Marybeth pausing to redirect Holden, who was busy poking a swath of green lichen.

At the top, Marybeth paced, already piecing together a plan. "If we try to get into the walls around the headwaters . . . maybe we could find whatever he's got in place to redirect the flow, long enough for us to get in."

"That's a good plan," Rusty said, and Marybeth froze. She looked like she might well up in tears of gratitude right then and there. And that was Rusty's fault. She determined to stop being so rough with Marybeth. To give her a chance. She'd moved heaven and earth to get here, after all.

Casey's eyes were on the sky. "Time's going fast," he said. "What if we split up? Two of us to the headwaters, two to stay here and give a signal if and when the water has moved."

"Perfect," Marybeth said, and with a hopeful look at Rusty, she stepped closer. "Maybe if we two head up—"

"Murse!" Holden elbowed Marybeth, pointing at the sky.

"Did he just call you 'Murse'?" Rusty asked.

Marybeth grimaced. "He has nicknames for everyone. Give it an hour, he'll be calling you *Rust*."

"Look!" Holden proclaimed. "Bald eagle. Right? Just like when we did *Embargo*, remember when we followed it and—" He started to take a long stride, following the course of the soaring bird, without a single thought toward the ground that dropped away beneath him. Marybeth grabbed his shirt, yanked him back, and none too soon.

"Close call again, Holden," she said breathlessly. "Eyes open, yes?"

He gave her a wink and a smile, pointing a finger at her with a click of his tongue. Rusty got the feeling this was a well-rehearsed dance between the two of them.

"On second thought," Marybeth said, "I might be needed here. Are you two up to scouting the headwaters? You might need this." She pulled a key out of her pocket in dark, scrolling metal. "Willa found a key cabinet when we were cleaning. This one was labeled *Falls*—I'd forgotten about it until today. Here's hoping it's the right fit."

Key or not, they'd find a way in. They'd climb in if they had to. Rusty opened her mouth to say as much.

"I'm not above scaling a wall if needed," Casey said.

Rusty's words halted into an odd croak.

"You okay?" Casey said. Looking genuinely concerned, blast it.

Rusty nodded, then started up the last bit of incline, leading the way to where a stone wall rose in perfect square around the river.

"You and Marybeth are good friends, I take it?" Casey asked. His interest was sincere, and she couldn't blame him for the bit of puzzlement she saw on his face.

"We were pen pals, a long time ago," Rusty said. "We'd never met, but we were inseparable, as contradictory as that sounds."

"Makes sense to me," he said. "I'm glad you finally got the chance to meet."

A pause, their feet crunching over the dry rocks of this high-country terrain. The afternoon sun beat down harshly at this elevation; the shade of the trees near the headwaters couldn't come fast enough.

"Your mountaineering skills are impressive." Casey made another attempt at conversation. "I saw your camp up at the ridge once and watched the way you bouldered just to get to some pinecones in a tree growing out of the cliffside there."

"Were you following me?"

He laughed. "No. The opposite, actually. When I saw you up there—

both times—I turned and went the other way. Didn't want to startle you. But if we're both out there, scouting the ridges and timberlines, we're bound to run into each other."

Rusty shrugged. "It's a big mountain."

"It is, at that. And yet someone has figured out how to make plum trees thrive, even up here."

Her attention snapped to him. "Plum trees?"

He smiled. Him and all that smiling.

"I . . . don't suppose you know anything about . . . some kind of smoke contraption set up there to ward off the frost . . ." Rusty measured her words.

"Oh good, you found it!" He looked so pleased. "That's the smudge pot. It's yours if you want it. We used to use them in the war to guide the planes in for night landings. We didn't complain about the extra warmth they brought, either. Did it work for your blossoms?"

Rusty swallowed. This man had been in her orchard. *Sam's* orchard. It was as good as sacred ground. And yet . . . hadn't he also saved the blossoms she'd feared were doomed?

"How did you know the blossoms needed help?"

Casey's face flushed, and he scooped a hand over the back of his neck, looking away. "I, uh . . ."

And she knew. After so many years of hiding her grief, locking herself away, shoving tears down so deep inside her . . . "You saw me that day."

"They . . . seemed to mean an awful lot to you."

Rusty jutted her chin out but it trembled ever so slightly. What was happening to her? Rusty, the fortress, was dissolving bit by bit into a sieve of emotions. She dropped her head. "They did," she said quietly. "They do." And then, meeting the eyes of the man who'd seen and held her tears, without her even knowing, "Thank you."

He considered her, his serious gaze lingering just long enough to tie her stomach up in knots.

"It was a pleasure, Rusty Bright. And the smudge pot is yours. I can show you how to light it if you like." And then, sensing her unease, he changed the subject, lickety-split. "Look," he said, gesturing ahead, where the stone wall rose above them to a height taller than Casey, which was saying something.

Rusty whistled low, pulling out the elaborate key—Gilman always did go overboard with theatrics—and approaching the wooden gate. "Let's hope this works," she said. "That'd be some wall to scale."

"Ah." He waved the thought off. "We could do it."

"We certainly could," Rusty said, offering him a smile for the first time. But with a heavy click of the key, she pushed the gate open, shoving it when it caught on bracken or bushes inside.

They stepped inside what felt like an enchanted forest, where the walls had created a world within a world. Winds trapped within had circled in a dance, dispersing seeds over the years where the mist of the river rose and descended, and where the ground responded by releasing from its grip entire carpets of larkspur and alyssum, climbing ivy, sprawling moss, and tucked-away patches of snow in the shadowed corner. Even the tangles of weeds had poetry to them here, *tap-tapping* against the walls and wrapping their ankles as they waded in to find a river at its leisure. A parched riverbed lay beyond it, and in the middle, a series of levees and dikes, where Gilman had coaxed the waters from their course and into weaving bands of streams, then released them unto their new home.

"Shall we?" Casey asked, a glimmer in his eye.

"Oh, we shall," Rusty said. And together, with the creaking of metal wheels and levers at each diverting dam, they maneuvered across the workings of Randolph Gilman's mind played out in hydraulic engineering, until the water began to glisten its way back to its original path.

Shouts soon sounded from below.

"Does that sound like a Holden-fell-off-a-mountain sort of shout, or a you-moved-an-entire-waterfall type of shout?" Casey asked.

"Can't say as I've heard either," she said, but gave her answer with a grin. "Let's find out."

Holden had not fallen off a mountain, and the water-sheened, slow-dripping face of the mountain proved they'd done their job. They made quick work clambering back down to the ledge and stopped to stare.

There, just as the diagram had hinted, was a gaping doorway to the mountain, square and set with beams. And inside it . . .

Galloping Goose Motor Number Eight.

Standing shoulder to shoulder with Marybeth Spatts, this stranger who was her sister, she was flooded with the thought that she would never have known this soul—certainly would not be standing here beside her right now—if not for the plucky machine before them.

It was burrowed, tilted and tired. One got the sense they were observing a baby bird that had attempted her first flight and crashed to the ground, helpless. Only this baby bird weighed seven tons, sang from two brass trumpet-like horns, and hadn't so much crashed as skidded with the force of the sky she'd just traversed, fishtailing to a stop in the gravel that had been laid to catch her.

It was a miracle she wasn't more mangled than she was.

It was Casey's eyes that were the widest. "Impossible."

Rusty tipped her head. "You were the one who figured out the plan."

"Sure, but that doesn't make it any less . . ."

"Incredible," Marybeth finished for him, laying her hand on the railing near the back steps. She rounded the far side of the Goose, and Rusty the near side, until they met in front and gazed upon a sight Rusty would never forget. She didn't know how a vehicle could be so endearing, but there was no other word for it.

The toothy metal cowcatcher grin of Motor No. 8 greeted them. Staring with darkened headlight eyes, and a dust-encrusted windshield devoid of glass, which lay in the gravel in a million shimmering pieces.

She stepped around to the passenger side of the cab and pulled open the door. It squawked like its namesake.

Rusty came around the driver's side and yanked open that door, leaning into the cab. She climbed in, perching where Phin had spent a good portion of his life. It felt strange for this place to be unoccupied by him. How many times had she seen him pull that rope to sound the horn? Playing the switches, knobs, and levers like music, always over the bass notes of the diesel engine rumbling away beneath hearts and souls.

Rusty blew out her cheeks. "How did the clue go?"

"Tunneling blight, she keeps the solution; coil the lash tight, begin restitution."

"Tunneling blight . . . what would that be?"

"Maybe the lash itself will give a clue." Marybeth pulled the belt out of her bag, along with the seam ripper. "Do you want to do the honors?" She held the box containing the belt and the small tool out to Rusty.

Rusty had stitched that tight, cinching up her disdain for Gilman along with all her hopes for Marybeth to someday open it, be captivated by what she knew it held.

"I always thought it'd be you," Rusty said.

There was a spark of delight in Marybeth's eyes, and she picked the stitches out as swiftly and carefully as she could. Unfolding the long length of leather slowly, Rusty leaned in with Marybeth to behold a sight she'd pored over for untold hours, all to no avail.

A single column of letters appeared all down the length of the leather strip, branded with precision.

"Is it a . . . message of some sort?" Marybeth said.

Rusty touched it gingerly. "It has to be. I tried everything over the years—forward, backward, scrambling, unscrambling, taking out key letters, substituting . . . and could never make hide nor hair of it. Neither could Dad."

Marybeth handed one end to Rusty and stretched the length out across the cab so they could see all the letters, one stacked neatly upon the next, for the entire length of leather.

```
DSNWEGTRMSHSAOAHS4.RNG,IASHEITEEMS
NEA2.IONTRINCLEANOCTRFFPW;OHTGOTEP,
RGUOEELTS-LSOHH.TTSSWENRRCOWIKUHCR
HWIERTENEOIGYTEAAEIGLSIBHIR.THFSAR
CBTNL.LNLEL*HTAOVTK,EHAMEGUEI3.NNC
UIWDLNLEATEDN4OIEL,NIIL.OS*SD,WLWG'-
```

"I've been wearing this all these years? And never knew?"

"All you needed was a seam ripper." Rusty grinned.

"There's the word *ten*," Casey spoke from Rusty's left, making her jump. He was leaning in—not crowding her but examining the letters.

"*Clean* . . . or maybe *lean*?" Marybeth said.

"And *tea*." Rusty pointed.

"You missed *goat*," Holden said with pride, pointing at the *G-O-T-E*. Marybeth gave him an indulgent smile and winked at Rusty.

"Now we're just missing the key to decode it. It has to be something in Gilman's riddle," Rusty said. "But I have no idea what."

"That's a scytale," said Holden, leaning over Marybeth to pull the rope attached to the horn. Nothing sounded, and he tried again.

"The engine has to be on for the horn to work," said Rusty, furrowing her brow at the puzzle that was Holden. "What's a scytale?"

"Do the headlights work?" He started punching keys, flipping switches. It would've been downright annoying if he didn't have the excitement of a ten-year-old kid.

"Holden," Marybeth said. He jerked his head up, knocking it on the ceiling and pulling out of the cab fast, hand to the back of his neck.

"Yep?" he rasped, in pain.

"What's a scytale?"

He stopped rubbing his neck, looking at Marybeth in rueful disappointment.

"From *Man Invisible*. Remember? Ace Archer's in the basement of the courthouse and he's given a secret message from the Brotherhood, all on a long strip of paper, but in order to decode it he has to . . ." He trailed his voice up and away dramatically, lifting a hand toward Marybeth as if to say, *Take it away, doll!*

"I . . . wasn't in that one," Marybeth said.

"You were my date to the premiere!"

Marybeth bit her lip. "It was a lovely evening, Holden. And you were splendid as Ace, you always are. It's no reflection on your performance at all, I promise, I just . . . I . . ."

This was going to be good. Rusty raised her eyebrows and smiled, leaning in as she rested her chin on her fist.

"I'd been up since four that morning for makeup and wardrobe, and on set all that afternoon, and you know how hot the lights are. Grauman's was just so cool and dark, and I must have felt just so safe in your presence—"

Oh, she was good.

"—that I . . . drifted off for a bit."

Holden's jaw dropped, and he staggered back as if she'd just stabbed him. "*Et tu, Brute?*" He fell to the ground.

Casey craned his neck to see over the hood of the Galloping Goose. "Is he . . . okay?"

"He's fine," Marybeth said. "I am sorry, Holden. You deserved better. *Ace* deserved better."

Holden sprang to his feet and said gravely, "Ace did deserve better. But I forgive you. And fair is fair since I slept through *Embargo.*"

"Yes, I know," Marybeth said.

"*How* did you know?"

"You do all things with great gusto, Mr. Huxley. Including your snoring."

"I *never.*"

"It was seismological."

"So about this Ace . . ." Rusty redirected, just as Holden's mouth opened to protest. "What did he do to decrypt the scytale?"

"Oh, easy. He needed exactly the right-sized cylinder. For him, it was an ancient rod hewn from the ruins of a ghost ship."

"Naturally," said Rusty.

"So we just need a cylinder to wrap it," said Marybeth. "Something just the right size in order to make the letters line up and reveal their order and meaning." She looked around the cab.

"It could be anything."

"But different sized cylinders will make the letters line up differently. So it has to be just the right one . . ." Casey mumbled something about circumferences and precision. "What did the riddle say?"

Rusty closed her eyes and recited, "Tunneling blight, she keeps the solution."

"Tunneling blight . . . something that's a cylinder . . . what would that be? The chimney from the woodstove in the back?"

"This thing has a woodstove?" Holden started toward the back, and they all followed.

Casey went in first, testing the flooring, making sure it was sound. "It's going to feel like the world's tipping, but you can come on in."

Inside, the industrious smell of diesel mixed with wood and metal summoned memories of watching the Goose gallop the ridges and rises of these mountains. Rusty and Sam used to race her, Phinneas always giving them a whoop and holler from his window as he feigned defeat, letting their victory soar high enough to crash down hard when he unleashed her engine and left them in the dust. Into which they had always collapsed, laughing. Spent.

Rusty braced herself against the frame of the door, letting the summer-baked memory wash over her.

Laughing. Spent. That's what life with Sam had been. Full to over-flowing, nothing held back.

That's what she'd missed so bad it sucked the breath out of her.

And yet—*spent.*

He'd never held back anything. Not one drop of love. And neither had she. That's what made it hurt so bad, but also, for the first time, some new conviction knocked upon her heart.

They'd spent their time, their love, their hearts. They'd poured it all in. Nothing left.

And that phrase . . .. *nothing left.* It didn't carry with it the cutting, hard edge of grief this time, but the gentle and sweet inkling that they had lived their story so full. True and loud, all the way to the end.

She'd lived alone in that cabin for years with all the never-got-to's swarming her for company. They never got to get married. Have kids. Race their kids against the Galloping Goose. Grow old together.

A flash of them together in that roiling dust of the Goose, red earth swirling about them as evergreen canyon walls rose up like a cathedral. Laughing and not just spent . . . but *whole.*

The beauty of it socked her good, and her eyes pooled. She swiped at them quick. What was *wrong* with her?

Whatever it was . . . it felt somehow . . . right.

Marybeth was busy wrapping the length of leather around the black chimney in the back corner, Holden and Casey watched with bated breath. Rusty wanted to know the code, too, of course, but something else tugged at her here in this metal time capsule.

The lost bag of mail. Could it be in here . . . still? After all this time?

For the past ten years, she'd had this foggy hope that somewhere out there, wherever the Goose was . . . there might be a last word from Sam Buckley in that bag.

That notion had kept her going more than she wanted to admit.

Now, if they could find that mailbag . . . she'd know. And the possibility would be snatched away, for better or worse. It knocked the wind out of her.

She made a quick search of the rectangular car. Nothing beneath seats, nor stashed against walls, nor near the stove—where once a mailbag had caught fire, and there'd been an outcry about finding a better spot for the mail. She'd think Randolph likely burned this bag, too, but knowing him, he'd never pass up the chance to hang on to something that might prove useful in his cowardly blackmailing ways.

But there was no sign of the mailbag now, and Rusty's heart was in her throat.

Marybeth made quick work of wrapping the strip around the black chimney, stacking the rounds beside one another. But as they all leaned in to examine the chaotic lineup of letters, it was quickly clear that this was not the right blight-tunneling cylinder.

"What else 'tunnels blight'?" Rusty asked. "The wheels, maybe?"

"The exhaust!" Marybeth said. Quickly she unwound the strip, and they filed out, looking for where the exhaust might exit the vehicle. It was in a stack up top, between the cab and the rail car. Rusty clambered up, using the seat as a step and hoisting herself to the roof. It gave a tinny *pop* in mild protest, and for a moment her heart was in her throat—she hadn't really thought that through. Typical of her.

Applause sounded. "Brava, Rust!" Holden cupped his hands and shouted.

Casey Campbell nodded with profound respect.

She carefully reached down for the scytale.

Marybeth handed it up, and Rusty gripped the pipe, examining it as she began winding the leather. "That's odd," she said, halting.

"What is it?" Casey asked.

"Something else is wound here," she said. "A length of wire, around and around, maybe five or six times. Should I just go over it?"

"The width of the cylinder must be precise, or the entire endeavor is doomed to certain failure," muttered Holden nonchalantly.

Silence reigned as everyone looked at him.

He shrugged. "So says Ace."

Rusty nodded and unwound the wire. Something clattered to the ground as she did.

Marybeth retrieved the rusted piece of metal from the gravel. "A key," she said. "What would a key this small go to?" It was nothing like the elaborate keys of Wildwood.

"Maybe this will tell us," Rusty said, and resumed winding the belt on the pipe, row stacked on row. As she neared the top, the metal morphed into sheer black, stained by the grime—or *blight*, according to Martin's riddle—of the diesel smoke. Grime covered her palms, but she didn't care. All these years . . . all these letters . . . lining up into something beautiful.

"It worked," she murmured.

Marybeth's joy was palpable. "What's it say?"

The words were jammed together end to end. She read aloud slowly, sorting the words and settling into the cadence of Martin Shaw's rhythmic riddle.

> "Drift with no snow,
> Lightning, no sky.
> Face without soul,
> Earth heaving sigh.
> Cart with no track
> Direct the bell
> Miles with no step
> Signals hear well*
> Messengers lead
> Amounting two score
> Blue lantern heed
> Where ceiling's a floor
> *3 4-4 1
> PS"

202

Marybeth pulled out a notebook—ever the prepared one—and asked her to read it again as she took down the words. Rusty saw it, the way her excitement took a turn halfway through. Her writing slowed, her smile faded, her face losing its bloom of color. She was realizing the same thing Rusty was.

"Face without soul . . . the face of a mountain," she said. "And a cart with no track, miles with no step . . ." She swallowed. "That'd be a hoist. It has to be. Don't you think?"

The very thing that had taken her father down into the belly of the earth and returned to her a man forever changed.

Rusty unwound the lash and tried to infuse compassion in her voice. "Sounds about right," she said simply, meeting Marybeth's eyes.

"A mine." Marybeth looked like she might be sick. She closed her eyes, her breaths coming quicker, shorter.

Rusty scrambled down, taking Casey's offered hand for her leap to the ground. When she pulled her hand away and saw the black mark her hand had left in his, she grimaced and mouthed a silent *sorry.* He shrugged and wiped it on his sleeve, giving a wink.

Holden withdrew a handkerchief and began jabbing swipes at the black smudge on Casey's flannel, but Casey pulled away. "Adds character," he said.

Rusty neared Marybeth and stopped. She was terrible at this sort of thing. Should she embrace her? Pat her on the back? Do nothing? And yet . . . this was the girl who'd burst into Rusty's own tangle of a heart and kept pouring light in, even when her own world grew dark.

Rusty lifted a hand toward Marybeth's shoulder but stopped short. It hovered awkwardly as she realized again she was covered in grime. Casey offered her his black-smudged sleeve, and she wiped her hand quickly there, giving him a grateful look, and then proceeded to give Marybeth three quick pats on the shoulder. Too bad her awkwardness hadn't rubbed away on Casey's plaid sleeve, too. She quickly clasped her hands behind her back. Marybeth faced her and didn't run or laugh at the pitifully attempted show of compassion. She looked . . . grateful.

And to her credit, she took a deep breath and rallied. "So I guess that leaves us with one question. . . . Which mine?"

Mercy

Which mine?

Mercy thought back to the map the brothers had on the wall at the mercantile. The store was closed now, the men doubtless home for dinner. She didn't suppose it would do to go banging on their windows, asking to be let into the store to look at the map of mines for undisclosed reasons.

It would have to wait for tomorrow. So the foursome headed back toward Wildwood, each lost in their thoughts for a time.

"So, all of this is yours?" Casey asked at length. She could nearly hear the *whip-snap-reel* of tape measures in his head as he assessed the cliffs and slopes that descended into Wildwood.

"For now," Mercy said.

Rusty cocked her head. "What does that mean, 'for now'? Fixing to leave?" The words were hard-edged, and Mercy couldn't blame her.

"No," said Mercy with quiet resolution. "No . . . but I've got an idea hatching. It's too crazy to share just yet, but also just crazy enough that if it works . . . it might just soar. I'd love for that to happen."

"Well, now you have to tell us," Casey said.

"Hear, hear!" said Holden, jogging to catch up from where he'd stooped to examine a stump. "Say it, Murse!"

"Yes, *Murse*, tell us," Rusty said, the edge in her voice replaced with mischief.

Mercy sighed, pulling up courage. "Well, *Rust*," she said, "Wildwood . . . it's far too big for one person."

"Not according to Randolph Gilman," said Rusty.

"And look how miserable he was. Though I think that has less to do with solitude and more to do with greed. I don't mind the solitude,"

Mercy said, and meant it. It was beginning to feel oddly like home. "But all those rooms, that big kitchen, the great hall . . . the lake, the towers, the falls. There's even a tunnel. . . . Holden, what would Pinnacle give to have a filming location like that?"

"They'd trip all over themselves," he said.

Mercy nodded. "And yet, there's something special here that I fear would be lost the moment it was invaded by cameras and lights. They're the dream factory . . . but this is the dream. There's no need here for manufactured enchantment. It's already here," she said, feeling the chase of it after her heart—how the rugged realness of this place was wooing her, speaking to her somehow. She didn't know what it was saying, but something was happening, in the depths.

"What if we opened the gates? Once a year, perhaps twice. Remember, Rusty, when you used to tell me about people coming in all their finery, all the way from Denver and sometimes even farther? And for what, a party?"

"You want to throw a party?" Casey asked.

Rusty grimaced.

Holden beamed.

"Not exactly," Mercy said. "Well, yes and no. After going to the requiem and seeing what the engine means to the town, I would love to make her reentrance into their lives something special. But it's going to mean keeping her location under wraps for a little longer—if you'll all agree. After that, after Wildwood is opened first to the community, I think—I mean I can almost see it—"

"Spit it out, Murse. We're with ya!" Holden's infectious grin warmed her heart and gave her courage to speak the dream aloud.

"I want to make Wildwood into a theatre. An outdoor forest theatre, with torches and an orchestra and all the magic you used to watch from the trees, Rusty."

Rusty kicked a pinecone, looking around.

"And Cracker Jacks at the concession stand," Mercy said, pressing on. There was no turning back now. "Gala level, but with touches of sheer delight. To bring people back to their youth and sweep them into an enchanted world all at once. Lights, a velvet runway, but in the forest— like a theatre in the round! Only a theatre in the ground. Would people catch that play on words? Or is it too . . . ?" She waved the thought off. "Doesn't matter. But if we charged by the ticket, and spread the play over three nights, instead of three acts all at once, they'd fill up the hotel, the boardinghouse. Some might even camp if we made it glamorous enough. I know something about glamorous camping, too, from our time in the Congo." She elbowed Holden.

"Glamorous camping is an oxymoron," Rusty said.

"Perhaps. But it has a future. Trust me."

"Trust her," said Holden.

"Oriental rugs on the ground, cots with fine linens, and suddenly a rudimentary tent feels like a lovely extravagant novelty to someone who's never camped before. We could fill a whole clearing with a city of tents. I could cook the beans Clark gobbled up on *Embargo*. I made those myself!"

"I never saw . . ." Rusty said.

"Neither did I," Holden said.

"I recall," said Mercy, with a smirk. "But Clark said he could die a happy man. From beans!"

The sun dipped below the ridgeline then, and Holden looked up. "Speaking of camping," he said, "where can a fella get a room for a night or twelve?"

"Twelve?" Mercy asked.

"I like it here," Holden said. "I can't work for another month, and Mother's always off at her bridge club—"

"Mother?" Rusty whispered to Mercy.

"That's right, bridge club," Holden said in response to whatever whisper he thought he'd heard. He caught Rusty's eye with a knowing look. "They really do love their bridges."

Rusty laughed, and Holden tilted his head at her, puzzled. She clapped her mouth shut and raised her eyebrows at Mercy in silent question. *That wasn't a joke?*

"How 'bout I take you over to Miss Ellen's boardinghouse?" Casey offered. "See if she has a room."

Mercy smiled at this, pleased at the thought of Holden Huxley taking his place at a table of miners. He'd stick out like a sore thumb and fit right in all at once. That was the paradox of Holden Huxley.

"And if she's full up," Rusty said, "maybe you could try Priscilla Murdock's." She said this with wide eyes and an air of great innocence, as if she were planting another stray cat on Miss Murdock's front step.

Mercy thought of Miss Murdock, who faced the canned peas forward just so on the shelf every time she came in. *"There's a particular way . . ."* she would murmur, looking sweetly pleased at the end result.

Pairing her with the forty-year-old child that was Holden Huxley, who needed near-constant supervision to save him from himself, might just be a perfect match.

Casey gave a friendly wave as the men sauntered off, and Mercy returned it—until she saw that he was looking at Rusty, who . . . could it be? Blushed!

"Is that guy real?" Rusty whispered, watching as Holden picked up a pinecone, tossed it in the air, and gave it a *crack* with a stick. "He seems like a lost puppy."

"That's the thing about Holden. His life is one long string of scripts. A thousand parts played. He can play a leading man with all the gravitas, sincerity, and wisdom in the world . . . but inside, he's an eternal boy, raised by the studio, with every need met before he has time to think it. So, in a sense, no, he's not real. And yet . . ." Mercy smiled. "You couldn't ask for a more genuine soul. He truly is as he seems. He'd give the shirt off his back for a stranger on the street. And then he'd swagger right down to wardrobe and pluck another silk shirt off the rack and toss it on, completely oblivious that it's likely a fifty-dollar shirt."

"I bet you could buy a fifty-dollar shirt at the drop of a hat, Spatts," Rusty said as Mercy led the way to their camp.

"Well, that's the thing . . . and what makes the whole idea of the forest theatre both a challenge and a necessity." She winced. "I don't have any money. I mean—I have some savings, but they're frozen at the moment—a misunderstanding. But for now . . . I haven't got enough to finish fixing this place up to the extent I'm imagining. But cleaning up Wildwood feels somehow right. The restoration of something time has laid waste to . . ."

She glanced at Rusty, uncertain whether to say more. "It feels like Wildwood should belong to the town, too. After it—or its owner— was the cause of so much pain for so many of them. But on a practical level—and correct me if I'm wrong—couldn't the town use the business a theatre might bring? The lodgers, people shopping in the stores? It's so quiet there most days. And with so many of the mines shuttering and nobody visiting . . ." She shook her head. "I see the way people pinch their pennies in the mercantile. They don't show it, Rusty, but they're hurting. They don't want to leave, but how will they be able to stay if this keeps on?"

"Don't you speak that question aloud down there in the village," Rusty said. "They all know it, and they walk around under the cloud of it every single day, doing their best to ignore it. The second someone speaks it aloud, the sky'll fall. And we only have a few square miles of sky here, what with the canyon walls reaching up to frame it. Don't do it."

"I won't. We don't have to. We can get them in on the solution without pounding the problem into them until they despair. We'll need everyone involved to pull this off. And for those who are still worried I'm some sort of Gilman relative, come to hold things over their head, maybe it would put them at ease."

"All that just by opening up Wildwood, eh?" Rusty said.

"By giving the Goose a grand welcome back party and inviting every one of them. Giving them an enchanting night of their own to help them catch the vision." Mercy took a breath at last. The idea was out there—and all the more daunting for having been spoken aloud.

She looked around. Above them, the wind blew through a stand of aspens. In the distance, Mercy Peak pointed at the sky, and wisps of snow blew off it in streaks, releasing the work left by a storm months ago. Sun dappled through clouds, spotlighting crevices and crags, patches of green evergreens.

"Wildwood Forest Theatre," she said. "What do you think? Will it fly?"

As she awaited Rusty's response, she realized how much hung on this moment. Rusty knew this place well. If anyone knew what would work here and what wouldn't, it was her.

But more than that, she realized, she longed for the vote of confidence from her truest friend.

At last, Rusty spoke. "If anyone can make that idea come to life," she said, "it's you, Marybeth. Spatts is strong, remember?"

CHAPTER 19

Rusty

Rusty nearly hadn't stayed. She didn't know how much more of the foundation shaking she could take. It seemed to happen in abundance in Marybeth's presence. And the campout . . . it opened something raw in her. The promise they would've shared on Rusty's wedding eve, which would never happen now.

But this blasted unraveling inside of her . . . Every time she tried to hang on to the old bitterness at being abandoned for so long and so entirely, she saw it in Marybeth's eyes: Her friend had grieved, too. Rusty wasn't the only one who'd traversed the last decade over a sea of loss. In the irony of ironies, Marybeth was the only one on the face of the planet who could understand what it felt like to have your pen pal best friend ripped away suddenly, inexplicably, and seemingly forever.

You can't ignore a bond like that. So, she'd gone off to the cabin with the promise of returning soon with a few supplies. When she came back, Marybeth had heated a skillet of corn bread over the fire.

"Is that nutmeg?" Rusty asked, settling down on a rock beside the campfire.

"Secret recipe," Marybeth said with a wink.

They ate in shared quiet, the air punctuated by the occasional fish leaping in the lake, the steady lap of waves, the evening song of the birds.

After they were done, Marybeth gathered the food supplies into bits of cheesecloth tied with twine. As if it was nothing, she slung a rope over two trees and hauled the bucket into the air. A sky-born pantry, away from the reach of bears.

"You're full of surprises," Rusty said, standing to help secure the ends of the rope.

"This?" Marybeth looked up at the bucket. "We spent some time filming in the High Sierra a few years back. This was my favorite part."

"Not smiling for the cameras and landing on magazine covers?"

"Not on your life." Marybeth laughed.

"I saw some magazines at Miss Murdock's. She pulled out a whole collection, you know. Let me see, what did they say . . . ? *Windsor Walks on Air.* Oh, and my favorite: *20,000 Leagues of Her Own: Star of Verne Adaptation Soars to New Heights as She Delves into the Sea.*"

Marybeth cringed.

"It's strange," Rusty said. "Seeing your face on that magazine and knowing you were the one who wrote me all those letters. Back when I was the only one who knew Marybeth Spatts."

Marybeth toed a pebble, lifting it into the water and watching its ripples. "I daresay you still are the only one." She shivered a little, stepping closer to the fire. "What do you make of the new riddle?" Marybeth asked, changing the subject. "Any idea what mine we should be looking for? I've been trying to remember the names I've seen on the map in the mercantile."

Rusty blew out her cheeks. "It depends. Martin Shaw spent time working most of the mines around here: Tomboy, Camp Bird, Lewis mine. He spent time in Gilcrest, too, which surprised everybody. Gilman was already distancing himself from his boyhood friends and had been for a long time, ever since the avalanche. And in each mine, there are names for the tunnels, hoists, drifts—"

"Drifts?"

"Yes, they're the tunnels that run horizontally along the base of a hill."

"As in . . . 'drift with no snow'?" Marybeth sat forward, her face aglow in firelight.

Rusty snapped to attention. "'Lightning, no sky . . .'" She let out an astonished laugh. "Lightning Drift."

"Is that one of the tunnels?" Mercy asked. "Where is it?"

"Inside the Gilcrest mine." She pointed past the village, deeper into the mountain range. "Handful of miles up that way, and then back down the other side a smidge. Maybe ten miles, all told?"

Mercy pulled back. "Ten miles?" And then pasted on a smile. "Well, what's ten miles for Spatts and Bright Adventure Company? It'll be nothing by the morning light. Or—afternoon light. I do have to work tomorrow morning. Would you be up for meeting up after that?"

"Wild horses couldn't stop me."

They retired into the boathouse, where two canoes were tied in place, bobbing gently on the water. They spread their bedrolls out onto the pillows that had already been placed in the boats.

"You're something else, Spatts," said Rusty, sitting in her canoe-bed. "For all the places I've slept, all over this mountain, I can't say I've ever slept on the lake. I thought I'd done it all . . . and you tromp into this valley, snap your fingers, and show me there's a whole other world I've never even thought of."

"I had a good friend once who taught me how to think outside the box."

Rusty lay still for a while, and Marybeth, too . . . but sleep was nowhere near. She drummed her fingers on her stomach and finally blurted out the question that had been following Marybeth around like a ghost. She wasn't going to answer it until someone dragged—er, invited—it from her.

"How come you left Hollywood, anyway?" Rusty said.

Silence, as the waves lapped. She waited, hoping it might stretch the invitation. And finally, Marybeth started to speak, telling of a world stranger than Rusty even imagined.

CHAPTER
20

Some days live forever in your mind, Rusty, no matter how you
try to forget.

—Marybeth, age 14

Mercy

February 1948
Building 9, Pinnacle Studios

The paper of Wilson P. Wilson's letter was growing soft from Mercy's
reading and rereading. But his words cut like a knife: *Just play your part.*

The soundstage buzzed with life. Mercy looked out at the sea of
people of every age, dressed in the medieval peasantry of France and
thrumming with unharnessed energy that, once "Roll film!" was cried,
would bring a bygone era to life.

Just play your part.

Where were his assurances of her being a standout? Where was his
promise that he'd make her something to remember? She closed her
eyes, and for a moment saw in his words not anger, but fear.

Wilson P. Wilson, monarch of Hollywood . . . was afraid.

And in reaction, he lashed out at her—and put children in harm's
way. What of *their* fear? What of *their* lives?

Negligible, he called the risk.

Maybe his building was negligible, amid his empire. But were the
people?

"Places, everyone!" the director shouted, clapping. Amid the scurry
of bodies, out of the corner of her eye, she spotted it: the dark scuttle
of a rat, edging the room and fleeing the set, out into broad daylight.

Her stomach flipped.

"The rats know when somethin's comin','" they'd said at Pa's mine.

Her words had choked up in her young throat, back then, and they'd been lodged there ever since.

Well, it was time to let them out.

"Roll film!"

"Spatts is strong," Mercy murmured.

"Cut! Line?" the director shouted.

The line coach adjusted her glasses, pointed at the script with a pencil, and looked at Mercy. "You're supposed to say, 'One life is all we have. To surrender what you are and live without belief . . . that's more terrible than dying.'"

But Mercy's mind was skipping around the script, pulling bits from Joan's words. "Go forward bravely. Fear nothing. Trust in God; all will be well."

"No," the line coach said. "That was an earlier scene. 'One life is all we have . . .' You know it. You had this down yesterday."

"I am not afraid; I was born to do this," Mercy said, standing.

"No, no, that's the next scene." The woman shook her head in frustration. "Do you need a break?" She turned to the director. "Could we get a break? Five minutes, she'll be fine."

"We're already behind schedule. We need this scene before the kids are off the backlot." He muttered curses at new regulations imposed by the current tutor of the studio's child actors. He pulled at his shirt several times. "Is it hotter than usual in here? Fine. Five minutes. Where are the extras?" He began to count children. "One . . . two . . . three . . ." He paused at an empty place. "Where's Girl Thirteen?"

Mercy sat on the edge of her seat, narrowing her eyes. Who was missing? She ticked off the names mentally and knew it right away—Tabitha Greer, with her wider-than-a-mile grin.

"Tabitha," she whispered.

"Thirteen! Where's Thirteen? Criminy." He slammed his clipboard on a chair and planted his fists.

Mercy spun on her heel and headed straight for the faux cave made of plaster. She knelt on hands and knees, and crawled inside. "Tabitha?"

"Miss Mercy!"

"What are you doing in here?"

Tabitha held out her fairy book, grinning and displaying a hole where her wiggly front tooth had been yesterday.

"Come on out, you goose." Mercy pasted on a smile. Tabitha scurried out after her, and the director pulled her up from the ground.

"Time's up. Get makeup over here. Plaster dust."

"We need to evacuate the building," Mercy said as an assistant touched up her face.

"Pardon?" He flipped a paper on his clipboard.

"We need to get everyone out. Now."

"Cute, kid. Right as we're filming the pinnacle scene. We gotta get this wrapped yesterday."

"The rats are running. The film stored in this building is unstable. Something's—" Mercy heaved a sigh. She sounded crazy, she knew. But she wasn't going to make the same mistake twice. "Something catastrophic is going to happen."

"Places, everyone!"

Mercy mounted the steps where she was supposed to give Joan's speech.

Lights. Camera. Action.

"Everyone," Mercy said, meeting the eyes of every actor, every person on set that she could, "get out. It is not safe in Building 9. You are in imminent danger."

"Cut! What's this?" the director said.

"Believe me or don't," Mercy said. "But I will not be filming."

And she walked out.

What could they do without the title role actress?

She made her way through a sea of gawking faces, uneasy murmurs, and angry tirades.

Outside, she watched from behind a tree as the building released a slow trickle of befuddled people. Searching for one face in particular . . . to no avail.

The sherbet-orange sun of Los Angeles sank low in the sky, behind the water tower. And when Mercy knew the building was empty, she stole back inside.

She searched the sets: the village street, the palace court, the battlefield, and the cave. "Tabitha?" she shouted, desperation crawling up her spine. "Tabbie?"

There was movement down the corridor, outside the sets. She ran toward it, tripping over a pile of lumber, falling flat on her palms and staring at the *Legacy Timber* logo stamped upon the beams that would be turned into sets . . . or go up in flames.

She smelled smoke.

The wrong kind of smoke. Not that of a rustic campfire or a warm hearth. This was the acidic, volatile smoke that pulled at the recesses of her mind. The same chemical smoke that lingered for days after the mine explosion.

Poisonous.

She was up, running. Yelling the girl's name. Screaming it. "Tabbie!" Rounding a corner. "Tabbie? Tabitha!"

Flames licked beneath the door to the film vault. Her heart slammed to her stomach. She couldn't be in there. Could she?

Placing her palms on the metal door, she retracted them quickly as the heat seared and her screaming morphed to sobbing—*Tabitha Greer!* She rammed the door with a two-by-four. "Give her up," she said, pulling in a ragged breath. Coughing it back out. *Give her up. Give. Her—*

The wood felt heavy, suddenly. A sound behind her, as the sprinklers started their pitifully weak rain. She turned—and there was Tabitha. Coughing. Hair in wet strings, falling over her face.

"Miss Mercy?" she said.

Mercy scooped that girl up with a strength she'd never known. Plowed her way through the passageways of black smoke into a darkness she'd imagined a thousand times down in that mine. Moving blindly, determined, ready to give up everything in order to burst at last through the door, into the spinning night.

Into the accusations.

Into the lies.

And into freedom . . . never to return again.

CHAPTER 21

Rusty

Rusty awoke to the sound of a whimper and sat up straight. That darn cat. She cursed the day she brought that thing home. She turned over, trying to get back to sleep, and it sounded again.

Distinctly less catlike.

The grog of sleep dripped away. She was in a boat. On the lake. With Marybeth Spatts in the next boat over . . .

And Marybeth was the one who'd cried out.

Rusty sat up. "Marybeth?" she whispered.

She was lying still, under the cover of silver moonlight. Rusty could only make out a vague silhouette, and it shifted a little as the same sound came again. Her slight form shivered.

You let those tears come, Marybeth Spatts, Rusty had once told her in a letter. Marybeth had confided how she wouldn't cry in front of her pa, because he insisted that Spattses were strong, and they didn't cry. That when the going got tough, they got tougher. Rusty had been so mad at that. Who said crying wasn't strong, too? She hadn't cried for Sam . . . but that was different. A different sort of strong. At least that's what she told herself.

Maybe it made sense that Marybeth had gone into acting. She'd had enough practice all her life long. A pang shot through Rusty's heart.

She had an extra blanket rolled up beside her. She'd brought it from home, smuggled it into the boat after Marybeth was already asleep, feeling as if it made sense to have it here tonight of all nights.

She stared at it, torn. Thought of the hand it had come from. The extraordinary kindness those hands had born, always. The world hadn't deserved him.

She leaned over the edge of her boat, careful not to rock Marybeth's. How was she going to keep from scaring her out of her skin? Clear her throat? Toss the blanket at her and quickly pretend to be asleep, hope she didn't notice?

Rusty was suddenly paralyzed. She'd never been good at this kind of thing. Give her a lock to pry open, a lizard to chase down, and she was your girl. But these sorts of delicate situations, where the hurts at hand were buried deep inside people and couldn't be fixed by giving it a good spit-and-wipe . . .

"Give them up" came the tear-soaked words, muffled in unmistakable tones of sleep.

She was *asleep* and crying?

Wonderful.

But she knew those words. She knew right where her friend was, caught in a nightmare that had held her captive far too long. Did it still keep her prisoner, as it had when they were young? Or was it brought on by the story she had just shared?

A shiver traversed the sleeping form again, and Rusty broke past her paralysis. She let her hand hover in indecision a moment before finally setting one on Marybeth's shoulder, in hopes of stilling the spirit that battled within her. And in that light touch, the shock of familiarity shot through Rusty. This posture—this holding of every muscle clenched, shoulders stiff, and bones pointy . . . this, she knew. Though her friend was warm and breathed, though she certainly lived, this was a fragile way of living. Like walking on ice and knowing it might crack beneath you and give way at any moment.

She let her hand linger on Marybeth, and at length her muscles began to ease, like a slow exhale that had been years in coming. Marybeth drew in a shuddering breath, reaching out and clutching her blanket so hard. As if she were a girl again, digging her fingernails into the dark soil. "Give them up," she said, a fresh tear running down her cheek.

Tears pricked Rusty's own eyes, a wave of warmth spreading inside her. She shoved it down. Forget that crying could be strong; it was for other people. Not her. She'd made that mistake in the plum orchard, thinking she was safe—only to have Casey Campbell witness her at her most broken.

"I don't know what to do," she whispered. To Marybeth. To herself. To God.

Should she wake her? Leave her asleep in this nightmare? But would it be worse to have her awake and find her tears had been witnessed?

Lifting her hand, she unfolded the blanket and held it out, ready to lay over her friend. Navy blue, with crisscrossing yellow lines of plaid. The one Sam had spread out as a picnic blanket so long ago.

A flash memory of his smile, that boyish grin that could steal any heart, made her close her eyes. Pull the blanket close to her heart, where something somewhere still beat, against all odds.

Her two dearest friends had been ripped from her. Her heart had borne the wounds, folded over on itself for knowledge that the second she unfolded, she'd bleed out.

And yet . . .

One of those friends had been returned to her.

A whole lot more stubborn and famous than before, but still . . .

Marybeth wasn't the only one who could be stubborn. In an act of sheer defiance over the prickly Rusty the world now knew, she opened up her arms, unfolding the blanket.

And with it . . . something inside of her unfolded, too.

Marybeth's form released a shivering sigh, her white-knuckled grip released the dark soil of the nightmare, and she stilled. Her breathing slowing, deepening.

Everything inside Rusty was a mess of a tangle or a tangle of a mess, she didn't know which. Likely both. It hurt. She might well bleed out, just like she'd feared.

But as she watched the slumbering form of her long-ago friend rise and fall in peaceful rest, something of that peace found its way inside of her, too.

* * *

"Get back, you fiend!"

Rusty sprang from her boat-bed, squinting through morning spears of light. Marybeth's boat was empty, not a sign of the girl or the plaid blanket. Rusty ran to the edge of the boathouse and around to the beach, expecting to see Marybeth facing down a bear.

There she was, one hand drawn up and over her head dramatically like she was in a sword fight, and the other arm extended, holding out a stick in place of a sword. Pointing it at . . . a raven.

Rusty snickered. She couldn't help it. Marybeth had surprisingly good form. She watched with growing respect and perhaps too much amusement as Marybeth parried and jabbed with a bird.

She noticed Rusty and startled, dropping the stick and blushing in a way that gratified Rusty greatly.

"Oh, I, um—I just—" She stooped and grabbed the stick again, pointing it at the bird that was doggedly going about its business, picking up the remnants of a biscuit that evidently had been dropped in the skirmish.

Rusty raised her eyebrows, smiling as she waited for Marybeth to untie her tongue, which only flustered her more.

"What *is* that thing? I didn't read anything about oversized crows in *Fearsome Creatures of the Lumberwoods*. Is it a mutant of some kind?"

"Yes. It is the vicious mountain mutant commonly known as a *raven*."

Marybeth looked askance. "That's not a raven. I've seen a raven."

"That's a raven," Rusty said with a shrug.

"That is the King Kong of ravens."

"The what?"

Marybeth shook her head, her perfectly curled hair looking not-so-perfect after sleeping in a boat and fencing with a mountain beast. "It's a movie about a giant gorilla who can demolish buildings with his sheer strength," she said. "It's"—she shook her stick at the blissfully unaware bird—"that."

"You come from a strange world," Rusty said, laughing.

"So you've said."

"Where'd you learn to swashbuckle like that? Were you secretly a pirate, and never told me?"

Marybeth looked sheepishly at her stick and then tossed it over the creek like a javelin. "Oh, that . . ." she said, blushing again. "It, um . . . well, it actually was a pirate movie. Anyway," she rushed on, quickly changing the subject. "How did you sleep?"

"Like usual," Rusty said. Which was true enough; Rusty rarely slept well. But Marybeth was awfully chipper for someone who'd spent the night crying in her sleep.

Rusty skimmed the ground, looking for the blanket, feigning nonchalance. Marybeth's haversack hung from the tree trunk by a nail. A stack of freshly split firewood was neatly stacked and formed a boundary wall to the camp, and the axe stuck in another log, awaiting its next use.

"You did that?" Rusty said, respect in her tone.

"You're not the only one who can swing an axe," Marybeth said with a smile as she poked the embers of a campfire and stooped to flip something in a skillet.

"And is that . . . bacon?" It smelled familiar but foreign. Salty but strange.

"In a manner of speaking," Marybeth said.

"What's that mean?"

She reached behind a rock and pulled out an empty blue rectangular can with bright yellow letters spelling *SPAM*.

Rusty recoiled. "Canned meat? Is it even meat? What *is* it?"

"What is SPAM . . . ?" Marybeth said philosophically, as if Rusty had inquired after the meaning of life. "That is the question of the ages. We lived off it for a month while filming in the Congo, so I learned a trick or two. You'll find I am a treasure trove of mostly useless skills, Rusty. But this one actually came in handy!" The bloom on her cheeks bespoke pride. "It's not bad, really." She sliced off a bit with the spatula, waited for it to cool, then offered it to Rusty. She reached out warily and put it in her mouth.

"Blech," Rusty said, spitting it out, kicking dust over it, and looking in horror at the skillet. "Sorry," she said, regret filling her at Marybeth's crestfallen look. "Maybe it's an acquired taste? Something for the Hollywood elite?"

"It's not that bad," Marybeth said. "Is it?" She sliced off a piece and ate it, tilting her head back and forth as if to say *Not bad at all!* and then repeated the process, tossing the King Kong raven a piece.

"Have you no pity?" Rusty said, aghast. "That thing doesn't deserve . . . *that*."

The bird hopped happily over, released a grating *caw!*, pecked at it once . . . twice . . . gave it a sideways glance with its beady yellow eye, and alighted swiftly into the air.

"You'll never be bothered by that bird again," Rusty said dryly. "I think you found the true purpose of SPAM."

Marybeth looked stunned, shifting her glance between the frying pan and the place in the bright blue sky where the bird had vanished.

A distant and mournful *caw* echoed from afar, and the space between them erupted in laughter.

Marybeth nodded her defeat. "Well," she said, "if I can't interest you in SPAM, at least let me thank you for this." She stooped and picked up a carefully folded blanket, sun glinting off the yellow threads. Rusty's jaw twitched, and she held her hands stiff at her sides.

Marybeth's eyes pooled. When Rusty still didn't move, Marybeth held it out tentatively. "This was his," she said, more a statement than a question.

Rusty swallowed hard, her answer clear. Marybeth nodded, fixing her eyes on the carefully folded wool. "I remember," she said. "About the picnic. The plaid blanket . . ."

Rusty swallowed harder. Shrugged. "We like our plaid up here."

"Like sunshine in the night," Marybeth said seriously. Offering the words like small gifts, each one wrapped in care. "That's what he said you were. And you said he was . . ."

Too good to be forgotten.

Marybeth spoke the words, and Rusty squeezed her eyes closed. She didn't know what to do about her memories living inside someone else's heart. She had no control there over keeping them buried. Marybeth could up and talk about them any second she chose. Summoning things long dead back to life.

And yet somehow, tucked deep inside her ire about it all, there was this grain of stubborn gratitude. To have someone else be a keeper of the things you held dearest felt safe. Scary, but safe. Dad had told her that about Marybeth, after the mining accident altered her pa so. *"You stick around for that girl,"* he'd said. *"Sometimes being a friend means being a keeper of their treasure in the times they can't hold onto it. You'll give it back to her one day, all the good things she's missing."*

"Thank you," Marybeth said, sliding her hand off Rusty's, leaving her warmth behind. She stepped back and clasped her hands in front of her, the picture of innocence. "For lending it to me," she said. "I must have been causing a disturbance last night."

"You're a ruckus-rouser alright," Rusty said, offering a half smile, to which Marybeth gave a weak laugh.

"Was I . . . talking in my sleep?"

"Somethin' like that," Rusty said. "About the miners, I think."

Marybeth nodded, her cheeks tingeing pink. "I'm sorry."

"Sometimes things sneak up on us," she said with a shrug. "Just how it goes. I'm starting to think when they do, we'd best turn around and shake hands with them, not just stuff them back in hiding. Nothing to be sorry for, Marybeth. Not one thing."

Marybeth's eyes sheened, looking so blue they were almost violet. "Well." She inhaled and drew back her shoulders. "Thank you, Rusty. I mean it."

They stood a moment, the silence unsettled. Marybeth looked around, and then up. Rusty looked around, and then down. They both looked at each other, then away.

"This is strange," Rusty said at last.

Marybeth let out a relieved breath. "Oh, I'm so glad you said it. It's *so* strange."

Rusty laughed. "Sort of like our ink knew each other, and our papers knew each other's hands, and I guess our hearts knew each other . . . but here we are, enfleshed and all."

Marybeth raised a finger. "And alive!"

"Resurrected from ten years of dead and gone," Rusty said, and for the first time, was able to laugh about the ridiculousness of that. "You know, you do have a flair for the dramatic. You really thought I was dead?"

Marybeth's laughter dropped away. "Nothing else could've kept me from being here. I mean it."

The words made sense. The circumstances were starting to. But Rusty's heart . . . it was going to take some time for it to understand, down to its depths. "Thank you for that," she said. "And I mean it, too. Now, speaking of strange, should we go track down a treasure or whatever on earth is hidden in that mine?"

"Yes." Marybeth dipped a bucket into the lake and sloshed water over the fire. "I've been thinking. That vow you told me about, the four boys . . ."

"The Blood Moon Boys," Rusty said ominously.

"Whatever happened to them? Did they just . . . drift apart? How does a bond like that get shattered? They can't have our excuse."

Rusty shook her head. "Something happened," she said. "Some kind of accident, long before I was born. All I know is Dad clammed up whenever the name of Reuben Murdock was mentioned. Reuben took himself away up into the mountains, became a hermit in the truest sense. Sometimes Dad would try to go see him, but he always came back silent and defeated and never would tell me what happened. They keep a chair for him still, by the fire in the mercantile. Just in case. That's the thing about Mercy Peak . . . they don't give up on you. Not even if it takes a lifetime."

"Is that what they did for you? After—after Sam?"

For months, folks had left casseroles on her porch. Knocked on her door, even when she'd refused to answer. There'd been bouquets of roses from Willa's garden. A stack of books to read—and a portrait of a cat—from Priscilla Murdock. Fresh-caught fish, bigger than you could shake a stick at, and Kurt and Angus trying to tiptoe away down the path as they bumped and elbowed one another.

And still Rusty had stayed away.

Mercy Peak had done its best to bring her back . . . but somehow, Rusty was only just now beginning to breathe again.

MERCY PEAK

A Screenplay in Three Acts

ACT II
SCENE 2: THE FIRST ARRIVAL

CUT TO MONTAGE MATCHING THE BELOW: A GLACIER CALVING.
TIME-LAPSE OF STORMING CLOUDS. MARYBETH, BACK TO
CAMERA, LOOKING SMALL AGAINST THE BACKDROP OF A STEAM
TRAIN.

NARRATOR

> Every day, astounding things are born with
> not a soul to know or see.

> A behemoth glacier at the top of the world
> might calve, shearing masses of ice into
> the ocean below with thunderous force. An
> iceberg is born—seaworthy mountain, fierce
> and formidable, setting waves into motion
> that will cross the world.

> The tiniest particle of water might move
> about in the womb of a cloud, and another
> and another, until their airborne dance
> sparks a force so fierce it warms, jolts to
> life, electric. A storm is born—water to
> light, searing and surreal.

223

A girl might summon every bit of courage
she has, come up short, and board a cross-
country train anyway. A pilgrim is born,
timid but true.

STEAM FLOODS THE PLATFORM AND SHE HESITATES, BOARDS
TRAIN. MONTAGE SHOWING SCENERY CHANGING FROM TRAIN,
MARKING HER PROGRESS ACROSS WOODS, PLAINS, AND
MOUNTAINS.

Our pilgrim is Marybeth Spatts. Exiled late
into the night, the voice of a tormented
father turning its torment on her.

Warned again and again by a faraway friend
that she would be poisoned by the man's
cruelty, in the end it was not she who
perished that night, but the man himself, at
his bitter end. She saw him buried . . . and
boarded a train.

An iceberg. A storm. A pilgrim. Each birthed
in isolated obscurity . . . and each sending
off ripples in their worlds, the universe
forever changed.

The final leg of her journey finds her
aboard Galloping Goose Number Eight. In the
locked cargo compartment behind her sits
a single bag of mail. She wonders if she
should have sent her own letter, to forewarn
her friend of her coming. Her friend, who'd
known her own loss after Silas Bright
succumbed to a winter sickness and left his
seat at the table far too empty. Marybeth
Spatts caught her friend's tears from afar
that year, and in return received a promise:
I'll save Dad's seat for you.

CUT TO MERCY PEAK DEPOT (EXTERIOR).

MARYBETH SPATTS, 19, STEPS OFF GALLOPING GOOSE MOTOR
NO. 8, CLUTCHING CARPETBAG. SHE STANDS UPON A PLANK IN
THE BOARDWALK WHERE TWO KNOTS MEET, GNARLED AND WORN

BY TIME. SHE PLACES HER FEET AROUND THEM AND SMILES—
SHE KNOWS THIS SPOT, THOUGH SHE'S NEVER BEEN HERE.

BEHIND HER, PHINNEAS TRENT, DRIVER, LEANS OVER IN THE
CAB, WHITE HAIR DISHEVELED FROM THE OPEN-WINDOWED
JOURNEY, MOUSTACHE GROOMED INTO CAREFUL HANDLEBAR
CURLS.

PHINNEAS TRENT

    You sure you're alright, miss?

MARYBETH

    [turning, disoriented] Hmmm? Oh, yes, I . . .

    [trails off, a little lost]

PHINNEAS

    [looking concerned] Miss Ellen's your best
    bet for a good room and a hot meal. Check in
    at the mercantile. They can direct you.

    [spots man in bowler hat] No journey
    today, eh, Mr. Gilman? [Mr. Gilman appears
    distracted]

MR. GILMAN

    [realizes he's being watched, puts a
    polished smile on] Not today, Mr. Trent. But
    you'll be staying through for this evening,
    yes?

PHINNEAS

    Yes, sir. I wouldn't miss—

WOMAN IN SIMPLE BLACK MOURNING DRESS CROSSES THE ROAD
IN THE VILLAGE, CLUTCHING HAND OF YOUNG GIRL. PHINNEAS
CATCHES HIMSELF AND NODS TOWARD THEM, AS IF THAT
COMPLETES HIS UNFINISHED SENTENCE.

MR. GILMAN NODS IN UNDERSTANDING, REMOVING HIS HAT
AND HOLDING IT TO HIS CHEST. MARYBETH LIFTS A HAND TO

ATTEMPT TO ASK A STRANGER FOR DIRECTIONS BUT NOTICES
THE STRANGER IS CLOTHED IN BLACK MOURNING GARB, AND
SHE RETRACTS HER HAND.

STRANGER MOVES DOWN PLATFORM AND INTO THE VILLAGE.
MARYBETH FOLLOWS, TAKING IN THE SIGHTS. SHE SPOTS THE
MERCANTILE, A RED-BRICK VICTORIAN BUILDING, AND GOES
INSIDE.

A MAN STANDS AT THE POST OFFICE WINDOW TO THE RIGHT,
WITH A TEENAGER, THEIR RESEMBLANCE STRONG. THE YOUNGER
MAN LOOKS STIFF AND APPREHENSIVE.

MR. JENKS

[hopeful] Any letter for us today, Angus?

ANGUS PIKE

'Fraid Phinneas hasn't brought in today's
mail yet . . . but don't you worry, young
man [directed at young Hudson Jenks]. Mail
often comes when you least expect it. Tell
you what. You come back later, after the—
[struggles]—the funeral. I'll aim to have
today's mail sorted before I leave for
that. You come back tonight, and we'll take
another look.

MR. JENKS

Mighty kind of you, but today's not a day
to go concerning yourself with that. [gives
a solemn nod, pats son, who is taller than
him, on shoulder]

MARYBETH WATCHES, FEELING CONSPICUOUS. SOMETHING IS
CLEARLY GOING ON HERE, SOMETHING TO WHICH SHE IS AN
INTRUDER. SHE EXITS THE STORE AND BUMPS INTO A BLOND
WOMAN, ABOUT FIFTY YEARS OLD, WHO IS LOOKING AT THE
SKY, HAND TO HEART.

MARYBETH

I'm—I'm so sorry. Are you alright?

226

WOMAN (WILLA JONES)

> [stumbling, righting herself] I'll be fine,
> don't you worry.

> You don't grow up in these parts without the
> wind toppling you a time or two. [laughs]
> Not that you're the wind, of course. [looks
> at Marybeth for first time] Oh—but are *you*
> alright? You're pale as a ghost.

MARYBETH

> [raises a hand to her cheek] I've . . . just
> had a long journey. [smiles weakly] But
> maybe you can help . . . I'm looking for
> Rusty Bright?

WILLA

> [smile freezes, solemnity taking over] Oh
> dear . . . you must be here for the funeral.

MARYBETH

> [stiffly] The—the funeral?

WILLA

> [looking at Marybeth with concern and takes
> her hand]

> Rusty told me once about a friend back east.
> . . . [shakes head]

> Oh dear. Words cannot express my sorrow.

> Such a loss—such a beloved soul.

> [struggles to contain emotion]

> Forgive me, I'm always getting ahead of
> myself . . . [voice fades out to indicate
> Marybeth's hearing becoming muddied in shock]

WOMAN KEEPS SPEAKING, LOOKING CONCERNED, BUT MARYBETH
CAN'T HEAR. SHE STUMBLES BACKWARD, MUTTERING AN
APOLOGY, AND WALKS NUMBLY THROUGH THE TOWN.

CAMERA FOLLOWS HER, FADING IN AND OUT OF THE PRESENT
WALK THROUGH A MOUNTAIN VILLAGE, AND BACK TO VOICE
OVERS OF RUSTY'S LETTERS WITH FILM MONTAGE SHOWING THE
PAPERS OVERLAID.

RUSTY'S VOICE

    "You've got a home here, Marybeth Spatts."

    "Spatts, you've got grit. Don't listen to
    anyone who tells you otherwise."

    "Confetti will fly when you come!"

    "You're the sister I always wanted. God
    just gave you to me through paper and ink,
    instead of blood."

    "We'll stay at Whistler's Bridge when you
    come. . . ."

CAMERA SHOWS MARYBETH SITTING ON THE OVERLOOK OF THE
BIG MEADOW, EYES PULLED TO THE REACHES OF THE PEAKS
WHERE RUSTY ONCE RAN. THINKING OF HER OWN FATHER'S
GRAVE, WHICH SHE'S ONLY JUST LEFT. WANDERING THROUGH
THE TOWN AS NIGHT FALLS, SHE STOPS IN FRONT OF
WHISTLER'S BRIDGE, A COVERED BRIDGE OVER FALLS CREEK.
MUSIC FADES TO THE SOUND OF THE WATER.

NARRATOR

    Marybeth Spatts, on the brink of her life
    beginning at last, believed that all was
    lost. As the snow fell in spiraling drifts
    of confetti, she shivered there upon the
    bridge's boards. Meanwhile in the dark skies
    above, a single bag of mail took flight.
    Paper born of the earth, and the trees,
    the skies, and the seas, fluttering unseen
    in the cargo hold of a rail car . . . and
    keeping in their folds the fate of Mercy
    Peak.

Folio of Field Notes, Volume V:
Marybeth Becomes Mercy
(Who Becomes Marybeth)

[Property of Sudsy McGee, Hollywood Biographer]

AUDITION NOTES

Elitch's Zoological Gardens
FOR SEASON: Summer 1938
NAME: Marybeth Spatts
AGE: 19
HEIGHT: 5'4"

DICTION: Slight twang, could use for southern roles or coach it out of her, possibly some mid-Atlantic training.

PRESENCE: Unspoiled but savvy. Conveys a sense of lostness. Air of innocence at first, but looks as if she's seen a thing or two. Sort of a wide-eyed doe look. Cast as the female ingénue? Tragic heroine? Lacks grit. Do not cast for complex roles.

PAY: Trade for room, board, and help with elephants.

BLOOMS
(Brilliant Lexicon of the Original Marybeth Spatts)

ENTRY NO. 58

Grit

As copied from dictionary at Denver Public Library, reached by bicycle from the elephant house before rehearsal.

(1) From the Old English word **grēot** meaning gravel, earth, dust. In emerging connotation, can imply a certain resolve, courage, or mettle.

(2) Personal notes: Spatts is strong. Get some grit.

Letter from Pinnacle Studios Legal Department

1938

From: Pinnacle Studios Legal Department
To: Marybeth Spatts

Dear Miss Spatts,

Pursuant to our policies regarding fictitious names for use in credits, please review the enclosed documents. Wilson P. Wilson has suggested Mary Windsor as your fictitious name. If this meets with your approval, please sign the enclosed and return.

From: Wilson P. Wilson
To: Pinnacle Studios Legal Department

She's suggesting Mercy instead of Mary? Good gravy. What difference does it make? It's close enough. We've got to wrap this up and get filming. Let her have it. She'll likely be a flash in the pan anyway, and we just need a body in that role for the last silent film. On to a new era of cinema, where actors have voices!

Transcript from Edie Valentine Radio Hour, 1943

WCMP Radio, New York
WABC, New York

[Triumphant music plays]

> *Golden Flaxe, the only breakfast cereal to bring the crunch to
> brunch presents: The Edie Valentine Radio Hour!*

[Live audience applause, dramatic music plays]

> *Tonight, Edie Valentine comes to you live from our radio
> playhouse here in New York with a very special guest. Please
> welcome Edie as she hosts the star of Pinnacle Studios
> Technicolor classic,* The Italian Escape. *The queen of the silver
> screen, with the single tear that flooded the world . . . ladies and
> gentlemen, Mercy Windsor!*

[Applause, poignant music plays]

> *Edie Valentine:* Welcome, Miss Windsor, and thank you for gracing
> our studio with your presence tonight. I don't suppose you'd give
> us an early glimpse of your next film?
>
> *Mercy Windsor:* Thank you for having me, Miss Valentine—
>
> *EV:* Oh, Edie is just fine.
>
> *MW:* [a pause] Edie . . . thank you for such a warm welcome. I can't
> begin to tell you what it means to me to be here with you.
>
> *EV:* The feeling is mutual, I can tell you! And let me tell you
> something else: Your studio certainly likes to keep your fans
> on pins and needles. We've been in close contact, asking if we
> might coax you to give us a monologue, an excerpt from your
> next film, but they won't budge an inch. They want to keep your
> acting for the screen, it seems.

[Audience groans]

> *MW:* They do know the value of a surprise, that's certain. [laughs]
>
> *EV:* I'm happy to say we've found a work-around that even Pinnacle
> Studios cannot protest. You're permitted to give a performance
> . . . so long as it's musical. So we've reached into our archives
> to pull out an audience favorite, and I wonder if you might do

231

me the honor of singing one of the lines for me. This one right here?

MW: [leans over sheet music at piano, where Edie Valentine seats herself and begins introductory chords] "Dr—Dream a Little Dream"?

EV: Yes, that's the one. Lend us your voice, dear? We heard you sing in *Embargo*. Do you know the song?

MW: I—[voice hoarse] . . . I—that is, I'm not certain—

EV: [a flash of compassion, noticing a gleam in Mercy Windsor's eye] Perhaps another song? "God Bless America" or—

MW: [takes a deep breath and puts on a smile] The song you suggested should be sung, Miss Valentine. I don't know that my voice could ever carry its beauty. Might we sing together?

EV: A duet, with *the* Mercy Windsor? [hand to heart, then an arpeggio of notes] What does our audience think?

[Wild applause. Piano keys play, joined by strains of violin from orchestra.]

EV and MW: "Stars shining bright above you . . ."

Marybeth, age 11

Dear Rusty,

Help! My feet are stained! They're purple. Purple!

We got five whole buckets of blueberries, and I had to get 'em preserved quick because they turn fast sometimes. But Pa came home in one of his moods and didn't want any noise, said all my stirring and such was liable to wake the dead. I was so mad at him, Rusty. I was just trying to put something in the cupboard for once. So he'd have something to eat. I stood there as it got darker and thought, Is he going to yell at me worse for being hungry or for making noise to make him something so he won't be hungry? *I used to wonder what "caught between a rock and a hard place" meant. Now I know.*

I got so fired-up mad, Rusty. It didn't seem fair. I got to thinking I was so tired of tiptoeing around him, and then it struck me—tiptoes don't make much noise.

So I washed my feet the best I ever have. Five times, water so hot I could hardly stand it. Cleaner than most people's hands

*have ever been in their whole life. And then, I pulled two buckets
close to each other, put a foot in each one, and just walked in
place in them till the berries were good and mushed and ready
for jam.*

Go ahead, make a joke about toe jam, I know you want to.

*I imagined I was walking away. Down this hill, down the
road, over the prairies far beyond us, up into your mountains.
I did it with all the buckets. Put the sugar in and walked some
more over those bucketed blueberry fields.*

By the time I was ready to boil it all up, he was snoring good.

I made four whole big jars, Rusty.

*But now my feet are purple, all the way up to my ankles.
What do I do?*

Marybeth

Rusty, age 11

Dear Marybeth,

Hail, the blueberry queen! You are my hero.

*Miss Murdock, who has carefully catalogued every cleaning
trick ever discovered, ever, says to soak your feet in milk. It works
for removing berry stains from the finest and most delicate of
fabrics. She asked what the stain was on, and I didn't think you'd
want me telling the Bastion of Civility about your feet, so I just
said "something great." So, try milk.*

Rusty

**MERCY ME!
STARLET MERCY WINDSOR
LENDS HANDS AND FEET
TO PAVEMENT OF GRAUMAN'S
CHINESE THEATRE.**

1940—The lovely face behind the single tear that flooded
the world lit the Los Angeles sky this week with her
smile. Tuesday evening, celebrating the premier of *Chase*

> *the Wind*, she laid her hands and feet in the wet cement
> as photographers sparked the night with flashes and
> reporters clamored for a word from the rising queen of
> the silver screen. When asked whether she had any tips
> for the ladies from the owner of these now-famed feet,
> she paused, smiled as if imparting a true secret, and
> said, "Soak them in milk."

Letter from Academy
of Motion Picture Arts and Sciences

March 1, 1949

Dear Miss Windsor,

As you are aware, in the most recent years of the illustrious history of the Academy Awards, we were honored to do our part to contribute to the war effort by crafting our time-honored Oscar trophies out of plaster, rather than our usual solid bronze, and then adorning them with the sheen of gold paint, that you might hold your well-deserved award in your hands even in the midst of a metal shortage.

Now, as we enjoy victory after the war, we are pleased to invite you to allow us to replace your trophy with a finely cast bronze version. As soon as you're able, please have your plaster Oscar delivered to us, and your new trophy will be in your hands in short order, with all our congratulations on your past success.

Letter to the Academy

Dear Academy of Motion Pictures Arts and Sciences,

With gratitude, I thank you for your benevolent offer to replace the plaster trophy.

However, a trophy composed of minerals, sand, and cement seems to hold a certain . . . grit . . . beneath all that gleam. I find that rather inspirational, and the trophy—kept now in a place

234

of particular honor—is a testament to that. If it's all the same to
you, I'll respectfully decline your generous offer, and thank you
for your recognition of my past role in the honored tradition of
your award.

Sincerely,
~~Mercy Windsor~~
Marybeth Spatts

Pa's gone. And somehow with him . . . the last bit of anchor I ever knew. He wasn't perfect . . . but there was a strength to him, and it's snuffed out like a light. I feel lost . . . free-falling with nothing to break the fall. The past years were hard, but at least they gave me purpose. At least there was some sort of shape to who I was or what I was meant to do. Now . . . it's gone, in a flash, and I feel so formless, like I might just float away. I pray that somehow, Pa's soul might rest in eternity, free of the dark that gripped him all these years. As for me . . . I'm never setting foot near a mine again in my life.

—Marybeth Spatts, age 19

Mercy

"You want to what?" Jim Hovel of Gilcrest mine slammed his ledger down on the desk, rattling the rust-spotted *Mine Superintendent* sign perched there. He looked over his spectacles at Rusty.

They could've used Holden's smooth talking or Casey's easygoing camaraderie, but they were off checking some of the other mines, just in case.

That left Rusty and Mercy to try and find a way past the straightlaced Jim Hovel, who didn't look like he was about to let two women into his tightly run ship on a fanciful whim. Vest pressed and buttoned, boxes on his ledger checked twice, pipe laid in perfect parallel to the desk's edge. His hat hung with nary a speck of dust on the hook behind him, even as a blast from below sent a shiver through the walls and up Mercy's spine.

She pressed her eyes closed and braced her fingertips on the solid strength of the desk in front of them. This was a bad idea.

"It's alright," she said softly, opening her eyes and spreading as gracious a smile as she knew and looping her arm through Rusty's. "We'll find another way—"

Rusty leveled her with a look that said *really?*

And she was right. There was no other way to retrieve whatever on earth Martin Shaw had planted there.

"We just have to check something down there, Jim," said Rusty.

He raised a brow. "You have to check something."

"That's right." Rusty lifted her chin.

"Such as . . . ?"

Rusty's eyes shifted to the side, and she appeared stumped.

"That's what I thought," said the superintendent, standing and planting his fists on the desk to dismiss them. "You girls go on back. Trust me, you don't want to go belowground."

Rusty's face went white. "It's—it's about my dad," she said in a fluster.

Mr. Hovel froze, his stern countenance faltering as his moustache twitched.

"This mine's not been the same since Silas," he said and crossed his arms over his chest, assessing the two of them. "Don't think I can let you in the mine, but tell me what this is all about and maybe I can send someone down for you. Did he leave something? We've got a lost heap out back, maybe if you checked there. It's been some time, but you never know. . . ."

Mercy thought quickly. "It's of a rather . . . personal nature, Mr. Hovel," she said. "We believe an old friend of Mr. Bright's may have left a message below for Rusty."

"Left a message."

Mercy nodded. Rusty bit her lip.

"What sort of message?"

"We're not sure, entirely," Rusty began, then rushed on. "But if you'll let us go down, say level thirteen or so—"

"Level thirteen? Not on your life. It's a blazing inferno down there."

Mercy remembered washing her father's shirts in the harsh lye soap, scrubbing her own hands raw to get the stains out of them. *"Heat of the underworld, Marybeth. Fit for no man."* But then again, the way he'd behaved had been fit for no man. And she'd weathered that all her life.

"We appreciate your concern," she said, drawing herself up and putting on her most polished presence. "But we don't mind all that. Do we, Rusty?"

Well, Rusty could muster some polish, too. She rolled her shoulders back, brushed her skirt with detached frivolity. Lifted her fingernails to examine them and said with aloof pomp, "That we do."

"You do." Jim looked satisfied.

"Not. Mind, that is, we don't. Doth. Doth not." Her fingernails were digging into her palm now as she tried to maintain her grand façade. "Ow!" She unfurled her fingers and shook her hand out, where she'd pinched her fingernails too hard into her palm. "We don't give a flyin' biscuit about the heat, Jim! C'mon. It's me. Rusty. Silas's Rusty. Just let us down. Twenty minutes, maybe thirty. Do it for Silas."

Jim looked at the clock on the wall, then his pocket watch. He flipped through his ledger, as if that might hold the answer he sought. Flustered, he set it down and leaned forward on his palms. "Fine."

Rusty's face broke into a smile. She took his hand and shook it hard. "Oh, you won't be sorry, you'll see—"

"Fifteen minutes." Jim pointed a finger. "No more."

Mercy thought back to the waterfall climb, the scytale. These were not fifteen-minute endeavors.

"Twenty-five," Rusty said. Bless her.

"Sixteen," Jim countered.

"Thirty," Mercy said.

They both turned and stared. She smiled sweetly.

Despite himself, a smile flickered at the corner of his mouth and he waved a hand. "Get on out of here. Tell Ricky at the hoist I said it was okay. Be as quick as you can. We need those cages and it's no joke down there. Wear those." He pointed at hard hats hanging on pegs.

Rusty let out a *pfff*, wrinkling her brow and waving her hand. Mercy nodded solemnly, grabbing two.

The superintendent shook his head. "Your father'd roll over in his grave if he knew I was letting you down there, Rusty Bright."

But Rusty was already out the door, waving a hollered "Thanks, Jim!" and pulling Mercy behind her.

Mercy's smile was short-lived. A zig around a cookhouse bordered in pines, a zag around a donkey-hitched ore cart and a man whose grin stretched wide at the sight of two women tromping toward the entrance, and suddenly Mercy's eyes went to the ground beneath her feet.

Give them up.

Mercy's breath came short. Shallow. She shook her head, shooing away the vision of young Marybeth, pounding the ground.

Give them up.

She sucked in a breath.

"You okay?" Rusty looked back at her, concern on her face.

Unable to muster a voice, Mercy nodded, then quickened her step to catch up and lead on. At the entrance, her feet stopped.

Rusty drew up beside her, tipped her gaze.

"It's nothing," Mercy said. Rusty looked from her to the mine and back again. She crossed to Mercy in two steps and took her hand. Without a word, she squeezed it. And when Mercy looked up, she saw Rusty's face etched in compassion. Not a bit of the hard exterior she'd worn like armor.

A rumble from below as another blast sounded. There was demolition going on down there. Dynamite. Fire in the hole. Blasting walls out.

Her stomach turned at the thought. She'd never go down, that's what she'd said. She'd go anywhere—the Congo. The frozen north. The rises of New York, the rivers of South America, the windy climes of the Sierra Nevada . . . She would—and had. But she'd never go underground.

She could not, would not, hear the sounds that reverberated through her father's world. That populated his dreams—his nightmares—and therefore hers.

"You want to go?" Rusty said.

The fear would not win.

"Yes," Mercy said. Most women spread lipstick on their smiles before film rolled. Mercy had to spread the smile itself on.

She did so now, took a deep breath and said, "Let's go."

The ore-cart track stretched before them. They entered the arched tunnel into a red-walled embrace, cool air wrapping them. Mercy's skin prickled as her eyes adjusted to the dark.

In silence, they continued until soon the walls seeped a liquid symphony, *drip-dripping* into puddles, their feet splatting in the thick muck. A sign overhead had been pounded into a beam, reading *DANGER: CLOSE CLEARANCE.* They ducked.

They passed another sign, this one tilted and tired, embedded in the mud. *DANGER: EXPLOSIVES.*

They exchanged a glance. Mercy gulped.

Men's voices tumbled down the corridor, lantern light tossing their otherworldly shadows against the curved walls. The shrill sound of a bell, the mechanical creak of a winch.

The smell was earth and grease, aged timber and dynamite. All of it, the smell of hope hard-sought and hard-won, dressed in calluses and denim.

They turned the corner and the tunnel widened as they approached the hoist, the operator's bushy brows furrowed in concentration. Only when he'd stopped the winch's metal grinding and another series of bells sounded—quick in sequence, then pauses—did he look up.

They stated their purpose, and he just blinked. Twice.

"Mr. Hovel says it's okay," Rusty said. He blinked again, setting the winch into motion and bringing the mechanical sound to life, the hoist clanking nearer and nearer.

He pressed the lever to the bell three times—their signal, apparently, to board. Mercy stepped toward the metal box, a far cry from the bright chrome elevator at Pinnacle Studios. Mercy unhooked the single chain that would be their barrier between themselves and the deep abyss, and stepped on.

"Level?" the hoist operator asked.

"We're to follow these signals," Mercy said, referring to her notes. She and Rusty had stayed up late making their best guesses at what the scytale's message meant, and they'd both reached back into their fathers' mining tales and agreed the numbers likely correlated to the hoist's signal codes. "'Three bells'—"

"That means men are on the cage," the man said with all the excitement of a potato. He seemed to sit still with ferocious intent, as if determined to see himself turned into a stalactite. "You're on the cage. What next?"

She nodded, trying to ignore how literal the word *cage* felt. "Then . . . four-four. And then one."

"One means to lower. And four-four—" The stalactite sat straighter. "That's level thirteen," he said, pointing at a sign behind him with signals posted for each level. Sure enough, *Level Thirteen: 4-4.* He looked over his shoulder, both ways.

"Very well," Mercy said. "Would you mind lowering us to level thirteen, please?"

"You must mean twelve," he said. "Or eleven."

"Four-four's where we're headed, mister," said Rusty, stepping into the box and knocking on it twice. "Tallyho, we're ready!"

The man shook his head slow, as if to say *your funeral . . .* He thrust two candles at them, along with a tin of matches. "There's no lights on that level." He looked them in the eyes for the first time. "You girls take care down there. Nobody's worked that level for years."

240

"Nobody? But . . . could you mean forty? Forty men working, yes?" Twoscore messengers. That's what the scytale had said. Someone down there must know.

"Nobody."

"So if a person were to say there were twoscore messengers . . ." Mercy tried to look nonchalant, as if this were the most natural conversation in all the world.

He leveled a look to faze her. She blinked, unfazed. At least on the surface.

"Messengers," he said, gesturing behind him. "Those sticks, jutting from the wall. They mark distance. Ten feet between each."

"Excellent," she said smoothly. "That's all we needed to know."

"Get on in, then. You ring the bell once down there if you want to come back up."

"How'll you know it's us? Not someone on another level?" asked Rusty. "Don't we need a code? The four-four?"

"I'll know. You won't be gone long."

And with another sequence of bells to signal their descent and level, they lurched into motion.

"See you in five minutes." The man settled back into his best stalactite impersonation.

"See you in thirty," Mercy said.

The operator gave one final shake of his head, and Rusty gave a playful wave of her fingertips as he disappeared from view.

The darkness grew darker.

The cool of the mine that had wrapped Mercy with a fleeting wave of reprieve grew hotter. She gripped the railing and her hand, sweaty, slipped. She lost her balance, colliding into the hard metal walls of the box, which came up only just above her elbow.

"Careful!" Rusty grabbed her, pulling her back and away from the rough dark insides of the mountain ribboning past them at a ruthless clip, which would not stop for life or limb.

Mercy tried to distract herself. Counted the levels they passed. *2 . . . 3 . . . 4 . . .* Squinted to see men at work deep within each level. Stooping, bending, reaching, drilling, hammering, mucking. *6 . . . 7 . . . 8 . . .* A rat skittered close to a candle, tipping a canteen and causing Mercy to jump back. *11 . . . 12 . . . 13 . . .* The embrace of the mountain fully around them, above them. The bottom of it at their feet.

They stepped off and rang the bell at the bottom, signaling that they'd completed their descent. And just like that, their metal chariot was rattling up the hoist until its echoes faded . . . and they were left in darkness.

Mercy wasted no time in lighting their candles. As their flames sprang to life, her heartbeat slowed a little. This wasn't so bad. Just another mine tunnel—*drift*, she corrected herself.

She held a candle up to the timber beam above them, etched with the timeworn words *LIGHTNING DRIFT*.

The tunnel loomed before them like a gaping yawn, a mouth stretched open to gobble them up. Rusty stepped forward, right into the mouth of the beast. She reached for a rectangular piece of wood jutting at an upward angle from the wall. "Our first messenger," she said. "We need how many?"

Mercy opened the paper where she'd written the clue.

> *Messengers lead*
> *Amounting twoscore*
> *Blue lantern heed*
> *Where ceiling's a floor.*

She folded the paper, placing it securely in the shirt pocket of the blue-checked gingham she'd dug out of the attic at Wildwood, where she'd also tucked the key that had been fastened to Motor No. 8's exhaust pipe. "Twoscore," she said. "So, forty?" She whistled low.

"They aren't too far apart," Rusty said. "With any luck, it won't take so long. What do you think that is, a quarter mile? Maybe less."

"It's been a very long time since my bones could measure miles," Mercy said. "Back home I marked the half mile by the biggest pine, three-quarters by the rusted mailbox in front of the burned-down cabin, and a mile by the way my little toe started to protest against my Mary Janes." She laughed. "I guess I got soft in the city. They drove us anywhere we needed to go," she said, trying to make light, trying to forget how this place seemed to smirk at her, to say *at last, you've come*. She closed her eyes for a second, trying to shake the indelible impression that she had come for a reckoning.

"Not according to *Harper's Bazar*," Rusty said. "'Mercy Windsor likes long walks on the beach and can often be spotted ascending the many stairs of Griffith Observatory to view the stars.'"

Mercy stopped walking, the *splat-splat-splat* of her shoes on mud echoing to a stop. "Where did you read a thing like that?"

"The Bastion of Civility, of course," Rusty said. "She blasts through the diner door with some magazine or other tucked under her arm and points out whatever nugget she's dug up about you. This town knows a whole lot about you."

Mercy sighed. So much for a fresh start. "Journalists wrote those things. None of them knew me."

"Well, none of them know about hiding deviled eggs under the chair cushion at the church picnic when you were ten, either."

"I'd forgotten about that," she said. "I only wanted to dispose of them without hurting Miss Larson's feelings, as the flies got on them terribly. I never guessed the mayor would sit in that seat. . . ." Mercy braced her hands on her stomach as she laughed. "Not my most illustrious moment, was it?"

Rusty turned, her mischievous face coming to life in the candlelight. "I've got a whole arsenal, Marybeth Spatts. Just you wait."

The laughter felt good. The walls, farther apart, the ceiling, higher. She started to walk again, resuming count of the messengers. They were nearly there, the bend in the tunnel ahead bringing them to thirty-five.

But around that bend . . . everything changed.

Rusty drew up to a halt.

Mercy bumped into her, causing them both to tumble forward and grasp for purchase, bracing themselves on the beam overhead and the respective walls to their sides.

"What on God's green earth . . . ?" Rusty said.

"You mean under it," Mercy replied.

Before them, the walls widened into a near-circle, and a pitch-black stretch of water glimmered.

"That's a lake," Rusty said.

Mercy swallowed. "That's a swamp."

"We can walk it." Rusty lifted her foot, and Mercy grabbed her arm, holding her back.

"Mine water," she said. "And it's been sitting for heaven knows how long. There's no telling what's in it. Arsenic . . . or rats rotting away . . . or—or—just don't touch it, Rusty," she said, her concern sincere. She'd already lost Rusty once. She wasn't about to do it again, to some black pit of poison.

For once, Rusty's indomitable spirit seemed to soften, something akin to compassion washing over her. "I think we'd be fine, Marybeth," she said, gentleness in her voice.

"Why would Martin place a clue just out of reach? Have us go to all that trouble, decoding the riddle, plummeting into the belly of the earth, finding our way down this dark abyss, only to stop here?"

"Maybe it wasn't flooded yet," Rusty said.

Mercy calculated. "If this place has been empty for decades like the man up there said, and if the flooding is the reason for that . . ."

"Martin would've known." Rusty scrunched her nose, thinking. "We have to remember he wasn't making it for us. He was making it for a mining baron, a miner, and a hermit. Why would he have put a body of water between them and whatever he wanted them to find?"

"Extra safety measure, so others wouldn't find it?" Mercy said. "Or perhaps . . . it could be that he wanted Gilman to have to face the conditions he'd created, see for himself what was going on down here."

Rusty nodded. "That's a fair guess. Still seems like he'd have made a way . . . stashed a raft or some such." She shone her candle around, bringing it close to the walls and the ceiling, revealing only splintered beams and rough-hewn rock the color of Rusty's hair.

"Maybe it's like you said. They could tromp across that easy enough . . . unless the bottom drops out somewhere in the middle." She sighed, wiping her forehead. It really was hot down here.

"Or take a flying leap," Rusty said. "I can't see how far it stretches." The darkness was so great, and their candles so small, it was impossible to say. "Maybe he just wanted them to swim."

Rusty froze, her candle's light catching something. "Or maybe he wanted them to use that."

The glow of her candle danced across a length of rope mounted to the top of the wall, where it curved into ceiling. It traveled deeper into the cavernous tunnel, skirting the perimeter, at least as far as the light would show, with brackets drilled into the rock to hold it in place.

"If we hold on to that," Rusty said, "and just inch our way along, finding footholds in the wall . . ."

Mercy lowered her candle and stopped when she saw a wide hole just big enough for the toe of a man's boot. "Like this?"

A jubilant laugh escaped Rusty. "Like that," she said, hoisting herself up. "And that." She reached her toe far in front of her, into another toehold. But when it came time to move her hands, she froze. "I can't do it with the candle," she said. "It'll catch the rope on fire."

Mercy stepped back, squishing her feet into the thick underground shoreline and gulping.

Here she was again, being clawed down by a mine. "We'll have to feel our way," Rusty said. "In the dark."

"I can't." Mercy's voice was thin. Like it might break in half, and she hated the way it sounded.

Rusty stepped down, and Mercy stepped back again, losing her balance in the slick muck. Her hands flung to the sides to catch her balance, and in one terrible, irrevocable motion, the candle flung right out of her hand.

Time slowed. The candle somersaulted in the dark air, flinging a spark like it was reaching out for dear life. It flickered, cast a light over the great black abyss, and then slipped right into it.

Splash.

Lost.

Mercy's breath hitched.

She was that little girl again. Everything inside her shriveled into a ball, helpless at the havoc within her. Her light, extinguished in the blink of an eye . . . just like her last and only hope had been, when Pa came out of the ground.

A hand came under her chin, gently tipping it up until she looked Rusty full in the face.

"Marybeth."

"R-Rusty."

"You can do this."

"I can't." Mercy's eyes flew to the sides, the roof, the floor, shadows everywhere. Darkness encroaching. All that dark that had knocked on their door all those nights, when Pa was lost in a stupor and she, with her too-small hands, kept the fire burning. To warm him . . . and to keep that dark back. Always, it had been just on the brink of overtaking her. And always, she'd been one breath ahead of it. How many nights had she sat up to stoke the fire, lest it go out? Felt the burn in her eyes, that want of sleep deeper than she was tall. But even then, slip of a thing that she was, she hadn't let it go out. Hadn't let the dark win.

And now . . . it was here. All around her.

Her throat began to close, the ground beneath her wavering like her resolve.

A hand landed on her shoulder, and she looked up.

Rusty, candlelight skittering over sun-kissed freckles.

"Marybeth," she said with a gentleness Mercy hadn't heard before. "Here." She held out her candle. When Mercy couldn't unfurl her fingers,

Rusty wrapped her hand around her friend's, and the warmth invited her fist to release. She placed the candle in Mercy's grip, then wrapped her own two hands around Mercy's. "There's light here."

Mercy nodded swiftly, chin up, trying to breathe, trying to choke the coming tears.

"You lost your pa down there in a lot of ways," Rusty said. And the words uncovered wounds that had been buried for so long, never given form or words, and never allowed to heal.

"Yes."

"It's a dark place," Rusty said. And again, the simple words gave form to this thing clawing at her. "Walls closing in, I imagine . . ." She put her hands on her hips.

"This isn't helping."

"You know what," Rusty continued, "that dirty old mine took an awful lot from you, Marybeth Spatts. And I know you swore up and down you'd never step foot near the likes of it, but here you are, and I think something's happening."

"What?" Mercy whispered.

Rusty looked around. "This place has a hold on you."

Mercy paused, then nodded fast. There was no denying it.

"Seems like a stranglehold," Rusty said.

"This isn't helping," Mercy said again dryly, letting out a somber laugh.

Rusty pointed her finger. "You get funny when you get panicked." Mercy smiled feebly. "Listen. Can you breathe?"

It didn't feel like it. But sure enough, breath was coming in and out of her lungs, her nose. She nodded. Small but sure.

"And can you wiggle your toes?"

She wanted to banter back at Rusty that she wasn't buying a pair of new shoes, so what did that matter, but she indulged and wiggled her toes inside her boots. She nodded.

"I bet you can walk, too. Here." Rusty offered her hand, a quiet invitation. "Take a step. I won't let go."

"*I won't let go.*" Just Rusty saying those simple words made a world of difference. Mercy took a step, then another, as the thrumming in her ears eased, and she began to hear again the musical drip of water.

"See that?" Rusty beamed like Mercy had just ascended Mercy Peak itself. "If you can do that, you can do twenty more steps. Keep my light."

"But you need it . . ."

246

Rusty turned, facing Mercy in a rare moment of solemnity. "*We need it. We're in this together. Spatts and Bright Adventure Company, remember? We promised we'd do this one day. You were a light to me more times than I can count. We find ourselves in shadowed spots . . . we share the light. It's what we do, you and me.*"

A montage of memories flitted through Mercy's mind—Rusty writing left-handed when she broke her right arm falling out of a tree, Mercy sending her a dip-pen she'd carved out of the left branch of a tree, insisting it'd help because it understood. Mercy not knowing what to write, how to live, how to keep on, after Pa went to the dark place . . . and Rusty, writing and writing, long letters, no matter how short or infrequent Marybeth's letters were, that long season. Rusty railing against Sam's absence, the indomitable force that she was untethered in a way Mercy hadn't seen before . . . and Mercy, sending Rusty a wooden box she'd built herself using stray nails, telling her to write down every moment she wished she was sharing with Sam, every time one came, so that one day when he returned, she could give it to him. All those moments, stored up to fill his heart and give her own heart some place to go, in its solitude.

Rusty was right. They shared the light.

She pulled in a breath, feeling her lungs ease past the constriction and fill deeply.

"Don't you turn back now, Marybeth. Spatts is strong. Right?"

"Prove it." Mercy let out a shuddering sigh, knowing her friend would relish a challenge.

"Okay," Rusty said and gave Mercy's hand a squeeze. "We'll prove it together."

And so, over an underground lake, perched on footholds slippery from the leaking earth, and with hands sliding over rough rope, Spatts and Bright Adventure Company found their way. Rusty held the candle out as far as she could while Mercy crossed. Mercy, hands rough from the rope, jumped down into the muddy path on the other side of the abyss and waited while Rusty blew out the candle, tossed it across. Mercy retrieved it by sound, lit it fast, and held it out for Rusty, who came into the periphery of the flame's glow none too soon.

In silence they walked, counting the last of the messengers until they stood, at last, in front of number forty.

Mercy shone the candle around. It looked largely unremarkable. She ran her hand over the walls—cold and damp to the touch. Rusty reached to the timber just over her head, doing the same.

"Odd place for a clue," Rusty said. "Not much different about it than any other part of the mine."

"So why here?" Mercy asked, her voice mingling with the continued music of the dripping walls. Her mind turned, pulling at the ropes of the riddle. "An abandoned level of a mine on the far side of an underground swamp . . . There has to be a reason he'd pick here and not somewhere easier for his friends to get to. What's remarkable about this place?"

"Nothing, far as I can see," Rusty said, then laughed. "Which isn't very far. It must have to do with the key. But what could need a key down here? There are no doors to speak of."

"Let's think. Other things that could be locked . . ."

"Treasure chest," said Mercy.

"Cabinet," said Rusty.

"Gate."

"Chains, with a padlock?"

"Trapdoor." They looked down. Nothing.

"Attic door." They looked up—and froze.

"What in the world . . . ?"

The candlelight bobbed in orange glow, stretching over a canopy of black-scrawled figures. Numbers, in every direction, scattered across the ceiling of the mine, as if someone had gathered up all the digits, one through ten, in duplicate and sometimes triplicate, and tossed them into the air.

Mercy reached up to touch one, tracing the number three. "Charcoal?"

"It's not smudging," Rusty said. "Like someone took a lit candle up there, writing with fire."

"There's no pattern, no rhyme or reason," she said. "What do we do with this?"

"Maybe it's an equation," she said. "Or coordinates?"

"Or a cipher," Mercy said. "Seems like something he would do . . ."

"Let's see that riddle again." They bent over the paper, reading. The words that had brought them to the mine, down the shaft, past forty messengers . . .

"This," Mercy said, finger on the last two lines. "It's the only part we haven't done yet: *Blue lantern heed, Where ceiling's a floor.*"

"Where ceiling's a floor—it has to be referring to this." Rusty gestured at the upside-down numbers hanging in chaotic constellation, where the ceiling above was, in essence, the floor of the next level up.

"But a blue lantern?" Mercy turned slowly, scanning the small space. A few piles of rocks, which they peeked under. A few alcoves left from mining—empty, but for old braces for candles—the splintery remnant of an old post, and holes someone had drilled but not blasted.

"We must be missing something."

"The postscript?" Mercy asked. "It's strange that there's nothing written after it."

"You always used to say the p.s. was your favorite part," Rusty said. "I never understood. Why not just stick it in the letter?"

Mercy smiled at the memory. She'd always saved the best bits for last. "Because it's special. Set apart."

"Well, nothing special about this one. It's empty."

"It is strange, though," Mercy said. "The S was crossed out, remember? You weren't sure if it was a flaw in the leather or something done on purpose."

Rusty closed her eyes, thinking. "It's the same depth as the rest of the engraved letters," she said. "And the placement looked intentional. . . ."

"Maybe Martin made a mistake while engraving but couldn't start from scratch?"

Rusty shook her head. "He was meticulous," she said. "Everything about all of this has been dialed in to the smallest detail. I think he took that S off on purpose."

"A riddle of its own?" Mercy asked.

"Postscript . . ." Rusty said, eyes darting to the ceiling and back around the room. "S is for script. Take the *script* off of *postscript* . . ."

"Post?"

Their eyes flew to the humble stub of a post, just a lonely half timber jutting from the ground. It was, in every way but one, entirely ordinary. Splintered and timeworn, forgotten here in the damp dark.

But on the side closest to the wall, where not a person would see as they tromped through this tunnel, two tiny hinges glinted dully in the candlelight. And opposite them: a small lock. Tarnished, blackened . . . waiting.

Silently, with a nod from Rusty, Mercy lifted the cold metal in her hand. She swallowed, inserted the key. *Click.*

It released its hold and Mercy carefully removed it, tucking it in her pocket before opening the tiny door to an alcove in the post, where someone had taken great care to carve out a cavity. Cavern within a cavern, mine within a mine. Treasure, in the form of a kerosene lantern that fit just so inside.

She removed it with care, holding it up in the candlelight as Rusty scrambled closer. Mercy turned the knob, lifting the candle to lend it fire, and the old relic ignited. Only instead of offering warm orange light, the glass glowed a deep, purply blue.

"Wood's glass!" Rusty exclaimed, rising onto her knees. "Dad told me about this. They used to coat the glass with something special to filter out the strongest parts of the flame. How'd he put it . . . *'There's a quieter light inside every light, Rusty girl,'* he said. *'You just can't see it, for the loud light all around.'* Ultraviolet, it's called."

"What's it for?" Mercy said. The color was strangely soothing, washing over her in indigo incandescence.

Rusty furrowed her brow. "They used it to encode things in the Great War . . . and I think they used it around here for spotting minerals. The assayers had some use for it, to tell what was what, long time ago. Dad said it gave some kind of glow to rocks that looked perfectly normal— fluorite, calcite, a bunch of other *-ites.*"

Mercy's eyes traveled the tunnel, watching the way the light mingled softly with the red-stone walls, the grey-stone walls. Lovely, but not glowing, not anything—

Her hand flew to her chest. "Like that?" She rose slowly, pointing at the ceiling.

"Jumpin' jackals," Rusty murmured almost reverently. She rose, too, holding the lantern up to the ceiling of numbers that were suddenly interconnected in a web of illuminated veins, ordering the jumble of numbers into a sequence.

The light from the candle leapt to take part, too, making the vein vanish right back into its camouflage inside the rest of the rock.

"We have to blow it out," Mercy said.

Rusty turned. "You sure?" she asked solemnly. She knew what it meant to Mercy. Maybe her friend couldn't feel the way the notion of extinguishing their single flame sent dread up her spine . . . but she knew this was a costly thing. A tiny flame could mean all the hope in the world to someone trapped in the dark.

Mercy spread her shoulders and nodded, jaw set. They'd done it long enough to get across the water, and she'd survived that. "We have to."

Rusty nodded. "Count of three?"

"One . . ." Mercy said.

"Two . . ." Rusty took Mercy's hand.

And this was it. Mercy licked the fingers on her other hand. Rusty's eyebrows shot up.

"Spit? From the queen of the silver screen?"

Mercy smiled. "How's the saying go? 'If it's worth doing, it's worth doing with something from deep down inside your soul'?" And ensuring that a theatric wink was the last thing Rusty would see, Mercy said, "Three," and pinched the flame into oblivion with a satisfying sizzle.

Mercy lifted her eyes.

It was brilliant. Breathtaking. As if light itself had shot through hard rock around them. Petrified lightning, blue-white and glowing.

Mercy lifted her hand to a wide vein of the webbing force. Tiny crystals met her touch, and a cluster of their dust came loose, showering around her in a luminous swirl. She spun slowly, mesmerized.

Lifting her eyes back to the trapped light above them, the topsy-turvy lining up in a map.

The two connected by a vein to a six. The vein traversing then to a sideways eight. And on and on, until the jumble became one long sequence.

Something welled up inside Mercy, billowing over the edges that had been so sharpened by fear, by the years and years of dark kept deep inside.

And yet here, in the oppressive dark that wrapped her tight and stole her breath . . . shooting through it was light. Embedded in rock. Which created the dark.

It was fractured and whole. And it was undoing something foundational, some crack so deep she'd never ventured to go there. The illumination hurt, like stepping from the dark straight into the high noon sun.

It hurt . . . but it healed, too.

Rusty rummaged for her pocket notebook and wrote like mad, muttering something about minerals blending into the many specks composing rocks like camouflage.

"Double-check me?" Rusty handed Mercy the notebook, and she dutifully confirmed the number sequence. As she did, Rusty wandered in a rare moment of spellbound silence.

"The numbers are copied right," Mercy said. "But what do they mean?" And how had a handful of candle-burned inscriptions on the roof of a mine ignited a light inside of her, too?

Rusty looked perplexed. "Was there anything more in the post?"

She squished across the mud and knelt, feeling around inside with apparently not even a qualm about creatures or spiders or cave trolls living inside.

"Eureka!" She pulled out what appeared to be a small hammer. Upon its handle was entwined another brass capsule. Rusty proceeded to untwist, unroll, and read in the now-familiar metered rhythm of their poet-prospector.

> "They rest beneath a steel frame
> And sing a silent song
> Traversing mountains,
> Honed in flame
> The Goose, she sings along
> So free these steel bars beneath
> Dear Motor Number Eight
> Place them in the Echoed Cove
> And then commence to play."

What the steel bars or the echoed cove were, Mercy did not know. But one thing was quickly clear.

"We're going back to the Goose."

Rusty

Rusty leaned her hoe against the cabin, dizzy from standing up straight so quickly after all that work. There hadn't been enough daylight left to get to the Galloping Goose and back before dark, so Rusty, on some crazy whim, had invited Marybeth to dinner at the cabin.

Marybeth had been awfully quiet since the mine, and Rusty got the sense that part of her was still down there. In her experience, busy hands helped a toiling mind find peace, so she'd handed her a garden hoe and invited her out into the twilight to help churn up the earth.

She had the place fenced in for the spring with a roll of wire mesh she'd scavenged from the factory at the old Peak View mine, lest the foxes and rabbits make a banquet of her carrots and such. She'd also brought back a covering to give shade to the things that preferred shadows. She took special care with those plants, feeling a blood-deep kinship with them. She had yet to put up the covering, but now was as good a time as any.

She flung the crinkly fabric out, pleased at the way it unrolled and lifted on a breeze.

"Oh my," Marybeth said, pausing for once from her work. "That was beautiful."

"Just some fabric on the wind," Rusty said.

"I've never seen winds like what you have here," Marybeth said. She pointed past a cluster of pines, where a meadow of tall grasses rippled in waves. "Something that can make a field of straight-growing rooted things ripple like water on the move . . . that's remarkable."

As if it had heard her and wished to show off, the wind chose that moment to twist the fabric violently, yanking Rusty forward. She flung the covering out again, but it twisted up worse.

"Could you—" She wrestled the next word as much as she wrestled the fabric. *Help* was not a word she was accustomed to speaking.

But Marybeth was there in a flash. She'd cleaned up in the creek earlier and somehow didn't look like she'd spent the day traversing the depths of the red-hot earth. She sported a green plaid flannel shirt tied at the waist, hair tied up in a white kerchief, and lips red, like she'd stepped out of an advertisement for canoes and lipstick.

Which felt like the perfect description of Marybeth Spatts, come to think of it. A combination of rugged and polished that somehow worked.

"Who'd you put makeup on for, the trees?" Rusty wished the biting words back as soon as she spoke them. Why did she always do that? She could've just said, *You look more like yourself today, Spatts.*

Marybeth's smile flickered briefly into a frown, but she rallied, smiling even broader than before. "Don't dress down for the garden," she said cheerily.

"What?"

"Just something I read once. Listen, if you'd seen how many truly horrid lipstick shades they've plastered on me over the years . . ." She rolled her eyes. "Enough to blind a bat."

"Bats are already blind."

"Enough to do it again!" She laughed, and Rusty couldn't help joining her. "I picked this one out myself. And I like it. So I wear it." She shrugged, as if that explained it all.

"You're not trying to impress a fella?"

Marybeth's expression slowly went flat.

"Ooooh," Rusty said. "You already *have* a fella. So? Who is he? Some billionaire? One of the leading men? Or wait—an overlooked cameraman, who is the only one who truly sees you for who you are but is shy of the spotlight? That's more your speed. I got it, didn't I? What's his name? You planning a wedding anytime soon? Maybe this could be your veil. . . ." She fluttered the fabric playfully.

"There isn't anyone," Marybeth said. "The papers would have you believe otherwise—that I'll spin about the ballroom with any of the leading men, give them all a turn having Mercy Windsor on their arms. And the studio arranged plenty of that. I even went on a few dates— mostly by accident—back in Hollywood."

"How do you go on dates by accident?"

"I thought they wanted to be friends."

Rusty snorted and stopped tying knots, staring at her friend, the doe-eyed ingénue. And sure enough, there were those doe eyes, naïve and wide, looking back at her. There was something tempered in them, too . . . a sadness, something not naïve at all.

"I just . . . I don't know, Rusty. Every time one of the other actresses gets engaged, the reporters ask when my turn is coming. People stare at my hand looking for a ring, so much so I started wearing gloves everywhere. The papers ask when I'll settle down and marry, as if everything before marriage is just . . . biding time. But . . ."

She trailed off, gathering her words and wrapping them in gentle courage, so that they didn't come out sounding like a tirade. "Didn't God make *this* time, too? Isn't there just as much purpose here? If He made it, how could it have less purpose than whatever's on the other side of marriage?" She paused, thinking. "Or on the other side of anything, for that matter. A career, or children, or some measure of success or other. How could the 'now' have any less purpose than whatever's on the other side?" She shook her head. "I think God made each moment and each moment matters. And what if—"

She swallowed, lowered her voice just in case those reporters were hiding behind trees. "What if I never marry? Would that truly be so shocking? The magazines make it sound as if it is the final piece of a jigsaw puzzle and the picture will never be complete without it. And perhaps for some, that's true. Beautifully so. But aren't there other pictures, too, outside of being part of a couple? Pictures that are just as beautiful? Just as complete, just as purposeful? Just as needed? And didn't God create each and every story—singleness and marriage alike—with just as much care and meaning? Because I feel like—I don't know, Rusty. Like my jigsaw pieces are scattered right here in these mountain folds. The people, the place, what we're doing. Perhaps someday there might be a marriage piece, but perhaps not. So." She paused. "What if I never do get married?" She pulled in a breath, as if the last coming question took the most strength to say. "What if that's not my story?"

Rusty stared.

"I'm sorry." Marybeth laughed. "You were just teasing, and I spilled every thought I've stuffed down for the past five years on the topic. I've never said it aloud before."

Rusty studied her friend. "Nothing shocking about that at all," she said. "I'm never getting married." And there was sorrow in her voice, too—but of a different sort. Marybeth heard it and laid her hand on Rusty's shoulder.

For once, Rusty didn't shrug it off. She stared good and hard at the ground and tried to figure out what to say next.

"I'm sorry, Rusty. I didn't mean—I wasn't thinking—"

"You did nothing wrong." Rusty pulled up her gaze, setting to work with too much speed, tying knot after knot after knot. Nothing was going to dislodge this shelter from these plants. Nothing.

"I didn't mean to make it about me," Rusty said. "It all matters, Marybeth. You're right."

Marybeth smiled. "Don't tell that to the ladies' magazines," she said dryly. "They might spontaneously combust for the scandal of such a notion."

"Miss Murdock's house would go up in flames. She's got rows of *Woman's Home Companion* on her shelves, organized by topic and going back forty years!"

"And yet she is a trailblazing bachelorette herself out here in this rugged country. . . ." Marybeth said, arching a brow.

"Ha! This country's not half as rugged as she is. She might surprise you."

"I believe it." Marybeth wiped her brow. "They had me on the cover once, holding up a jar of blueberry preserves and telling how to make the best preserves."

"They did not."

Marybeth shot Rusty a conspiratorial grin.

Rusty leaned in. "Did you tell them about the toe jam?"

"I did not."

Rusty held in her laughter. Marybeth Spatts was full of surprises.

They worked together in silence awhile, and Rusty felt Marybeth's furtive glance on her.

"What?"

Marybeth shook her head. "Nothing."

"You keep looking at me."

"Well, it's just—" Her eyes sparked a little. "You'd better be careful if you're set on not marrying. Seems to me there's someone out there who's noticing you."

Rusty's cheeks flamed. "I don't know what you mean."

"Casey Campbell, like the soup? He couldn't stop smiling at you when we were propping up the falling shed yesterday."

They'd come across the forlorn outbuilding on the way to the water-fall, and Casey had insisted they could fortify it in five minutes' time, or at least start the process.

"Maybe he just really likes propping up falling sheds," Rusty said. "Can you blame him?"

Marybeth gave her a look. "He's noticing you. Mark my words."

"Well, he'd better stay away if he knows what's good for him."

"Be kind, though," she said. "He seems jolly and rugged, and I think he is, but he's not a stranger to loss."

"What do you mean?"

Marybeth shook her head. "I don't know the whole story . . . only that he once had a younger brother. Sorrow recognizes sorrow, and I saw it in him. Just . . . be kind, yes?"

Rusty cleared her throat and welcomed the return of blessed silence.

Marybeth's mouth tugged into a half smile as they finished tying the fabric to the fence posts. The wind rippled over it, too, and Marybeth tilted her head. She got that look on her face—the one that said an idea was taking root and working fast.

"What is it?" she asked. "The fabric. It's so fine." She fingered it. "Nylon?" She looked at the sky. "That'll be good for protecting from storms, too."

Rusty nodded, following her gaze upward. "Monsoon season isn't until late summer. Spring, we only get rain showers. But come those hotter months, it'll let loose daily and almost always late afternoon. Looking like it might be a zinger tonight, though."

Marybeth's eyes flashed with delight. "Truly?"

Rusty's brows shot up. "You fancy the rain? Most people aren't too keen on summer storms."

"I'd give anything for it," Marybeth said. Then a shadow crossed over her face. "That could put a damper on the plays, though. If the forest theatre idea flies."

"The storms usually let up by five or so. You'll be fine if you're planning evening performances."

"All the same, it'd be nice to have something like this for the audience and the stage. We can't exactly issue rain checks for a once-a-summer performance."

Marybeth's eyes moved around the clearing, landing on objects as if she was considering solutions and tossing them out one by one. "Umbrellas for everyone, perhaps? Or—where did you get this fabric? Was there more?"

Rusty laughed. "You're going to be sorry you asked that. It's more than you ever could want."

"Not for what I'm thinking."

"Oh, I think it is." She glanced at the sun. "We've got enough light if we hurry. Follow me."

Fifteen minutes later, they broke through into a clearing, twigs and leaves in their hair from bushwhacking the short route up to the old mine. "I know this place," Marybeth said. "From the map. Part of the Peak View mine, right?"

"That's right. It's shut down now."

"Gilman property."

"Right again. The Gilmans bought it a few decades back." Rusty led the way to the old mess hall, which was half-rock, half-timber, an attempt to keep the walls dry during winters when the snowbanks climbed and stayed, sloping up to cover right over the rock portions of the walls.

At the door, she paused, making sure Marybeth was still with her. "Which makes you the proud owner of . . ." She flung the heavy wood door open. It creaked its weary welcome, and they stepped inside a room shot through with sun shafts and light-swimming dust. "Ten thousand surplus parachutes!"

"What?" Marybeth turned slowly, taking in the sight of tables littered with a few defunct sewing machines and racks of carefully folded white parachute bundles.

"Well, maybe not ten thousand, exactly. But a few hundred, at least. Give or take." Rusty shrugged.

"But—why?"

"Mine dried up—first of gold, then of workers, when so many went to war. Mr. Gilman was gone, and some distant nephew was executor of his estate. Same one you bought Wildwood from, I imagine. He was running for mayor or some such back east and thought it'd be good publicity to offer up his 'family facilities' to the war effort. With most of the Mercy Peak men part of an airborne paratrooper infantry, he thought there was some kind of poetry in letting the town they came from make parachutes. The man had some kind of soft spot for soldiers. Had served as one himself, a long time ago. There was some story about him pulling a spent shell out of a crater in the earth, right in the middle of a midnight shelling. He had a funny name—Chester something or other. Anyway, the factory here provided jobs to the women back home at a time when they were sorely needed, provided a boost to the war effort, and made him look awful good for his campaign, which I believe he won."

"So this is . . ."

"Yours. Yep. Congratulations, Marybeth Spatts. You are officially the owner of twenty fancy costumes, a pyramid of terrible cereal, a befuddling amount of SPAM, twenty thousand yards of unusable fabric, and precisely two actual outfits."

Marybeth laughed dryly. She stepped slowly through the scene before her, weaving in and out of sun shafts, trailing her hand along tables where Mercy Peak women had toiled for three years, blisters on their hands and aches in their hearts. Missing their sons, brothers, beaus, husbands, and praying their stitches made here on solid ground might make those men fly. Bring them home safe and sound.

Marybeth laid her hand on a pile of parachute bundles and closed her eyes. "And the men?" She turned tentatively, facing Rusty.

Rusty swallowed around the burn in her throat. "Most returned," she said. "Three didn't."

Tears welled in Marybeth's eyes. How? How, when she'd never known those men, did tears come so readily? She had a tender heart. A strange mix of protectiveness and cynicism stirred in Rusty.

"The ones who came back, they call them the Caterpillar Club. Men who flew once, in all this 'silk.' People say the mines will pick up again, and they'll have more work. But until then, they're doing what they can to get by. Some are at Gilcrest, others mining farther away. . . . Casey Campbell thinks his ski hill idea will give some of them jobs." Rusty shrugged. "He's hopeful."

Distant thunder rolled high in the mountains.

"We'd better get back," Rusty said. "It's not safe to be out in it. Lightning gets to striking—mostly up by the ridges, but sometimes down lower, too. We should go, unless you want to be stuck here all night."

Marybeth looked like she wouldn't mind that one bit but pulled herself away as Rusty led the way back to the cabin.

BLOOMS

(Brilliant Lexicon of the Original Marybeth Spatts)

ENTRY NO. 98

Condensation Nuclei

As defined by Marybeth Spatts

(1) Bits of dust, smoke, or salt that raindrops form around inside clouds. Then the drops move around and bump into one another. When they collide, they combine and get heavier and heavier until the cloud is so heavy it can't hold it in any longer . . . and it rains. All because of dust.

Mercy

Mercy closed her eyes and listened, a smile spreading across her face.

The rain came down in sheets upon the rooftop, running down the windows in rivulets, mapping journeys. Even Confetti the Cat was under its spell, curled up in perfect peace beside the fire. On the woodstove, Rusty's copper kettle bubbled in a friendly roil, tossing coffee grounds around inside in its hearty hammered belly as Rusty pulled two tin mugs down from a shelf.

"Let me help," Mercy said. "What can I get? Sugar?"

"There's honey in that cupboard."

Mercy opened the far cupboard, up against the wall where Rusty had pointed. Rusty busied herself with toasting bread over the woodstove flame on a long prong, and Mercy's stomach rumbled. How was fresh toast so much more appetizing to her than the finest spreads Hollywood had to offer? No seafood cocktail, no pâté or caviar. Just bread and butter, and it did her good.

And honey. She snapped back to attention and scanned the contents of the cupboard. On the bottom shelf, a few tins of beans. On the next shelf up, a tray, and on the top shelf, a box that said *LETTERS.*

Mercy halted. Was that . . . *her*, in that box? Her words? Her heart?

Without thinking, she pulled them to the ledge of the shelf, feeling all the years, all the laughter, all the tears that this box might contain.

"Seems like another life," Rusty said, turning the toast slowly while watching Mercy.

Mercy noted the twine wrapping it crisscross like a gift—and how tight and full the collection of knots was at the top. As if the person doing the tying meant to never again untie them.

Mercy smiled sadly and pushed the box back in. "Do you ever wonder how we were matched up together to begin with? No one else in my class had a pen pal in Mercy Peak. They were all over in Telluride. My teacher was going to write to get it sorted out and get me matched with someone over there. Said she didn't have extra postage to be sending a separate envelope every time we wrote. I didn't want another pen pal—I wanted you. So I asked if I could keep you and told her I'd bring my own stamps. I used to sweep floors at the mine office to earn stamp money."

Rusty stopped turning the toasting stick for a moment. "You never said . . ."

Mercy smiled. "Doesn't matter. There was plenty of dirt to be swept there, and I used to think, watching bits of it swirl in the sunlight, how dirt could change a life. It made it so I got you as a friend." She lifted her gaze to Rusty's. "That changed everything."

Rusty narrowed her eyes, and hope flickered inside Mercy. They'd left the mine changed today, something cinched tighter between the two of them.

"I don't think a single other soul from that class kept writing to their pen pal after that first year." She smiled, trying to lighten the atmosphere. But she was here for honey. Returning to the task at hand as Rusty returned her attention to the toast, she pulled out the tray on the second shelf, thinking it might be hidden near the back. As she held it in her hands, she saw it was no tray at all—but a framed picture.

Beneath a thin layer of dust, a freckle-faced Rusty, about sixteen years old, smiled so broad it felt like the frame might crack. Her eyes were scrunched shut, face turned slightly toward the person next to her.

A young man. Dark curly hair tousled, smiling not at the camera, but at Rusty. Looking like he was pleased at having made her laugh—but more than that, looking at her with pure adoration like Mercy had never seen before. Not in real life, and not on-screen, where the best actors were paid the highest dollars to shower adoration convincingly upon their counterparts.

This was real. So real it gripped her heart and squeezed it tight, her breath coming thin and shallow as if the moment could somehow be broken between these two smiling souls.

She was transfixed. This was Rusty as she knew her. Her buoyant pen pal who would take on the world and crack a joke that could mend a broken heart and who could infuse courage like iron, strong enough to grow wings of steel.

The long quiet must have piqued curiosity in Rusty. "Can't find the honey?" she said, and turned to help, halting when she saw what Mercy held.

For a moment—just a fleeting moment—Rusty's hard façade was gone. Vanished clean away, leaving a new person before her. Broken. Raw. Hurting so much it seemed to pulse out of her, and Mercy longed to catch these rays of pain, gather them up, hold them.

Rusty shook herself from the trance. This was the woman who'd slammed doors and stormed out of rooms and spoken piercing words without a second thought. What would she do now?

But there was no wrath in the steps that approached. They were tentative, drawing near.

She didn't speak a word. Just stared at the picture, eyes welling. She pursed her lips and lifted the corner of her worn apron. Slowly, as if it might burn her if she moved too fast, she wiped away the dust, while Mercy held this frozen, glass-plated moment in time. Finally, Rusty reached her hands around the frame and gingerly took it. Mercy could almost hear the ratcheting of bolts as her friend used every tool she had inside to fasten her feelings down, pack them back away.

Rusty cleared her throat. "Honey's in the other cupboard."

Watching her friend from the corner of her eye, Mercy retrieved a glass jar with its wooden dipper and brought it to the table. She poured steaming coffee into the mugs through a strainer, while her friend remained spellbound.

She pulled a chair out for Rusty, then took a seat herself, and waited. At last, Rusty joined her, eyes fixed on the picture still as she set it down in front of them.

"I haven't looked at that in . . ." She blew stray hairs out of her face, an action Mercy knew would help dry the tears that threatened. Mercy wished she would let them fall, let the storm come, let it wash over her. That she would ride the release of it.

"It feels like another life," her friend finally finished.

Mercy nodded, considering what to say. *I'm so sorry. I wish he was still here. I wish you were, too.*

But Rusty *was* here. The stalwart, stoic, storm-holding vault in human form before her was still Rusty. And what sort of friend would Mercy be if she was only interested in the vibrant version of Rusty she'd only known through letters? Weren't friendships born for such times as this? Wasn't a 'brother born for adversity'? Rusty's heart was wounded, deeply. If it had been a broken bone, some visible ailment or injury, wouldn't Mercy visit her in any hospital, offer her arm as she learned to walk again?

A broken heart was just as real as a broken bone . . . and it took longer to heal.

"He's just like I pictured him," Mercy said.

"Guffawing like a gorilla?"

"Overflowing with adoration for you," Mercy said, reaching out her hand and looking tentatively at Rusty, asking silently, *may I?*

Rusty released her hold, tilting it toward Mercy.

Mercy held it gently, running her thumb over the frame, which looked like it had been built by hand.

"It was a gift," Rusty said. "Sam, he—he roped me into taking that picture. Some traveling photographer that came with the circus when they led all those elephants and tigers up the mountain. He gathered those beams from the wreckage of an old mine we'd found once, where he vowed to me that someday he'd find treasure and make me rich."

"And what did you say to that?"

Rusty's mouth tugged into a reluctant smile, and she rolled her eyes. "I said I was already rich since I had him. Can you believe that? What a sap I was. But it was true."

Mercy smiled but shook her head. "I think that's the most beautiful thing I've heard."

"You would."

Mercy handed the picture back and watched her friend's hand hover hesitantly before taking it. "Is it hard to look at?" she asked, venturing a question.

Rusty pursed her lips and finally gave a single nod. "Looking him in the face . . ." she said. "It also means looking his absence in the face." She paused, but Mercy felt more pulsing in the air. Rusty wasn't done yet. Finally, in a whisper that slipped out beneath barely held-in tears, she said, "That's a mountain too steep for me to climb, Marybeth Spatts." She blew out her cheeks and gave a dry laugh. "And now you know all there is to know about me and the last ten years. It's been me and a whole heap of not climbing that mountain. Simple as that."

Mercy studied her friend, and tentatively laid her hand on Rusty's. "Seems you've done a lot of living in that time," Mercy said. "That in itself is a big mountain climbed."

"I don't know about that," Rusty said.

"You once told me that getting to the end of the day is a miracle worth giving thanks for when your world's turned upside down," Mercy said quietly. "I don't think I ever told you this, but those words got me through a great many days."

Rusty looked Mercy in the eyes. Something new there—a recollection that Mercy, too, knew well the terrain of grief.

"You had a very long road with your father," Rusty said.

Mercy nodded. Her throat tight, she pushed the words out. "You got me down that road, Rusty. I wish I'd been there to do the same for you."

Rusty blinked fast, breaking eye contact. "Sheesh, this rain," she said. "You'd think the sky was weeping. That's about enough of my sob story."

"I didn't see much sobbing," Mercy said with a wink.

"Quit it. I'll cry when I'm good and ready, and I just don't think that's ever going to happen, so you can give it up. Our time is better served doing something productive."

CHAPTER

25

Sometimes you gotta go back to a claim you never thought you'd go to again. You never found what you were hoping for. But when you read the land farther up the hill, it changes the story. The *mountain* changes the story, see? There's more to it. You see where things farther up mighta landed, down there. You gotta go back.

—Martin Shaw

Letter from Rusty to Mercy, age 10

Dear Marybeth,

~~Seasons Greetings!~~ ← *I wrote that because it sounded nice and I've heard folks say it. Fall is my favorite season, and this being October, I thought it'd be just the right way to start things out. But the teacher says it means "Merry Christmas" and made me cross it out. I should just say plain old "hello," but all those other fancy greetings just got a ring to them, you know?*

Anyway, I'm writing because. . . I have for you a map!

In school, we learned about something called cartography, which isn't about carts, by the way. It's mapmakers, which I think could be a great job to have. I made this map of Mercy Peak for you to use when you finally come.

You will see the church that captured the cat, the mercantile where you need to go if you need information (and I guess also if you need supplies), and the diner whose kitchen is run off a tractor motor out back whenever the power goes out, which is nearly every afternoon in summers during monsoon season. The diner sign says Jim's Diner *but we all started calling it the J.D. . . . Not for Jim's Diner, but for John Deere, since that's what really runs*

*the place, even if Jim thinks he does. It's a fine eatery, my dad
says, and also the only one, so I hope you like tractor-cooked
food.*

*And my faaaavorite part of the map is the back lot of Wild-
wood, where I never yet have been able to get without being spotted first by Mr. Gilman's henchmen or hounds. See it? It's labeled*
Hic sunt dracones.

*Did you know that in the olden days, before they knew what
was all over the surface of the earth, they mapped the parts
they knew and in the places that they didn't know, they put this
phrase:* Hic sunt dracones.

GUESS WHAT THAT MEANS.

If you guessed something about Dracula . . . Wrong!

But if you guessed something about dragons . . .

Why, Marybeth Spatts, you are a certified genius.

It means HERE BE DRAGONS.

*The teacher said it was a fancy way to say, "Be careful, it's
dangerous here because we don't know what's out there because
we haven't explored it yet."*

Isn't it grand?

*Write soon! When you get here, we'll go dragon hunting at the
back lot of Wildwood. Sound like a good itinerary? (Look that
word up, it's a good one.)*

> *All my sympathy (Isn't that a fancy closing? Let's see
> the teacher make me cross that out . . .),*
> *Rusty*

Mercy

Hic sunt dracones.

Mercy and Rusty sat in the idling Big Green, staring down the overgrown road before them . . . the road that led into the wilderness.

"You sure this is a good idea?" Mercy asked, foot firmly on the brake.

"It's the only way up to the top of the falls in a vehicle, at least according to Gilman's maps," Rusty said. "Besides, it's us or no one."

"Or Holden or Casey," Mercy said.

"Casey had to get his reports written up for his partners and sent off
in the mail, and Holden went to help him with some measurements.

They won't be back for hours. We could wait if you want, or . . ." Rusty said, with a glint in her eye. "Come on, say it. 'It's us or no one!'"

Mercy checked the sun, which was inching too fast toward the western canyon wall. "Daylight waits for no man," she said, and sat up straight.

Rusty waited, drumming her fingers on the dashboard.

Mercy sighed. "It's us or no one."

"That's more like it!"

Biting her lip, she eased her foot off the brake, onto the gas pedal, took a deep breath—

"Yoo-hoo!"

She slammed her foot onto the brake and the truck stalled, lurching to a halt.

"Smooth," Rusty said, recovering from the rag-doll jerking. They both turned to look behind them and spotted Priscilla Murdock, waving at them from the road. She wore a tailored suit of powder blue, outlined in crisp white piping.

"What is the Bastion of Civility doing out here in the wilderness?" asked Mercy. She creaked the door open, got out, and greeted Priscilla.

"I brought pickled eggs," she said, as if it were the most natural explanation in all the world. She walked toward them with the barest hint of a limp, beaming with pride as she held up a jar like it was a trophy.

"Thank you, Miss Murdock," said Mercy. "I'm afraid we were just headed up the mountain, or else I'd invite you in—"

"Oh?" Her eyebrows shot up, and she twisted her gloved hands. "What adventure!"

Rusty was beside them now, looking at Miss Murdock quizzically. "You say that like it's a . . . good thing."

"Isn't it, though? Nothing like a gust of fresh air to fill the lungs and renew the constitution!" She cocked her elbow and swung her fist sideways at the word *gust*.

"You once told me that adventures were horrid things and a sign of uncouth character."

"Did I?" She blushed, smiling. "Well, now, that doesn't sound like me, does it?"

Rusty's eyes shifted.

"But now you mention it, Holden Huxley *did* say something about you being interested in that old treasure Martin Shaw was always on the hunt for, God rest his soul."

Rusty speared Mercy with a glance. Mercy dropped her gaze. She should've warned Holden better about keeping things mum.

The threesome stood in the path in an awkward silence. Finally, Priscilla Murdock cleared her throat. "I want to come."

Mercy startled. "Come? As in . . . ?"

She twirled a gloved finger at the rusty pickup truck. "Wherever you're going in that," she said. "If you're going to go about hunting this . . . treasure"—she spun her hand in the air, like she was wrapping the word up tight in a cocoon—"there's a particular way . . ." She was growing more agitated, her measured words speeding up as if she was losing careful control.

Rusty caught the gloved hand, which had begun to shake. And caught the woman's eyes, too. "Is this about Reuben?" she asked, compassion delivering the words.

Priscilla's chin trembled. "Someone has to look out for you girls," she said at last. "That's all."

Mercy couldn't grasp all that was happening, but she couldn't risk the woman being hurt. "I'm sorry, Miss Murdock," she said. "We only have the two seats—"

"What do you call that?" She pointed at the back of the truck.

"You mean the bed of the truck?"

"It looks spacious. I'll sit there. Let's go." The woman tromped forward with the force of a hurricane.

"I don't think we can stop her," Mercy whispered to Rusty.

"I don't think we should."

"What? Why? She'll find out about the Goose—"

"I can take care of that. But I think there's more going on here. Remember the Blood Moon Boys?"

"Of course."

"Reuben . . . the quiet one . . . he's her older brother."

"The one who disappeared into the mountains?"

"Never to be heard from again, yes. To hear it told, she adored him and followed him around like a puppy. She's never given up hope that he might come back someday."

Mercy looked at the woman, struggling in her pencil skirt to climb into the truck as her high heels clanked against it.

"Here, let me help you." Mercy rushed to her aid.

"Miss Murdock, if you come with us, you are solemnly sworn to not utter a word of what you see."

Priscilla crawled on her knees to the center of the truck and sat. "On my honor," she said, adjusting her hat.

"You know, you could sit inside," Rusty said. "I'll ride out here."

"Not on your life, Ruby Bright. I can only make it in and out of there so many times." She pointed at the tailgate of the truck. "Don't make me do that more than I have to."

"Alright, well . . . hold on tight. This might be the ride of your life," Rusty said.

"I'm counting on it."

By the time they'd bounced up the mountain on a road carved by a thousand storms and hardened by the high mountain sun, they were all lucky to *be* alive.

The doors slammed as Rusty and Mercy exited, making their way to the back, where a green-faced Priscilla Murdock leapt out like a newly released gazelle.

When they unlocked the headwater wall gate, her crossed arms uncrossed. When they redirected the flow of waters, her sour expression morphed into scrutinizing interest.

"It's incredible," Rusty said to Miss Murdock. "These little brooks, when they meet all together, the way they turn into a force to be reckoned with."

When they descended to the ledge and stood in the dark frame, her narrowed eyes grew round. And when they entered and saw the Galloping Goose, her hand raised to her mouth in a rare moment of speechlessness.

"That's—"

"Galloping Goose Number Eight," Mercy said when Miss Murdock appeared to not have the words.

"But how . . . ?"

"Randolph Gilman," said Rusty.

"But why . . . ?"

"That is where the treasure comes in." They told her what they knew, all the way up to the most recent clue, which Rusty pulled out and read.

> "They rest beneath a steel frame
> And sing a silent song
> Traversing mountains,
> Honed in flame
> The Goose, she sings along

> So free these steel bars beneath
> Dear Motor Number Eight
> And place them in the Echoed Cove
> And then commence to play . . ."

"So there are steel bars underneath this behemoth that will be some kind of key?" Miss Murdock said with an air of either incredulity or enthusiasm—it was difficult to tell with her.

"That's what we aim to find out," said Rusty. And in short time, the three women were under the carriage of Motor Number Eight's rail car, lying on their backs like so many mechanics.

"It's made of tie plates," Priscilla said. "I remember Reuben talking about it. He helped Martin down at the railworks when they were building it, on one of Martin's sabbaticals from the mountains. He only came down from prospecting when he was forced to by weather or injury or the need for funds. He was laid up pretty bad one winter with a broken leg but wouldn't sit still for the life of him. He got a job working on the engine, and when Martin dropped one of the plates, Reuben told him to do it again and picked out a tune on his guitar in the same key. Said that vehicle would be downright musical, made of old tie plates like that. He let me come one day, and I remember thinking what a thing they were creating, how they were lucky to have such good friends. And those men were good to the core, letting me tag along so often with Reuben. Until . . ." Her voice trailed off.

"Look at this," Priscilla redirected, pointing. "These bars here." Several of them, all of different lengths, were stretched between two parallel bars, secured with bolts. "They don't seem to be serving any structural purpose."

"You're right," said Rusty. "And look at their markings . . ." She pointed at one of the rusted rectangles about the length of her forearm, each one engraved with a scattering of dots, and each scattering different. Three dots in a triangle there, five in a circle there, a peak shape, a flower shape, and so many more.

"It looks like a glockenspiel," said Mercy.

"Gesundheit," said Rusty.

Mercy laughed, then grew serious, studying them. "It's an instrument like a xylophone. We had one in the studio's orchestra. And if we're supposed to strike these with that hammer . . ."

"In the number sequence given on the mine ceiling . . ." Rusty added.

"Then it matters what order they're in."

"Should you try it?" Priscilla asked.

"It says it's to be played in the Echoed Cove . . . but it couldn't hurt to try it here."

Mercy pulled out the small hammer, and Rusty read her the numbers. Together they counted bars and *pinged* each until it was clear that this was nothing more than a gathering of random notes. That there must be some other order in the place Martin had wanted them played.

Using the wrenches they'd brought and a good deal of mustered strength, they freed the bars from the frame and bundled them up in burlap sacks, coming out streaked with grease and grime.

"How could a song possibly tell us the whereabouts of a treasure?" asked Mercy on the way back down. They were scrunched up in the cab, Rusty insisting Priscilla join them inside this time.

Priscilla sighed. "Reuben would've loved this. Or hated it. Those boys all felt differently about the treasure after the avalanche."

Mercy wanted to ask but didn't have the heart to force it.

Rusty, it seemed, didn't have the heart to *not* force it. "What happened?"

Priscilla shifted in her seat. As if she wasn't sure she should—or could—go back to what she was about to say. She took another deep breath and looked out the window, the pines slapping the glass.

"Martin Shaw was so certain he'd found a vein in an adit—that's an entrance in the earth." She looked at Mercy, not knowing that Mercy well knew the terms of the world of mining. "I begged my brother to let me come."

Mercy tore her eyes from the road long enough to see the woman's soft smile.

"I'm the youngest," she said. "By quite a bit. I forget sometimes that you younger generation don't remember all of us Murdocks. By the time I was in high school, my brothers and sisters had moved away to the corners of the earth. Or at least Colorado. Breckenridge, Crested Butte, Boulder, Creede . . . we're all over the place. By the time my parents began to need help as they aged, I was the only one left. Not that I minded. But as my peers were marrying and starting families, I was tending to the roots of mine. It's an honor I don't take lightly. . . . It's just that my story unfolded in a way that most don't see, and many don't understand." She sighed. "I miss them all. Especially Reuben."

"Was he the oldest? If he was friends with my father . . ."

"He was the second oldest. I love them all, but he and I . . . we shared something special. I overheard Martin talking about the adit, and I begged Reuben to let me come. I was his shadow back then—I'd go anywhere he'd let me. Perhaps it was his quiet nature, in the midst of a bustling house, or perhaps it was the way he always would hesitate before going out that front door"—she smiled fondly at the vision— "and tip his head at me, inviting me to come . . . but he was the one my heart beat for the most in all this world. That day, though, he wasn't going to let me come. He said it was too far, too cold. 'Not today, Rill.' He was the only one who called me that, and the only one I'd ever allow to give me a nickname, vile things that they are. No offense," she said to Rusty, who shrugged.

"But I put on my red mittens and ran after him anyway. He laughed—he had the gentlest laugh, and he used it more than his words—and said I could come, but I had to stick right by him. When we got to the chute they liked to travel up, I could tell he was nervous, worried about something. And then we heard it." She stopped, shaking her head. "Like— thunder, but coming from the mountain itself. As we looked up, the white of the snow fractured and dropped, disappearing. To a twelve-year-old, it felt like two things twining together that never belonged: terror at the tremble of the earth and wonder at seeing clouds rise up where none had been before."

"Avalanche," Mercy whispered.

She nodded. "And in the backcountry, with no one else around for a rescue, we knew we were doomed. When the mountain starts coming down, you're minutes away from the end, if not seconds."

"Unless you get an air pocket," Rusty said, pushing her way into the story with urgency. "Say you got an air pocket."

"I did," she said. "It was a small one, but when the force of that avalanche came down, it pushed bits of the mountain in front of it and that debris swept me right off my feet. Like I was floating, only float- ing turned into a tumble, a twist—just blue sky and dark, blue sky and dark, and that was the only hint I had about which way was up. Looking back, I know it's impossible, over the roar of that beast, but I could have sworn I heard Reuben calling for me, and all I remember thinking was just *Reuben.* And praying *Please be alright. Please be alright.*"

The girls gulped, neither of them having the courage to jump ahead in the story.

"I thought I'd died." Priscilla laughed without mirth. "There in the dark, with the snow pressing in on me, every bone in my body its captive. I couldn't budge an inch, and my arms and legs were bent in ways I can't even begin to comprehend."

The limp.

"It was so dark . . ." Her voice choked a bit, lip trembling. The woman's armor cracked, letting Rusty and Mercy see the world so carefully contained inside the woman's carefully constructed world. "It got difficult to breathe. The mountain had tangled me up with it. I only knew it was claiming me, quickly."

"Were you afraid?" Rusty said.

"At first, yes. Everything in me kicked against it. I wanted to live, but mostly I wanted to make sure Reuben lived. But then, something happened, right there in the dark, when not a soul in the universe knew where I was. I can't—I can't explain it, but it was so sudden, and so thick, and heavy, and warm, and good—it was simply . . . comfort. Peace. Like the God who made those mountains to begin with looked down at that avalanche and found me, wrapping me up, and wherever He was, the fear began to fade.

"So I waited. It felt so long. Things started to slow down, and that prayer was my companion, even as it slowed in the murky place of my mind. *Please let Reuben be alright.*"

Give them up. Mercy's heart pounded with the desperation of the prayer she knew too well. *Give them up.* It gripped her and pulled her into the avalanche right along with twelve-year-old Rill.

"I could feel a darkness even darker closing in, my whole body relaxing, letting go of its fight." Her voice grew hoarse as she struggled to continue. But did so, haltingly. "And then—someone's hand broke through. Punched in, found my hand . . . and my hand went limp in theirs. The next thing I knew, I opened my eyes to light so bright it hurt, and yet it flooded me—my lungs, too—as I gasped to pull in breath. There was Reuben, his eyes streaming tears. They looked so blue—so very, very blue, rimmed in red, and with his face pulled in a desperation I've never seen before or since. He held me in his arms, and he was yelling my name, I could see, but couldn't hear. *Rill! Rill! Rill, please!*

"And then when I pulled in that breath, he pulled me in, too. His embrace so much like what I'd felt inside the avalanche cocoon . . . but human. He'd been only three steps ahead of me, joking about his long strides. The force of the avalanche pushed him into an alcove of the chute, and the debris closed over the opening like a door, leaving him and his friends safe. And me . . . buried somewhere behind him. I didn't think of the experience as it must have been for him until many years later. How he must have felt, looking out over that broken snowscape and knowing his sister was buried somewhere beneath. To this day, I don't know how he found me. He'd been on rescues before—most men around here have—and they don't always end well. He had every reason to give up hope. But . . ." She choked up, voice growing thin. "He never gave up on me." She sniffed, dashed a tear away with her hand, and then as if remembering the cruciality of handkerchiefs, fished one out of her embroidered handbag—which, of course, she'd brought along on their trek up the mountain in a rusty old truck.

"It was himself he gave up on. He was never the same after that. He never could forgive himself. I still followed him around like a shadow, and he was the one who coached me through learning to walk with crutches, helped me learn to walk again on my own two feet when it came time. Always with an arm to offer me. But there was another shadow over him after that, too . . . and it followed him, always. One day, he just followed it up into the mountains . . . and has never returned. I could hardly bear to see him go but wished even more to see him out from beneath that shadow. Missing him was . . ." She paused, folded her hands tightly in her lap and nodded. ". . . *is* . . . so heavy. Truth be told, Ruby Bright, that infernal cat was my saving grace sometimes."

"What?" Rusty's eyes grew round.

"Why do you think I was so adamant you take him when you isolated yourself up there on the mountain? I knew what it was to be alone. To lose somebody. It's about time you finally took it."

Rusty's jaw dropped, and she stared at Mercy, who stifled a smile.

"Anyway, Reuben wrote to me over the years. He isn't far but has never been able to bring himself back. He walks over to Silverton or Ophir; sometimes the postmarks even read Durango. I think he took a little of me with him in his pocket. Maybe he doesn't realize he took most of me. I always hoped he would find a nice girl, be blessed with a family. If any man was ever meant to be a father . . ." She shook her head. "That great big heart of his, in all its quiet giving. But he never did. His letters grew less frequent. I worry for him, that he's off up there, disappearing into himself." She dashed her eyes with her handkerchief. "As you might imagine, I like order. Safety. Tangling with the mountain will do that to you, I suppose. And I don't like cold. But I also don't like defeat. So I remember the sight of his hands reaching down into the dark for me . . . and I reach for him. I hold onto hope for Reuben. That perhaps someday, I'll see him filling that doorframe once more. I asked him outright, once, to come home. I didn't hear back from him for many months, and the letter that came after that didn't mention my question at all, just as if I'd never asked."

"Maybe about . . . ten years ago?" Rusty asked.

She furrowed her brow and nodded. She gave a quivering smile. "You two hold onto each other, yes? Brothers . . . sisters . . . they're too easy to lose."

Rusty and Mercy exchanged a look.

"And as for those musical bars," Priscilla said, an air of hope in her voice, "you need Willa Jones."

Folio of Field Notes, Volume VI:
Wildwood Forest Theatre Preparation Documents

[Property of Sudsy McGee, Hollywood Biographer]

Mercy's To-Do List
June 1948

☐ Need restroom facilities at each stage venue. Note to Angus.

☐ Electricity for spotlight. Borrow John Deere from diner for generator?

☐ Announce open house for town to preview venue. Surprise with reveal of the G.G. Call it . . . "A Wildwood Evening of Enchantment"?

☐ Get headliner for flagship production. Holden Huxley?

☐ Pick play for flagship production: *The Light Princess*? Requires lake and castle . . . both of which we have. Cave scenes questionable.

☐ Tunnels are like caves. Find out how big of an audience could fit in Randolph Gilman's tunnel. Could it be lined with long rows of seats going down and actors performing as they walk down the aisle and back?

☐ Box office: Wildwood's gatehouse?

☐ Telegraph Sudsy

☐ Business model does not allow for rain checks. Set up awnings for all future stages and seats: Rusty and Casey to hang parachutes as coverings.

☐ Music: Talk to Willa Jones. Meeting at Opera House 10 A.M.

WESTERN UNION

JUNE 13, 1948
TO: MERCY WINDSOR AKA MARYBETH SPATTS
WILDWOOD MANOR—MERCY PEAK
FROM: SUDSY MCGEE
HOLLYWOOD HERALD

DEAR MISS WINDSOR,

COMING OUT FROM HIDING, I SEE. DID NOT EXPECT
THAT. IN RECEIPT OF YOUR INQUIRY RE: PLAY VENUE.
SEEN SOME SCHEMES IN MY DAY. THIS ONE TAKES
GUTS IN MORE WAYS THAN ONE. YOU WILL NEED A
HEADLINER NAME TO DRAW CROWDS THAT FAR. WILL IT
BE YOU? YES, WILL DO A PRESS RELEASE IF YOU GRANT
EXCLUSIVE INTERVIEW WITH PERMISSION TO ASK FIVE
QUESTIONS OF MY CHOOSING ON ANY TOPIC. NO HOLDS
BARRED.

WESTERN UNION

JUNE 14, 1948
TO: SUDSY MCGEE
HOLLYWOOD HERALD

MR. MCGEE,

MAKE IT THREE QUESTIONS AND YOU'VE GOT A DEAL.

WESTERN UNION

JUNE 15, 1948
TO: MERCY WINDSOR
WILDWOOD MANOR—MERCY PEAK

MISS WINDSOR,

YES TO 3 QUESTIONS . . . IN PERSON. MUST KNOW IT'S
REALLY YOU. MATTER OF JOURNALISTIC INTEGRITY.

CHAPTER
26

I'm not afraid of you.

—Mercy Windsor, on the set of *Embargo*,
to a pit of slithering serpents

"I'm not afraid of you," she said. The same words she used to utter before entering any new film set, as if it could convince her that she didn't feel like running off and burying her head in the sand. Only this time, she wasn't staring down a soundstage, but Hannafin's Opera House of Main Street, Mercy Peak. She hadn't thought she'd ever come near a stage again—or even a building containing one, for that matter—but here she was. Pulling the heavy carved door with both hands, throwing her weight into it like a tug-of-war with time itself.

She stepped inside, eyes pressed closed, and took a moment. This was not Grauman's in Hollywood. This place could be Grauman's grandfather, and held within its empty walls the echoes of finery and festivities long gone. Now, this was the place Ralph and Nancy Mosely came each week, hauling their own popped corn and blankets, and sharing with the other few stragglers who dared partake of such an ancient pastime as the silent theatre.

"Oh good, you're here!" A friendly female voice echoed slightly. Willa gave her a million-watt smile and guided Mercy up the aisle. A red carpet had been laid some decades before, judging by the places it was worn.

"Miss Murdock's doing," Willa said.

"Pardon?"

"The carpet. Prissy says that if we are to have a movie house, it shall be a movie house worth contending with the West End of London." She leaned in. "Between you and me, nobody here quite knows what she's talking about, but Prissy fares best when given her lead." She winked.

"Prissy . . . as in Priscilla Murdock?"

Willa's laugh filled the auditorium. "That's right. We were school-mates. I've never been able to shake calling her Prissy, much to her chagrin. She made the change when we were teenagers and she had her eye on a senior over in Telluride. She thought her full name sounded more sophisticated."

"What became of the senior in Telluride?"

"He's still a senior in Telluride . . . just a senior of a different sort now." Willa winked. "His name is Tom, and he's a confirmed bachelor, last I knew. He never was quite as awestruck by the sophisticated name as Priscilla had hoped."

Mercy followed Willa up the aisle and to the base of a stage. The whole place smelled of mellowed wood and cinnamon, and she could almost envision the memories of a thousand town meetings spinning under the stage lights.

"Now, about that piano . . ." Willa started. "Rusty says you're need-ing music for a play?"

That was the pretense, true as it was, for Mercy coming here today. Willa uncovered the instrument and plunked a few keys playfully. They left a hollow after-echo, a sign it hadn't been tuned in some time, but soon Willa was covering over that by playing a few plucky measures of "The Entertainer."

Mercy clapped when she stopped, delighted at the brightness filling the hall from this humble instrument.

"It's a player piano," Willa said, "so you'll have all the scrolls we have available for your play, if you wish. If any of them are suited to your play."

"Oh, but I was hoping—" Mercy stopped herself. "That is, I don't mean to presume, but everyone says you have magic in your own music."

"Do they?" Willa blushed. "This town is prone to exaggeration . . . they're too kind. And you're one of us now; you're ours when you live in Mercy Peak, so you'd better get used to it." She shook her head, but the smile on her face told Mercy the words had tickled her.

"May I hear one of your own pieces?"

At this, the woman grew uneasy, looking over her shoulder furtively. "Oh, I—well, there's a reason I'm not a concert pianist." She was a lovely woman, her blond hair sprinkled with silver, deep smile lines beginning to trace her face. "I play for the silent films because it's everything I love best—the music, the story, a chance to bring it to people and lift their hearts—but no one is looking at me. I wasn't born for the spotlight."

"I understand the feeling," Mercy said, and meant it. "What if I . . . wandered a bit? Explored the theatre while you play to your heart's content? No eyes on you. Only ears. Anything that's a delight to you."

Even her laugh was musical. "Well, how can I refuse that?"

True to her word, Mercy began to walk the hall, hands clasped behind her back as she took it all in like a patron at an art museum. The music lifted from beneath her, swelling in climbing notes, tumbling in cascades, a tune that felt alive and full of the player's soul.

Mercy ran her hand over timeworn rails and well-loved seats, lifted her eyes to the balcony above, and marveled. For its small size, the opera house was a vestige of a glamorous time, right out here in the rugged embrace of the mountains. At the peak of the mining boom, ladies in lace dresses on the arms of men in bowler hats would've frequented this place, right alongside miners who'd come down from the mines. What a world it must have been, back in those days.

She stood in the center aisle and lifted her eyes to the roll-up stage curtain, which bore a hand-painted scene of a gondola in Venice. It was a masterpiece, depicting an ancient water city that seeped with tales untold. It drew her close. What pairing of imagination and skill had brought such a scene right here into the mountains?

"I love that painting," Willa said, her notes dropping to a natural close. "When I was a girl, a traveling painter came through town offering his services and was hired to paint this." She laughed. "Actually, it wasn't just him—he and his wife were a traveling pair, he plying his mural-painting ability from town to town, while she ran something of a peddler's wagon and chased their little girl around—just a wee thing with dark curls like springs and a laugh that pealed like a ringing bell, filling up the little clearing they occupied in the trees at the edge of town. The peddler's wagon was so . . ." She searched for a word. "It was just magical. There's no other word for it."

She pointed at the long, narrow black boat in the mural. "See that gondola? Imagine a boat like that, strapped to a wagon and selling books. That's what they brought with them! The woman—she told me of her gondola in Venice, its cabin stocked, every nook and cranny, with books so colorful and titles so sparkly they were like treasure to behold. They brought a smaller version of it for its American tour—not a gondola, but something like it—a sandolo, I think it was called? It had belonged to a family friend, who had rebuilt it after it had been destroyed in a terrible storm decades before. He had bequeathed it to them, and though its age and state made it no longer seaworthy, this young man was determined to give it new purpose. Its story held personal meaning to him, though I'm not sure what it was. In San Francisco, he secured the front portion, with its black paint and gold flourishes, to a wagon—a peddler's wagon unlike anyone had ever seen before, its hull packed with books. Imagine a contraption like that, coming trundling into this valley." Her laugh tumbled with genuine joy.

"I'd prayed all my life to someday see the ocean. I was born and raised here, high up in these mountains, and you can imagine that for a miner's family with six children, a trek halfway across the country is no small matter. My father wanted so badly to give me my dream, and when that sandolo rolled into town, you should've seen his face light up. *'Look at that, Willa. God strapped the sea to a wagon and brought it straight to you!'* He went home and got that month's milk money and told me to go pick out any book I wanted. When I protested, he waved me off and said he'd get the milk some other way, like trade digging post holes for the dairy farmer. I climbed up that wagon's ladder and flipped through books for a whole day, and the woman just delighted in that. I had pulled a whole stack of books out, trying to decide between them, and she said in this enchanting Italian accent, *'It is impossible to choose, no?'* She led me to a picnic blanket she'd spread beneath a tree, with pillows making a throne of the tree trunk. *'Read,'* she said. I asked which one, and she laughed and said, *'All of them, to your heart's content!'* And I did—for the whole two weeks they were there, I finished my chores at home, and every afternoon scurried off for the gondola wagon and the picnic blanket and my stack of books."

"Which book did you choose?"

Willa dipped her head and laughed. "I'd like to say it was some great classic—*War and Peace* or *David Copperfield* . . . but I was a young girl full of fancies and a vision for the sea. I chose an illustrious volume called *Legends of the Waves*. Nothing but sensational lore," she said conspiratorially. "Davy Jones, the Flying Dutchman, the vanished ship *Jubilee*. The woman—Vittoria—she listened as I chattered away about the ocean. She'd listen with her daughter held close on her lap, or let her little girl sit with me while she helped other customers. She painted our town bright with her books, and I think we needed it. So many were moving away—leaving empty houses, and leaving our hearts emptier, too.

"She would bring me a cup of hot tea, poured from a pot she kept warm in a special chamber in the boat. I'd bring a sandwich and split it with her little girl. It became our ritual for those two weeks. And then with a wink, she'd leave me alone for hours and hours. The last day, she asked to borrow back the book I'd chosen. *'Just a—how do you say? Formality. I will return it, I promise!'* She kept it overnight, and when she returned it, the inside cover had been painted by her husband. An ocean scene just for me and the words: *'The Bounding Sea, for Willa.'* And then he wrote something else, too . . ." Willa narrowed her eyes, as if reaching for the precise words. "*'Whenever you wish to see the ocean, just look up. The sky is painted blue by that faraway sea you can't see, and the clouds are just bits of flying ocean, visiting you from afar.'* Vittoria read that part aloud and lingered over her husband's words. I remember the way she let her fingertips hover over them, the way she sniffed a little. *'That is my husband,'* she said. *'He has learned to see things in a different way—it is always so beautiful to me.'*"

Willa looked up, settling her eyes on the painted curtain once more. "They returned to Venice soon after; they called the peddler wagon their 'Great American Tour' and sailed from San Francisco a month or two later to return to their bookshop there. But every time I've opened that book, I've thought of them. Every time I've seen a cloud in the sky against that backdrop of blue, I've remembered I live in a world where when I can't see the ocean, God sends it straight to me. So great a kindness, this world is. I sometimes think, when our dreams seem impossible to us, perhaps we just haven't seen yet how God will chase after our hearts with those very dreams, in the unlikeliest ways. It took a storm-battered boat, restored splinter by splinter, to teach me that."

Mercy thought of the false skies she'd sat beneath in the soundstages at Pinnacle. She'd watched the painters once, and marveled at their artistry. Had she ever thought of the vaulting sky above in the same way? A living, moving work of art?

Willa, bright with her memories, continued, "And every time I've played along with the movies, I've had that scene to keep me company."

"Your playing truly is beautiful," Mercy said.

"You're too kind."

"I'm not just saying that to flatter. Your talent could rival any musician I've had the pleasure of hearing. And a great many more, too." She thought quickly, trying to find a way into the question she ultimately needed to ask. "How do you choose what to play with each film?"

"I'm not sure I have a specific method," she said, forehead scrunched in thought. "Some movies I pull out a tried-and-true villainous string of chords for treacherous scenes; some I weave in bits of classical pieces. And there have been a few over the years—a very few—that inspired their own original score."

"Oh?" Mercy folded her arms atop the piano and rested her chin there, loving this glimpse into Willa's art. "What set them apart?"

"It's—it's hard to explain." Willa seemed a bit sheepish. Mercy, recognizing one who'd stumbled into something they weren't ready to speak of, offered another route into the conversation.

"Could you . . . play one of them for me?"

Willa pondered, then nodded. She closed her eyes.

The notes began, soft tiptoes that traversed small climbs and trilled down again. Like raindrops on a puddle, the notes fell into the air and released rings of expanding echoes into the room. Whimsical and endearing in the occasional minor note, like a child learning to walk, and tossing in a small leap every now and again. The climbs grew, taking on heights, pausing to ponder, soaring into an unexpected flight that filled Mercy from the inside. It gripped hold of her. Held her captive, breath hushed, as the notes tiptoed now into her own heart in a way that somehow *knew* her, moved her, left her aching.

Willa's fingers slowed as the notes descended a slow cascade into a soft, bright melody. Tapping at her heart with distant familiarity until the notes lined up, sure and certain, into the opening refrain engraved on Mercy's soul.

Stars shining bright above you . . .

Mercy's eyes welled with unshed tears, and when Willa lifted her own gaze to meet hers, she resisted the urge to dash the tears away, hide them in that locked-away place. Silence was its own song, between them, until Mercy at last spoke. "H-how—how did you do that?"

Willa pressed her hands together between her knees, looking at her lap. As if she, too, found it difficult to put words there. "That one . . . was special," she said. "It was a movie that landed here at a time when I was . . . struggling. Life hadn't gone as I'd once hoped, though I'd never told anyone that. Growing up in such a full house, there was always noise, always joy, always bits of strife, too, but that just comes and goes, you know. I always thought, I'd like that, too, someday. A merry house full of life, children to tend."

Mercy's heart pricked. She thought of Willa's cottage overlooking the river, the way it seemed an outpost of life—with wild roses and bright green grass, music spilling from within. It was, indeed, a merry house full of life—but she knew there had been no young hands to tend.

"I've made my peace with the way my life has unfolded," Willa said. "It's a beautiful life, grace upon grace at every turn. But every now and then, that old longing comes, though the time for it is past. I've never married; there will never be children. The times when that old sorrow bubbles back up . . ." She lifted her eyes to the painted screen, her voice thick. ". . . I tell myself, *'Don't forget, Willa, how great a kindness this life is.'* And I don't. I don't forget that." She smiled sheepishly, sniffing and looking at Mercy, whose own voice was caught in her throat. "But all those years I learned this instrument, I always thought there'd be someone to play these notes for. Perhaps even . . . a lullaby."

Mercy looked away, feeling the other end of that unmet longing. *Was* this world a kindness? A world where one woman longs for a child to play her lullabies for, and a girl on the other side of the country lies alone at nights, wishing for even the embrace of a parent? Her breathing drilled deep to the place where the hard questions lived— and she pulled it quickly back up, taking shallow breaths. Finding a smile for Willa, encouraging her on. This was not about her own story, after all.

Willa continued, "And then one day, we got a reel in. I came here to preview it, as I always do, to make notes about what music to play in which scene. It was a silent film and the crowd always likes a jaunty tune to match the big antics, so I was practicing along, and then this girl appeared on the screen."

Mercy's fingers, which had been tracing the edge of the piano, stopped. She swallowed.

"As I watched her, I felt I knew her somehow. Not because of any mystical connection—it is only a screen after all. Just flickering lights and film. But just . . . something in her eyes. As if she'd seen some things, and rather than hide it away as so many of us are apt to do, she allowed it to connect us. To the story, to her, to everyone else in the room. She was playing a young mother receiving news that her child had died."

Mercy was frozen. Certain that if she shifted even a bit, some crack in this moment would swallow her up, and she'd be right there on that set again. Hot beneath the lights, squirming beneath the scrutiny of director, producer, and others. The memory was so clear. . . .

After the third cry of "Cut!" And the third tirade to "Make it real, sweetheart!" the costume mistress had come over and knelt, untying her boot just to tie it again. "Pretend them away," she'd murmured, so quietly Mercy had wondered if the woman had been talking to herself.

She'd peered at the woman, bewildered, ready to crawl out of her own skin to escape this place. But where in all the world could she have gone? She had nobody. No place was home. No money for a train ticket or hotel room.

The costume mistress grasped her hand and leaned in. "Just forget them. Tune them out. You ever hear a radio?"

Mercy had nodded.

"Turn those voices into static—tune them out. Just like a radio knob. Yes?"

Mercy nodded, still in a haze.

"Now, tune in to the music, whatever will play when this is shown. The way the people will feel. These people who are just as real as you and will see something real in you, too. Think of their sorrows, think of their courage. Do this for them. Those old codgers barking at you— they'd wilt under these lights. They can't do what you're doing. Don't be cowed by them; they're just a bunch of bluster."

Mercy knew they were far more than bluster. But it helped to think of them sweating under these lights and trying to play a widow who was both heartbroken and courageous all at once.

Heartbroken, Mercy knew. Courageous . . . well, that would be where the acting came in.

"And whenever you need a break, just a minute to take a breath and clear them out, you just tie that shoe or have me do it. Any time you need to, whether it's untied or not. Just let 'em try to make a fuss about that." And with a wink, the costume mistress stepped away.

She'd closed her eyes. Mercy hadn't lost a husband, but she'd lost her one true friend. Thinking of Rusty, she let the tears come—but held them back, just enough. Just enough to keep Rusty hers and not share that dearest soul with untold millions. Or more likely, dozens—who would come to see a silent film, in the age of talkies? Still. Rusty felt too precious to share . . . and too important not to share.

So, the cameras rolled. A single tear spilled. Mercy turned the voices off-camera into radio static and imagined a faraway song.

One that never could have sounded as haunting, as captivating, as soul-filling, as Willa's sounded today.

Feeling the piano player's eyes on her now, and the way her own cheeks burned, she stooped to tie her shoe—and found only buckles.

She stood slowly. There was nowhere to go. Nowhere to hide.

But it was Willa who looked near ready to bolt.

"That girl on the screen . . . I can't explain it. But suddenly, every moment over the years that I'd dreamed of playing a lullaby, perhaps for a dreamed-of child of my own, those notes I'd laid to rest along with that hope . . . they rose up and wove into that scene. Her delivery of that performance was so real, I—well, I wanted to gather her up in her moment of grief, like a mother would. I—I hope that doesn't sound presumptuous. I'm a stranger, I know, and I would never presume to—"

She was flustered, her words picking up speed until she halted them, lifted her eyes, and met Mercy's. "Rusty had vanished from us not too long before, and we were all missing her, too. She used to go around humming that tune, 'Dream a Little Dream.' So it made its way into the song." She paused and met Mercy's eyes. "For whatever it's worth, dear girl . . . that lullaby was for you."

The words hung between them like notes themselves.

"It's silly," Willa rushed to say. "I shouldn't have said all of that. I hope I didn't—"

And then it was Mercy reaching out and taking Willa's hand. The same fingers that had held a thousand beautiful notes.

"Thank you," she said simply.

All those nights she'd lain awake, heard the neighbor's lullabies in the next shanty down . . . All those empty spaces, filled. Decades later—and somehow, sweeter for it.

"It means more than I can say." Her voice was thick. She longed to explain. To spill her own account into the one Willa had risked sharing and let the frayed edges of both meet together. And someday, she prayed, she would. Someday, when she'd managed to find voice enough again.

Mercy was up against a wall in this conversation, and Willa seemed to sense it, offering a gentle conclusion. "That song was special because that girl was special. I knew it then . . . and I know it even more now."

The words shook something loose in Mercy, something so true and good she didn't know what to do with it. She fumbled her way through asking Willa if she might "lend her musical expertise" tomorrow and gave warning that it might involve a hike. Willa beamed at the chance to go, and Mercy wished she could explain better what they'd need her for . . . but she didn't quite know the answer to that herself.

She rowed the length of the lake back to Wildwood, thinking on what Willa had said. *"You're ours."*

She'd been plenty of people's. She'd been Ralston Spatts's girl. Hollywood's queen. Pinnacle's property. Leading lady to this actor or that. But in those lights, "ours" meant possession and control.

Willa's sweet voice, the way her own broken story wrapped around the word *ours* . . . it meant belonging and freedom.

And to belong . . . didn't one have to be known?

And to be known . . . didn't one have to let people in?

This was a practice Mercy knew nothing about. No one had ever knocked back from the other side of that door before, pouring right back into her. No one since Rusty, anyway.

It was terrifying. Look what losing Rusty had done to her. Her heart wouldn't survive another shattering like that one. It hadn't even survived the first shattering.

And yet that night, as she retreated again to her boathouse, the walk through Wildwood didn't feel quite as empty. Just down the mountain, there were people she liked. And who perhaps even liked her back a little.

CHAPTER
27

Rusty

"Maybe we should walk," Rusty said. She, Willa, Marybeth, and Casey Campbell looked up the steep slope. They could've used Holden's utter disregard for danger just now . . . but he'd returned to Hollywood to go on a date he'd forgotten about, promising to make it back in time for the open house at Wildwood.

The old Peak View mine tram hung above them, the way the miners used to traverse the mountain to work, by night or by day, rain or shine.

A breeze blew, and the hanging bucket creaked. Clouds gathered, a slow-tumbling migration. Rusty shivered.

"I tested it out last week," Casey said. "It's a little worse for the wear, but it runs. They built this solid, that's for sure."

"And this is the best way to Sea Glass Lake?" Marybeth asked.

"And the Echoed Cove," said Willa. "If that's where you need to be, this is the best way. There's a climb, to be sure, but it's treacherous in its own right, with loose rock from the mine tailings over so many years. Once we're at the top, it'll be a short walk down into a basin where the lake is. Then all you have to look out for is Sasquatch," Willa said, with a twinkle in her eye.

"Sasquatch?" Marybeth said. "As in . . . Bigfoot?" She looked delighted.

"Friend of yours?" Rusty said dryly, thankful for the diversion.

"You might say that."

"Right," Rusty said. "I forgot I'm talking to Frankenstein's girlfriend. Mythical creatures populated your dinner table beneath a crystal chandelier, no doubt."

Instead of protesting, Marybeth held up a finger. "Frankenstein's *monster*'s girlfriend. But Sasquatch was an entirely different creature.

Why, when they were filming—" Marybeth seemingly became aware of the three sets of amused eyes on her and halted. "Never mind. I take it Sea Glass Lake has its own share of lore?"

"Oh, this is a *true* story," Willa said. "Only a few years ago, the Jenks children were skating on Sea Glass Lake. The ice broke, and Poppy fell in. It was terrible, truly—but to hear her sisters tell it, a great tall being covered in fur emerged out of nowhere, diving in to rescue the girl."

"So the Mercy Peak Bigfoot is a heroic sort of cryptid, then," said Casey.

"Oh yes. There have been other incidents—a lost goat who had wandered away in a blizzard returned mysteriously to its home. A set of giant footprints were found, leading the way. Oh, and once, Priscilla's cat was stuck at the top of a tree near Ruby Rock, howling for days on end. One morning it was found safe in a crate on her porch, and a branch had broken off the tree in the middle of the night, as if someone had climbed up in secret. Our Sasquatch is really more of a Robin Hood," Willa said proudly.

Rusty feigned interest in the tales she'd heard a thousand times, but inside, her stomach was mush. She didn't know what was wrong with her. She'd been to the lake before, always by foot and by the backcountry trails. She'd always wanted to ride the tram—had even stowed away in it once, under one of the two benches in the bucket. But her father had spotted her braid and sent her packing. She'd sworn to Sam that one day she'd ride it, and he swore right back that he was going to make it happen for her.

Someday.

A pit opened in her stomach, ready to swallow her right up.

She loathed pits.

"Let's do it," she said, and set her jaw and her courage.

"Should one stay behind while the other three go up?" Marybeth asked.

"Better to split up in pairs," Rusty said. "So no one's alone. J-just in case."

"Good idea," said Willa. "And perhaps one Mercy Peak local in each pair in case we get separated somehow?"

"Excellent plan," said Marybeth, smiling a little too brightly. "Willa, may I claim you as my partner?"

This delighted Willa. The spark in Marybeth's eyes when she looked at Rusty and Casey did not delight Rusty.

The two women climbed into the oversized bucket and sat.

"Take this." Casey handed Marybeth some sort of radio, army green and chipped, with two black speaker-like apparatuses.

"A radio?"

"Handie-Talkie," Casey said. "Army surplus, from the war. Just push this button to talk, and I'll hear you." He held up an identical unit. "I can talk to you, too. Let me know when you're up and ready for us."

"You're certain they work?" Marybeth asked, ignoring the way Rusty was staring daggers at her. Casey answered in the affirmative, giving a few instructions, and then he flipped the switch. The metal pulley jolted into slow action, and the women were off, flying overhead where hundreds of miners had been borne up over the years, only to descend again into the earth.

She didn't like this. The closer they got, the closer she was to living her dream—and living it incomplete.

"Rusty?" Casey's voice, always friendly, was gentle beside her.

She jerked to face him much too fast. "Hmm?" She feigned nonchalance.

He pinched his brows. "Are you okay?"

"Of course," she said, laughing nervously. "Why wouldn't I be?"

Casey studied her, waiting. That wasn't what people did. All those people, after Sam . . . they'd knock on her door and ask, *Are you okay?* and then ask a thousand more questions that she didn't have answers for. *When will you come back down? What do you need? What can we do?*

"Fine," she said, realizing he was still just . . . waiting. "I'm fine." She smiled.

He shrugged. "Good," he said, as the pulley slowed to a stop and the bell rang. "Because it's our turn."

She laughed nervously again. Drat. She wished she could stamp those nervous laughs out on the ground like she was squishing bugs. He helped her into the old bucket like some fine gentleman across the sea might've helped a lady into a carriage or a chariot. Her hand trembled in his a bit as she looked down at the ground, at the seat across from her, and saw—for just a flash of imagination—Sam.

And he was gone. Gone then, gone still, gone forever.

And she was still here, taking steps without him.

But this one felt more tender than usual. The tram jerked into motion, jolting her so she gripped the bench tighter than she needed to.

"Hey," Casey said, his face all concern.

She was sidled up into the corner of her bench, the whole rest of it stretching cold and empty next to her.

Tentatively, he moved from the opposite bench to hers, leaving plenty of space between them. And more tentatively still, he reached out, into that void . . . and laid his hand on hers.

She winced. Not because it was painful—but because of the warmth. It pricked something in her heart. It told her *you're not alone* . . . which went against everything her heart was shouting.

Alone, alone, alone, that's all she'd been the past ten years. All she thought she'd ever be. She'd come to terms with that . . . hadn't she?

And then blasted—or blessed—Marybeth Spatts blew into town, resurrecting all kinds of things long dead.

Including her heart. Which beat louder under the warmth of Casey Campbell's touch.

Finally, she looked at him.

And he still did not speak. He searched her eyes, and his smile was sad, and genuine, and knowing.

Her breathing slowed under his gaze, and she held it for the first time.

"You're probably wondering why I'm acting like a cat in a roomful of rocking chairs," she said.

"Not really," he said. "Mostly just wondering if you're alright."

Clearly the man could see she wasn't. So she could either try and fail to pretend she was, or just spit it out.

"I guess I'm not, really," she said. "But it's hard to explain. And truth be told, it's ridiculous. I'm getting all worked up about something a decade old—more than a decade."

"Something to do with Sam?" Casey asked, again with features only lined in gentle sincerity and genuine interest.

"Who told you about Sam?"

His eyebrows went up. "You do know you live in Mercy Peak."

At this, she laughed. This time it was easy and gentle and so . . . natural. Which felt completely unnatural. "So, everyone, then?"

He looked up, as if calculating. "Yes," he said. "Yes, I think it officially was everyone."

She laughed again, then ran her free hand along the edge of the tram. "We were going to ride this together one day," she said. And in speaking it aloud, there was sadness . . . but an odd sort of sweetness, too. As if the memory had been there, sitting upon her heart, waiting to be given form in words.

The tram slowed to a creaky stop, and Rusty sat up straight. Casey looked down the slope, and then up.

"Everything's fine" came Marybeth's clear voice. "We'll be back in operation shortly!"

"Wonder what that's all about," Casey said.

It was about a meddling so-called friend who couldn't mind her own business, Rusty thought. But said only, "Yes, I wonder."

"Guess we may as well enjoy the view," Casey said. And bless him, he was not looking at her when he said it, making eyes at her like some terrible double-meaning line from a movie. He was looking out at the treetops they were passing, so close they could touch them.

Rusty reached to do just that, brush her fingers through the evergreen boughs. And as she did, she froze.

"Look," she said. A low cloud, wispy in its tendrils of mist, reached back. Settling in her palm, cooling her skin with its ethereal touch. "Willa calls clouds *flying seas*," she said quietly.

Casey moved carefully back to the other bench and slowly reached out, careful not to rock the tram much. His hand, large and calloused from days spent climbing this mountain, chopping wood for campfires, and stringing lines for measurements, looked endearingly out of place there, holding the most delicate form of water known to man.

The joy of it spun in Rusty, stretching her cheeks wide into a smile. He looked at her, and she laughed.

"Think we're the first two humans in history to hold a cloud together?"

That tickled her even more. "We might just be," she said. And then the tram jolted into its upward crawl again, bringing them straight into the heart of the cloud's embrace as it wrapped around them, cloaking them from the world beyond and spinning misty tendrils between them, too. Every glimpse she got of Casey, as they moved into the heart of the cloud, he had his eyes fixed on her. He had smiling eyes, she decided. He seemed to be all ease and affability . . . but there was a depth to his warmth. As if it had been hard-won.

In the safety of the cloud, as if a spell had been cast where anything could be said and welcomed and even forgiven . . . he spoke out of that depth.

"I'm sorry you aren't here with Sam," he said, punctuating the statement with a small, somber nod.

Rusty's smile melted away, yet somehow in the words he offered there was peace. And the walls—those walls so firm and strong she'd spent so many years hammering up around her heart with rusty old nails—they eased a bit at the joints.

"Thank you," she said simply. She wanted to say more but didn't know what, and the tram came to her rescue, slowing to a stop.

"Welcome to our foggy kingdom," said Willa.

Casey opened the door to help her out, an action Marybeth looked entirely too pleased over.

Rusty smiled sweetly at her friend but spoke through gritted teeth. "I'm on to you."

Marybeth responded with the most innocent doe-eyed look she'd ever seen. Rusty rolled her eyes. "Onward," she said, and led the way down the trail, unheeding of the distant roll of thunder.

They crested a small rise, and Rusty slowed, as she always did for the first glimpse of this lake. It was something to behold, as evidenced by Marybeth's airy gasp, hand to heart.

"Oh my . . ." She shook her head in wonder.

"I know," Rusty said. No matter how many times she saw it, the otherworldly blue of this lake pierced her heart straight through. It was beyond any name they had for colors in this world—it was turquoise in crescendo, aqua in fortissimo, and so beautiful it almost hurt.

"That's so blue it almost hurts," said Casey. Rusty snapped her gaze to him. "In a good way." He raised his hands.

"In the best way," Rusty agreed.

"What makes it that color?" Marybeth asked, still awestruck.

"Minerals in the water," she said. "There's nothing like it, don't you think?"

"The Echoed Cove is . . . that way." Willa pointed. "I've never seen the lake in mist like this before," she said. "I'm a little disoriented."

The mist brought the scene to life, moving over the waters in swirls, slipping in and among treetops, winding around their feet. It wasn't so heavy it suffocated; rather it had the effect of lifting the whole of creation, including them.

They followed Willa's lead, the metal bars divided between the foursome's burlap bags slipping against one another in an eerie sort of minor song to accompany their trek.

On the opposite side of the lake, red earth mingled with emerald trees, each descending right into the lake, not even leaving a shore, as if the mountain rushed to claim the waters and call them her own.

They reached an alcove, a sideways dome of sorts. Rusty, along with every other child who'd had the privilege of growing up on the shoulders of these mountains, knew the great secret of this cove.

"If you stand inside and speak softly," she said, "the curve of the alcove will snatch up your voice and project it out over the lake. And the lake picks it up and carries it all the way across, so that someone on the other side of the lake can hear you clear as day."

"That can't be true," Marybeth said. "Is that true?" She looked at Willa.

"As true as can be," Willa said. "We can try it before we go, if you like. But right now, I imagine you might be interested in this." She gestured at the back of the alcove, where the wall met a ledge halfway down and pegs had been secured at various intervals in two parallel rows.

"A frame for the instrument," Willa said. "Don't you think?"

Rusty set the bag down, and without a word, stooped to pull the metal bars from within. "Which ones go where? The space between the holes is all the same. And you said they don't go in the typical order, right? With the bars getting incrementally larger, left to right?"

"Right." Marybeth pulled up a bar. "Otherwise we could have played the sequence anywhere. It has to come down to these." She pointed at the etching of dots on it. "Some sort of code?"

Casey crouched to examine the pegs in the rock. "Look," he said. "The dots are here, too." He ran his finger over a place in the wall just above where it met the ledge. "This one has dots in a circle," he said. "Does it have a match?"

It did . . . and so did each of the others. They made quick work, the four of them each pulling out bars, finding their spots, until what stood before them was the most jagged, forlorn-looking glockenspiel anyone had ever seen . . . and you couldn't help but love the uneven row of metal.

Casey scratched his head. "Shouldn't they be in ascending order?"

Rusty shook her head. "He wanted them scrambled. So we—or the Blood Moon Boys—would have to come to this particular spot to find the right order."

"Why here, I wonder?" Willa said.

"The moment of truth." Marybeth held up the hammer. "Let's hope we find out. Willa, would you do the honor?"

Willa took the hammer and stepped up to her instrument, inlaid into the very mountain. "What do I play?"

Marybeth nodded at Rusty, who pulled out the numbers in sequence that she'd written down from the mine ceiling.

Rusty read the numbers one by one, waiting for Willa to strike each note. She did . . . and the effect was as if someone had opened a music box, with metallic notes tiptoeing their shine out into the mist and billowing to fill the whole basin. Mingling with the clouds note by pleasant note, until the familiarity of the song took form around them, cementing its identity the moment it struck three of the same notes in progression.

"*It is well* . . ." said Casey. "A hymn. Right?"

"It's . . . beautiful," Rusty said, her heart echoing with the way the notes were at once mournful and hopeful.

"Why that song?" said Willa. "Could there be a clue in the words? 'When peace, like a river, attendeth my way . . . When sorrows like sea billows roll; Whatever my lot, Thou hast taught me to say . . . It is well, it is well with my soul. . . .'"

Rusty's heart ached around the words. What would it be to hold sorrow and be able to say such a thing? She knew the writer of the hymn had suffered loss upon loss.

"It's as if he wants it played for someone," Marybeth said. "He imagined Randolph and Silas would be on this hunt together. Perhaps it had particular meaning to them?"

Willa put her hand on Marybeth's arm. "Reuben Murdock," she said. "The last time anyone saw him in Mercy Peak was at church one Sunday. He always sat in the back. I asked him why, once, and he said he didn't want to be in anyone's way. He was always overly conscious of his height," she said fondly. "But that Sunday . . . I remember watching him during the closing hymn, from across the aisle. He was looking at his sister, and his own eyes welled up. A single tear dropped to the floor, and as everyone else was singing, he just . . . slipped out the door. Nobody saw him after that."

Rusty could relate. And yet the man's tale cast light on a truth she should have known long ago: She wasn't the only one hurting in these mountains. She'd walled herself away with her own pain so it wouldn't bleed out on everyone else, but had they been aching, too? Those people knocking on her door . . . had they been offering compassion, born of their own deepest hurts?

Sam's parents had left after his funeral, to care for a relative up near Breckenridge. They wrote, and so did Rusty . . . but along with all of the others who had tried to reach out, she'd distanced herself from them.

The thought smote her.

"But what are we to do with the song?" Marybeth asked. "We're missing something. There's no key for where to go from here."

"Perhaps he left a message, of some sort?" Willa asked.

Rusty pulled herself out of her reflections. "Like in the mine," she said. "There were the numbers on the ceiling, and then the metal capsule containing the next riddle." She rummaged in her sack. "Like this." She held up the tarnished brass cylinder.

"Where would he hide something like that around here?" Casey ran his hand along the top ledge of the cove, coming up with only dust. "Maybe a chink of some sort, or an engraving in the rock."

"He was a prospector," Willa said. "They staked their claims in jars sometimes—attached to posts or buried in piles of rocks . . ." She looked around.

Marybeth crossed the alcove, to a mound of rocks at its entrance. Rusty joined her, and together they unpiled rocks until the beautiful sound of stone on metal sounded, and Rusty pulled out another capsule.

With haste, she opened it, unrolling the paper within and handing it to Marybeth, who read,

> "First of four, and then you'll see
> The answer on this inland sea
> Three rhymes reveal the letter . . ."

Willa was already in action, calculating. "First of four," she said. "Can you play it this time?"

Marybeth handed Rusty the hammer, and the weight of it in her hand was more than the hammer warranted. As if each note she played was an invitation for her heart to step up and live those words. She plinked them out, releasing them into their misty waltz over the lake, over her soul . . .

When peace like a river attendeth my way . . . Peace. A flash of Sam, splashing through the river, reaching back for her, giving her his smile, his heart, his time, his life.

When sorrows, like sea billows roll . . . Sorrows. A flash of Kurt holding a telegram to his heart, there at her step. The red in his eyes, and she'd never once seen that man cry. The hat to his chest. The way he caught her hand and squeezed it when she read the message, and her hand fell, her heart fell, her everything fell.

Whatever my lot, thou hast taught me to say, it is well . . . it is well . . . with my soul. Playing the climbing notes felt like someone was laying steps before her soul, beckoning her to step upon them.

It is well . . . with my soul. . . .

"There," Willa said. "Four of the same note in a row." It hung among them, rolling out and across the lake.

Willa fingered a phantom piano in front of her, feeling out the music. "It's a C."

"Which completes the rhyme," Marybeth said. "Which letter rhymes with *see* and *sea*?"

> "First of four, and then you'll see
> The answer on this inland sea
> Three rhymes reveal the letter . . ."

"C," Casey said. "'First of four' . . . Is there a place with four C notes in a row?"

Willa hummed lightly, and when she approached the run of four Cs, spoke the words. "Well with my soul . . ."

"*Well,*" Rusty said in a choked voice. The hardest word for her to reconcile her heart to.

"Well . . ." Marybeth repeated. "If Martin was writing this for Randolph and Silas, could it have something to do with one of their wells?"

"We don't have a well," Rusty said, then winced and corrected herself. "I mean I. I don't have a well. My sink pumps from the creek, and I boil as needed."

"So . . . to Wildwood's well?" Marybeth said. "But what should we do with these?" She lifted one of the metal bars.

"Leave them," Rusty said. "They belong here. This is where Martin intended them to be. There has to be some reason he wanted that song played here, of all places. He could've built this apparatus anywhere at all . . . and I don't think he'd make Dad and Gilman haul all of this out here just because."

Marybeth set the bar back in its place. "You're right," she said. "There has to be a reason."

They packed up the rest of their things and began to file out of the alcove into the mist—and straight into Martin Shaw's reason.

Listen. Not to me. Listen to what you're looking at. Cracks aren't cracks; they're places water mighta washed gold out of. See an adit? That's an entrance to a mountain. In a world where mountains can have doors, you never know what'll happen. An adit doesn't mean someone beat you to the treasure. It means they saw something there. And maybe you will, too. Listen to what's there and listen to what's not there. You'll hear the story.

—Martin Shaw

Mercy

The man before them loomed like the peaks. Tall and thin, rugged with a beard to his chest, brown peppered in white. His clothes were worn but clean, boots patched and patched again. Thunder rumbled in the distance, and one could easily believe this man had summoned it by his very presence.

"Sasquatch," mumbled Casey.

"Reuben Murdock," murmured Willa, who took a small step back, her cheeks flushing.

"M-many happy returns of the day, sir," Rusty said, drawing herself up and sticking her hand out.

He looked at her hand like it had just fallen from outer space.

Mercy looked at her friend curiously.

"What?" Rusty whispered.

"That means *happy birthday*," Mercy said.

Rusty's smile wobbled. She dropped her hand to the side.

The man took a deep, slow breath, and Mercy got the sense that when he exhaled, he might just blow all the fog away with it, and some of the snow on the peaks, too. *Grandfather Mountain* came to mind, looking at him.

But when he breathed out, he simply uttered two low, rumbling words. "That . . . song . . ."

The foursome exchanged glances.

It was Willa who spoke, stepping timidly forward. "I believe it was meant for you, Reub—Mr. Murdock."

He shifted his gaze slowly to rest on her. For every bit of rugged, hard exterior on this man, his brown eyes were the complete opposite: kind, gentle. They housed sorrow and depth. A whole universe, in those eyes. They settled on Willa.

"It's difficult to explain," she said. "But that song was put into place long ago by Martin Shaw. I believe it was for you."

A deep-drawn sigh from Reuben. "Martin . . ."

"He seems to have planted a series of clues, you see," Mercy began. "Meant for his friends, as part of a—" Willa shook her head, but it registered too late as Mercy's words trailed out—"treasure hunt."

Reuben bristled. "Thought he gave all that up."

Mercy bit her lip. Oh dear.

Reuben spoke again. "He should've given all that up." He turned and started to retreat into the mist. Thunder rumbled again, as if calling the man home.

"Mr. Murdock!" Mercy said, running to catch up to him. She was dwarfed in his presence and felt suddenly like Jack who'd climbed the beanstalk into the giant's realm above the clouds. Only instead of a beanstalk, she'd taken a tram, and instead of hoarding gold, this giant wanted to take himself as far from it as possible. "Please, Mr. Murdock—" She reached out, taking his rough hand.

He stopped in his tracks, looking down at her hand, then at her face.

"Your sister," Mercy said.

His eyebrows drew up, hope flooding his expression for a split second.

"She longs to see you," Mercy said. "Please—will you come down with us?"

He pulled his hand back, looking in the direction of the valley, and then up to where the mist hid the steep-sloping peaks.

"Too late for me," he said.

"It's never too late," Mercy said. "If there's one thing I've learned in Mercy Peak, it's that it's never too late. If—if not now, perhaps soon . . . ?"

"July tenth!" Rusty piped up

Mercy looked at her, puzzled. The night they would reveal Motor 8 to the town?

Rusty nodded, encouraging Mercy on. It didn't seem the right venue for this reticent man, but perhaps Rusty knew something she didn't. "I have a gathering planned at Wildwood—"

"Gilman place," he said gruffly.

"Yes. Well, it was, once. But not anymore. I want to make it into something good. I want to give the town back something from the place that took so much from them, and—well, the second Saturday in July—July tenth—will be the gathering. Priscilla will be there." Mercy pleaded with her expression. "It would mean . . . everything to her."

"She doesn't want me."

"Oh, but she does!"

"I wrote her once. I asked."

"I don't think . . ." Mercy trailed off, wanting to make sure she was remembering correctly.

"I asked—if she wouldn't mind me coming home, if she'd put a candle in the window. I watched for weeks after that. There was no candle."

Mercy swallowed. "Reuben, would this have been about ten years ago?"

He pressed his eyes shut, shaking his head almost imperceptibly. "Not sure," he said. "Time out here . . . but it was long ago."

Mercy nodded. "There's a chance she never got that letter, Mr. Murdock."

His eyes flashed a moment of desperate hope—and quickly flickered to resignation. "Not likely."

"Say you'll come," Mercy said, her mind scrambled. A gathering perhaps wouldn't hold much appeal to him, after all this time. "Or if you'd rather not join us that evening, you know where to find her. I know she'll want to see you. She speaks of you with so much love."

"Sh-she does?"

"I have never heard a sister adore her brother so much as she does you. Please come."

She left with his promise that he would think about it . . . and with her eyes set on the well at Wildwood.

Rusty

June 1948

The well in the courtyard of Wildwood, squarely between the two back turrets, was giving up no secrets. Rusty and Marybeth circled it in opposite directions, stopping when they met. Casey had stayed in the mountains to complete his survey work, and Willa was inside, scrubbing away, bless her heart, to make way for the event she was brimming with excitement for. Marybeth had tried to send her home, tried to pay her, tried everything, but Willa refused, stating she was "just overjoyed to see this old place coming to life again."

"Well," Rusty had said. "This should be easy. No riddle to decipher, no rhyme . . . Surely it's just tucked behind a loose stone or something."

It was not. The stones were not dry-stacked but seamed together with mortar, and none showed any promise of being loose. They ascended the turret stairs and looked down on it, hoping for an answer in aerials—with no luck. They hunted around the courtyard. They lowered the bucket and pulled it back up, finding it full of only water. They shone flashlights down into the well, searched for loose rocks or capsules or anything at all . . .

To no avail.

Finally, they sat in the courtyard, backs against the summer kitchen, and stared.

"Well?" Marybeth asked, laying her cheek on her bended knees and looking Rusty's direction.

Rusty snorted. "Well?" She mimicked the position, and they both stared until their shoulders shook with tired laughter at the joke.

"This is a fine kettle of fish, Ruby Bright," Marybeth said.

Rusty jerked her head up. "Now, don't go calling names."

"Desperate times . . ." Marybeth sighed. "We've survived an inferno mine, a rickety tram—"

"And traitorous tram operators who strand their innocent friends in said trams—"

"A high-altitude trek on a steep mountainside—"

"And don't forget the killer waterfall."

"Yes!" Marybeth threw up her hands in exasperation. "We've done it all! And this is what's going to stump us? A glorified pile of rocks?"

They sat in silence for a moment, the cry of a blue jay falling like an upside-down question. "Do you think . . ." Rusty began, not quite knowing how to put it into words. "I keep thinking about Reuben. The look on his face . . . like in hearing that song, someone had given food to a starving man."

"I've never seen anything like it," Marybeth murmured.

"I can't help thinking . . . the riddles, the clues—they don't feel like they were only intended as a safeguard for treasure. There's something more at play. It's like you said—he could've built that apparatus any-where. But he put it out there, where it would carry, and out there where he knew Reuben would have a chance of hearing."

"With that particular song . . ." Marybeth said.

"And the other clues, too—subterranean, in the mines, where my dad lived his days."

"And everything with the Goose—the scytale, the frame—all things for a devotee of Newton's Laws . . ."

"He was doing this for them," Rusty said, conviction in her voice.

"Almost like he—like he was trying to fix something broken with this treasure hunt. Resurrect something dead. Heal something hurt."

"Maybe he did," Rusty said, looking sideways at Marybeth.

Marybeth met her glance and smiled. A small dimple, and for a moment Rusty could picture her as the coal-streaked schoolgirl who'd written her, all those years ago. "I think he did," she said. "I wish I'd known him. He seems like a man whose waters ran deep." She grew pensive, and then sat up with a jolt.

"*Deep waters*," she said. "There's a tunnel running under this well. Or right around it." Rusty scrambled to her feet, and the two dashed into Wildwood, down into the cellar through the kitchen, and stood at an arched wooden door, stalwart and black-hinged, looking like it belonged in a medieval castle rather than in the Rocky Mountains.

"Have you been in here?" Marybeth asked.

Rusty shook her head. "No. You can bet I tried, but it was always locked, and that housekeeper always close by. You?"

Mercy shook her head. "I tried but haven't been able to find the key." They stared at the heavy bronze padlock for a moment before exchanging a look.

"You thinking what I'm thinking?" Rusty asked.

"I wish I knew someone who was handy with locked doors and rusty nails." She bit down on her smile and dashed away, returning with a not-so-rusty nail.

Rusty set to work. "Feels strange doing this without a cat wriggling under my arm."

"If anyone can do it, it's you," Mercy said. And on cue, the scraping nail clicked the lock to glorious liberation, dropping to the stone floor as Rusty carefully removed the padlock. They pushed together on the door, tumbling into darkness—and straight into a rock wall.

"What . . . ?" Rusty placed her hands against it, feeling her way across as her eyes adjusted and confirmed: the tunnel was as blocked off as could be, walled in.

Mercy groaned. "Not this again . . ."

"I thought you said you hadn't been here before."

"Not this particular blocked-off rock wall tunnel, no. But on set . . ." She tipped her head. "The good news is, I have practice knocking down walls like this."

"You can't tell me they used real rocks on a Hollywood set."

"The director insisted. Said nothing else would fall correctly or give me the correct amount of terror in my eyes."

"Well then," Rusty said. "Lead the way, terror-eyed ingénue."

The hour that followed was a blur of treks to the shed, hauling hammers, chisels, sledgehammers, and chipping away chinks until one rock came loose . . . and then another . . . until it was ready to fall in one mighty blow.

"Would you like to do the honors?" Marybeth handed the sledgehammer to Rusty, who curled her fingers around the handle and swung it back behind her. Summoning every bit of injustice doled out by the hands of Randolph Gilman, as far back as she could remember, she wound them up, held her breath, swung the hammer, and with a mighty *crack*, the wall came tumbling down.

They backed up to safety, then stepped through the swirling dust and into the dark beyond. It was cold—nothing like the mine had been.

To her knowledge, only Randolph had ever traversed this path. And for the first time . . . she felt sorry for the man. Down here in the dark, buried by his own machinations, isolated by his actions. Building this tunnel to escape the cold above, but perhaps it was even colder, down here, alone. No one to see him. No one to help.

Marybeth shone a flashlight as they made their way to the stretch just below the courtyard, where a wide stone pillar stood front and center.

The well.

They circled it and repeated their actions from up top. Trying stones. Searching the perimeter, the ceiling, the floor, the beams—

And there was nothing.

Until, eyes adjusting, Rusty spotted something nestled against the wall, just behind one of the support timbers. A canvas bag, covered in dust.

Marybeth drew up beside her and cast her light on it, illuminating stenciled letters in big, bold black.

U.S. MAIL

They were silent. Spellbound. How many words . . . how many years . . . how many lives . . . were touched and held in the rustic fibers of that bag?

What would this mean for Mercy Peak?

Rusty's fist pressed into her heart.

With all the care in the world, they brought it up out of the tunnel and settled it safely in the turret room. They backed away from it, staring.

"What now?" Rusty asked.

Marybeth turned to face her. "You decide, Rusty. There could be something very important in that bag for you. . . ."

And that's what she was afraid of. Desperately hoped for it and desperately feared. For all these years, she'd held out hope . . . and as long as the bag was gone, she could keep holding out hope. But now . . .

"Let's wait." Rusty backed up, inching toward the door.

Marybeth held the top of the bag in her hand. She looked at Rusty— and saw straight through her. Saw the pulsing question filling the room: *Is it there?* Saw the way Rusty's fear reached out to harness it, lock it away.

Rusty jutted out her jaw.

Marybeth waited, compassion on her face.

"I—I can't." She pursed her lips, then burst out with the question itself. "What if it's not there? At least if I don't know . . ."

"There's hope."

Rusty nodded.

Marybeth rested her hand on the bag. The bag that could hold Sam's words.

"Rusty?" she said finally.

"Hmmm?"

"What if it *is* there?"

She worked her jaw. If it was, it had waited all this time. It could wait a little longer. Or a lot longer.

"What if I looked for you?"

Rusty's eyes burned. "I can't stop you," she said. Part of her desperate to cry out, *Yes! Look!* Part of her desperate to run. "I'm going to search the well again."

"So that's a yes?" Marybeth spoke as Rusty turned.

She froze, heart aching . . . and whispered, "Yes."

Back outside, time crawled. The well gave up no secrets. The more time that passed, the more her chest ached, and it felt like she was losing Sam all over again. Every second erasing another shred of barely-there hope.

At last, Marybeth emerged back into the courtyard . . . hands empty. The pain on her face said it all. Without a word to explain, she approached Rusty, slipped her hand into Rusty's too-empty one, and shook her head.

A chasm threatened to break wide open and swallow her whole. Rusty gulped, nodded fast, and blazed right over it all. "Losing daylight," she said, sniffing. "We've gotta get that well clue."

"It could wait," Marybeth said.

"We're so close."

Marybeth nodded solemnly. "Do you want to talk about it?"

Rusty squared her shoulders. "I think we should refuse to be defeated by a glorified pile of rocks," she said, gesturing at the well.

Marybeth's concern settled over Rusty, but bless her, she didn't speak another word about it. "Yes," she said. "Yes, no dastardly pile of rocks and metal shall prevail!"

Rusty smiled, shoving all thoughts of phantom letters into the shadows. "Rocks and metal got nothing on us!"

Marybeth laughed, then narrowed her eyes. "Wait . . ." She strode to the well, gripping one of the metal bars that held up the well's small, thatched roof. "That's it, Rusty Bright! You're a genius. We've been focused on the rocks all this time. What about the metal?"

Rusty clambered up to stand on the edge of the well a little too quickly. Her foot caught on one of the stones, and her heart jumped into her throat as she lost her balance, teetering toward the dark abyss of the well. Marybeth's arm shot out, gripping Rusty's—and none too soon.

They both froze, breathless.

"Be careful," Marybeth whispered.

Rusty gulped and nodded. She took a deep breath and ducked under the roof to see where the pipe ended, a foot or so beneath the roof's peak. It was capped neatly, and Rusty wasted no time in unscrewing the cap. She felt around inside the pipe.

"Nothing," she said, heart sinking.

Marybeth hopped up quickly and scrambled to check the other pipe.

"Be careful!" Rusty said.

Marybeth opened the top with a *screech* that made them both shiver. She felt around inside the pipe swiftly—and then stopped. Bit her lip over a smile.

"There's something in here," she said, pulling out a long brown rolled-up piece of leather. Marybeth handed it to Rusty and climbed down. They knelt, unrolling the leather together to reveal a large circle and a scattering of letters and numbers, engraved like the belt had been.

The etchings were a mix of chaos and order—arranged in concentric circles, from the inside to the outside of the circle. But the letters themselves were placed at odd angles—some upside down on their circles, some right-side up, some at angles. There were no words, no apparent pattern, nothing to tell them what this meant. And no brass capsule.

Scrolling among and between the circles of letters was a pattern of filigree, a single small hole at its center. Tendril-like lines, cut through with a knife, in a spoked pattern from the center. Familiar, somehow.

"Look," Rusty said, leaning in to see the outer ring more clearly. Script flowed around the entire circumference of the circle.

> *Time shall pass,*
> *By time arranged.*
> *One face shall last,*
> *By time unchanged.*
> *Place the pin*
> *Anchored fast.*
> *A careful spin*
> *Reveals the last.*
> *Look upon white earth's demise.*

New chasms dawned;
The sun does rise.

"What are these numbers?" asked Marybeth. Beneath the words, a second circle of engravings was spaced out with care.

4:17 5:29 3:75 4:14 6:07 1:10 9:15 6:16

"Times?" Rusty asked. "Time shall pass, by time arranged . . . one face shall last . . ."

"Times . . . a face . . . It's a clock," Marybeth said, her smile breaking unbridled across her face. "Look at this filigree—it matches the face of the clock above the town hall. Doesn't it?"

"It does . . ." Rusty said. "How are we supposed to get up there without causing a ruckus? It's right smack-dab in the middle of town, and someone's always watching down there."

Marybeth twinkled with mischief. "You always did want to get up in that tower, Rusty."

Rusty blew her cheeks out.

"You're not going to like this idea," Marybeth said. "I'm not sure I like it myself."

"Spit it out, Spatts."

"We take a cue from Randolph Gilman and use a gathering as a diversion."

The words unwound inside Rusty. Her eyes shifted from side to side as Marybeth's meaning—and all it signified—became clear.

"He used Sam's funeral as a diversion to steal the Goose. And we use *his* sorry attempt at stealing the Goose . . . as a diversion to find this treasure, once and for all?"

Marybeth nodded slowly. "What do you think? We don't have to—"

"Let's do it."

I'm not afraid of heights, Spatts. Are you? People are afraid of heights 'cause they could fall. Truth is, you could fall flat on your face on a boulder, walking right there on the ground. Falling could happen anywhere.

—Rusty, age 13

Rusty

July 1948

Casey Campbell, like the soup, was making a spectacle of himself. Climbing up trees like he was some kind of bear. Some plaid-wearing, bearded, lopsided-grinning bear.

"Toss one up!" he hollered down from his perch. He braced himself on the branch above, and Rusty lobbed the bundled parachute to him.

Things at Wildwood were at a very strange standstill. The hunt for the treasure had propelled itself forward into ever-increasing intensity . . . and then come to a screeching halt as they bided their time, awaiting the night of the gathering.

Marybeth and Rusty did plenty of covert study of the town clock, but until they could get close enough to match the filigree to the clockface for the right orientation to try and find whatever missing piece they needed to solve it . . . they could do nothing.

So, they doubled down on Wildwood preparations. Shining it up on a shoestring budget, every preparation doubling as a step toward welcoming the town, but also as a stairstep toward its future as a forest theatre.

Rusty and Casey were getting a rhythm down, with five of the parachutes already spread out like awnings and strung taut. It had started in complete disaster, with the first two looking like limp and pitiful over-sized handkerchiefs and drooping from the trees with strings dangling. But they'd worked and worked at them until—miracle of miracles—Marybeth's vision began to manifest in the forest.

Marybeth said her head was swimming with possibilities for plays that could be performed with the backdrops out here, and in addition to this forest stage, she had plans for them to string parachute awnings at the shore of Gold Leaf Lake near the boathouse— *"the perfect spot for a symphony,"* she'd said—as well as over the courtyard, and even at the far reaches of the property where it abutted Ruby Rock and Emerald Gulch beyond.

That girl always had seen things upside down, and that fact was sealed as Rusty vaulted another parachute—which was made to float down, not be tossed up—and it landed with a satisfying thud in Casey Campbell's hands. He worked to unpack and unfold. Rusty climbed the ladder to receive strings he cut and handed to her, affixing them to branches until it began to find a tension.

Rusty studied him while he studied the strings, his calloused hands working the knots. He was lost in his own thoughts . . . until he looked up so suddenly Rusty nearly lost her grip and toppled right off the lad-der. He reached out and gripped her forearm, his blue eyes piercing with mingled concern and curiosity.

"Woah there, slick."

Rusty's face flamed. At being caught looking at him. At nearly losing her balance. She'd made it this far in the last ten years without getting knocked over—and that was saying something. What business did he have coming along and ripping the balance out from right under her?

"You okay?" he said, continuing his untangling efforts once she'd settled back on the rungs.

Rusty let go with both hands and resumed tying, just to let him see for himself. "Fine. Peachy. Perfect, thank you."

"Glad to hear it," he said, and reached up. "What's this?"

Rusty climbed higher to see that he held an aged piece of rope in the tree. It looked to have weathered many a winter, all brown and knotted.

"There's another one." Casey pointed to the next tree.

"And another one over there," Rusty said, looking behind her. "It's an old trick for winter. The miners used to mark the trails by tying ropes or rags in the trees, once the snowpack covered the trails entirely and got so high they could just reach up and tie something on. They were always looking for ways to not get lost in blizzards, and it was a way to help out their fellow miners, too, on their way up and down the mountain. But . . ." She spun, looking around. "This is private land. There would've been no miners traveling through here."

She blinked, picturing Mr. Gilman's maps. His cryptic check boxes. She could swear some of them were located right about here. . . .

"I'll have to tell Marybeth," she said.

Casey nodded, getting back to work. "You sure you're okay, slick?"

"Fine, why?"

"I mean—you were looking awfully hard, earlier."

"At what?"

He looked up and grinned. The cad. "You tell me."

"I . . . it was just you— untangling knots so fast, that's all. You have a lot of experience with that?"

"You might say."

Silence settled over him as they kept on working.

"I . . ." She cleared her throat, looking at him tentatively. "I was sorry to hear about your brother," she said at last.

Blast. That wasn't casual conversation. She was so bad at this.

But he didn't seem offended. He slowed his work, not taking his eyes from the mass of knots, her words seeming to burrow into their crevices as he proceeded with caution.

At last, a nod. Wordless, from the man who was a fountain of words.

Something inside Rusty ached like an open wound. She kicked herself and hoped she hadn't opened a wound like that in him. But there was no taking the comment back. It could just flop around like a rope on fire inside of him, lashing out and causing lesions . . . or maybe she could release a second rope, one to twine around it, tame that fire-rope. If she could say something right, for once.

"I . . ." She cleared her throat again. Thought about the things no one asked about with Sam, though she wished so hard they would. "What made him laugh?"

Casey's hand stilled. Rusty couldn't see his face, the way his head was tipped down over his work, dark hair falling over his forehead.

Now she'd gone and done it. Pushed too hard, right in where she wasn't wanted. Hadn't she hated when people had done that to her after Sam? *After Sam.* She hated that phrase. There should be no *after.* Hadn't Sam well and truly lived? And yes, there was a line in the sand somewhere, where he stopped being there, a line that went so deep it hurt. And yes, there was a distinct before and after, where things fell starkly on one side or the other. But the one thing that didn't fall neatly into one or the other . . . was him. The Sam who spent his life, and spent it well. Rusty refused to stop remembering him.

It gave her courage to wait. See if maybe Casey Campbell did, in fact, want to talk.

"What made him laugh . . ." He repeated Rusty's question as his eyes went fathoms deep, no laughter there at all. "No one's asked me that before." He seemed . . . stumped.

"Was he a . . . solemn child?" The words felt stiff, and Rusty winced. *Ruby Adaline Bright, why do you always have to be sticking your nose—*

And then a low sound, rolling like slow currents of the river. Laughter.

Casey's whole face lifted as he met Rusty's gaze. "Solemn child," he said. "Not exactly. Let's see . . . one thing that made him laugh—that's going to be hard to narrow down. That kid's laugh could light a city. But more than that, he made others laugh. Once, he tried for four days straight to catch this salamander he had his eye on. Spot, he called it." Casey looked over and his eyes were shining with something Rusty hadn't seen before.

"You lived near a pond or something?"

A laugh. "Not exactly." He secured a bit of parachute, enough that they had a roof over their heads, and he hoisted himself to sit on the thick branch he'd been steadying himself against. It brought him nearer to Rusty's ladder, and he smelled clean and sharp like the pines all around.

"We lived in a shacktown," he said, his mouth pulling to the side.

Rusty's words from the day they'd met came flying back. *"You crawl out of one of the old prospector shacks . . . ?"* Her face burned. "A Hooverville?" Rusty had heard of them, colonies of shanties springing up when everything spiraled down for so many in the country.

He tipped his head, an ironic smile painting his face as he lifted a hand to spell out the name in invisible lights. "Hollywood on the Tideflats." He laughed. "That's what they named it back in Tacoma."

Rusty didn't know where that was but didn't want to say so.

"Up in Washington," he said. "Right on the ocean. It was no life for a kid. But we had no place to go, so the whole camp just ignored the fact that my brother was only ten and took us both in."

"Was it a hard place to live?"

He stilled.

"Sorry," she said. "Stupid question."

"Not stupid," he said. "Most people don't even ask. They just say, 'I'm sorry,' but they aren't really sure what they're sorry for. They don't know what to say, or care to ask about it."

"It was hard in some ways, yeah," he said at last. "Cold. Wet. But . . . at least it wasn't lonely."

A pang inside, and Rusty tamped it down fast. But he saw it—and obviously regretted it.

"Sorry, I didn't mean—"

She shook her head. *Redirect.* This wasn't about her. "You knew the people?"

"We got to know them fast. Everyone sort of took my brother under their wing, let him tag along to shipyard work or lumbering or helping with repairs. Houses were made out of everything you can imagine—old street signs, tar, scraps of tin or wood . . . you name it. You know the houses people used to order from Sears and Roebuck?"

Rusty brightened. "Yes," she said. "You should've seen the spontaneous parade that erupted in town when Al McQueen got himself one." She laughed. "I did a jig on his roof, before it was a roof."

"Did you now?" Casey's eyes filled with mirth. He crossed his arms and studied her. "I imagine you've got quite a few tales like that to tell. Those feet of yours seem like they were made for dancing."

She swatted the musing away. "Another lifetime," she said. "So . . . did you live in a kit house?"

"In a manner of speaking," he said. "We lived in the wood from the shipping crates of one of those kit houses. Among other things."

"Such as . . ."

"Flap of corrugated tin I caught in a windstorm. Wreckage washed up on shore after a storm, probably from two or three different boats, judging by the different woods. One of them, we got the plank where the ship's name was painted."

"Which was . . . ?"

"*The Good Fortune.*"

Rusty burst out laughing, and so did he—and it was something. People always talk about the magic of a baby's laugh, and it's true. But to hear the belly laugh of a man who's been to war and back, who is built of loss and has somehow lived to tell . . . it was a different sort of magic. Not the enchanting kind, but the sort that pricked an ache inside, where the good and the beautiful collided with the hard and the heartbreak.

He wiped a tear, his laughter subsiding, and as he took a deep breath, he grew thoughtful. "We got a lot of kicks out of people calling our shack 'the Good Fortune place.' But you know, in a lot of ways, it was. We were poor as dirt, but we had a lot of good, hardworking people around who looked out for us. We had bonfires on the beach, where anyone who'd caught anything that day would share the bounty with anyone who didn't. We had a roof over our heads, and one night when it flew right off in a windstorm, the next day a tarp appeared—same day a tarp went missing from one of the other homes, and when I asked the guy about it, he said he'd been meaning to get rid of that wall for some time, that he wanted a sea view. We had doors for a roof, windows for walls. . . . It makes you see possibilities in a lot of things you never would've before."

"And your brother . . . that's where he found his salamander?"

"Yeah. A marsh on the outskirts. He caught that thing, named it Spot, and took it around the whole camp showing him off. Made him a home in an old pickle jar, put sticks and grass inside. When I had to talk to him later about maybe letting Spot go, it broke the kid's heart—but he rallied. Gathered everyone up for a 'See Spot Run' bon voyage party. We had a bonfire, popped corn, and released that salamander back into the wild with a mighty cheer from all those men."

"I can picture it," Rusty said. "I like him." This she said with conviction.

"My brother? Or Spot?"

"Both," she said. And then tentatively, walking the question out upon the floor Casey had laid with the telling of his story, she asked, "What was your brother's name?"

A smile. A single syllable. "Cal." She recognized his tone—all the longing, all the warmth, all the ache and love wrapped up just in a breath.

"Cal," she said, and matched his smile.

"I used to call him 'Cal the Kid.'" He laughed. "Just a stupid nickname and he hated it—but loved to hate it, if you know what I mean."

"Yeah," she said. "I do know a thing or two about nicknames."

"That's a story you're going to tell me," he said, pointing a finger and lifting a corner of his mouth in mischief.

"Maybe." She shrugged a shoulder. "But I want to hear Cal's first. He loved to hate it?"

"'Just wait,' he'd say. 'Time's not on your side, old man. I'll be three feet taller than you someday, old man.'" He lifted his eyes, meeting Rusty's. "I was sixteen and six feet tall when he called me 'old man,' by the way." These details he peppered the story with only begged more questions. Sixteen, and raising a ten-year-old?

But the moment didn't need more questions. Just an invitation to continue this spilling of words and story. "Ambitious." Rusty infused the word with appreciation.

His smile grew a deep dimple. "That kid was going to lasso the moon. Half the time, he got his inches and feet mixed up. But he was also a big dreamer, so it's impossible to tell; he probably did mean three feet. I was always telling him 'Shoot for the moon, kid'—so maybe he measured that distance in three feet." Casey gripped the branch he sat on and dropped his gaze, smiling as he remembered.

He must have felt Rusty's study, because he met her eyes and didn't look away. Held them in a way that was invitation, searching like he already saw the question that was pounding inside of her.

And then he just waited. Like he knew and wanted her to ask.

"I want to ask you a question," she said, too direct.

"Please do."

"I'm worried it will be too—" *Personal. Nosy. Terrifying.* "—too much."

"Please don't."

"Ask, or worry?"

"Please don't worry. Ask away, Rusty Bright. I'm an open book."

She gulped. "How . . . does this go?" It wasn't a complete question, and she floundered over words as he waited and watched. "When you— when you lose someone. You seem so—I don't know. Complete. I . . ." Her voice grew thick, and she rushed to finish. "I don't feel that way. How . . . how do you make it through?" She swallowed and lifted her eyes to him. Her throat, her heart, they ached. But this man had something that she was desperate for. "How does it turn out?"

How does it turn out? There. She'd shoved her heart out of her chest in five short words. She wanted to gather them back up, keep them in the dark.

But they sat there in the silence, pulsating.

And he repeated them, picking them up and holding them in his

314

steady timbre. "How does it turn out?" He pulled in a breath and released it. "How do you make it through?"

She looked at her hands, where her thumbs twisted together. She wanted to dig a big old hole in the ground and hide inside, pull one of the flightless parachutes over herself.

"A day at a time," he said. "Sometimes less. Sometimes . . . a minute or a second at a time. Sometimes more. Until someday it becomes . . . a memory at a time. Maybe with tears, maybe with laughter, maybe both. And maybe, if you're lucky, a friend to share that memory with." He paused. "Like you and Cal and that salamander. No one's ever asked me what made him laugh," he said. "Thank you, Rusty." Her name wrapped in his voice felt oddly at home.

She mustered a smile. "I wish I could've known Cal. And Spot."

"Me too," he said. "You said I seemed complete. Trust me—there've been plenty of times when I've been anything but. Railed at the sky, at God, rewritten the story in my head a thousand times so Cal would be here today and if one of us had to go, it'd be me. But for whatever reason . . . this is the story we're living. How do you make it through? I don't know that we ever do. *Through* sounds like there's an end to the loss, and I can tell you right now I'm never going to forget Cal or stop missing him. I'll never be who I was before he was gone. So, in a way, his absence will always be a part of me. That piece won't come back. I'll never be . . . complete, so to speak. But . . . I can be whole. Even while missing him. The day I stop missing him, please bash me over the head with a skillet or something."

Rusty sputtered a laugh and wiped at her swimming eyes. He dug in his pocket and handed her his handkerchief.

"In some ways, losing someone becomes a part of you. But I guess the question is, what sort of part? A bitter part? That was me, for a long time. Cynical, short-tempered. Isolated."

"You?"

"I know. I'm one big package of likeability now," he said, raising an eyebrow and pasting on an incorrigible grin. Rusty had the sudden urge to swat him, and he seemed to know it. His expression challenged her to do it.

But she wanted to know the end of what he'd been saying. "What changed?"

"Cal. That kid . . . grinning at everyone with a gap where he'd knocked out his front tooth climbing a tree."

"Wonder where he got that propensity." Rusty eyed the branch he sat on.

"Some great and worthy American hero he looked up to, I guess," he said, and she nearly did whack him that time. "Back in the war, we were up in the Dolomites, we were encamped in the middle of winter. I went to the stream to fill my canteen and slipped on a patch of ice. But I got up, filled my canteen at the stream, and caught my reflection as I stood back up. I looked cold and hard and empty. Tired. And not just from the war. For the rest of the day, I couldn't get the ice or the stream out of my head. Both water—but one harmed, while the other gave life. I thought of Cal, tromping through marshy land with bare feet. Would he want to be held in a cold, hard, unmoving place of ice? That was the home my heart was giving to his memory. I hated that. And I realized I had a choice in what sort of home my heart was. It could be a place of life and movement and hope, like that stream. Or I could carry on as I was, bitter and growing colder and harder by the day. Cal didn't deserve that."

"Neither did you." The wind rippled over the parachute, Rusty's knot coming untied until the white fabric draped down around the two of them, catching on branches and walling them away from the rest of the world. Making Casey feel that much closer—and Rusty's heart that much louder.

She reached to turn away, tie it back, but he caught her hand. Gently, and only for a moment, but it was enough to make her lift her eyes, despite everything rebelling inside, and meet his gaze. Blue, and steady, and seeing.

"Neither do any of us," he said, his voice tripping over a ragged breath. "The more I live, the more convinced I am that we were made to be held. Not to hold bitterness. But it was so much a part of me, I didn't know how to end it."

Rusty gulped. Nodding. Knowing.

"I couldn't let go. Not alone, anyhow. It was like the grip of my heart was frozen shut around it. So . . . maybe it's stupid, but I realized there are two ways to release a frozen-shut grip. Pry it loose, finger by finger, until it breaks . . . or set it in the sun. Thaw it out. Let the sun do its work."

"And your sun was . . ."

"Don't go running, but it was—and is—the Maker of the sun."

"God," Rusty said. She couldn't look at him. Fixed her eyes on one of the ropes above him, which was coming loose. She wanted to cinch it tight but wouldn't dare reach across this man. If she got even an inch closer, he'd feel her pulse sculpting the air between them.

"You know Him?"

She nodded slowly. "We're acquainted."

"Glad to hear it." The wind picked up, rustling the branches around them.

"Not sure He's too keen to know me, though," Rusty said. "I more resemble that frozen water." She blew a loose strand of hair out of her face. "And I know that like your ice patch, I have been the cause of pain. Not sure He'd care to get too close."

"That's exactly what He cares to do."

"But I don't—" Her voice caught. "I don't know how. All that thawing. I don't—" Her words tripped to a halt.

"You don't have to." He filled in the silence. "Water is not in charge of its own thawing. But . . ." Hesitancy girded his voice.

"Say it. It's alright."

"It'll never thaw if it hides away in the shadows."

Her defenses rose. "Puddles don't have feet."

"But you do. You get to choose how close you get to the sun."

A long silence, and he began tying the ropes again. Lifting their parachute walls, exposing them again to the rest of the world.

His words sat inside Rusty in a place she didn't know what to do with, didn't know was even there anymore. She climbed down from the ladder, and he followed.

"You ask good questions, Rusty Bright."

The smile came naturally then, even as the ache in her throat remained. "I like hearing about Cal," she said. "I hope you'll tell me more."

"I'd love that more than anything."

As she made her way down the ladder, his voice stopped her. "Rusty Bright?"

"Casey Campbell?"

"I'm going to ask you a question, too."

She waited, tilting her head.

"Not now. I'm just giving you fair warning, so you can get used to the idea."

"How am I supposed to get used to the idea if you don't tell me what the question is?"

"Just . . . get used to getting used to the idea. I'm going to ask you something, so just know to expect it."

"You are . . . unexpected," she said. And he brightened.

"Thank you," he said, and walked away with a whistle, as if they hadn't just exchanged hearts and held each other's wounded places in the overstory, of all places. He looked over his shoulder, gave a salute-turned-wave, and vanished.

Folio of Field Notes, Volume VII:
Fire Investigations + Miscellaneous

[Property of Sudsy McGee, Hollywood Biographer]

LOSS INVENTORY REPORT

Pinnacle Studios
INCIDENT TYPE: Fire
DATE: 2.14.1948
TOTAL LOSS ESTIMATE: $2,500,000

Indirect Financial Losses

Expected income from *Joan of Arc,* whose filming has now been terminated
Set/cast/crew expenditures from *Joan of Arc*
Future construction costs to repair damaged building

Known Physical Losses

Miscellaneous set construction, *Joan of Arc* set
All film reels housed in Building 9, west end film vault
Partial loss of Reel Number 10 from *Joan of Arc,* from active use on set, remains presently missing

Find Reel 10

Interview with Mercy Windsor

Interview Transcript of Biographer Sid "Sudsy" McGee
with Mercy Windsor, screen name of Marybeth Spatts

DATE: June 24, 1948
LOCATION: Jim's Diner, Mercy Peak, Colorado
ORDERED: S. McGee: Preposterous Pete's Grits
M. Windsor: Cinnamon donut

SG: It's a bold move, Miss Windsor, coming out of hiding.

MW: "Marybeth" is fine.

SW: You'll find that the article will have a more widespread printing, and a larger public response, if you use your screen name.

MW: Very well.

SM: And as agreed, you'll allow my five questions?

MW: We agreed on three, Mr. McGee.

SG: You can't blame me for trying. Three it is. Your time being short, I'll jump right in. First question: Why this village in Colorado?

MW: I suppose . . . it was the only place that ever felt like home.

SG: So you grew up here, then.

MW: In a manner of speaking. But I'd never spent more than a day here until this spring.

SG: So you mean—

MW: [tapping wrist] Time, Mr. McGee. Do you have your second question prepared?

SG: What do you have to say about Wilson P. Wilson, president of Pinnacle Studios?

MW: [Picks fork up. Sets fork down. Looks at donut. Takes a bite. Swallows.] Wilson P. Wilson believes he made me, and he also believes he destroyed me. Certainly, he did his best to disgrace and erase Mercy Windsor. But Mercy Windsor was never me. I—I and every person—am made of more than can be destroyed by man. I am . . . a soul. And so are you, Mr. McGee. And as hard as it is to feel the truth of this, so is Wilson P. Wilson. The truth is . . . I pity him. He will make and destroy many others, or at least believe that he has. I am just a flash on the screen in a long succession of flashes on a screen. But in Mercy Peak—and I hope you'll put this in the press release, Mr. McGee—in Mercy Peak, my name is not written on a two-second screen credit. My handprints are not impressed into a square of cement that can be cut away and stored in a dark back room after I have fallen from grace. In Mercy Peak, the fingerprints of God himself are impressed upon the mountains. In Mercy Peak, my very soul is held in those same hands. Not ushered into hiding at the first sign of scandal. In Mercy Peak, the red carpet is a mountain that rises up to meet my humble feet and carry me to heights and depths I've never known. The air is wild, the winds are free, the people are good and real, and life is true. What do I have to say about Wilson P. Wilson? . . . He hurt me. He has hurt a good many others. But in all that hurt, he cannot keep me from being healed. And I—I wish that healing for him, too, someday.

SG: [long pause]

MW: Mr. McGee? Did you have a third question?

SG: I—well, I—that is, yes. You just—that wasn't what I was expecting.

MW: Me either, Mr. McGee. I think that's the most beautiful part.

SG: My final question is . . . what happened the night of the fire?

MW: [shoulders slump] I cannot answer that.

SG: Then, as per our agreement, I cannot print the press release, Miss Windsor.

MW: Spatts.

SG: Pardon?

MW: Nothing. I'm legally bound not to speak with a member of the press, Mr. McGee, about the events of that evening. But if you someday find that you are no longer in the employ of that institution and still wish an answer, you'll know where to find me. And, Mr. McGee . . . I hope you'll still find it in your heart to print the release. Many good people are depending upon it.

Mercy Windsor Rises Again?

SILVER SCREEN TIMES, DENVER TRIBUNE, SAN FRANCISCO CHRONICLE, RENO EVENING POST, SALT LAKE CITY HERALD, FLAGSTAFF EVENING POST, ALBUQUERQUE GAZETTE

July 1, 1948—Mercy Windsor, former queen of the silver screen, whose whereabouts have been unknown these past four months, has surfaced at last in a small town deep in the mountains of Colorado. While many may imagine she has been in hiding, waiting for the tide of a storm of scandalous press to pass before attempting to ascend the heights of Hollywood once more, Miss Windsor has something else entirely in mind.

In a leap from "star" to "director," she plans to open a one-of-a-kind forest theatre venue, showing twice-yearly productions on outdoor stages scattered throughout the property of the castle-like Wildwood Estate. She describes Mercy Peak as a place where "the air is wild, the winds are free, the people are good, and life is true."

She hopes to debut this autumn with three days and three nights of theatrical enchantment in the village of Mercy Peak, to which the public is invited. She, along with the Wildwood Forest Theatre troupe, will be mounting a stage adaptation of George MacDonald's beloved fairy tale *The Light Princess*. It will be a play in three acts, featuring one act per evening, with a full day of events in between each and catered al fresco preshow dining. The venue will change each night, with a forest theatre, a lakeside stage, and a palace-like courtyard offering what Miss Windsor is calling "living sets." And none other than Holden Huxley will take the role of the male lead.

Tickets are limited and can be purchased by contacting the Mercy Peak Mercantile by telegram or phone and inquiring with Marybeth Spatts, clerk. Lodging information will be available there as well.

It may not be the story the public imagined for the fallen star, but according to Miss Windsor, "The stars in Mercy Peak cannot be lassoed to the ground by scandal and headlines. They are there for all to see and to be swept away into hope and awe. The stars here aren't found by looking at screens . . . but by looking up. I hope you'll come and see."

1910
Kurt Pike to TwinPages Publishing Company

Dear TwinPages Publishing Company,

My brother Angus saved up coupons off your Swift Rider comic books for thirteen months and ordered the Blue Lightning slingshot. It's great, but I was holding it over a cliff by accident—sort of—and then I dropped it by accident—really—and Angus is sadder'n a hound dog. I'm sending you a dime; it's all I got in this whole world. Will it buy a new Blue Lightning?

1915

Dear TwinPages,

It's me, Kurt again. Here's another dime. I send one every time I get one. Are you keeping 'em together? When you get enough, send that slingshot.

1920

Dear TwinPages,

Got any of those slingshots? I still feel pretty bad, and while my brother's likely forgotten, he's getting married soon, and I think it'd be a good joke to give him his old favorite thing as a wedding gift. Got any on hand? Here's a dollar to add to the coffers.

1930

TwinPages,

Kurt Pike here, co-owner of Mercy Peak Mercantile. Don't mean to make a pest of myself, but here's the rub: Old sore spots came up in an argument the other day. One thing led to another, and wouldn't you know, it all came down to me holding that stupid slingshot over that stupid cliff when my brother and I were just kids. He wrapped all our arguments ever up in that and painted a line down the center of our business, saying we do best with clear lines between us.

Heaven help me, send that slingshot if you got any in the backroom. I'll pay anything.

For Display at the Mercy Peak Mercantile, the J.D., the Feed Store, and the Depot

**A Wildwood Evening
of Enchantment**

The Mercy Peak Citizenry is cordially invited
for punch, light refreshments,
and the music of Willa Jones and Hudson Jenks.

There will also be a performance
by Holden Huxley
with a special surprise guest.

Wildwood Forest Theatre
Saturday, July 10
7 P.M.

BLOOMS
(Brilliant Lexicon of the Original Marybeth Spatts)

ENTRY NO. 42

Raze

(1) To utterly destroy

Raise

(1) To lift higher

Question: Are they opposites? Or is it two sides of a whole story? Ask Rusty what she thinks.

Rusty

"You could fit a whole slew of people up here." Rusty drew up next to Marybeth, surveying the scene. Wildwood's high meadow, looking down on Gold Leaf Lake, was mid-transformation, being outfitted for the elevated camping experience Marybeth envisioned for patrons of the forest theatre. They were making good progress, on track for the reveal in less than two weeks.

The Caterpillar Club had razed the odd stumps, along with a few trees, and cleared debris, even raking it so the ground felt like freshly spread icing on a cake, ready to be decorated.

Marybeth laughed. "I never understood that word."

"*People?* I don't understand them, either."

"*Slew*. Why would you call a group of people a *slew*? It sounds like stew. As if they're all about to be devoured forthwith."

"I don't know, it just sort of . . . rolls off the tongue. Slew. *Slew*. Slew, forthwith!" Rusty gestured grandly toward the sky with an open hand on this last rendition, as if she were Hamlet battling with the question of *to be or not to be*. "Try it, you'll like it!" Rusty grinned mischievously and set to laying pathways to each tent with rocks, opening up to a central fire ring.

The men had pulled out the mattresses from the empty barracks at Peak View mine and, to hear Angus tell it, beat them until not a shred of dirt could remain—and had a mighty good time at it, too, judging by the whoops and hollers that could be heard. The mattresses were bleaching out in the sun now on the outskirts of the clearing.

Miss Ellen, Willa, and the war girls they'd called out of factory retirement had kicked the parachute factory back into a flurry of industrious vision, staffed by coverall-clad girls who moved about in an indoor blizzard, white threads flying, nylon fluttering, transforming stacks of unused parachutes into tents, ready to make a fluttering, gossamer city of the high meadow.

Rusty would've called it crazy, but she'd seen what Marybeth had done with an ordinary boathouse. She had a gift, it seemed, for making something plain as mud into something extraordinary. They were getting so close, Rusty could picture Marybeth's vision: The glow of firelight casting shadows of content theatregoers in their finery. The sun rising in the morning, casting the soft pink alpenglow upon white fabric rippling in morning breezes, giving the guests a wake-up they'd not soon forget. Music playing as the moon rose each night—

"Drat," Rusty muttered.

"Everything alright?"

"I forgot to borrow the phonograph from Miss Ellen for up here," she said.

"That's alright," Marybeth said. "We've got time." She smiled. "Can't you just imagine it? The music, with the only other sounds a chorus of frogs, a symphony of crickets, an owl . . . it will be so serene—"

WHOMP-WHOMP-WHOMP-WHOMP-WHOMP

A deafening sound roared in, pulsing through her. A helicopter. Descending, behemoth-like, upon Marybeth's vision and flinging dust with gleeful abandon into all the standing mattresses. Holden was back.

"Hooooldeeeen!!!" Marybeth cried as the Prince of Pinnacle waved jubilantly from the window. Marybeth and Rusty scrambled to cover the mattresses with tarps.

He hopped down and strode over with a spring in his step and exultation on his face.

He started shouting, and though she couldn't hear him, his meaning was clear: He had arrived! He was happy to be here! Let the Evening of Enchantment begin!

Finally, the great machinery powered completely down, and after a hollered greeting until their hearing recovered and the last of the tarps were laid, Marybeth asked, "Frank could spare his helicopter again?" He was up and down into the sky more than a cloud. He probably had a song about it.

"Eh." Holden shrugged a shoulder. "It's probably fine. Mother's going to—" His grin froze and faded. "Mother! I forgot to tell her I was leaving again!" Pinching his forehead into deep, folded thought, he closed his eyes until he landed on a solution. "Sammy," he hollered at the pilot. "When you get back to the city, be a zinger and wire Mother's driver, will you? He'll ring her at the club, who can send a waiter to tell her I've left." He nodded, satisfied. "Now. Where to, sis?"

Marybeth smiled. "I think you're free for the afternoon, Holden. We're just starting to put things in place to show people around on Saturday, let them start to catch the vision. I'm thinking of putting a few of the tents up, should anyone wish to camp out that night."

He whistled low, then said, "Sure thing, Murse. They're gonna love it!" And then he was off like a bolt of lightning, waving over his shoulder and spouting something about finding Casey and catching some fish.

Rusty began to head down the path, too, but Marybeth stopped her. "Do you have time to talk?"

"Now?" Rusty said. "I was going to string up the tin-can lights. The Jenks girls were hammering designs into them today, so they should be ready."

"Please. Just a few minutes?"

Something in her voice made Rusty pause. "Maybe just a few." She pointed at the sky, where the grey clouds were turning purple-slate over the peak, which matched the foreboding hue. "That doesn't look good." Distant thunder rolled, ushering them on.

Marybeth started to walk, leading the way up toward the border between Gilman and Bright land. And Rusty knew—this would not be just a few minutes. A blue jay swooped above them, alighting on a branch and mocking Rusty for being caught in the clutches of whatever was coming.

Which came presently.

"Rusty . . ." Marybeth began. "I, um . . . well, you know the fairy tale we're planning for the first play . . ."

"About that stubborn princess who won't cry? Sure."

"Well, I was just thinking—I've been worried about you. Since we found the mailbag, you've been . . . quiet."

She shrugged. "Some people are quiet."

Marybeth gave her a look, as if to say, *Since when did you fall into that category?* A branch shook above, the blue jay watching on. Somewhere near, water rushed. Rusty shook her head. "It's not like your Light Princess fairy tale," she said. "The princess just . . . sheds a tear and the evil spell is broken and love floods in. . . . I wish it were as simple as that. But a tear is just a tear. And talking about there being no letter—" Her voice cracked. "It doesn't change the fact that he's gone."

Marybeth considered and nodded.

"Just say it," Rusty said.

"Say what?"

"Whatever Spatts-ism you're going to say. I can see it in your eyes. Things you say that seem simple but really aren't. You did it a billion times in those letters."

"You always seemed to like it."

"That's beside the point."

"Fine. I was just—I was just thinking—well, this fairy tale gets it right, in some ways. There is no magical tear."

"What are you talking about? She cries, and the curse is broken, the lake is fixed, happily ever after. The end."

Marybeth looked flustered that whatever she'd hoped for here wasn't working. "You're the most courageous person I know," she tried again. "Make no mistake about that. And sometimes tears are just tears, and words are just words. All I'm saying is, if they do come . . . if you go there, to the hard place. Just know . . . you're already loved. You've got a whole slew of people loving you."

"You said *slew*."

"So I did."

"Let me guess. You want me to tap into my true feelings. Dig down deep. Is that right?"

"I'm just worried about you, Rusty."

"I'm fine." She thought of the tram ride, taken without Sam. She thought of Casey's words in the trees, about thawing ice and things that made her heart hurt . . . in a good sort of way.

"I'm fine," she repeated. Her lip quivered. She bit down hard on it. The traitor. She sped up, crossing the empty tracks near Ruby Rock. She kept on, kicking up the forest floor until they broke through, out near a trickling branch of the river.

Marybeth followed. Touched Rusty's elbow. "Tell me again that you're fine," she challenged, though her voice was gentle.

Rusty jutted her chin out.

"Tell me you don't understand a woman who can't cry."

Rusty turned her back on Marybeth.

"Tell me you don't understand a woman who won't . . . mourn."

At this, a dam broke inside Rusty, and the words spewed out. "Sam's gone. His words are gone. And—" She stopped, fumbling over the last, most terrible part. "He was never mine to mourn!" She broke free. "We were supposed to be each other's forever. But that never happened—and I feel like I can't—I shouldn't—"

"What?" Marybeth asked, her face sincere. "Mourn him . . . as if you'd made your vows?"

Rusty walked on, staring hard at the ground. "I'm a never-married widow. Which is impossible. It's an oxymoron. It's stupid."

"*Never* is a terrible word," Marybeth said, hurrying to keep up.

"Yes." Rusty's feet carried her blindly.

"You told me that once."

"Yes."

"You also said impossible things were perfect imperfections."

Rusty looked askance at her. "How do you remember these things?"

"You make an impression. Rusty—" Marybeth grabbed her arm gently, and Rusty stopped. Sniffed.

"Losing Sam was terrible," Marybeth said. "But being his . . . and him being yours . . . was perfect."

She couldn't take much more. This pounding thing, it was liable to burst right out of her chest. She drilled her gaze into the ground—and it was ground she knew. Ground where once, a golden-threaded plaid blanket had been laid. Where a boy, good as gold, true as could be, took her around in a circle, laying her hands where he had buried pits of plums, just to give her a ring. Her thumb stroked her empty left finger, where a ring had never been. Her feet shuffled in the soil where her plum ring encircled her, body and soul.

She could see his lopsided grin, the dimple on one side. How when she looked up at him, dark curls caught the sun and his laugh carried her to a place good and true. She blinked, and the image was gone.

Just like him.

The rain was coming down now. Good. Let it come. The sky could weep all it wanted—she wouldn't.

Because the truth was . . . if she did, she'd never be able to gather those tears back up. Stuff them all back in the locked box marked *Sam*. She'd never—she'd never be able to uncross that line. And she didn't want to leave the boy with the sunlit, wild hair behind. Ever.

She dropped to her knees, right on this ground where she'd sat with him and promised to be his forever . . . someday.

Marybeth was silent.

Rusty cursed the silence.

Marybeth took a step forward.

Rusty glared at her through the cursed silence.

Seethed at her through the glare through the cursed silence.

Marybeth stopped, her blue eyes resting on Rusty and blast it all, there was no pity in them. It would've been easier if there was. Rusty knew the signs well—it's what drove her up the ridge to begin with, to get away from the softness of people's pity and into a jagged terrain that matched her heart better.

Don't you come closer. Don't you do it, Marybeth Spatts. Don't—

She did it. In those muddied red velvet heels, sinking into the mud and poking holes, poking holes in the wall Rusty needed no holes in.

She closed the gap between and Rusty did not look at her. Couldn't, wouldn't. Anything she said would bounce right off, wrong words because there were no right words, and muddy up whatever friendship there was between them.

She knelt.

"You'll ruin your dress," Rusty said lamely.

Marybeth scooted forward, her only answer a great muddy *squish*. Dress ruined. Marybeth heedless. Still not saying anything about Sam. Still not backing away from Rusty not looking at her. What was wrong with her?

Rusty drew back—and Marybeth paused, letting her breathe. And then slowly, carefully, she leaned forward.

She picked up Rusty's hand, which clutched pebbles and muck. And just held it, right there in the rain.

"Rusty?" she said. Just her name, and somehow the two syllables tapped twice on that brick wall inside—*tap, tap*—until it cracked.

And Rusty looked up.

"Was he yours when he brought you those plums from his father's tree?"

Rusty lifted a shoulder into a half shrug and dropped it, both of them knowing the answer.

"And was he yours when he cleaned up the cuts from the cat you rescued?"

Her eyes were hot, now. Hot and brimming.

"And was he yours when he came out here, and he planted something invisible—to give you a ring?"

Rusty swiped at her eyes. No one was going to know it wasn't just rain. It was rain that made her eyes sting and blare red, like she knew they had to be doing. Blotchy like the rest of her when feelings got all wretchedly big inside.

Something inside reached up, asking to be let out. Choking her on its way up. Shaking her heart until her shoulders shook, too, and she clamped it down hard because what if it came out? What if after all this time, the flood came out? And what if it pulled her under? Drowned her? Emptied her out until she was an empty shell, nothing but an empty shell? So the storm rose inside of her as the storm outside dwindled into a soft rain and hid, she prayed, the single tear that escaped.

She looked away.

And Marybeth scooted forward on her knees, muddier and muddier.

A hand on Rusty's shoulder.

Releasing Rusty's hand. Moving her other hand to Rusty's other shoulder.

Bracing her. Like she knew it was coming.

But she wouldn't let it. Rusty shook her head no, telling it so. She held on. Ten seconds more, breathing in shaky through her nose, shaky back out, until that breath hitched on a single bump inside somewhere.

"Your . . ." Marybeth began.

Rusty winced. Shook her head with her eyes pressed shut like the darkness inside could black out this moment, black out what was coming, black out all that had ever been and all that had never been.

And that was the hardest of all. All that had never been.

". . . Sam," she finished.

My Sam.

His name.

Her Sam. Two words Rusty had danced around, so tight were they locked in a glass cube somewhere dark, a place of woulda-beens, coulda-beens, never-beens. It hurt.

"Your Sam, Rusty."

Three words. Inside the heat rose, strangled, and she shook her head to shake off the shaking until rising, rising, the floodgates opened.

Ten years of tears, melting into the rain. Ten years of tight-held grip, melting into Marybeth Spatts.

And there was Rusty—all of her, poured out, into the arms of her long-lost friend.

She didn't know how long they sat there. Somewhere in the deluge the day had slipped its hand into the sunset of night, and stars came out in pinpricks.

The silence was thick and full, the night holding all she had given, and pouring something strange back into her so that somehow—what remained was not a void, but a slow filling of something nameless and new.

Rusty didn't know what to do, what to say. Whatever happened next felt like it had to be some monumental word or act, a bridge to carry her over the chasm of this night where she'd let loose the sorrow of a thousand souls. Something polished, something profound.

"Well, Rusty," Marybeth said, perhaps sensing this same poignant ethereal hinge that their lives seemed to swing upon. She would know what to say. She was the one with the poise. "You've entirely drenched me in snot."

Her face was serious.

"Don't think a little snot makes everything right again," Rusty said.

"I wouldn't dare," she said in her most dignified silver screen accent. "I just believe we should acknowledge that I can now add to my résumé, 'human handkerchief.'"

"You think that's gonna get you back into the good graces of Hollywood?"

"If that doesn't do it, nothing will," Marybeth said.

Rusty looked at her a second. She looked back. For a moment, both solemnly serious and then, in the twitch of a corner of her mouth, something bubbled up inside . . .

And they laughed. All those years and letters, papers and pledges, secrets shared and secrets held, brimming up from long-ago pages and twining around the laughter of two friends.

A gift's a gift, plain and simple. Not just when someone sees it.

—Mr. Jenks, Sr.

Mercy

Mercy turned the key to the ignition in Big Green and stared down the driveway out her back window with determination.

"Would you like me to drive?" Willa sat beside her on the truck's bench, clutching her purse on her lap and looking concerned over the way Mercy beheld the driveway like a fearsome foe.

"Thank you, Willa," she said. "But this driveway and I have unsettled business, and I'm settling it one backward-drive at a time."

The seat creaked beneath Willa as she turned to survey the scene, gulping at the sight of the tree that had done battle with the side mirror, the tire tracks disappearing into ditches on either side. She pursed her lips and nodded resolutely. Bless that woman. "You show it who's boss, Marybeth."

And she did. For the first time, she made it all the way down the curving driveway, backward, without stopping once. She went at the pace of an inchworm, but she harmed neither tree nor truck. Backing out onto the dirt road, she pulled over, foot on the brake, and lifted her hands from the steering wheel ever so slowly.

"I . . . did it," she said, staring at the road ahead. She felt Willa's smile before she saw it.

"You did it!"

Mercy turned to face her, a laugh bubbling out. "I did it!"

"Anyone ever tries to tell you can't do something, Marybeth Spatts, you just take them down this driveway." Willa winked, and they were on their way.

They had begun sorting through the mailbag, making plans to deliver the envelopes the night of the gathering. But there were a few letters that seemed to warrant a more . . . personal delivery.

Hudson Jenks's was one of them.

The road to the Jenks place was little more than a dirt turnoff, nearly overgrown by shrubs. Mercy had passed it a few times and never thought much of it. But as branches pressed up against the truck windows and they bounced down the uneven rivulets that only the peculiar magic of a forgotten road can produce, the road slipped behind a fold of the mountain she'd never known was there.

The tunnel of branches intensified into nearly a solid curtain over the jouncing terrain until suddenly, it lifted. They broke through into a clearing, and Mercy eased her foot onto the brake, feeling her jaw drop. "Where . . . *are* we?"

"The Jenks place," Willa said, enjoying Mercy's awe with a twinkle in her eye.

"No, this is—this is what the movie people search the world over to find. They'd call it . . . I don't know, never-never land or Shangri-la or paradise. The Jenks place?" She shook her head, taking it all in.

They were in a valley above the valley below—she'd heard Kurt call that a *hanging valley*, and it felt for all the world like a living loft. Everything was lush, so lush and green, with long meadow grass waving, a merry creek bubbling its welcome, and trees lining the road up to a white-steepled structure with a bright blue door. Stacked rock walls surrounded everything, giving the effect that everything here stood upon a castle-worthy foundation of stone. Steps built into the rolling grass rises, walls built around beds of blooming larkspur. Aspens shimmered silver-green as they pressed up against the windows of the white clapboard building, steepled and stout and standing, too, upon a stacked-rock foundation seamed with tufts of bright green moss. The leaves of the aspens created living stained glass, green with a few early gold leaves, where aged clear glass dripped into petrified time.

"Mercy Peak has another church?" She shook her head. "Rusty never mentioned . . ."

"Jenkses' place," Willa said again, simply.

"*This* . . . is the Jenks place?"

Three blond heads spilling out the door answered the question as the children rushed toward the truck. Mercy turned off the ignition and just stared. "Green Meadow Spires," she murmured. "I thought it must be referring to stone spire formations on the mountain or something. Not—"

"Actual spires?" Willa said, and Mercy nodded. "I'm sure they'll fill you in. It's a good story."

Mercy walked toward the house, clutching the letter and marveling at this small utopia. "Hello, Poppy!" she said, taking the offered hand of the youngest of the Jenkses, who had become Mercy's fast friend on her frequent trips into the mercantile for peppermint sticks. Poppy bounced on her toes and tugged Mercy inside, chattering about two butterflies she'd chased from a patch of clovers.

Daisy, Hudson's wife, with her tight blond curls blowing in the breeze, greeted her at the door, welcoming her in and through what once must have been a small reception area. Neat hooks were lined up on the wall, with jackets tossed onto them, as if the children flung them on like a ring toss. Three pairs of saddle shoes in stair-step sizes dotted the floor. One pair was placed neatly against the wall, laces curled inside. One pair was bright white and stiff as a board, as if they'd never been worn, and yet one of them rested against the other akilter. And the last pair was tossed with wild abandon, one flung to the far wall, the other still spinning in the center of the room.

Watching the three girls, Mercy thought she could guess whose were whose. Poppy's feet were stained green from running unshod across the grass. Fiona, the middle girl, settled in on a stool beside a window inside the house, tucking her bare feet just so behind the stool legs, picking up a book, and neatly slipping the bookmark into the back pages. And Molly, the eldest, had disappeared, but pounding footsteps up a staircase somewhere said she was on the move, and fast.

"Sorry for our tangle of a mess," Daisy said in her lilting Irish brogue. She bit her lip, twisting a dish towel in her hands and surveying the room. Where pews would have been, there was now a gathering of cheery mismatched chairs and a worn blue settee. Beyond that, a round table waited to play host to the next meal, with places set. In the center of the table, a chipped white pitcher of fresh-picked mountain lupine splashed color and life, and in its small shade, three thin storybooks with golden spines were stacked at delightful diagonals, with one in particular showing wear upon its golden spine.

"I see no mess," Mercy said. "Just lovely life."

Daisy blushed and beamed at the same time, exuding gratitude.

Mercy thought of her sparse shanty in Swickley's Crossing, devoid of possessions. She thought of her sparse mansion in Hollywood, devoid of people.

This scattering of energy and joy . . . this was beautiful.

A thump sounded above, and Daisy listened for a moment before letting out her breath.

"Molly," she said. "She'll be practicing handstands."

"As she would," Willa said, laughing. "She had a rope tied between two trees outside the school a few months ago and was attempting to walk on it."

"Ah yes, the tightrope-walker phase," Daisy said, cheek dimpling as she smiled. "What brings you girls out this way? It's been a bit since we've had visitors."

"You're lucky I didn't know about your piece of paradise here," Mercy said. "I'd have been knocking at your door to see if we could set up camp in your meadow for the theatre!"

Daisy beamed. "Hud is fit to burst, he's so excited for your Wildwood theatre. It's not often he gets to offer his music to an audience."

"He'll bring the plays to life," Mercy said, and meant it. "Is he . . . about? We have a small delivery for him."

"Aye, he'll be in from the pasture any minute," said Daisy. "Can I offer you ladies some tea? I've got hot water in the kettle."

Offering to help, Mercy followed her into the kitchen—which appeared to be a log cabin, butted up against the church, with thick logs and chinked seams, sunspots piercing through and setting the air dancing. Mercy sucked in a breath.

"Are you alright?" Daisy asked.

"Oh yes, I—" She felt like someone had kicked the wind out of her . . . or transported her back ten years to the cabin she'd left behind, sealed up with so many memories inside. "It, um—it feels like a miner's shanty," she said, mustering a smile.

"Right you are," Daisy said. "Everything in this meadow was brought down from a wee town up near the ridge when their mining up that way stopped. Cabins and houses went pretty quickly. People put them on skids, hitched them up to the pack mules, and moved these little worlds all over the mountains. You'll spot them behind houses and barns, if you look—they all have the same look. Square and simple, just like you see here. For most, they've used them as outbuildings or bunkhouses on the cattle ranches. Ours became a kitchen. But after the houses were moved, the church remained, and it was the one Hudson's father helped build when he was a boy. He was needing a bigger house for the growing Jenks boys, Hud included, so those men moved the church down here to their little valley, and here we are," Daisy said. "Living in the silent echoes of hymns."

A burst of laughter sounded from Poppy, who tickled Fiona's feet where she read on the stool.

The door opened, letting in a whistling tune as Hudson tromped inside.

"Here he is now." Daisy pulled down another cup from the open shelf and poured the tea, bringing the tray to the scattering of chairs. "We have visitors," Daisy said, and Hud greeted them all with a grin.

"What brings you ladies out here? Something about the gathering?"

"Actually . . . we've . . . brought something for you, Mr. Jenks."

Willa nodded encouragingly as they all sat down, and Mercy held the envelope facedown in her lap. "It's . . . difficult to know where to begin."

Hud pulled a wriggling Poppy up on his lap, then spotted the letter. His face grew somber; an in-person delivery of a letter seldom carried good news, Mercy knew.

Eager to put him at ease, she said, "It's—nothing to worry about" but could think of nothing else encouraging to say. She didn't know what news it held, nor how it would affect the man. Her best course was to let him read it for himself.

"Here," she said, holding out the letter. He reached out to take it. "It's a long story, but . . . we recently found the lost mailbag that went missing with the Goose so long ago. This was in it."

His hold on the envelope froze as realization set in. Yellowed and worn, its corner lifted in a breeze from the open window, as if it were offering sheepish apology for its late arrival.

Hudson pulled it slowly to himself and turned it over. His breath escaped in a single laugh. "Never in a thousand years . . ." He shook his head. "We waited and waited for this. My father, especially. I don't know what was worse—the waiting, or the way he hid his disappointment with his big, bearded smile every time it wasn't there."

Daisy took the seat beside him and slid her hand under his, lacing their fingers together. The notes those fingers had played . . . but it wasn't a bow or strings they held now. It was his future . . . in the past.

"I don't know if I even want to know," he said.

Willa nodded. "No one would blame you either way, Hudson. You can open it, you could burn it unopened, you could carry it in your violin case as a story to be told. Whatever you choose to do . . ." She looked at Mercy, who picked up the explanation.

"We just wanted to see it safely into your hands."

Hudson nodded. A clock ticked from the wall, and a smaller tumble than before sounded from above. Fiona turned a page in her book, furtively looking over its top at her father. Daisy squeezed her husband's hand. Poppy hummed a tune.

A sudden clamor from Fiona's corner sounded as she—the quiet one—hopped up and rushed over. "Oh, for Pete's sake, Pa," she said. "You have to open it. Aren't you dying to know?"

This time the laugh that emerged from Hudson was deep and buoyant. "Are you?"

"Yes! Open it. Please?"

A few seconds passed as he stared at the envelope, then slid his music-making, cattle-tending hands into the aged seal and released the victorious sound of a *rip*. "Go get your sister," he said. "We do this all together."

Poppy dashed up the stairs to the steeple-room-turned-bunkhouse and was followed back down by a rosy-cheeked Molly.

"It came?" she said. "After all this time!" Chatter broke out, and Willa and Mercy rose to leave.

"No, stay," Hudson said. "You're a part of this, too, now." He opened the paper, its folds crackling like tiny stiff bones.

"'Dear Mr. Jenks,'" he began, then looked up at them. "Ha! Imagine that, calling a seventeen-year-old kid *mister*." He laughed nervously.

He cleared his throat, reading aloud an introductory paragraph about the magnitude of auditions, and of choosing participants from such a sea of talent.

And then came the part they were all waiting for.

"'It is no small matter, then, to inform you that—'" His voice broke off. Green eyes welling, he gave a small shake of his head. "'That—'" His voice was thick.

Fiona stood, crossing the small circle and kneeling at her father's feet, laying her head on his lap and embracing his legs. "Should I . . . ?"

He nodded, handing her the letter.

Fiona tucked her feet behind her, her gingham dress spreading out around her knees as she lent her clear, high voice to words written long before she'd been born.

"'It is no small matter, then, to inform you that you, being among our top applicants and displaying unparalleled talent, skill, and dedication, have been accepted to the New York Conservatory for Musical Arts.'"

Unbridled joy erupted as Molly leapt out of her seat, picking up Poppy and spinning her around in a circle. Daisy clasped her hands over her smile, eyes pricking with tears.

Fiona beamed at her father, who still sat speechless.

"There's more," she said, and continued joyfully. "'In addition, we are pleased to offer you a full scholarship . . .'" Fiona slowed, her words tempered now. "'. . . that will provide for tuition, room, and board, in exchange for your willingness to take part in our school's ambassador program. As part of the ambassador program, you will be invited to perform at private concerts in some of New England's finest homes, from Newport to Cape Cod, as well as summer vacation colonies along the Atlantic coast, continuing up through the state of Maine. The season will culminate in a charity musicale for our generous patrons, hosted at Carnegie Hall. If the above is agreeable to you, please reply within the month, so that we may reserve your spot before moving on to our waiting list.'"

Hushed joy swirled among the hollow sorrow of a missed chance. The astonishment of such an opportunity.

"Hudson . . ." Daisy said. "It's wonderful."

All eyes landed on Hudson, who had yet to speak. He scraped a palm over his jaw, shaking his head. "All those years . . ." he muttered. Leaning back, he folded his arms over his chest. His eyes glistened as he let his gaze settle on each of his girls.

Daisy's face fell, her pretty features tugged down into dawning sorrow. "Think of all you missed . . ."

Hudson was silent, riding the current of her words as he shook his head. "Think of all I would have missed if I'd gone," he said. "This . . ." He took Fiona's hand. "This is a performance I wouldn't miss for the world."

Daisy sniffed, then sprang to her feet, dusting her hands on her apron. "We're celebrating," she said. "It's never too late! How often do you get accepted into one of the world's top conservatories? What should it be? Gingersnaps? Haystacks?"

"Both!" piped up Molly, and rushed into the kitchen to help.

* * *

Later, walking in the hanging valley as the Jenks girls gallivanted in all their various forms, Willa and Daisy picked chamomile blossoms for Daisy to dry, and Mercy held the gate open for Hudson as he led a cow out to pasture, then returned to survey his family.

It was the golden hour, sun skimming everything in haloed light.

"You don't regret it?" Mercy said, breaking the silence.

Hudson pulled in a long breath, stuffed his hands into his pockets. "I think . . . I regret my father not knowing. He worked so hard for it—I wanted it for him, even more than for me," he said. "His pride in me didn't change one bit when that letter never came. But I'd have loved for him to get it."

"Maybe he does know," Mercy said. She'd seen his tombstone in the churchyard, the way it was always adorned by wildflower bouquets in varying sizes. "I wonder, sometimes, if God lets our loved ones know the good things happening here."

"Maybe." He smiled. "Either way, there's not a drop of sorrow where he is, and for that I'm glad. And you know, there was hardly a drop of sorrow when he was here, either. He had cause enough for it, we all do, especially with mining drying up quick as a blink in the town he was born in. But he never dwelled there. Most men left in anger that the silver deposits that had been so rich ended up being so shallow."

Rich but shallow . . . Mercy blinked away images of her yawningly empty home in Hollywood.

"Your music . . . it stirs people deeply, Hudson. There aren't many who can make a whole living with that, but I believe what that letter says. You'd have been one of them."

Hudson folded his arms over his chest. "Maybe, maybe not. Maybe whoever was next on the waiting list needed it a whole lot more than I did. Maybe I'd have missed Daisy entirely if I'd have gone. Did you know she moved here in a covered wagon, all the way from Leadville?"

"No, I didn't."

"God's honest truth. A covered wagon, in the 1930s. Not as rare as you might think in these parts. With men chasing mining or cattle or sheep, shifting them around season to season, they had to get their families from one place to the next somehow. Good roads for cars aren't abundant in these mountains; automobiles even less. So there came Daisy that very summer, along with her whole family, bringing a blast of life to Mercy Peak along with the best Irish soda bread anyone had ever tasted. She danced with me at a barn dance one night, and I knew, her hands in mine, she was different. Special."

He looked across the meadow, where she stooped to pick up Molly's flung shoe and chase her down with it, scooping Poppy up with her free arm and twirling her as she went.

"You were right," Mercy said.

"Who'd have thought I'd get to open a letter like that . . . with a family I never even dared to dream of all those years ago? People who weren't even born when it was written? Who might never have been born if I'd have gotten it?" He paused. "Can't say as I understand what made the Goose disappear . . . but part of me wants to rise up and bless it, for what it's ended up meaning for me. I might've missed out on Newport and Carnegie and all those other places . . . but I got to play my father into heaven, as he crossed that threshold. I got to play my daughters into the world." He choked up. "Someday, maybe I'll get to play at their weddings."

"You might be busy walking them up the aisle," Mercy said, smiling gently.

"Who's to say I can't do both?" He laughed and pulled the letter out from his pocket, tapping it with one hand onto his open palm. "There was a time when I wanted this so bad I could hardly breathe. Could feel the want of it pressing down on my chest like a weight. I never really let on, as Pa wanted it enough for both of us. But seeing how it's all turned out, I think . . . I think I got the better end of the deal here." He nodded resolutely.

"Do you think you'll always wonder?" Mercy ventured. "What would have happened if you'd gone?"

He looked around, the wind sifting through tall grasses, evening light peaking at its most golden. He scuffed a foot on one of the stone steps built into the hillside. "I used to sort rocks up at the mine," he said. "Up near Ruby Rock. Men would bring rocks and boulders in the ore carts to go down and get crushed, get all the gold and minerals out into sediment. But sometimes the rocks that came were too big to fit inside the machine. If the man up top couldn't break it in a quarter hour of jackhammering, he'd toss it out a door that opened straight into the sky, along with the other waste rocks. The pile at the bottom would just grow and grow, and it was my job to clear them away to make room for new rocks. I could see some of them glimmer, and I asked the super about it. He told me it'd cost more than we'd make to get that amount of gold out of that size of rock. He told me to roll 'em down the hill and let the treasure return to the earth."

Mercy laughed. "So, there's gold-filled rock tumbling around the sides of these hills?"

"More like gold-speckled. And not so much tumbling around the sides of these hills as . . . embedded in them." He waited, a glimmer in his eye, as he scuffed his feet again.

"You mean—surely not all of this . . . ?" She studied their valley with new eyes. The stone-embraced flower beds and steps, the foundation of the church-home.

"Not all of it, no. A lot of it is just the waste rock. Though I take issue with the word *waste*. Just look at it now, holding up all kinds of life. That's no waste. But yes, tucked in among them . . . The supers looked at me like I was crazy when I asked if I could bring them home instead of rolling them down the hills, but they said it was fine. So, there's gold all around us," he said, letting his gaze linger as the sun alighted on his daughters, playing a game of blindman's bluff, stumbling and laughing in chase.

"Will I always wonder?" He pondered, then shook his head. "Maybe sometimes. But mostly, I'll just think—they took an awful lot of gold out of these mountains. Far away, and it never came back. Some of it . . . it was created here, and here it was meant to stay, and it's made a fair place for a home, I'd say. Maybe I was meant to stay, too. Reckon sometimes that's where the treasure is."

"You're a remarkable man, Hudson Jenks," Mercy said. "With a re-markable family."

"It's a remarkable life, I'll give you that," he said. A cow mooed behind him, ambling up and draping its head over the wooden fence. "And I have a fenced-in, four-legged herd of an audience who can't escape." He stroked the beast's face. "No matter what they think of my playing. How many ambassador musicians can say that?"

And with the spotlight of the setting sun on the man who would never grace the stage of Carnegie Hall, the evening dawned with the world a little more beautiful.

CHAPTER
33

Mercy could hear the pleasant clatter of silverware on dinner plates, coming from the lantern-lit banquet table, laughter sprinkled amid happy conversation. It was a beautiful cacophony, the dining song comprised of a potpourri of china in mixed patterns, borrowed from every willing home in Mercy Peak, with a few miners' tin mess kits, which the men among the attendees seemed to be relishing, as well as piling with relish, this night of the cookout.

Mercy paused, taking in the sight before her. Her breath caught. The sea of smiling faces, young and old and everywhere in between. The parachute awning above fluttered as an evening gust rippled through. The tin-can lights clinked pleasantly, flickers of light flashing from within and from the glass miners' lanterns placed at every table and the torches that flamed at the edges of the courtyard.

On the lawn beyond the courtyard a handful of people had left their dinner to dance beside a big galvanized bucket campfire they'd set out, where Hudson Jenks wielded his bow so tenderly the strains reached inside of Mercy and made her ache. And then her eyes froze on one astonishing sight.

There was Rusty.

Standing in front of Casey Campbell, who held his hand out to her, steady and sure, even as Rusty stared at it. As if to accept was to take her own life in her hands.

"Oh, Rusty . . ." Mercy murmured, her hand landing on her own heart, eyes welling. Saying a silent prayer that her friend—who had hurt so much, so deeply, so long—would take that hand. Open that heart, which she knew was already beginning to beat for the man before her.

Inch by inch . . . she did.

Casey, bless that man, enfolded her hand so slowly, so surely. Slipped his arm around her back—nothing tentative about the motion at all, but rather all restraint, all to make sure she was not rushed. That she would know this was a safe place.

And they danced. There, surrounded by the people Rusty had exiled herself from for so long. There, in the light she'd hidden from, in the warmth she'd kept herself from. Mercy saw it: the dawning of a smile, as Rusty dipped her head, then lifted it, meeting Casey's eyes.

Mercy's heart swelled, and she shook her head at herself. "Enough eavesdropping, Spatts," she said to nobody and turned to prepare for the next event . . . for which she could hardly wait. She found Phinneas and gave him the bag. She was about to make her announcement, after Hudson's song drew to a close, when a whisper sounded behind her.

"Spatts!" Rusty beamed, glowing, flushed and out of breath.

Mercy turned to face her, sliding her hands under her friend's elbows and biting her lip to keep from smiling too big.

"Yes, Rusty?" she said.

"That man . . . *danced* with me." She laughed, dropping her hands to her sides and making her emerald skirt swish. Then her face went slack, stricken. "I danced with him." Hands moved to cross over her stomach. "Oh. Oh no. What's he gonna think?"

"I imagine he is inordinately happy, and that's all there is to it," Mercy said, giving Rusty's elbows a squeeze. "I think he would dance you to the moon, if you would let him."

"The *moon*." Rusty looked horrified. "What was I thinking?" She started to pace. "What was I doing, why did I *do* that? What if he thinks— what if—and what about Sam? Marybeth, I'm—I'm not ready for this."

Mercy placed her hands on Rusty's shoulders, holding her friend gently still. "You're not ready to move your feet in a simple box shape in time with music, with a fellow who is pleasant and kind, and whose company you enjoy?"

Rusty gulped. "It wasn't just moving in a box. It was a *dance*, and you know it. And you know how that goes. Next thing you know he'll be bringing flowers and asking for moonlight walks—"

"Rusty?"

She wrung her hands and looked at Mercy, her fear palpable.

"Did you enjoy the dance?"

Rusty gulped.

"Do you enjoy Casey?"

She averted her eyes.

"This is okay. You are okay. Casey is okay."

"What does that even mean, *OK*? It's two letters, and nobody even knows what they stand for. Old kin? All clear, spelled real bad? Whatever it is, it's not okay."

"But *you* are. *This* is. Just . . . breathe."

Rusty, miraculously, obeyed. She clamped her jaw shut, nodded desperately, and pulled in a slow breath.

"Casey is a good man. It's going to be o—"

"Don't say it!"

"All will be well."

"A well is a deep dark pit of murky water. Put that in your lexicon."

"All will be *well*, and you know exactly what I mean."

Rusty planted her hands on her hips and blustered out a sigh. "Distract me."

Mercy nodded, not missing a beat. "Anything for you, Rusty Bright. Here." She gestured to the steps she'd been about to announce from. "You get to tell everyone about the mail."

Before Rusty could protest, Mercy stepped up and said, "Ladies and gentlemen," tapping a spoon on a crystal glass until she had everyone's attention.

"As we've been readying Wildwood for its new life, we've made some exciting discoveries that we wish to share with you tonight. The first of which we hope will bring delight to many of you here. Rusty?"

Mercy stepped back and relished the way Rusty slipped into the tale of discovering the bag in the dusty confines of the deep dark tunnel, which, she added, was on its way to being cleaned up so they'd all have a warm way from town, once the weather turned, for the autumn play ahead. Phinneas took up the bag on cue and made a happy spectacle of making deliveries.

Murmurs of disbelief washed into waves of surprise and delight, peppered with the sound of tearing paper, envelopes opening, pages fluttering.

Rusty drew up next to Mercy and surveyed the scene. "Well, you did it, Spatts."

"Did what?"

"Made Mercy Peak your home. I always knew you'd fit in here. Mind you, when I told you to come, I never thought you'd be buying the castle in the canyon and saving the town with your forest theatre. . . ."

"That remains to be seen," Mercy said, but her heart overflowed at Rusty's vote of confidence. "But I am thankful to be here."

A silence settled between them as they watched the smiles grow as people read their mail and shared with one another the wonder of a lost thing, found.

Rusty was oddly pensive beside her. Mercy cleared her throat. "I know what you might be thinking. . . ."

"I don't doubt it. But there's no use in dwelling on it." She looked over the crowd with a sad smile as people opened letters. One woman held out a birthday card, laughing that this was sent when she still kept track of years. Twenty-year-old Elmer Drysdale held up a quarter, which had been sent to him by an uncle upon the occasion of him getting a tooth knocked out.

Phinneas looked jollier than Saint Nick, hauling that old mailbag over his shoulder and doling out envelopes as if they were gifts, indeed.

Priscilla Murdock held a stack of decade-old catalogues and magazines to her chest, watching with joy and a small sigh of wistfulness.

Rusty elbowed Mercy. "Look," she said, pointing at the tree line behind Priscilla. A figure emerged in silhouette, and as he approached the soft glow of the torches, the stoic features of Reuben Murdock appeared. He was clean-shaven, and as he stopped and took in the scene, he removed a worn black hat from his head, holding it to his chest, sad eyes settling on Priscilla.

He took a small step back, but Mercy caught his eye and let her smile speak volumes of hope to the man. It seemed to fill him with just enough courage to close the space between himself and his grown kid sister. He tapped her on the shoulder and hung his head.

Priscilla turned, her petite form reaching only to his shoulder. As she looked up and up . . . the catalogues slipped from her hands, and she trampled them, throwing her arms around her brother in an unrestrained and wordless embrace.

Reuben remained stiff as a board, not knowing what to do. But as the moment stretched on and the Bastion of Civility remained in that embrace with no sign of leaving . . . slowly, his arms came up around her . . . and he held his sister.

Mercy wiped a tear.

Rusty, too, though she looked chagrined to be caught crying—again. "That's—beautiful," she said, voice raspy.

"All these long-lost words . . . if we could see what's happening in each and every heart this instant," Mercy said.

"We'd be bowled clean over," Rusty said. And she meant it, Mercy could see, though her smile flickered as she began to study the flagstones beneath her feat.

This was the moment. "If you'd had word from Sam after all," Mercy said, "would you want to read it?"

Rusty scuffed a foot. "Doesn't matter. We searched that bag how many times?"

"But imagine—"

"I can't." She flashed a pained look at Mercy, a silent plea. "It hurts, Marybeth."

Mercy slipped her hand into Rusty's. "But if you didn't *have* to imagine . . ."

"What do you mean? There's no letter, and it's alright. It'll be alright, anyway."

Mercy pulled something from her pocket and pressed it into Rusty's palm.

Rusty lifted it beneath the flickering light of the tin cans and torches. She opened her mouth, but no words emerged. Only a choked croak of disbelief.

Her eyes flashed to Mercy. "H-how—?"

"Your dance partner," Mercy said. "He found it while he was up tuning the Goose and working on the headlights with Ralph Mosely. He said it was wedged between a seat and the wall, like the Goose was just holding onto it tight for you all this time."

"Casey Campbell?" Rusty looked for him in the crowd, and found him with Kurt and Angus, admiring the slingshot Angus held and bending over it with boyish joy. She could hear him from here. "Is this Blue Lightning? *The* Blue Lightning, as in Swift Rider's slingshot?"

Rusty looked back down at the envelope, then back at Casey. "Why didn't he deliver it himself?"

"He said he thought with how much Sam meant to you, it would be best coming from a good friend. Someone you felt . . . safe with. He said I would know better than he when the time would be right."

Casey turned, as if he could feel their stares. He caught her gaze above the crowd, above the happy din. He saw the envelope, and the smile froze on his face, something deeper growing in his eyes. The corner of his mouth pulled in, and he gave a single nod.

Rusty's eyes welled, and all she could do was mouth the words *thank you*.

He gave a sad smile, and then he stuffed his hands into his pockets, pulled reluctantly back into the banter with the brothers, though he glanced back at Rusty, concern on his face.

"Is . . . the time right?" Mercy asked.

"Now or never," Rusty said and slowly slipped her finger under the flap that Sam had sealed for her.

CHAPTER
34

Rusty

On the front, in handwriting so familiar and dear it made her smile, was her name. *Rusty Bright, Mercy Peak, Colorado.*

Slowly, she pulled out the paper inside and began to read.

Dear Rusty Bucket,

We lost a friend this week. It's hit everyone hard. The work we're doing is dangerous, more than usual. We all know there's risk, but we all look out for each other, too. Sometimes though . . . things still happen. The camp's quiet, strange-quiet. It's got us all thinking . . . I think all will be well, Rusty. I'll be just fine, and we'll have our home, and our promise there in the place the river carved out for us.

But just in case . . . you deserve more than silence. So I've given this letter to my friend to send if I meet the end. If you're getting this . . . Rusty, I'm sorry. You'll want to sock me on the shoulder good, like the first time we met. Do you remember? I'd slipped on the high road above Whistler's Bridge and slid a good ten yards before you caught up with me, pulled me to my feet, and gave me a good talking-to. You told me never to almost die in your presence again, and by the way, you were Rusty, and who was I?

You had the fire of the sun in you, Rusty. I got a glimpse of it and was never the same. My heart was yours then and has been every moment since.

I've met my end early. But, Rusty . . . don't let it be your end, too.

The world needs the girl who can jimmy a lock with an old

350

nail and climb mountains with bare feet. Who can stare lightning and life in the face, not afraid of either, and fill everyone around her with courage. I wish the whole world could know you. They'd be different if they did. If there ever was a way.

Sunshine in the night, Rusty. That's what you are. Don't forget.

I wanted it to be me, who'd get to hold that sunshine all our lives. Back in that ring of plum trees, I told you I hoped you'd be my Someday Forever.

Now . . . well, it's not so different. Just flip the words around, and it's still true. We'll be in Forever together . . . Someday. The promise isn't gone. Just changed a little. And when we're there, I want to hear all your tales. Every single one. I wouldn't miss it for the world, Rusty girl.

So go live. It's what you were made for. Climb the canyon walls. Stare down that lightning. Let the world see and know you.

Sunshine in the night, Rusty. That's what you are.

Don't forget.

> Love,
> Always.
> Sam Buckley

How does that boy say so much with so little? She could see him. As her eyes welled and her heart filled, she could see that boy. Looking up at her with his green eyes and freckles when he fell on that high road. She hadn't known he'd fallen in two ways that day. Had been oblivious for so long to the ways he'd cared so well for her. Given her his life long before he ever pledged to.

Marybeth watched quietly as Rusty let her tears fall in silence. "It was good?" she asked.

Rusty nodded. "It was good." The letter. The life. All of it. She pressed the letter to her heart, then tucked it inside her skirt pocket. It seemed right, on this night, to have Sam's words in her pocket. *Go live.* She took a deep breath, feeling lighter and fuller, all at the same time.

Casey came over, looking between them. "I . . . don't mean to interrupt."

Rusty gave him a smile. It was all she could do to keep from throwing her arms around him in a lumberjack embrace and thanking him for giving her this last, perfect gift from Sam.

"You're not interrupting," she said.

His eyes lingered on her a moment, then he shook his head slightly, as if to bring him back to the moment. "Ralph is on the Handie-Talkie. We're ready to go with the falls on your cue." He was talking to Marybeth, but his eyes kept coming back to Rusty.

Marybeth nodded and took a deep breath, taking her place on the step. This time, Rusty clinked the glass, then stepped aside when everyone was ready.

"Friends," Marybeth said. "First . . . I want to thank you for the very deep privilege of getting to call you friends. I've had very few in my life, and the close ones I have known have taught me one priceless thing: hope. I now know it in each one of you, because you took me in. A stranger from afar, living in a house that held shadows, and yet . . . you gave me a home. Helped me fling the shutters wide and begin to rebuild. It's meant . . . more than you'll ever know. You've given me a second chance at life . . . and so it is my very great honor to give something to you in return. A second chance for something I hope you'll all be as overjoyed to see as I was. Casey?" She held out her hand for the radio, pushed the button, and spoke the agreed-upon code words. "The Goose flies at midnight."

People started to look around, understandably puzzled. And then someone pointed toward the mountainside where, in the last streaks of twilight, the waterfall began to pull to the side, like a curtain drawing back, into two, maneuvered at the headwaters by Nancy Mosely. And as they did, two bright lights ignited, side by side. Turned on by Ralph, who'd been secretly toiling for the past days to turn the Goose and fix what he could.

Hushed and befuddled murmurs skittered over the crowd. Marybeth bit her lip, waiting—and there. A spotlight flicked on, shining to illuminate the beaming, gleaming, friendly face of Motor No. 8.

It was Phinneas who realized it first. "It's her!" he cried, taking off his pinstriped cap and tossing it in the air with a *whoop*. "Our Goose!" And cheers erupted, followed quickly by a deluge of questions—*How? When? What in the world?*

"And now, to present you with the tale of the Galloping Goose and her flight across the canyon, to the best of our surmising, is the one and only . . . Holden Huxley."

Holden took the stage, ready to give a dramatic delivery of the account of what happened with the Goose that night. Every bit of endearing, maddening naïveté dropped away from him as he stepped into the role he shone in: that of leading man. He held them rapt in his grasp as his voice rose and fell, hesitated, sprang upon them at just the right moments. Willa's piano accompanied, her skill as a musical storyteller on full display . . . all while Marybeth and Rusty slipped away to the village below.

CHAPTER
35

Rusty

"This is it," Rusty said.

"Let's hope," Marybeth said. She gave a pull to the trapdoor in the ceiling of the town hall, and Rusty reached up to pull the rope that brought down the ladder. "You said this building was donated by the Gilmans?"

Rusty nodded, beginning the climb. "Randolph Gilman commissioned it, and it was Martin who did the work on the clock tower. Randolph got all up in arms that Martin made it so fancy, said he wouldn't pay. Martin just whistled on, working away, and said, *'No extra charge.'*"

They emerged into the dark of the clock tower.

"Got your lantern hat?" Rusty asked.

Marybeth put her miner's helmet on, lighting up the lamp on the forehead.

"Rusty," Marybeth said, stopping short of crossing the threshold, and grabbing Rusty's arm, "did you ever think we'd be here? That first letter . . . who could have imagined one day it would bring us to this?"

"Sneaking like bandits into a clock tower in the middle of the night with miners' lamps and a vendetta against a man long dead who stashed a stolen train-that's-not-a-train inside a mountain?"

"Yes."

"No. I did not imagine this." She paused, considering. "Well . . . not precisely, anyway."

Marybeth gave her a quizzical look, to which Rusty shrugged, looped her arm through Marybeth's, and together, they stepped into the yawning dark.

Rusty unrolled the large leather disc, and Marybeth set to searching the room. They'd puzzled all week over what the riddle might mean.

Time shall pass,
By time arranged.
One face shall last,
By time unchanged.
Place the pin
Anchored fast.
A careful spin
Reveals the last.
Look upon white earth's demise.
New chasms dawned;
The sun does rise.

4:17 5:29 3:75 4:14 6:07 1:10 9:15 6:16

They had theorized everything from sewing, to a boat's anchor, to a spinning top—with Martin, one just didn't know. But they'd settled on a great hope that he might have hidden here whatever they needed, just as he'd done with the blue lantern in the mine.

"How're we ever supposed to climb out there without falling clean off?" Rusty said. She held up the leather round, looking between it and the clockface, and back. "Or maybe . . ."

She pulled a cinder block over to where the opaque glass was lit from inside and stepped up on it. She held up the leather to the clockface, twisting it in a steady circle until—

"There!" Marybeth said. The filigree cutouts matched perfectly with those on the cast-iron framework that held the glass. There was a peg in the center, which the hole in the leather fit on snugly. Metal clips sat at the ready in four places around the edge, and Rusty used them to attach the leather in place.

"Now what?" Rusty said.

Mercy looked around. "We're still missing something to decode it with. Let's hope this room holds more secrets for us."

The girls began searching the small square room, top to bottom, in opposite directions, until they met back at the clock.

"Nothing?" Rusty said.

"Nothing."

They looked again. "Hold up," Rusty said. "Here." She crouched by a metal vent. "What would you need a vent for in here?"

Marybeth knelt and started to pry the black metal loose, noticing how the scrolling black metal matched the scrolling filigree on the clockface.

"Martin Shaw was something of an artist, wasn't he?"

"He was a Renaissance man if ever there was one." Rusty reached in as Marybeth pulled the grate away, pulling out a green velvet drawstring bag. She opened it and slid out two brass instruments. "It's a . . . compass?" She held up a hinged instrument. "And a . . ." The next piece was a semicircle, engraved with numbers over its arc. "A protractor?"

"The compass looks like something Randolph Gilman had in the turret room, with all those measuring and drafting instruments," Marybeth said. "I've never seen one quite like this, though. What does it do?"

"Not much besides draw circles. See, a pencil can attach here, in this grip." She showed a clamp on the side of one of the two pointed lengths of the large instrument, which was the length of Marybeth's forearm. Rusty reached into the bag, but there was no pencil.

"Maybe we don't need the pencil? Let's see . . ." Marybeth stood and approached the clock.

"These times." She pointed at the first one, 4:17. "If we set the pin there . . ." She placed the pointed end of the compass on the number and started to spin it, as the riddle indicated. It caused the opposite compass leg to point at various places along the way, crossing several letters and numbers. They wrote them all down, repeating it with the next time and the next until—

"3:75?" Rusty said. "That can't be right."

Marybeth stared. "Or maybe we haven't been right. Perhaps they're not times at all." She picked up the protractor. "Each of the clues has catered to one man's strengths, yes? And Gilman would've known just how to use this. You said it had something to do with angles?"

Rusty pulled the instrument down, showing how the two metal bars could be moved. Place them closer to each other and the angle number grew smaller. Farther apart, and the number grew.

"So, what if we placed the pin in the center . . . point its counterpart at the number on the clock it corresponds to . . ."

"Four, for the first number?" Marybeth asked.

"Yes, and then—the angle should be 17 degrees. That will give it a direction but place it somewhere different from the four itself. Where does that land us?"

Marybeth shrank the angle until the compass pointed squarely at a tilted letter *R*.

A thrill shot through Rusty. "Next," she said. "5:29."

Marybeth maneuvered it to its new position and angle size. "U."

They continued the process, until they had eight letters, lined up on Rusty's notepad.

RUBYROCK

"Ruby Rock," they said in unison. A place they'd traipsed past a thousand times on this journey already.

"Your namesake?" Marybeth asked. "What do you suppose it means?"

Rusty read the last stanza of the riddle once more. "'Look upon white earth's demise. New chasms dawned; The sun does rise.'" She gulped. "Ruby Rock is at the head of Emerald Gulch."

"The site of the avalanche?"

"White earth's demise."

They were going back to where it had all fallen apart.

Don't be afeared of a mountain to climb. There's a mountain! So
climb it, whydontcha! Sure, it's hard. But one step ain't too bad.
So do that, and then do it again. All the way up.

—Martin Shaw

Mercy

Look upon white earth's demise. New chasms dawned; The sun does rise.

They determined it had to mean sunrise. Sunrise at Ruby Rock,
looking toward the slide site up Emerald Gulch . . . which happened
to be nestled against Mercy Peak.

They'd returned to the dissipating party at Wildwood and to the
boathouse for a fitful rest of a few hours, then rose early to make the
trek by lantern light. The stars blinked in and out of thin clouds as they
made their way there. It began to sprinkle—the sort that would soon
be gone, Mercy thought, judging by the wisps of clouds and the bright
moon above.

They sheltered beneath the parachute awning in front of Ruby Rock
and waited for the sun to come.

"What are we looking for, do you think?" Mercy said.

"Your guess is better than mine," Rusty said. "But it seems he wants
us—or rather wanted my father and Randolph and, I imagine, Reuben—to revisit the place that tore them apart. To look toward it at
sunrise, where a new chasm is."

"Can you imagine . . ." Mercy said, "if what opened that chasm was
what nearly took their lives?"

"I don't know what to make of that," Rusty said. "It's either terribly tragic or completely beautiful. Something good coming out of something so awful."

"It feels like the deepest good is what Martin was trying to do. All of these riddles had to be years in the making. If he really discovered gold or silver or something of worth that long ago . . . he could've ridden off and been a rich man. But instead—he just stayed. Sowing words and thoughts and riddles and rhymes into all these rocks . . . in order to heal."

They talked on about the men, the brotherhood lost, until the sky began to whisper the palest pink of dawn. Emerging from their covering, they stood at Ruby Rock, looking west to the gulch.

The sun was climbing, the pink curtain of light descending farther as it crested the hill opposite Mercy Peak. Gatherings of pines at the base of the mountain and leading up to it were shaded still, but with the mountain illuminated behind it, it gave the effect of a pink-glowing arrow, pointing down.

"Do you suppose . . . ?" Mercy began.

Rusty shrugged. "'The sun does rise', he said. I think a glowing, sunlit arrow on a mountainside is as close to 'X marks the spot' as Martin Shaw gets." She squinted to where the tip of the arrow on the mountain was. "That's the Three Trees," she said. "Angus has a plaque in the works about them."

Mercy let out a breathy laugh. "That's what I thought, too. But look—when the light hits it like that . . . look at the one in the middle." She stepped away.

Rusty looked again. A tree on the left, a tree on the right—and in the middle, a form that was almost identical to the others in shape, but as the direct light accentuated the emerald of the pines, the one in the middle stayed black.

"Either that one is in some kind of shadow . . ."

"Or it's not a tree at all."

"What, then? A crevice?"

"There's only one way to find out," Rusty said. "You said you wanted to climb Mercy Peak someday. . . . Are you ready, Mercy Windsor, to meet Mercy Peak up close?"

Mercy's eyes traveled up, up, up. Had it always been this steep? The slope looked much gentler from afar. The climb ahead was going to be nearly vertical in some spots. How would they do it?

"I'm ready," she said. But as she took a step, motion from the corner of her eye caught her attention.

Two does, foraging the blackberries along the river. One of them with a few faded spots. She gripped Rusty's wrist to stop her and motioned at the deer. Rusty gave her a look that said, *Are you crazy? What are we waiting for?* But something in Mercy told her to wait.

The deer approached the mountain, which was as good as a wall. Where would they go? Mercy watched as the older doe picked her way up a ledge—just the slightest outcropping that traveled up like a zig without its zag. Soon, the ledge retreated into the mountainside, and the deer stepped up to the next one, like a sideways stair, and continued her journey up.

Mercy turned to Rusty and whispered, "There's our path."

Rusty nodded solemnly. "You first."

Mercy approached the mountain and set her foot upon its narrow red outcropping. She pressed her eyes closed, saw the flash of a camera, the flash of memory, saw heels on a red velvet carpet.

But this was real.

She pressed her hand to the mountain, stone against palm.

Flash. She was kneeling in front of Grauman's, Wilson P. Wilson pressing her hands into wet cement.

But this was true.

She took a step, and another, and another, climbing—ascending—to where the air was clear. Pure. Crisp. Cleansing.

Flash. A headline: MERCY WINDSOR CLIMBS TO THE STARS.

But this was life. So rugged it scraped. So beautiful it ached. A laugh tumbled out of her, her face turned skyward, and she soaked it in.

With the first light of dawn touching her, cascading over her with actual starlight . . . she stepped out of the shadows for the first time in her life. Here, where the Creator of the universe pressed His world into her hands. Where He had her—plain old Marybeth Spatts—inscribed on the palm of His hand.

Her breath came short and quick. Her heart overflowed with the truth of it. Whatever they found or did not find in this mountain . . . this was a place of treasure.

"You okay?" Rusty said.

Mercy opened her eyes. "Yes," she said. So simple, so true, it was astonishing.

"Well, uh . . ." Rusty cleared her throat. "I don't want to rush you—seems like you might be having a moment you could maybe fill me in on later—but, um . . . I don't know if I can perch here much longer without splatting to the ground."

Mercy gasped. "Sorry!" And the climb was a scramble, then. Their feet like those of the deer, but a little less sure. Zigging and climbing, all the way up to the Three Trees that were growing out of stone.

"That's a lesson in perseverance," Rusty said, looking at them. "Trees right out of rock. Life right where it looks impossible."

"And what about that?" Mercy said, approaching the phantom tree, which was no tree at all.

It was a fissure. A near-perfect rectangle splitting the rock in two. Or rather, a place where once two slabs had been seamed together by some unifying force—the bit on the left mineral-stained darker than the slab on the right.

"What was here?" Mercy said.

Rusty let out a low whistle. "Something softer than the two rocks. It eroded faster."

"Like . . . gold?"

"Could be. Could not be. Martin Shaw sure thought so," she said. "Look."

On either side of the fissure stood a stone mound, stacked with care and topped with rocks inscribed with the initials *M. S.*

His claim.

"So the gold is . . . gone?" Mercy said.

Rusty shook her head. "If it's there . . . if that's what was in this spot . . . sure, it might've eroded. Time, elements, life . . . that's just what it does. But it doesn't mean the gold is gone. Just means"—she took out her pick from her belt—"you've gotta dig a little. Hunt the ground below. Whatever held these two together, it's still there."

"Or maybe it's deeper in," she said, pointing to where Martin's initials were scraped just inside the chasm.

Above them, the chasm grew wider.

"This . . . isn't right," she said. "Gilman has detailed surveys of all of this terrain in the turret room. There's no chasm on his maps."

"Something must have happened since the time those surveys were taken," Rusty said. "Something to open it up, like an earthquake, or—"

"An avalanche."

The avalanche that had nearly killed the Blood Moon Boys, and Priscilla Murdock, too . . . Could it have opened up the vein of treasure they'd been searching for when that happened?

"If I climb a little higher," Rusty said, "I can get in there."

Mercy's stomach tumbled. She did not cherish the thought of people she loved going into tight spaces. But hadn't they done just that? The mine . . . the tunnel . . . even the clock tower. With each step, the hold of that old North Carolina mine loosened its grip on her a little more.

"I'm coming, too," she said.

The going was rugged. Bits of rock cascaded when footholds weren't as sure as they looked, and handholds flaked right off. But as they ascended deeper into the rift, they were soon able to stand side by side, staring at what appeared to be a dark opening.

"That has to be the work of Martin Shaw," Mercy said.

Rusty crouched down, examining the rock all around it. "But why here?"

Mercy joined her. She dusted the ground, raking away rocks and dirt, following the path until she was on all fours, head inside the adit, examining the walls. Her eyes adjusted to the darkness. She brushed the hard chiseled side to her right . . . and then she saw it.

Glimmering in a streak, like a river at sunset, suspended in the rock.

"A vein," she whispered.

"What?"

Mercy backed out so that Rusty could see.

"Jumpin' jellyfish," Rusty said when she saw it. "I've never seen anything like that. Gold is caught up in the rocks in tiny flecks, usually. Not veins so fat you can trace them—and it just keeps going back."

She backed out, and the girls just looked at each other.

"Whose is it?" Mercy asked. "It's not Gilman land."

"And it's not Bright land. It's nobody's so far as I can tell—except it *is* a clearly marked claim, which means . . ."

"It belongs to Martin Shaw's heirs and successors. Of which there are none."

"Unless you count a certain document signed by four boys."

"Reuben," Mercy said, and a laugh so deep bubbled up inside.

The man with the saddest eyes and the sorrowed heart and the fledgling home with his sister was about to be the richest man in these mountains, if her guess was correct.

"Reuben." Rusty's hand flew to her heart. "The gentle giant of Mercy Peak . . . oh dear. Oh, the mine people will descend on him like a flock of vultures, wanting to invest in this and that and pick him clean and—can you even imagine? He was shell-shocked just seeing the four of us out there by Sea Glass Lake. What'll he do with pressure like that?"

Mercy thought of the man. "We'll have to ask him what he wants.

But it seems to me, a man like that, who's looked out for this town from these ridges for decades now, without anyone ever even knowing . . . I think he'll be just the man to put the town back on its feet with a thriving mine—if he wants to. And I know a very willing investor," she said, then shrugged. "If I can ever get my funds released."

They sat awhile longer, silence settling as the mountain cradled them where it had broken open and bled . . . and then gathered up and held.

At length, they started the trek back down. It was a strange sort of wonder that entranced them, and it wasn't until they were nearly down, on a ledge just above Ruby Rock, that Mercy turned to look up at Rusty, and speak. But as she did, her foot slipped.

"Take care, Marybeth!" Rusty cried, but the words were cut off as a slide of rocks broke loose where Mercy tried to cling to the mountain . . . but caught only air.

I think you do have wings, Marybeth.

—Rusty Bright, age 15

There were some things that were never meant to be hers.

Sure as her name was Marybeth Spatts, she would never be rocked to sleep.

Never be tucked in.

Never have her own lullaby.

Never be told "take care."

Never have someone there to catch her if she fell.

"Never's a terrible word," Rusty had once said. *"Don't say it."*

And now here, as blackness and muffled sounds engulfed her, she swam in a sea of never and always and yes and forever . . . she could see it.

All her days, life had told her *never.*

And now . . . all of creation was telling her *yes.* Yes, that sort of love was meant for her.

It was in the rocking of a boat by the hands of lapping waves, as she, grown as could be, slept like a baby.

It was in the hands of a friend she'd believed lost laying a blanket over her trembling form in the middle of the night.

It was in the fingers of a woman who had longed to be a mother . . . playing her first and only lullaby for a stranger on a screen.

It was in Rusty's words, before the great darkness. *"Take care, Marybeth!"*

And all she remembered after that was a flutter.

A great fall, her body sinking fast to the earth, and then that great rush of wings around her . . . followed by dark.

A dark she swam in for she knew not how long. After all those years under the soul-piercing stage lights, this place felt different. The darkness was sweet, somehow. In it, she heard snatches of piano, offering a song in sweet pieces.

"Stars shining bright above you . . . night breezes seem to whisper 'I love you . . .'"

Her eyes fluttered open.

A face—hair like copper, sprinkled in freckles and sun—smiled.

"Spatts," she said, as if she'd just spoken the greatest treasure in the world.

Slowly, Mercy's senses began to clear. She heard the strains of the river nearby, and a window showed the blossoms of wild red roses peeking through, as if they were checking on the patient within. She was at Willa's house, and Willa was playing the piano in the next room.

"Wh-what happened?" Snatches of images began to flit through her mind. The clock tower . . . the sunrise . . . the alpenglow on Mercy Peak . . . a gold vein . . .

"I fell," she said.

Rusty's face crumpled as she expelled a breath and said, "Yeah, you did. I thought I'd lost you for good." She swallowed, hard. "Don't do that again, you hear?"

"Don't . . . fall?"

"Or at least if you do, make sure it's not clean off a mountainside."

"I thought I heard . . . wings. Some kind of fluttering? How did I— How am I here?"

"You don't remember?"

Mercy shook her head back and forth on the pillow beneath her.

"Well, that was done by the hands of every single person in this town that you enlisted to help with your crazy parachute awning idea. Kurt, Angus, Hudson, Daisy, the Jenks girls . . . me and Casey . . ."

"I fell on the parachutes?"

"By Ruby Rock," Rusty said.

She'd fallen from the sky and been caught by the hands—or at least the work of the hands—of these people. Her . . . family. Tears sprang to her eyes. "I guess flightless birds can fly after all."

"Told you they were the best. So, flightless bird, Doc says you're going to be okay."

"You said *okay*." Mercy mustered a mischievous smile.

"See? Already being a joker . . ." Rusty chattered on, and Mercy's smile went all the way through her. For a moment, she was ten again, picking up that first wordy letter from a stranger across the miles who would change her life forever.

She sat slowly up, her head pounding, her heart so full it was sure to burst. Willa entered, ushering in a bashful Kurt, who offered her a slingshot to try. Soon Priscilla Murdock was there, fluttering with the news that the patient had awoken, with Holden Huxley on her heels like an obedient puppy, and her reticent brother standing off in the corner, keeping watch, missing nothing. The man who'd lost everything, now holding a fortune in his hands. Mercy wondered if anyone had told him yet.

Soon the Jenkses were trailing up the path outside, and the cottage was bursting with life. The day passed in a steady flow of visitors and meals, story and laughter. Mercy took it all in, letting her gaze hop across each conversation until it landed, at last, on the sunset outside.

Sunsets here were more an experience than a sight. They marked the soul. Pierced it, rearranged things with all that shifting color and light, and sealed it up again, a little more whole than it was before. The streaks of color across the sky just now were no exception.

Rusty had told Mercy that Martin Shaw had once told her that all the streams and thunderstorms and waterfalls running through this mountain were carving it away, tiny bits at a time . . . including the smallest pieces of gold. So small, no man on earth would ever be able to harvest them. They'd be swept down those mountains, across the country, out to sea, washing the wide world in gold, nobody even stopping to notice it rocking back and forth in every single wave of every single ocean.

Mercy watched the gold of the clouds slip into coral, and the coral shift to fleeting pink, lifted by shadowed bits in grey-tinted purple, a touch of royal, right here at sunset. All of it bent and mixed and moved upon those clouds as if in response to some unseen, cosmic conductor who whispered not *crescendo* but simply *majesty* . . . and the colors, the clouds, the light, the shadows obeyed.

Willa's words about the clouds being a flying sea twisted up in Mercy and she wondered—was that gold up there, right now? Washed from the mountains, lifted from the sea, and igniting the sky as starlight struck it and sank behind the mountains?

How extravagant a kindness this world was.

She'd seen so many lights in the past ten years, all of them blinding her. This . . . was more luminous by far . . . and it filled her. Brought tears to her eyes. As if God himself were reaching around her heart in this moment and whispering, *All of this. For you. To know me. To be known by me.*

The Academy could keep their gold statues. Grauman's could dig up her handprint. But nothing . . . nothing . . . would ever erase this moment.

This sunset.

This miracle.

This life.

Epilogue

Folio of Field Notes, Volume VIII: *Final Documents*

[Property of Sudsy McGee, Screenwriter]

WINDSOR'S WINNING COMEBACK

OWEN HASKELL, HASKELL AND KLINE,
FOR THE *NEW YORK REVIEW*

MERCY PEAK, CO: In a display of sheer dynamism, leading lady and newcomer to the stage Ruby Bright dazzled the audience into loving a sometimes-unlovable princess and cheering when she crossed an impossible threshold to shatter an age-old curse. In a turn of Hollywood-level irony, it was a tale of a single flood that brought tears to the world . . . directed by the owner of the single tear that flooded the world long ago in a land far away.

This viewer is hopeful, to say the least, that the Wildwood Forest Theatre will become a tradition and mainstay. Mercy Windsor makes production an art form of its own, and the Mercy Peak Theatre Troupe displays gumption enough to enchant. Not to be missed.

> ## WILSON P. WILSON UNDER INVESTIGATION FOR WILLFUL NEGLIGENCE
>
> HOLLYWOOD, CA: Pinnacle Studios president Wilson P. Wilson is under investigation relating to the recent discovery of a partially intact film reel found in the debris of Building 9, which was ravaged by flame last February. A source, who wished to remain unidentified, said that the footage in question was from Reel 10 of the never-completed *Joan of Arc* film. Wilson offered no comment.

MOTOR NO. 8 INCIDENT REPORT

United States Postal Service
San Juan Regional Headquarters
Montrose, Colorado
Incident Report
DATE OF INCIDENT: October 2, 1928
INCIDENT TYPE:

- ☐ Weather
- ☐ Animal
- ☐ Criminal
- ☐ Deliver misdirection
- ☑ Other: *Wind!*

PERSONNEL/ROUTE INVOLVED: *Phinneas Trent, driver of Engine No. 8, Rio Grande Southern Railway*

REPORTED BY: *Phinneas Trent*
RECORDED BY: *Viola Burton, Montrose Postal Office*
METHOD OF REPORT: *Telephoned from Mercy Peak Mercantile*
CORRESPONDENCE AFFECTED: *Miscellaneous personal post and two bags of mail from Telluride school and Mercy Peak school, each bound for Pan-American Youth Correspondence Program*

DESCRIPTION: (As dictated by Phinneas Trent to Viola Burton)
What was it like? I'll tell you what it was like! Felt like the Slide-Rock Bolter slammed into us with the force of a thousand winds! No, you can't file it under weather. Yes, wind is weather. But this was something more, I'm telling ya! It felt like the wind and the engine had some arrangement to have it out at that crossing. The hardest wind I've felt in my thousand years on this route pummeled through with enough force to derail her! That's right, derailed. Strangest thing. It roared down the mountain so fierce I slammed the gas pedal down, and she just took her sweet time, inching forward like she was saying, "Nah, let's just wait here and be a part of this." I didn't want to be a part of that, thought it'd kill us all! Me, the engine, every bit of mail. But it just jostled her till she hopped right off the rails. We got her back on and secured her so good she'll never leave the rails again, not by any natural means. But the mail was shook up fierce, like the malts Kurt Pike makes. What's that? No, not now, Kurt. [muffled conversation in mercantile background] Maybe in a minute, I'm talking to Miss Burton. Miss Burton, it was like an earthquake or something. You get any other reports like this? I swear it can't have been just my engine, not with a force like that. Felt like Providence herself was blowing through and had a bone to pick with the mail, bent on mixing it all up. I got it all sorted—Telluride school letters in the bag intended for North Carolina, Mercy Peak kids' letters heading to Virginia. Counted 'em and everything. What? Could some have gotten mixed up? Well, sure, I told you, they were all mixed up, but I know the kids and which ones live where, got it all sorted, promise. So, if it's all the same, just write this down as situation sorted and we can call it a day, but look out for that wind out there! Say, you have dinner plans, Miss Burton? You like malts?

When Hollywood Ousts Her . . .
Can the Queen of the Silver Screen
find a home—and a missing rail car—
in the mountains of Colorado?

MERCY
PEAK

a major motion picture filmed on location

Starring . . .

HOLDEN HUXLEY as *HIMSELF*

DEBBIE REYNOLDS as *RUSTY BRIGHT*

DICK VAN DYKE as *SAM BUCKLEY*

CARY GRANT as *CASEY CAMPBELL*

BURL IVES as *PHINNEAS TRENT*

JIMMY STEWART as *HUDSON JENKS*

CONFETTI THE CAT as *HIMSELF*

MOTOR NO. 8 as *ITSELF*

And debuting . . .

MARGARET SWIFT in the role of
MARYBETH SPATTS in the role of
MERCY WINDSOR

Written and directed by Sidney McGee
With music by Willa Jones

Historical Note

There were seven Galloping Geese that traversed the San Juan Mountains starting in the 1930s. All seven are in existence today (one of them being a replica), still bringing delight—and some even carry passengers once again.

While Motor 8 is a work of fiction created for this story, it must be acknowledged that the phrase *Goose Number 8* is sometimes used to refer to the San Cristobal motor briefly used on the San Cristobal Railroad. The motor didn't operate as planned and was eventually parted out. The term is also used in the San Juan Region in reference to a now-retired "parade" Goose, created for Fourth of July parades and other celebrations. Special thanks to Joe Becker and the Galloping Goose Historical Society for providing insight into the nuances of "Motor 8."

Author's Note

Dear Friend,

When I started this book, I set out to write a friendship tale: pen pals, adventure, a lovable rail car, the great and undeserved kindness of this life. But as I completed one of the final read-throughs before this book went to print, I stepped back and saw a theme I hadn't known was there and the way it seemed to beat through with a pulse in nearly every story thread: Willa's. Priscilla's. Hudson's. Rusty's. Casey's. Marybeth's. Reuben's. Even Kurt and Angus and the Blue Lightning slingshot.

Each of them, in different ways, knew or hoped for one life—and then something happened, or didn't happen, resulting in a life that looked very different from what they'd once imagined.

In this, there was hardship. In this, there was healing. In this, there was hope. In this, there was wholeness in the end. Because it boils down to this beautiful promise from Joel 2:25—*"I will restore to you the years that the swarming locust has eaten. . . ."*

God was at work in each of their lives. Sometimes quickly, sometimes over years, to restore what had seemed utterly lost. This is what He does—He reaches into the void and breathes life.

I may not know the details of your story, my friend. But I know the God who made your heart . . . and I know that He is in the business of redeeming and restoring. Composing a deep and personal lullaby just for a girl who had long given up the hope of knowing such a love. Sending a sky-born ocean and a mountain-roving boat to a landlocked, sea-dreaming girl. Creating molecules and music in such a way that a cove and a lake might deliver a lifeline through acoustics to the most isolated soul. Delivering dreams across miles and decades, sometimes in a form entirely different from what we ever could have imagined.

I'm praying that He reaches into your own story today with a flash of that same light, and this unshakable truth: You are His good creation. Your life is on purpose. This day—even this very moment—has such rich purpose. The Maker of the mountains holds your very heart, and that's a great big mighty something.

And as Rusty would say . . . "something's something."

Like Mercy stepping from the silver screen into the wilds of the mountains, I hope that as you step from the pages of this tale, you'll behold a story more life-filled and beautiful than anything that could ever be composed on paper: your life. For "He has done all things well" (Mark 7:37).

To quote the Joan of Arc words that gave Mercy courage to live her life: "Go forward bravely. Fear nothing. Trust in God; all will be well."

Amanda

Acknowledgments

I owe a million thanks to Mike, Mitch, Richard, and Ethan of Knotts Berry Farm. Jim, Andre, and John at the Chollar Mine in Virginia City, Nevada. The entire stellar Bethany House team. Charlie Giordano and the Colorado Railroad Museum. FRS '22 readers, who asked for a main character who was single. The gentleman in the food truck line. Jennifer Walchle, Erika Hays, Mimi McKinnis, Sabrina Newcomb, G. K. Chesterton, Wendy Lawton, Dr. Jonathan Rogers. Ben and kids—there are pieces of my adventures with each of you tucked into these pages—I love you! The two mountain ranges that shaped this book: the Rockies and Sierras. And to the Maker of those mountains: With the same hands that sculpted the very earth, you reach for my heart and the gratitude takes my breath away.

For extended acknowledgments and the stories behind each of these names and places, please visit AmandaDykes.com.

Discussion Questions

1. Rusty and Marybeth's friendship was one for the ages . . . and yet for nearly twenty years, they'd never met face to face. What is it about letters that offers the chance to bind people together? Have you ever had a special pen pal or received a piece of mail that held great importance to you?

2. For years, Rusty chose "the frigid grip of isolation" over the "sea of community, compassion, currents she knew were kind." Why is it sometimes tempting for us to choose isolation over community? Has there ever been a time when community surprised you in a good way?

3. What are Marybeth and Rusty's main personality differences? How did those complement or challenge their friendship? Have you experienced a friendship or relationship where a different personality proved to be a gift?

4. Consider the things Mercy lends her voice to—or doesn't lend her voice to—throughout the book: scripts, lullabies, warnings to her father and to Wilson P. Wilson. How does her use of voice grow or change throughout the story?

5. Would you rather live in Rusty's cabin, Mercy's Celestial Climes, or Wildwood Estate? What about camping in the boathouse or running the traveling book boat/wagon?

6. If you had to dine tonight on a Classic Hollywood menu (Cobb salad, pineapple cake, crème brûlée, salmon puffs, caviar, etc.) or a Mercy Peak menu (chili and corn bread, biscuits and gravy,

Boston brown bread, blueberry pie), which would it be? What would you add to your chosen feast?

7. There are some elements tucked into the book that serve as "echoes" of one another. Pinnacle Studios has the initials P. S., for example, which is an important component of letters to Marybeth. Can you think of any others?

8. While watching "the burst," Miss Ellen says, "When the mountain cracked open, it seemed like our hearts did, too, even wider—but then we saw what it made way for. . . . It's a daily reminder that light will break into our darkness." Can you think of other examples, personally or in history or other stories, when something broken has been redeemed into a place of light?

9. Joel 2:25 (esv) says, "I will restore to you the years that the swarming locust has eaten." In Mercy Peak, Marybeth experienced the unexpected fulfillment of dreams she had long given up on (a lullaby just for her, being rocked to sleep, finding a family who cherished her). How did other characters experience the theme of restoration in their own lives? Can you think of a time when God pursued you with a long-held dream but in an entirely different form than what you'd imagined?

10. At the end of the book, we learn that a movie (in the fictional world) is in the works! Who would *you* cast to play the characters of this book?

Amanda Dykes is the winner of the prestigious 2020 Christy Award Book of the Year, a *Booklist* 2019 Top Ten Romance debut, and the winner of an INSPY award for her debut novel, *Whose Waves These Are*. She's also the author of *Set the Stars Alight* and three novellas. A former English teacher, Amanda is a drinker of tea, dweller of redemption, and spinner of hope-filled tales who spends most days chasing wonder and words with her family. Find her online at AmandaDykes.com.

More from Amanda Dykes

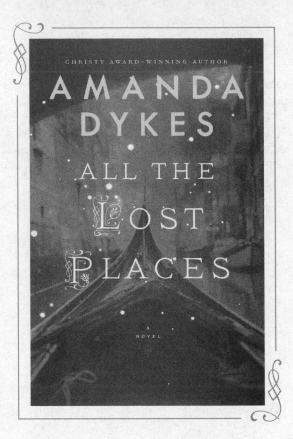

Discovered floating in a basket along the canals of Venice, Sebastien Trovato wrestles with questions of his origins. Decades later, on an assignment to translate a rare book, Daniel Goodman finds himself embroiled in a web of secrets carefully kept within the ancient city and in the mystery of the man whose story the book does not finish: Sebastien.

Available now wherever books are sold.

Sign Up for Amanda's Newsletter

Keep up to date with Amanda's latest news on book releases and events by signing up for her email list at the link below.

AmandaDykes.com

FOLLOW AMANDA ON SOCIAL MEDIA

AmandaDykes, Author   @Amanda_Spins_Stories   @AJDykes

More from Amanda Dykes

Discovered floating in a basket along the canals of Venice, Sebastien Trovato wrestles with questions of his origins. Decades later, on an assignment to translate a rare book, Daniel Goodman finds himself embroiled in a web of secrets carefully kept within the ancient city and in the mystery of the man whose story the book does not finish: Sebastien.

All the Lost Places

Mireilles finds her world rocked when the Great War comes crashing into the idyllic home she has always known, taking much from her. When Platoon Sergeant Matthew Petticrew discovers her in the Forest of Argonne, three things are clear: she is alone in the world, she cannot stay, and he and his two companions might be the only ones who can get her to safety.

Yours Is the Night

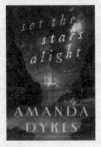

Reeling from the loss of her parents, Lucy Claremont discovers an artifact under the floorboards of their London flat, leading her to an old seaside estate. Aided by her childhood friend Dashel, a renowned forensic astronomer, she starts to unravel a history of heartbreak, sacrifice, and love begun two hundred years prior—one that may offer the healing each of them seeks.

Set the Stars Alight